The Barrens and Others

THE Barrens AND Others

F. PAUL WILSON

A Tom Doherty Associates Book • New York

THE BARRENS AND OTHERS

A Forge Book
Published by Tom Doherty Associates, Inc.
175 Fifth Avenue
New York, NY 10010

Forge® is a registered trademark of Tom Doherty Associates, Inc.

Library of Congress Cataloging-in-Publication Data
Wilson, F. Paul (Francis Paul)
The Barrens and others / F. Paul Wilson.—1st ed.
p. cm.
"A Tom Doherty Associates book."
ISBN 0-312-86416-7 (alk. paper)
1. Horror tales, American. I. Title.
PS3573.I45695B3 1998
813'54—dc21   98-23591
                                  CIP

First Edition: December 1998

Printed in the United States of America

0 9 8 7 6 5 4 3 2 1

COPYRIGHTS

CONTENTS

The Barrens and Others

1987

This was the year I started my career as annual bridesmaid to the various literary awards in our field. "Dydeetown Girl," a novella edited by Betsy Mitchell and published the year before in Baen's *Far Frontiers*, made the final ballot for the Nebula Award from the Science Fiction Writers of America. It didn't win but I was happy to see it recognized as a superior piece of science fiction.

My short fiction output during the first half of 1987 was limited to "Wires," a novella-length sequel to "Dydeetown Girl" (instigated by Betsy Mitchell, who asked, "What happens to all those children people aren't supposed to be having?"), which she published in Baen's *New Destinies*. Otherwise, I spent the winter and spring setting up the Nebula weekend for SFWA and blazing through the latter half of *Black Wind* in a white heat. I had little time for anything else. But as I was recharging during the summer, Paul Mikol called and asked me to lead off *Night Visions 6*.

I hesitated. *Night Visions* was Dark Harvest's annual showcase anthology in which two established authors and an up-and-comer are each given carte blanche to do whatever they wish with thirty thousand words: Ten three-thousand-word short stories or a single thirty-thousand-word novella, or anything between—whatever suits them. I'd long admired the *Night*

Visions series. And why not? Its list of contributors was a *Who's Who* of horror fiction.

My problem was time. Something happened to me after I hit forty. Something turned up the rheostat on the creative juices. Throughout my thirties I'd always been one novel ahead of myself—Dutch-ovening the characters and ideas of the next book while I wrote the current one. After forty, the ideas exploded. By the summer of 1987 I'd already begun the novel that would become *Reborn* (working title: *Hanley's Heir*), and I had another half-dozen novels plotted out in my head, plus an idea for the novella that would eventually complete the "Dydeetown" stories, plus I wanted to expand "The Tery" to novel length. And all the while I was practicing medicine full-time while trying to be a good husband, and a father to two teenage daughters. Where was I going to find the time for another thirty thousand words by the end of the year?

So I said, "Sure, Paul. Count me in."

Allow me to explain.

It's hard for a writer who's paid his or her dues to say no to an editor's request for a story. Most writers go through years of frustration at the beginning of their careers trying to cajole editors into simply looking at their work. And if they can make a sale it's a bonanza, no matter how low the word rate.

I was no exception. I wrote for years without a sale, seeing every story rejected with Pavlovian regularity by every paying (and nonpaying) market I knew. I even kept track of editorial changes, so that as soon as a new name took the helm of a magazine, I could resubmit the stories rejected by his or her predecessor. It got so confusing after a while that I had to design a flow chart to keep things straight: a grid with the magazines listed along the horizontal axis and the stories listed along the vertical. When a story was rejected by *Analog* it immediately was put into an envelope addressed to *Amazing* and sent off in the next day's mail. A check mark was placed in the *Amazing* box next to that story, and the *Analog* box earned a big black X. When it came back from *Amazing* it was sent off to *Fantasy & Science Fiction* and the *F&SF* box was checked. Ad nauseam. I burned up a *lot* of postage in those days and, quite literally, can paper a wall with all the rejection slips I collected. (I've saved every single one, and someday I may do just that.)

So maybe you can understand how someone who hung on through that process might find it nigh impossible to force the word *No* past his lips when asked—*asked!*—for a story.

I'm learning, though. It's taken me years and a few occasions of being unable to deliver on a promised story, but I'm learning.

Dean Koontz wrote a generous introduction to *Night Visions 6*, and Berkley published the paperback edition as *The Bone Yard*.

So here are those three stories . . . all set in the same town. I called it "The Monroe Triptych."

"Feelings," the first of the three *Night Visions* stories, came easily. It's a simple just-deserts-cum-voodoo tale, based on a real-life malpractice scam in Florida.

I set the story in the imaginary Long Island north shore Gold Coast town I'd created in 1985 while writing *The Touch*. I'd put a lot of work into The Incorporated Village of Monroe then, going so far as to draw a map of the waterfront and the downtown area. I knew it almost like my own hometown. A good place for a yuppie ambulance chaser to live if he had roots on the Island.

For those of you who get off on interstory connections, the very fact that it's set in Monroe ties "Feelings" and the other two stories in the triptych to *The Adversary Cycle*; and you'll notice Dr. Walter Johnson mentions his brother, a GP who remained in their hometown, "a foggy little place on the coast . . ." That other Doc Johnson practices in Greystone Bay (see *Soft & Others*). Some readers might recall that Howard's father is the lead character in "The Last One Mo' Once Golden Oldies Revival" (also in *Soft & Others*).

Writing this one was almost as enjoyable as writing "Cuts."

FEELINGS

"Five million dollars, Mr. Weinstein? *Five million?* Where did you come up with such an outrageous figure?"

Howard Weinstein studied his prey across the table in his office conference room. Until today, Dr. Walter Johnson had been little more than a name on a subpoena and interrogatories. His C.V. put his age at fifty-one but he looked a tired old sixty as he sat next to the natty attorney the insurance company had assigned him. His face was lined, haggard, and pale, his movements slow, his voice soft, weak, his shoulders slumped inside a gray suit that looked too big for him. Maybe the strain of the malpractice suit was getting to him. Good. That might spur him to push his insurance company for an early settlement.

"Five *million?*" Dr. Johnson repeated.

Howard hesitated. *I'm* the one who's supposed to be asking the questions, he thought. This is my show. But he had asked his last question and so the deposition was essentially over. He wanted to say, *It's my favorite number,* but this was a legal proceeding and Lydia's fingers were poised over her steno machine's keyboard, awaiting his reply. So he looked Dr. Walter Johnson straight in his watery blue eyes and said, "That's the compensation my client deserves for the permanent injuries he suffered at your hands due to your gross negligence. He will suffer lifelong impairment—"

"I saved his life!"

"That is hardly clear, Dr. Johnson. It's up to a jury to decide."

"When you sue me within my coverage," Dr. Johnson said, staring at his folded hands where they rested on the table before him, "I can say to myself, 'He's doing business.' But five million dollars? My malpractice coverage doesn't go that high. That will ruin me. That will take everything I own—my house, all the investments I've made over the years, all the money I've put away for my children and future grandchildren—and still leave me millions in debt. You're not just threatening me, you're threatening my family." He looked up at Howard. "Do you have a family, Mr. Weinstein?"

"Is that a threat, Dr. Johnson?" Howard knew the doctor was making no threat, but he reacted instinctively to keep the defendant off balance. He had no children and had divorced his wife three years ago. And anyway, he wouldn't have cared if the doc had been threatening her.

"Oh, no. I was simply wondering if you might have any conception of what this sort of threat does to someone and to his family. My home life is a shambles. I've had constant stomachaches for months, I'm losing weight, my daughters are worried about me, my wife is a wreck. Do you have any idea what kind of misery you cause?"

"I am more concerned with the misery you caused my client, Dr. Johnson."

The doctor looked him square in the eyes. Howard felt as if the older man's gaze were penetrating to the back of his skull.

"I don't think you feel anything for anyone, Mr. Weinstein. You need a real lesson in empathy. Do you even know what empathy is?"

"I have empathy for my clients, Dr. Johnson."

"I sincerely doubt that. I think the only empathy you know is for your bank account."

"Okay, that's it," Howard said, nodding to Lydia at the steno machine as he closed his case folder and rose from his seat. He had let this go on too long already. "The deposition's over. Thank you for your cooperation, Dr. Johnson. We'll see you in court."

He ushered out the defendant and his attorney, then stepped over to where Lydia was packing up her gear. "Let me see the end of that tape," he said.

"Howie—!"

Ignoring her mild protest, he opened the tape compartment and pulled out the long strip of steno paper. As he scanned through it, looking for where Dr. Johnson had begun running off at the mouth, Lydia said:

"You're really not going to ruin him, are you? You're really not going to take everything he owns?" She was thin, dark-haired, attractive in a brittle sort of way.

Howard laughed. "Nah! Too much trouble. It's S.O.P.: Ask for an exorbitant amount, then settle for somewhere near the limit of his coverage. Taking all his assets—which I could probably get if we go to court—and going through a long liquidation process would be a big hassle. Best thing to do is get that big check from the insurance company, take my forty percent, then move on to the next pigeon."

"Is that all he is? A pigeon?"

"Waiting to be plucked."

He knew there was something wrong with the metaphor there, but he didn't bother to figure out what. He had found the spot he had been searching for on the tape. He marked it with a pen.

"Stop the transcription here."

"Why?"

"It's where the doc made his closing sob story about threatening his family and—"

"—your empathy for your bank account?" She smiled up at him.

"Yeah. I don't want that part in the deposition."

Her smile took a mischievous twist. "I sort of liked that part."

"Ditch it."

"I can't do that."

"Sure you can, Sis."

Her smile was gone now. "I won't. It's illegal."

In a sudden surge of anger, Howard ripped the offending section from the tape and tore it into tiny pieces. He never would have dared this with any other licensed court stenographer, but Lydia was his sister, and big brothers could take certain liberties with little sisters. Which was the main reason he used her. Her name had been Chambers since her wedding four years ago, so no one was the wiser.

He tossed the remains in the air and they fluttered to the floor in a confetti flurry.

Lydia's lips trembled. "I hate you! You're just like Dad!"

"Don't say that!"

"It's true! You're just a 'Daddy Shoog' with a law degree!"

"Shut *up*!" Howard quickly closed the door to the outer office. "I told you never to mention him around here!"

He prayed none of the secretaries had heard. One of them might get to thinking and might make the connection. She might find out that Lenny Winter, the fifties d-j known as "Daddy Shoog," was really Leonard Weinstein, Howard's father. And then it wouldn't be long before it was all over Manhattan: Howard Weinstein was the son of that fat balding guy doing the twist and shilling his "One Mo' Once Golden Oldies" albums like Ginsu knives *("But wait! There's more!")* on late night TV commercials.

God! He'd never be able to maintain credibility at another deposition, let alone conduct a court case.

He had made every effort to avoid even a faint resemblance to his father: He'd grown a thick, black mustache, he took care of his hair, combing in a style his father had never used when he had a full head of it, and he kept his body trim and hard. No one would ever guess he was the son of Daddy Shoog.

Had to hand it to the old jerk, though. He was really cleaning up on those doo-wop retreads, especially since he was forging the inconvenience of paying royalties to the original artists.

"Too bad you inherited Dad's ethics instead of his personality. The only reason I come around is because I'm family. You've got no friends. Your wife dumped you, you've—"

"*Your* marriage didn't last too long either, Miss Holier Than Thou."

"True, but I'm the one who ended it, not Hal. You got dumped."

"Elise didn't dump me! I dumped *her*!"

And did a damn fine job of it, too. Left her without a pot to pee in. God, had he been glad to be rid of her! Three endless years of her nagging, "You're never home! I feel like a widow!" Blah-blah-blah. He'd taught her the folly of suing a lawyer for divorce.

"So what have you got, Howie? You've got your big law practice and that's it!"

"And that's plenty!" She pulled this shit on him every time they argued. Really liked to twist the knife. "I'm just thirty-two and already I'm a legend in this town! A fucking *legend*!"

"And what are you doing after lunch, Mr. Legend? Going down to St. Vincent's to scrape up another client?"

"Hey! My clients are shitbums. You think I don't know that? I know it. *Damn,* do I know it! But they've been injured and they've got a legal right to maximum recovery under the law! It's my duty—"

"Save it for the jury or the newspapers, Howie," Lydia said. Her voice sounded tired, disgusted. She picked up her steno gear and headed for the door. "You and Dad—you make me ashamed."

And then she was gone.

Howard left the files on the desk and went into his private office. He ran a hand through his thick dark hair as he gazed out at Manhattan's midtown spires. What was wrong with Lydia? Didn't she understand? The malpractice field was a gold mine. There were million-dollar clients out there who hadn't the vaguest inkling what they were worth. And if he didn't find them, somebody else would.

He'd come a long way. Started out in general practice, then sniffed the possibilities in liability law. Advertising on TV had brought him a horde of new clients, but all of them combined hadn't equaled the take from his first medical malpractice settlement. He had known then that malpractice was the only way to go.

Especially when you had a method.

It was simple, really. All it took was a few well-compensated contacts in the city's hospitals to let him know when a certain type of patient was being discharged. One of Howard's assistants—Howard used to go himself but he was above that now—would arrange to be there when the potential client left the hospital. He'd take him to lunch and subtly make his pitch.

You couldn't be *too* subtle, though. The prospective client was usually a neurosurgical patient, preferably an indigent sleazo who had shown up in the hospital emergency room with his head bashed in from a mugging or a fight over a bottle or a fix, or who'd fallen down a stairway or stumbled in front of a car during a stupor. Didn't matter what the cause as long as he'd wound up in the ER in bad enough shape for the neurosurgeon on call to be dragged in to put his skull and its contents back in order again.

"But you're not right since the surgery, are you?"

That was the magic question. The answer was almost invariably negative. Of course, the prospect hadn't been "right" *before* the surgery, either, but that was hard to prove. Nigh on *impossible* to prove. And even if the potential said he felt pretty good, he usually could find some major complaint when pressed, especially after it was explained to him that a

permanent postsurgical deficit could be worth somewhere in the neighborhood of seven figures to him if things went his way.

Yeah, they were druggies and winos and all-purpose sleazos and it was
an ordeal to be in conference with one of them for more than just a few
minutes, but they were Howard's ticket to the Good Life. They were the
perfect malpractice clients. He *loved* to stick them in front of a jury. Their
shambling gaits, vacant stares, and disordered thought patterns wrung the
hearts of even the most objective jurors. And since they were transients
with no steady jobs, friends, or acquaintances, the defense could never
prove convincingly that they had been just as shambling, vacant, and disordered before the surgery.

In most cases, the malpractice insurer took one look at the client and
reached for his checkbook: It was settlement time.

Yeah, life was sweet when you knew the bushes with the best berries.

Lydia was still fuming when she reached the garage downstairs. She handed
in her ticket and found herself waiting next to Dr. Johnson. He nodded to
her.

"Can't they find your car?" she said for lack of something better.

He shrugged. "Seems that way. Goes with the rest of the day, I guess."
He looked tired, haggard, defeated. He smiled suddenly, obviously forcing
it. "How'd I do up there?"

Lydia sensed his desperate need for some hope, some encouragement.

"You did very well, I thought. Especially at the end." She couldn't bring
herself to tell him that his final remarks were shredded on the floor of the
conference room.

"Do you think I have a snowball's chance in hell of coming out of this
with the shirt on my back?"

Lydia couldn't help it. She had to say something to ease this poor man's
mind. She put her hand on his arm.

"I see lots of these cases. I'm sure they'll settle within your coverage
limits."

He turned to her. "Settle? I'm not going to settle anything!"

His intensity surprised her. "Why not?"

"Because if I agree to settle, it's as much as an admission that I've done
something wrong! And I haven't!"

"But you never know what a jury will do, Dr. Johnson."

"So I've been told, over and over and over by the insurance company. 'Settle—settle—settle!' They're scared to death of juries. Better to pay off the bloodsucking lawyer and his client than risk the decision of a jury. Sure! Fine for them! They're only thinking about the bottom line. But I did everything right in this case! I released his subdural hematoma and tied off the leaking artery inside his skull. That man would have died without me! And now he's suing me!"

"I'm sorry," Lydia said. It sounded lame to her but it was all she could say. She felt somehow partly responsible for Dr. Johnson's misery. After all, Howie was her brother.

"Maybe I should have done what a lot of my fellow neurosurgeons do: Refuse to take emergency room calls. That way you don't leave yourself open to the shyster sharks prowling around for a quick fortune. Maybe I should have gone into general practice with my brother back in our home-town. A foggy little place on the coast . . ."

He rubbed a hand across his eyes. "Looks pretty hopeless, doesn't it. If I go to court, I could lose everything I've worked for during my entire career, and jeopardize my family's whole way of life. If I settle, I'm admitting I'm wrong when I know I'm right." His jaw tightened. "It's that damned greedy bastard lawyer."

Although Lydia knew the doctor was right, the words still stung. Howard might be a lot of things, but he was still her brother.

"Things have got to change," Dr. Johnson said. "This kind of abuse is getting way out of hand. There's got to be a change in the laws to control these . . . these Hell's Angels in three-piece suits!"

"Don't hold your breath waiting for tort reform," Lydia said. "Ninety-nine percent of state legislators are lawyers, and they're all members of law firms that do a thriving business on liability claims. You don't really think they're going to take some of the bread and butter off their own tables, do you? Talk about conflict of interest!"

Dr. Johnson's expression became bleaker. "Then there's no hope of relief from the Howard Weinsteins of the world, is there? No way to give him a lesson in empathy, in knowing what kind of pain he causes in other people."

Dr. Johnson's car pulled up then, a maroon Jaguar XJ.

"I don't know how to teach him that lesson," he said. "My brother might, but I certainly don't." He sighed heavily. "I honestly don't know what I'm going to do."

"Keep fighting," Lydia told him as she watched him walk around the car and tip the attendant.

He looked at her over the hood of the Jaguar. There was a distant, resigned look in his eyes that made her afraid for him.

"Easy for you to say," he said, then got in and drove off.

Lydia stood there in the garage and watched him go, knowing in some intangible way that she would never see Dr. Walter Johnson again.

"He's dead! God, Howie, he's dead!"

Howard looked up at Lydia's pale, strained features as she leaned over his desk. He thought, *Oh, no! It's Dad! It'll be in the papers! Everyone will know!*

"Who?" he managed to say.

"Dr. Johnson! The guy you deposed last week in the malpractice case! He killed himself!"

Relief flooded through him. "He killed himself? Did he think that would let him off the hook! The jerk! We'll just take his estate to court!"

"Howard! He was depressed over this suit. You drove him over the edge!"

"I did nothing of the sort! What did he do? Shoot himself?"

Lydia's face got whiter. "No. He . . . he chopped his hand off. He bled to death."

Howard's mind suddenly went into high gear.

"Wait a minute. Wait. A. Minute! This is great! *Great!* It shows tremendous guilt over his negligence! He cut off the appendage that damaged his patient! No, wait! *Wait!* The act of suicide, especially in such a bizarre manner, points to a deranged mind. This means I can bring the hospital executive committee into the suit for allowing an obviously impaired physician to remain on the staff of their hospital. Maybe include the hospital's entire department of surgery, too! Oh, this is big! *Big!* Thank you, Lydia! You've just made my day! My *year!*"

She stood there with her mouth hanging open, looking stupid. "I don't believe you."

"What? What don't you believe? What?" What the hell was wrong with her, anyway?

"Isn't there a limit, Howard? Isn't there a place where you see a line and say to yourself, 'I can't cross over here. I'll cause too much pain on the other side.' "

He smiled at her. "Of course there is, Sis. And as soon as I find it, I'll let you know."

She didn't smile at the joke. Her face was hard, her eyes icy. "I think Dr. Johnson asked a good question last week. *Do* you have feelings, Howie? Do you ever feel anything for anybody but yourself?"

"Get off the soapbox, Sis."

"Gladly," she said. "Off the soapbox and out of your slimy presence." She turned toward the door, then back again. "Oh, by the way, I think you should know about Dr. Johnson's hand. You know, the one he cut off? They can't find it."

Howard fluttered his hands in the air. "Oooh! I'm scared! Maybe it will come crawling after me in my sleep tonight!"

She spun and slammed out the door. Howard immediately got on the intercom to his receptionist. "Chrissie? Get hold of Brian Jassie down at the coroner's office."

Missing hand? That sounded awful weird. He wanted the straight dope on it. And Brian Jassie could get it for him.

Brian had all the details by four P.M.

"This is what we got so far," he told Howard over the phone. "It's a strange one, I tell you."

"Just tell me what happened, Brian."

"Okay. Here's how they think it went down. About ten o'clock last night, at his Fifth Avenue office, this Dr. Johnson ties a tight tourniquet just above his right wrist with neat little pads to put extra pressure over the main arteries, and whacks off his hand. Records show he was a southpaw. There's evidence that he used local anesthesia. Well, he must have, right? I mean, sawing through your own wrist—"

"Brian!"

"Okay, okay. After the hand is off, there seems to be an interval of about half an hour during which we have no idea what he does, maybe some ritual or something, then he sits down, lowers his stump into a bucket, and loosens the tourniquet. Exsanguinates in a couple of minutes. Very neat, very considerate. No mess for anybody to clean up."

A real nut case, Howard thought. "Why do you say he was involved in some ritual?"

"Just a guess. There were candles all around the room and the histology department says the hand was off for around thirty minutes before he died."

"Then you have the hand."

"Uh, no, we don't."

Howard felt a little knot form in his stomach. "You're kidding."

" 'Fraid not. The forensic team looked everywhere in the office and around the building. No hand."

So Lydia hadn't been pulling his chain. The hand really was missing. Well, that would only reinforce his contention that Dr. Johnson was mentally unbalanced and shouldn't have been allowed to practice. Yes, he would definitely bring the hospital executive committee into the suit.

Still, he wondered about that missing hand. He sat there smoothing his mustache and wondering where it could be.

The package arrived the next day.

Chrissie brought it to his desk unopened. It had come by Federal Express and was marked "Personal And Confidential." Howard had her stand by as he opened it, figuring it would have to be shoved into somebody's file—most of the "Personal And Confidential" mail he received was anything but.

Chrissie began to scream when the hand fell out onto his desk. She kept on screaming all the way down the hall to the reception area. Howard stared at the hand. It lay palm up on his desk blotter, a deathly, bled-out white except at the ragged, beefy red wrist stump. The skin was moist, glistening in the fluorescent glare. He could see the creases that ran along the palm and across the finger joints, could even see fingerprint whorls. A faintly sour smell rose from it.

This had to be a joke, Lydia's way of trying to shake him up. Well, it wasn't going to work. This thing had to be a fake. He'd seen those amazingly lifelike platters of sushi and bowls of sukiyaki in the windows of Japanese restaurants. What was it they called the stuff? *Mihon.* That was it. This was the same thing: expertly sculpted and colored plastic. A gruesome piece of anatomical *mihon.*

Howard touched it with his index finger and felt a faint pins-and-needles sensation run up his arm and all over his skin. It lasted about the time between eye blinks and then it was gone. But by then he had realized from the texture of the skin and the give of the flesh underneath that this wasn't *mihon*. This was the real thing!

He leaped out of his chair and stood there trembling, repeatedly wiping his finger on his suit coat as he shouted to Chrissie to call the police.

Howard was late getting out of the office that day. The endless questions from the detectives and the forensic people had put him far behind schedule. Then, to top everything off, his last call of the day had been from Brian at the coroner's office. According to Brian, the forensic experts downtown said that the hand had definitely belonged to the late great Dr. Walter Johnson.

So now he was shook up, grossed out, and just plain tired. Irritable, too. He snapped at the Rican garage attendant—Jose or Gomez or whatever the hell his name was—to move his ass and get the car up front pronto.

His red Porsche 914 squealed down the ramp and screeched to a halt in front of him. As he passed the attendant and handed him a fifty-cent tip— half the usual—he could almost feel the man's animosity toward him.

No, wait . . . it was more than *almost*. It was as if he were actually experiencing the car jockey's anger and envy. It wormed into his system and for a moment Howard too was angry and envious. But at whom? Himself?

And just as suddenly as it came it was gone. He was once again just tired, irritable, and anxious to get himself out to the Island and home where he could have himself a stiff drink and relax.

Traffic wasn't bad. That was one advantage of leaving late. He cruised the LIE to Glen Cove Road, then headed south. He stopped at the Mac-Donald's drive-thru just this side of the sign that declared the southern limit of "The Incorporated Village of Monroe." He ordered up a Big Mac and fries. As he handed his money to the pimple-faced redheaded girl in the window, a wave of euphoria rolled over him. He felt slightly giddy. He looked up at the girl in her blue uniform and noticed her fixed grin and glazed eyes.

She's stoned! he thought. *And damned if I don't feel stoned, too!*

He took his bagged order from her and gunned away. The feeling faded almost immediately. But not his puzzlement. First the lot attendant and now the kid at Mickey D's. What was going on here?

He pulled into his spot in the Soundview Condominiums lot and entered his town house. It was a three-storied job with a good view of Monroe Harbor. He'd done some legal work on the land sale and so had been able to get in on a preconstruction purchase. The price: one hundred and sixty-nine large. They were going for twice that now.

Yeah, if you knew the right people and had the wherewithal to take advantage of situations when they presented themselves, your net worth could only go one way: Up.

Howard pulled a Bud from the fridge and opened up the Styrofoam Big Mac container. As he ate, he stared out over the still waters of the Long Island Sound at the lights along the Connecticut shore on the far side. Much as he tried not to, he couldn't help thinking about that severed hand in the mail today. Which led his thoughts around to Dr. Johnson. What was it he had said about empathy last week?

I don't think you feel anything for anyone, Mr. Weinstein. You need a real lesson in empathy.

Something like that. And then a week later he had sat down in his office and cut off his hand, and then had somehow got it into a Federal Express overnight envelope and sent it to Howard. *Personal And Confidential.* And then he had let himself die.

. . . a lesson in empathy . . .

Then the hand had arrived and Howard had touched it, felt that tingle, and now he seemed to be able to sense what others were feeling.

. . . empathy . . .

Yeah, right. And any moment now, he'd heard Rod Serling's voice fill the room.

He finished the beer and went for another.

But let's not be too quick to laugh everything off, he told himself as he nibbled on some fries. Law school had taught him how to organize his thoughts and present cogent arguments. So far, there was a good case for his being the victim of some sort of curse. That would have been laughable yesterday, but this morning there had been a real live—no, strike that, make that *dead*—a dead human hand lying on his desk. A hand that had once belonged to a defendant in a very juicy malpractice case. A man who had said that Howard Weinstein needed a lesson in how other people felt.

And now Howard Weinstein had encountered two instances in which he had experienced another person's feelings.

Or thought he had.

That was the question. Had Dr. Johnson done a number on Howard's head? Had he planted some sort of suggestion in his subconscious and then reinforced it by sending him a severed hand?

Or was this the real thing? A dead man's curse?

Howard decided to take a scientific approach. The only way to prove a hypothesis was to test it in the field. He tossed off the second beer. Time to hit the town.

As he gathered up the MacDonald's debris, he noticed a dull ache all along his right arm. He rubbed it but that didn't help. He wondered how he could have strained it. Maybe it was a result of jerking away after touching that hand this morning. No, he didn't remember any pain then. He shrugged it off, pulled on a sweater, and stepped out into the spring night.

The air was cool and tangy with salt from the Sound. Too beautiful a night to squeeze back into the Porsche, so he decided to walk the few blocks west down to the waterfront nightspots. He had only gone a few steps when he noticed that the ache in his arm was gone.

Canterbury's was the first place he came to along the newly renovated waterfront. He stopped in here occasionally with some of his local clients. Not a bad place for lunch, but after five it turned into a meat market. If AIDS had put a damper on the swinging singles scene, you couldn't tell it here. The space around Canterbury's oval bar was smoky, noisy, and packed with yuppie types.

Howard squeezed up to the bar and suddenly felt his knees get rubbery. He leaned against the mahogany edge and glanced at the fellow rubbing elbows with him to his right. He was downing a straight shot of something and chasing it with a few generous chugs of draft beer. There were four other shot glasses on the bar in front of him, all empty.

Howard lurched away toward the booths at the rear of the room and felt better immediately.

God, it's happening! It's true.

As he moved through the crowd, he was assaulted with a complex mixture of lust, boredom, fatigue, and inebriation. It was a relief to reach the relative sanctuary of the last booth in the rear. The emotions and feelings of the room became background noise, a sensory Muzak.

But they were still there. On the way from the city it had seemed he needed physical contact—from the garage attendant, the girl at Mickey D's—to get the sensory input. Now the feeling seemed to waft through the air.

Howard shut his eyes and rubbed his hands over his temples. This couldn't be happening, couldn't be real. This was the stuff of *Twilight Zone* and *Outer Limits* and *Tales from the Darkside*. This sort of thing did not happen to Howard Weinstein in little old Monroe, Long Island.

But he could not deny his own experience. He had felt drunk before noticing that the guy next to him was doing boilermakers.

Or had he?

Maybe he had unconsciously noticed the guy with the ball and the beer as he stepped up to the bar and his mind had done the rest.

It was all so confusing. How could he know for sure?

"Can I get you something, Mr. Weinstein?"

Howard looked up. A well-stacked blonde stood over him with a tray under her arm and her order pad ready. She was thirtyish with too much make-up and too-blond hair, but on the whole not someone he'd kick out of bed. She was dressed in the standard Canterbury cocktail waitress uniform of short skirt, black stockings, and low cut Elizabethan barmaid blouse, and she was smiling.

"How do you know my name?"

"Why shouldn't I? You're one of the more important men in Monroe, aren't you?"

She was interested in him. Howard couldn't read her thoughts, but he sensed her excited response to his presence. She was probably attracted to money and power, and apparently he represented a modicum of both to her. There was a trace of sexual arousal and an undercurrent of anxiety as well.

Anxiety over what? That he'd give her the cold shoulder? He tried to see if he could affect that.

"Nice to be recognized," he said, "especially by such an attractive woman" . . . he craned his neck to see the name tag centered on her cleavage . . . "Molly."

The anxiety all but vanished and the sexual arousal rose two notches.

Bingo!

He ordered a Chivas and soda. He was ready for her when she returned with the drink.

"Looks like you'll be working late tonight, huh?"

He could feel her excitement swell. "Not necessarily. It's still the off-season so it's not really crazy yet. When the tables are kinda slow like tonight I can usually get off early if I ask."

"Why don't you ask. I've got no plans for the evening. Maybe we could think of something to do together."

Her sexual arousal zoomed.

"Sounds good to me," she said with a smile and a wink.

Howard leaned back and sipped his scotch as he watched the gentle sway of her retreating butt.

So easy! Like having all the answers to a test before you sat down to take it.

This was a *curse?*

What a night!

Howard walked along the waterfront through the morning mist. He was still a little weak-kneed. He'd had loads of women over the years, plenty of one-night stands, even an all-nighter with a couple of pros. But never, *never* anything like what he had experienced last night.

As soon as they got to Molly's apartment and begun the foreplay, he had found himself tapped into her feelings. He could sense her excitement, her pleasure—he was more than just aware of it, he was actually experiencing it himself. He could tell when he was going too fast or not fast enough. He found he could toy with her, tantalize her, bring her to peaks but keep her from going over the top. Finally he brought her to an Everest and leaped off with her. Her climax fused into his and the results were shattering. She was left gasping but he was utterly speechless.

And that had only been the first time.

Molly had finally fallen asleep telling him he was the greatest lover in the world, really meaning it. Howard had drifted off with her, thinking it wouldn't be bad if that message got around to all the attractive single women in town. Not bad at all.

He had awakened early and Molly had wanted him to stay but he had begged off. He was catching a new emotion from her: She was starting to get lovey-dovey feelings for him—or at least thought she was. And why not? Decent looks, money, power, and a great lover to boot.

What's not to love?

Those feelings tripped off sirens and red lights for Howard. Uh-uh. No love. Just good times and fun and stay loose. Love meant trouble. Women started thinking of marriage then.

He felt her hurt and disappointment as he left, trailing vague promises of getting together again real soon. But he couldn't go home just yet. He was too excited, too exhilarated. This was great! This was fantastic! The possibilities were endless. He walked on, exploring them in his mind.

A siren broke into his thoughts. He looked around and found he was in front of Monroe Community Hospital. An ambulance was racing up the road. As it neared, he felt a growing pressure in his chest. His breath clogged in his throat as the pain became a great lead weight, crushing his sternum. Then, as the ambulance passed and pulled into the approach to the emergency entrance, the pain receded.

Whoever was in that ambulance was having a heart attack. Howard was sure of it. He watched as the ambulance attendants carried someone into the emergency room on a stretcher. Heart attack. No doubt about it. Just one more bit of proof on the side of this so-called curse Dr. Johnson had laid on him. And it would be so easy to confirm. Just go up to the reception desk and ask: *Did the ambulance get here with my uncle yet? The man with the chest pain?*

He started across the lawn toward the four-story brick structure. As he neared it however, he began to feel nauseous and weak. His head pounded, his abdomen burned, ached, cramped, and just plain hurt. Every joint, every bone in his body hurt. He began to wheeze, his vision blurred. It all got worse with each step closer to the hospital but he forced himself on until he reached the emergency entrance and opened the door.

. . . pain . . . fear . . . pain . . . hope . . . pain . . . grief . . . pain . . . rage . . . pain . . . despair . . . pain . . . joy . . . pain . . . pain . . . pain . . . pain . . .

Like a physical assault from a Mongolian horde, like a massive torrent from a sundered dam, like ground zero at Hiroshima, the mental and physical agony flooded over Howard, sending him reeling and stumbling back across the driveway to the grass where he crumbled to his knees and crawled as fast as he could away from the hospital. Anyone watching him would have assumed he was drunk but he didn't care. He had to get away from that building.

He felt almost himself again by the time he reached the sidewalk. He sat on the curb, weak and nauseous, swearing he would never go near another hospital again.

It seemed there were drawbacks to this little power of his after all. But nothing he couldn't handle, nothing he couldn't overcome. The advantages were too enormous!

He had to talk this out with somebody. Brainstorm it. But with whom? Suddenly, he smiled.

Lydia lived in the garden apartments on the downtown fringe, a short walk from here.

Of course!

Howard had looked like he was on drugs when Lydia opened the door to her apartment. She had been in the middle of a nice little dream of being married with two kids and no money problems when the pounding on the door had awakened her. Her brother's face had loomed large in the fish-eye peephole so she had opened up and let him in.

That proved to be a mistake. Howie was absolutely manic. While she made coffee he stalked around her tiny kitchen waving his arms and talking a mile a minute. Watching him, she thought he might be on speed; listening to him, she thought he might be on acid.

But Howie didn't do drugs.

Which meant he had gone crazy.

"Do you see what this means, Sis? Do you *see*! The possibilities are endless! Can you imagine what this will let me do at a deposition? If my questions are getting into a sensitive area, I'll *know*! I'll sense the defendant's fear, his anxiety, and I'll keep hitting those sore spots, pushing those secret buttons until he comes across with what I want. And even if he doesn't, I'll know where to look for the dirt. Same's true with cross-examinations in the courtroom. I'll know when I've hit a nerve. And speaking of courtrooms, I thought of something that's even better—even *better*!" He stopped and pointed a finger at her. "Juries! Jury selection!"

Lydia stirred the boiling water into the instant coffee—decaf, for sure. She didn't want to hype him up even the tiniest bit more. "Right, Howie," she said softly. "That's a good point."

"Can you imagine how I'll be able to stack the jury box? I mean, I'll *know* how each juror feels about the case because I'll ask them point blank. I'll say, 'Mrs. So-and-so, how do you feel about the medical profession in general?' If I get some sort of warm glow from her, she's out, no matter what she says. But if I get anger or envy or plain old spitefulness, she's in. I can pack a jury with doctor-haters on all my malpractice cases!" He giggled. "The settlements will be *astronomical*!"

"Whatever makes you happy, Howie," Lydia said. "Now why don't you sit down and drink your coffee and take it easy." She had heard about Dr. Johnson's hand winding up on his desk yesterday. The shock must have got to him. "You can lie down on my bed if you want to."

He was staring at her.

"You think I'm nuts, don't you?"

"No, Howie. I just think you're feeling the strain of—"

"Right now I'm feeling what you're feeling. Which is a lot of disbelief, a little anxiety, a little fatigue, and a little compassion. Very little compassion."

"You don't need a crystal ball or a voodoo-hoodoo curse to figure that one out."

"And you've got a low backache, too. Right?"

Lydia felt a chill. Her low back did hurt. Her period was due tomorrow and her back always ached the day before.

"Half the world's got backaches, Howie."

"You've got to believe me, Lydia. There's got to be a way I can—" His eyes lit. "Wait a minute. I've got an idea." He began yanking the kitchen drawers open until he got to the utensils. He pulled out a paring knife and handed it to her.

"What's this for?" she said.

"I want you to poke yourself here and there on your body with the point—"

"Howie, are you nuts?"

"Not hard enough to break the skin; just enough to cause a little pain." He took the pen from the message pad by the phone and pointed to the kitchen door. "I'll be on the other side of the door there and I'll mark the spots and number them on myself with this pen."

"This is crazy!"

"I've got to convince you, Lydia. You're the only one in this world I trust."

Damn him! It had been like this all their lives. He always knew what to say to get her to go along.

"Okay."

He got on the other side of the swinging door. Lydia put her back to it and poked the knife point at the center of her left palm. It hurt, but certainly nothing she couldn't bear.

"That's one," said Howie from the other side of the door.

Lydia turned her hand over and jabbed the back of her hand.

"That's two," Howie said.

Lucky guesses, Lydia told herself uneasily. For variety, she poked the point gently against her cheek.

"Very funny," Howie said, "but I'm not writing on my face."

The words so startled her that the knife slipped from her grasp. As she grabbed for it, the blade sliced into her index finger.

"Hey!" Howie said, pushing through the door. "You weren't supposed to cut yourself!"

"It was an acc—" And then she realized. "My God, you knew!" She sucked her bleeding finger. *He knew!*

"Of course I knew. As a matter of fact, for an instant in there I actually *saw* the cut on my finger. Look here. Even drew it for you. See?"

Lydia did see: A half-inch crescent was drawn in ink across the pad of Howie's right index finger, perfectly matching the bloody one on her own.

Suddenly Lydia was weak. She lowered herself into a chair. "My God, Howie, it's really true, isn't it?"

"Sure is." He stood over her, beaming. "And I'm going to milk it dry." He turned and started toward the door.

"Where are you going?"

"Back to the condo. I need some sleep, and I've got a lot of thinking to do. Don't make any plans for dinner tonight. I'm treating. Lobster and champagne at Memison's."

"Aren't we generous?"

"Make reservations for two."

And then he was gone. Lydia sat there trying to accept the fact that something that simply didn't happen in real life was happening in hers.

On the way home, Howard kept well away from the hospital. As he walked he realized that the courtroom was small potatoes, just a springboard into politics. *United States Senator Howard Weinstein.* He liked the sound of that. He'd know who to trust and who to boot. And after he'd built up his power base, maybe he'd go for the White House.

Hey, why the hell not?

He was tempted to stop by his father's place out on Shore Drive and see what he was up to. He hadn't heard from the old man in a couple of weeks. Might be interesting to see how Dad really felt about him. And then again, it might not.

He went straight home.

His right arm started bothering him at the front door. The ache was worse than he remembered from last night. Just to test a theory, he walked back outside again. The pain disappeared by the time he got to the parking lot. It reoccurred when he returned to the condo.

Which meant that someone nearby had a bad case of bursitis or something. So why the hell didn't the jerk do something about it?

Howard was too tired to worry about that now. He downed a couple of shots of scotch to calm his nerves and crawled under the covers. As he closed his eyes and tried to ignore the throb in his arm, he realized that he felt a little sad. Why? Or did the emotion even originate with him? Maybe somebody else nearby was unhappy or depressed about something. Was he getting more sensitive or what? This could get confusing.

He pushed it all away and wrapped himself in dreams of dazzling courtroom prowess and political glory.

The pain awoke him at four in the afternoon. The aching throb in his right arm was worse than ever. He wondered if it had anything to do with touching the hand. Maybe Dr. Johnson was getting even with him after all.

That was not a pleasant thought.

But then why would the pain stop as soon as he left the condo? He couldn't figure this out.

He phoned Lydia. "How about an early dinner, Sis?"

"How early?"

"As early as possible."

"I made reservations for seven-thirty."

"We'll change them."

"Is something wrong, Howie?" There was a hint of real concern in her voice.

He told her about the pain in his arm. "I've got to get out of here. That's the only time it stops."

"Okay. Meet you there at five-thirty."

That was when the peasants ate, but the pain wouldn't allow Howard to be snooty. He took a quick shower and hurried outside before his hair had dried. Blessed relief from the pain came at the far end of the parking lot.

"I'll take that one," Howard said, pointing out a big-tailed two-pounder in Memison's live lobster tank.

"Excellent choice, sir," the waiter said, then turned to Lydia. "And you, Miss?"

"I'll have the fish dinner, please."

Howard was surprised. He sensed a skittish reluctance in her. "No lobster? I thought you loved lobster!"

She was staring at the tank. "I do. But standing her and pointing out the one I'm going to eat . . . somehow it's not the same. Makes me feel like some sort of executioner."

Howard couldn't help laughing. "I swear to God you're from Mars, Sis. From *Mars*!"

When they returned to the table, Howard refilled their tall, slim champagne glasses from the bottle in the bucket. He watched a fly buzz angrily against the window that ran alongside their table. Outside at the marina, the boats rocked gently at their moorings. He savored the peace.

"You're awful quiet, Howie," Lydia said after a moment.

"Am I?"

"Compared to this morning, you're a sphinx."

Howard didn't know what to tell her, how to say it. Maybe the best thing to do was to lay it all out. Maybe she could help him sort it out.

"I think I'm having second thoughts about this special 'empathy' I've developed," he said finally. "Maybe it really is a curse. I seem to be getting increasingly sensitive. I mean, as I walked over here I got rushes of feelings from everyone I passed. There was this little kid crying on the corner. He had lost his mom and I found myself—*me*—utterly terrified. I couldn't move, I was so scared. Thank God his mother found him just then or I don't know what I'd have done. And when she whacked him on the backside for running off, I felt it. It hurt! The kid was the worst, but I was picking up all sorts of conflicting emotions. It was almost a relief to get in here. Good thing we're so early and it's almost deserted."

"Why'd you have our table moved? To get away from that fat guy?"

Howard nodded. "Yeah. He must have stuffed himself from the buffet.

I thought my stomach was going to burst. I couldn't enjoy my dinner feeling like that. And if he's going to have a gallbladder attack, I don't want to be near him."

The fly's buzzing continued. It was beginning to annoy him.

"Howard," Lydia said, looking at him intently. She only called him Howard when she was mad or really serious about something. "Can this really be happening?"

"Don't you think I've asked myself that a thousand times since last night? But yes, it's real, and it's happening to me."

He signaled their waiter as he passed. "Could you do something about that fly?"

"Of course."

The waiter returned in a moment with a fly swatter. He swung it as Howard was pouring more champagne.

Pain like Howard had never known in his life flashed through his entire body as his ears roared and his vision went stark white. It was gone in an instant, over as soon as it had begun.

"My God, Howard, what's the matter?"

Lydia was staring at him, wide-eyed and ashen-faced. He glanced around. So were the other people in the place. He felt their disapproval, their annoyance. The waiter began sopping up the champagne he had spilled when he had dropped the bottle.

"Wh-what happened?"

"You screamed and spasmed like you were having a seizure! Howard, what's wrong with you?"

"When he swatted that fly," he said, nodding his head in the direction of the retreating waiter, "I . . . I think I felt it."

Her disbelief stung him. "Oh, Howard—"

"It's true, Sis. It hurt so much for that one tiny second there I thought I was going to die."

"But a fly, Howard? A *fly*?" She stared at him. "What's wrong?"

Suddenly he was very hot. Terribly hot. His skin felt like it was on fire. He looked down at his bare arms and watched the skin turn red, rise up in blisters, burst open. He felt as if he were being boiled alive.

. . . boiled . . .

His lobster! The kitchen was only a few feet away. They'd be cooking it now—dropping it live into a pot of boiling water!

Screaming with the pain, he leaped up from the table and ran for the door.

Outside . . . coolness. He leaned against the outer wall of Memison's, gasping and sweating, oblivious to the stares of the passers-by but too well aware of their curiosity.

"Howard, are you going crazy?" It was Lydia. She had followed him out.

"Didn't you see me? I was burning up in there!" He looked down at his arms. The skin was perfect, unblemished.

"All I saw was my brother acting like a crazy man!"

He felt her concern, her fear for him, and her embarrassment because of him.

"When they started boiling my lobster, they started boiling *me*! I could feel myself being boiled alive!"

"Howard, this has got to stop!"

"Damn right it does." He pushed himself off the wall and began walking down the street, back to his condo. "I've got some thinking to do. See you."

Lydia was having her first cup of coffee when Howard called the next morning.

"Can I come over, Sis?" His voice was hoarse, strained. "I've got to get out of here."

"Sure, Howie. Is it the arm again?"

"Yeah! Feels like it's being crushed!"

Crushed. That rang a bell somewhere in the back of her mind. "Come right over. I'll leave the door unlocked. If I'm not here, make yourself at home. I'll be back soon. I've got an errand to run."

She hung up, pulled on jeans and a blouse, and hurried down to the Monroe Public Library. A *crushed arm* . . . she remembered something about that, something to do with the Soundview Condos.

It took her awhile, but she finally tracked it down in a microfilm spool of the Monroe *Express* from two years ago last summer . . .

Howard looked like hell. He looked distracted. He wasn't paying attention.

"Listen to me, Howard! It happened two years ago! They were pouring the basement slab in your section of condos. As the cement truck was backing up, a construction worker slipped in some mud and the truck's rear wheels rolled right over his arm. Crushed it so bad even Columbia Presbyterian couldn't save it."

He looked at her dully. "So?"

"So don't you see? You're not just tuned in to the feelings and sensations of people and even lobsters and bugs around you. You're picking up the *residuals* of old pains and hurts."

"Is that why it's so noisy in here?"

"Noisy?"

"Yeah. Emotional noise. This place is crowded, I mean *jammed* with emotions, some faint, some strong, some up, some down, some really mean ones. So confusing."

Lydia remembered that these garden apartments had been put up shortly after the war—World War II. If Howard could actually feel forty-plus years of emotion—

"I wish they'd go away and let me sleep. I'd give anything for just a moment's peace."

Lydia went to the medicine cabinet in the bathroom and found the bottle of Valium her doctor had prescribed for her when she was divorcing Harry. She shook two of the yellow tablets into her palm and gave them to Howard with a cup of water.

"Take these and go lie down on my bed. They'll help you sleep."

He did as he was told and shuffled off to the next room, moving like a zombie. Lydia's heart went out to him. She called a friend and begged her to take the steno job she had lined up for this afternoon, then settled down to watch over her big brother.

He slept fitfully through the day. Around dark she took a shower to ease her tension-knotted muscles. It helped some. Wrapped in her terrycloth robe, she returned to the kitchen and found him standing there looking worse than ever.

"I can't stand it!" he said in a voice that sounded as if it were going to break into a million jagged pieces. "It's making me crazy. It's even in my dreams! All those feelings! *I'm going nuts!*"

His wild eyes frightened her. "Just calm down, Howie. I'll make you something to eat and then we can—"

"I've gotta get outta here! I can't take it any longer!"

He started for the door. Lydia tried to stop him.

"Howard—"

He pushed her aside. "Got to get *out*!"

By the time she threw on enough clothing to follow him, he was nowhere to be seen.

*   *   *

The night was alive with fear and joy and lust and pain and pleasure and love, emotionally and physically strobing Howard with heat and light. He needed relief, he needed quiet, he needed peace.

And there, up ahead, he saw it . . . a cool and dark place . . . almost empty of emotions, of feeling of any sort.

He headed for it.

She got the call the next morning.

"Are you Lydia Chambers, sister of Howard Weinstein?" said an official sounding voice.

Oh, God!

"Yes."

"Would you come down to the Crosby Marina, please, ma'am?"

"Oh, no! He's not—"

"He's okay," the voice said quickly. "Physically, at least."

Lt. Donaldson drove her out to the buoy in a Marine Police outboard. Howard sat in a rowboat tied to the bobbing red channel marker in the center of Monroe Harbor.

"Seems he stole the boat last night," said the lieutenant, who had curly blond hair and looked to be in his midthirties. "But he seems to have gone off the deep end. He won't untie from the buoy and he starts screaming and swinging an oar at anyone who comes near. He asked for you."

He cut the engine and let the outboard drift toward Howard and the rowboat.

"Tell them to leave me alone, Sis!" Howard said when they got to within a couple of dozen feet of him.

He looked wild—unshaven, his clothes smudged and wrinkled, his hair standing up at crazy angles. And in his eyes, a dangerous, cornered look.

He looks insane, she thought.

"Come ashore, Howard," she said, trying to exude friendliness and calm confidence. "Come home now."

"I can't, Sis! You can explain it to them. Make them understand. This is the only place where it's quiet, where I can find peace. Oh, I know the fish are eating and being eaten below, but it's sporadic and it's far away and I can handle that. I just can't be in town anymore!"

Lt. Donaldson whispered out of the side of his mouth. "He's been talking crazy like that since we found him out here this morning."

Lydia wondered what she could tell the lieutenant: That her brother wasn't crazy, that he was suffering from a curse? Start talking like that and they'd be measuring her for a straightjacket, too.

"You can't stay out here, Howard."

"I have to. There's a gull's nest in the buoy and the little birds were hungry this morning and it made me hungry, too. But then the mother came and fed them and now their bellies are full and they're content" . . . he began to sob . . . "and so am I and I just want to stay here near them where it's quiet and peaceful."

She heard the lieutenant growl. "All right. That does it!"

He stood up and signaled to shore. Another larger boat roared out from the marina. There were men in white jackets aboard, and they were carrying something that looked like a net.

"He'll be asleep for awhile yet, Mrs. Chambers," said Dr. Gold. "We had to inject him with a pretty stiff dose of Thorazine to quiet him down."

It had been horrifying to watch them throw a net over her own brother and haul him into the bigger boat like a giant fish, but there had been no other way. Howard would have died out on the water if they had left him there.

She had spent most of the morning signing papers and answering countless questions on Howard's medical and emotional history, family history, current stresses and strains. She had told Dr. Gold everything, including Howard's receiving the hand in the mail two days ago. *God, was it only two days ago?* Everything . . . except the part about feeling the pain and emotion of other people . . . and animals and even insects. She couldn't bring herself to risk trying to explain that to Dr. Gold. He might think she was sharing her brother's psychosis.

"When can he leave?" she asked.

"Not for twenty-eight days at least. That's how long he's committed. Don't worry too much. This appears to be an acute psychosis precipitated by that grisly incident with the severed hand. We'll start his psychotherapy immediately, find an appropriate medication, and do what we can to get him on his psychological feet again as soon as possible. I think he'll do just fine."

Lydia wasn't too sure of that, but all she could do was hope. At least the Monroe Neuropsychiatric Institute was brand new. It had opened only last winter. She had heard about it, but since she never came to this part of town, she hadn't seen it until now. It seemed pleasant enough. And since most of the patients here were probably sedated to some degree, their emotions wouldn't be too strong. Maybe Howard had a chance here.

Dr. Gold walked her to the door.

"In a way it's sort of ironic that your brother should wind up here."

"Why is that?"

"Well, he's one of the limited partners that developed this little hospital. All of the limited partners got a certified historic rehabilitation tax credit for investing, one of the few goodies remaining after tax overhaul."

"Rehabilitation?" A warning bell sounded in a far corner of her mind. "You mean it isn't a new building?"

"Oh, my goodness, no. We've cleaned it up to look spanking new, but in reality it's a hundred and fifty years old."

"A hundred and fifty—"

"Yes. It was abandoned for such a long time. I understand it was being used for dogfights before we took it over. Even used it as a place to train young fighting pit bulls. Trained them with kittens. A sick, sick—" He stared at her. "Are you all right?"

"Dogfights?" Oh, God, what would that do to Howard? Wouldn't the residual from something like that send him right up the wall?

"I'm sorry if I upset you."

"I'm okay," she said, steeling herself to ask the next question. "What was the building originally?"

"Originally? Why I thought everybody knew that, but I guess you're too young to remember. Up until the late 1960s it was the Monroe Slaughterhouse. One of the busiest in the—"

He stopped as the sound came down the hall—a long, hoarse, agonized scream that echoed off the freshly painted walls and tore into Lydia's soul.

Howard was awake.

The idea for "Tenants" had been wandering through the back of my mind for years. A simple little story about an escaped killer who thinks he's found the perfect hideout from the law in a remote house. The old coot who lives there is crazy: He keeps talking about his tenants, but he's alone in the shack. Or is he?

I could have set it anywhere, but I chose Monroe. Not only because I'd set "Feelings" there but because I was squeezing out these stories between sections of *Reborn*; that novel is also set in Monroe and I saw a possible connection. I'd envisioned *Reborn* as the first part of a long roman-fleuve that would unite my three previous novels, *The Keep*, *The Tomb*, and *The Touch*, into a six-book cycle. But why were all these strange things happening in Monroe? Why had the *Dat-tay-vao* been drawn to Monroe in *The Touch*? Was it all random, or was there a reason? I realized *Reborn* contained that reason. So if the old guy in "Tenants" has some strange boarders, maybe they too wound up in Monroe for a reason. The locale had no direct effect on the novelette itself, but it gave me a little extra kick to know I was connecting it to the cycle.

Gus and his tenants surface again briefly in *Nightworld*.

TENANTS

The mail truck was coming.

Gilroy Connors, shoes full of water and shirt still wet from the morning's heavy dew, crouched in the tall grass and punk-topped reeds. He ached all over; his thighs particularly were cramped from holding his present position. But he didn't dare move for fear of giving his presence away.

So he stayed hunkered down across the road from the battered old shack that looked deserted but wasn't—there had been lights on in the place last night. With its single pitched roof and rotting cedar shake siding, it looked more like an overgrown outhouse than a home. A peeling propane tank squatted on the north side; a crumbling brick chimney supported a canted TV antenna. Beyond the shack, glittering in the morning sunlight, lay the northeast end of Monroe Harbor and the Long Island Sound.

The place gave new meaning to the word *isolated*. As if a few lifetimes ago someone had brought a couple of tandems of fill out to the end of the hard-packed dirt road, dumped them, and built a shack. Except for a rickety old dock with a sodden rowboat tethered to it, there was not another structure in sight in either direction. Only a slender umbilical cord of insulated wire connected it to the rest of the world via a long column of utility poles marching out from town. All around was empty marsh.

Yeah. Isolated as all hell.

It was perfect.

As Gil watched, the shack's front door opened and a grizzled old man stumbled out, a cigarette in his mouth and a fistful of envelopes in his hand. Tall and lanky with an unruly shock of gray hair standing off his head, he scratched his slightly protruding belly as he squinted in the morning sunlight. He wore a torn undershirt that had probably been white once and a pair of faded green work pants held up by suspenders. He looked as run-down as his home, and as much in need of a shave and a bath as Gil felt. With timing so perfect that it could only be the result of daily practice, the old guy reached the mailbox at exactly the same time as the white Jeep-like mail truck.

Must have been watching from the window.

Not an encouraging thought. Had the old guy seen Gil out here? If he had, he gave no sign. Which meant Gil was still safe.

He fingered the handle of the knife inside his shirt.

Lucky for him.

While the old guy and the mailman jawed, Gil studied the shack again. The place was a sign that his recent run of good luck hadn't deserted him yet. He had come out to the marshes to hide until things cooled down in and around Monroe and had been expecting to spend a few real uncomfortable nights out here. The shack would make things a lot easier.

Not much of a place. At most it looked big enough for two rooms and no more. Barely enough space for an ancient couple who didn't move around much—who ate, slept, crapped, watched TV and nothing more. Hopefully, it wasn't a couple. Just the old guy. That would make it simple. A wife, even a real sickly one, could complicate matters.

Gil wanted to know how many were living there before he invited himself in. Not that it would matter much. Either way, he was going in and staying for a while. He just liked to know what he was getting into before he made his move.

One thing was sure: He wasn't going to find any money in there. The old guy had to be next to destitute. But even ten bucks would have made him richer than Gil. He looked at the rusting blue late-sixties Ford Torino with the peeling vinyl roof and hoped it would run. But of course it ran. The old guy had to get into town to cash his Social Security check and buy groceries, didn't he?

Damn well better run.

It had been a long and sloppy trek into these marshes. He intended to drive out.

Finally the mail truck clinked into gear, did a U-turn, and headed back the way it had come. The old guy shoved a couple of envelopes into his back pocket, picked up a rake that had been leaning against the Ford, and began scratching at the dirt on the south side of the house.

Gil decided it was now or never. He straightened up and walked toward the shack. As his feet crunched on the gravel of the yard, the old man wheeled and stared at him with wide, startled eyes.

"Didn't mean to scare you," Gil said in his friendliest voice.

"Well, you sure as hell did, poppin' outta nowhere like that!" the old man said in a deep, gravelly voice. The cigarette between his lips bobbed up and down like a conductor's baton. "We don't exactly get much drop-in company out here. What happen? Boat run outta gas?"

Gil noticed the *we* with annoyance but played along. A stalled boat was as good an excuse as any for being out here in the middle of nowhere.

"Yeah. Had to paddle it into shore way back over there," he said, jerking a thumb over his shoulder.

"Well, I ain't got no phone for you to call anybody—"

No phone! It was all Gil could do to keep from cheering.

"—but I can drive you down to the marina and back so you can get some gas."

"No hurry." He moved closer and leaned against the old Torino's fender. "You live out here all by yourself?"

The old man squinted at him, as if trying to recognize him. "I don't believe we've been introduced, son."

"Oh, right." Gil stuck out his hand. "Rick . . . Rick Summers."

"And I'm George Haskins," he said, giving Gil's hand a firm shake.

"What're you growing there?"

"Carrots. I hear fresh carrots are good for your eyes. Mine are so bad I try to eat as many as I can."

Half blind and no phone. This was sounding better every minute. Now, if he could just find out who the rest of the *we* was, he'd be golden.

He glanced around. Even though he was out in the middle of nowhere at the end of a dirt road that no one but the mailman and this old fart knew existed, he felt exposed. Naked, even. He wanted to get inside.

"Say, I sure could use a cup of coffee, Mr. Haskins. You think you might spare me some?"

* * *

George hesitated. Making coffee for the stranger would mean bringing him inside. He didn't like that idea at all. He hadn't had anybody into the house since the late sixties when he took in his tenants. And he'd had damn few visitors before that. People didn't like coming this far out, and George was just as glad. Most people pried. They wanted to know what you did way out here all by yourself. Couldn't believe anybody sane would prefer his own company to *theirs*.

And of course, there was the matter of the tenants.

He studied this young man who had popped out of nowhere. George's eyes weren't getting any better—*"Cataracts only get worse,"* the doctor had told him—but he could plainly see that the stranger wasn't dressed for boating, what with that blue work shirt and gray denims he was wearing. And those leather shoes! Nobody who knew boats ever wore leather shoes on board. But they were selling boats to anybody with cash these days. This landlubber probably didn't know the first thing about boating. That no doubt was why he was standing here on land instead of chugging about the harbor.

He seemed pleasant enough, though. Good-looking, too, with his muscular build and wavy dark hair. Bet he had an easy time with the girls. *Especially* easy, since from what George understood of the world today, *all* the girls were easy.

Maybe he could risk spotting him a cup of coffee before driving him down to the marina. What harm could there be in that? The tenants were late risers and had the good sense to keep quiet if they heard a strange voice overhead.

He smiled. "Coffee? Sure. Come on inside. And call me George. Everybody else does." He dropped his cigarette into the sandy soil and stomped on it, then turned toward the house.

Just a quick cup of coffee and George would send him off. The longer he stayed, the greater the chances of him finding out about the tenants. And George couldn't risk that. He was more than their landlord.

He had sworn to protect them.

Gil followed close on the old guy's back up the two steps to the door. Inside was dark and stale, reeking of years of cigarette smoke. He wondered when was the last time George had left a window open.

But being indoors was good. Out of sight and inside—even if it stank, it was better than good. It was super. He felt as if a great weight had been lifted from him.

Now to find out who made up the rest of the *we*.

"Got this place all to yourself, ay?" he said, glancing quickly about. They were standing in a rectangular space that passed for a living room/dining room/kitchen. The furniture consisted of an old card table, a rocker, a tilted easy chair, and a dilapidated couch. Shapeless piles of junk cluttered every corner. An ancient Motorola television set with a huge chassis and a tiny screen stood on the far side of the room diagonally across from the door. The screen was lit and a black chick was reading some news into the camera:

"*. . . eriously injuring an orderly in a daring escape from the Monroe Neuropsychiatric Institute. He was last reported in Glen Cove—*"

Gil whooped. "Glen Cove! Awright!" That was the wrong direction! He was safe for the moment. "Fan*tas*tic!" he yelled, stomping his foot on the floor.

"Hey! Hold it down!" George said as he filled a greasy, dented aluminum kettle with water and put it on the gas stove.

Gil felt the customary flash of anger at being told what he could or couldn't do, but cooled it. He stepped between George and the TV set as he saw his most recent mug shot appear on the screen. The black chick was saying:

"*If you see this man, do not approach him. He might be armed and is considered dangerous.*"

Gil said, "Sorry. It's just that sometimes I get excited by the news."

"Yeah?" George said, lighting another cigarette. "Don't follow it much myself. But you got to keep quiet. You might disturb the tenants and they—"

"*Tenants?*" Gil said a lot more loudly than he intended. "You've got *tenants?*"

The old guy was biting his upper lip with what few teeth he had left and saying nothing.

Gil stepped down the short hall, gripping the handle of the knife inside his shirt as he moved. Two doors: The one on the left was open, revealing a tiny bathroom with a toilet, sink, and mildewy shower stall; the one on the right was closed. He gave it a gentle push. Empty: dirty, wrinkled sheets on a narrow bed, dresser, mirror, clothes thrown all around, but nobody there.

"Where are they?" he said, returning to the larger room.

George laughed—a little too loudly, Gil thought—and said, "No tenants. Just a joke. Creepy-crawlies in the crawl space is all. You know, snapping turtles and frogs and snakes and crickets."

"You keep things like that under your house?" This was turning out to be one weird guy.

"In a manner of speaking, yes. You see, a zillion years ago when I built this place, a big family of crickets took up residence"—he pointed down— "in the crawl space. Drove me crazy at night. So one day I get the bright idea of catching some frogs and throwing them in there to eat the crickets. Worked great. Within two days, there wasn't a chirp to be heard down there."

"Smart."

"Yeah. So I thought. Until the frogs started croaking all night. They were worse than the crickets!"

Gil laughed. "I get it. So you put the snakes down there to catch the frogs!"

"Right. Snakes are quiet. They eat crickets, too. Should've thought of them in the first place. Except I wasn't crazy about living over a nest of snakes."

This was getting to sound like the old lady who swallowed the fly.

Gil said, "And so the next step was to put the turtles down there to eat the snakes."

"Yeah." As George spooned instant coffee into a couple of stained mugs, Gil tried not to think about when they last might have had a good washing. "But I don't think they ate them all, just like I don't think the snakes ate all the frogs, or the frogs ate all the crickets. I still hear an occasional chirp and croak once in a while. Anyway, they've all been down there for years. I ain't for adding anything else to the stew, or even looking down there."

"Don't blame you."

George poured boiling water into the mugs and handed him one.

"So if you hear something moving underfoot, it's just one of my tenants."

"Yeah. Okay. Sure."

This old guy was fruitcake city. As crazy as—

. . . Crazy. That was what that college chick had called him that night

when he had tried to pick her up along the road. She was cute. There were a lot of cute girls at Monroe Community College, and he'd always made it a point to drive by every chance he could. She'd said he was crazy to think she'd take a ride from a stranger at that hour of the night. That had made him mad. All these college broads thought they were better and smarter than everybody else. And she'd started to scream when he grabbed her, so he'd hit her to make her stop but she wouldn't stop. She kept on screaming so he kept on hitting her and hitting her and hitting and hitting . . .

"You're spilling your coffee," George said.

Gil looked down. So he was. It was dripping over the edge of his tilted mug and splashing onto the floor. As he slurped some off the top and sat on the creaking couch, he realized how tired he was. No sleep in the past twenty-four hours. Maybe the coffee would boost him.

"So how come you live out here all by yourself?" Gil asked, hoping to get the conversation on a saner topic than snakes and snapping turtles in the crawl space.

"I *like* being by myself."

"You must. But whatever rent you pay on this place, it's too much."

"Don't pay no rent at all. I own it."

"Yeah, but the land—"

"My land."

Gil almost dropped his coffee mug. "*Your* land! That's impossible!"

"Nope. All twenty acres been in my family for a zillion and two years."

Gil's brain whirled as he tried to calculate the value of twenty acres of real estate fronting on Monroe Harbor and Long Island Sound.

"You're a fucking millionaire!"

George laughed. "I wish! I'm what you call 'land poor,' son. I've got to pay taxes on all this land if I want to keep it, and the damn bastards down at City Hall keep raising my rates and my assessed value so that I've got to come up with more and more money every year just to stay here. Trying to force me out, that's what they're up to."

"So sell, for Christ sake! There must be developers chomping at the bit to get ahold of this land. You could make 'em pay through the nose for a piece of waterfront and all your money worries would be over!"

George shook his head. "Naw. Once you sell one little piece, it's like a leak in a dam. It softens you, weakens you. Soon you're selling another piece, and then another. Pretty soon, I'll be living on this little postage stamp surrounded by big ugly condos, listening to cars and mopeds racing up and down the road with engines roaring and rock and roll blasting. No thanks. I've lived here in peace, and I want to die here in peace."

"Yeah, but—"

"Besides, lots of animals make their homes on my land. They've been pushed out of everywhere else in Monroe. All the trees have been cut down back there, all the hollows and gullies filled in and paved over. There's no place else for them to go. This is their world, too, you know. I'm their last resort. It's my duty to keep this place wild as long as I can. As long as I live . . . which probably won't be too much longer."

Oh, yes . . . crazy as a loon. Gil wondered if there might be some way he could get the old guy to will him the property and then cork him off. He stuffed the idea away in the *To Be Developed* file.

"Makes me glad I don't have a phone," George was saying.

Right . . . no phone and no visitors.

Gil knew this was the perfect hiding place for him. Just a few days was all he needed. But he had to stay here *with* the old guy's cooperation. He couldn't risk anything forceful—not if George met the mailman at the box every day.

And from a few things the old man had said, he thought he knew just what buttons to push to convince George to let him stay.

George noted that his guest's coffee was empty. Good. Time to get him moving on. He never had company, didn't like it, and wasn't used to it. Made him itchy. Besides, he wanted this guy on his way before another re-mark about the tenants slipped out. That had been a close call before.

He stood up.

"Well, guess it's about time to be running you down to the marina for that tank of gas."

The stranger didn't move.

"George," he said in a low voice, "I've got a confession to make."

"Don't want to hear it!" George said. "I ain't no priest! Tell it somewhere else. I just want to help get you where you're going!"

"I'm on the run, George."

Oh, hell, George thought. At least that explained why he was acting so skittish. "You mean there's no boat waiting for gas somewhere?"

"I . . ." His voice faltered. "I lied about the boat."

"Well ain't that just swell. And who, may I ask,"—George wasn't so sure he wanted the answer to this, but he had to ask—"are you on the run from?"

"The Feds."

Double hell. "What for?"

"Income tax evasion."

"No kidding?" George was suddenly interested. "How much you take them for?"

"It's not so much 'how much' as 'how long.' "

"All right: How long?"

"Nine years. I haven't filed a return since I turned eighteen."

"No shit! Is that because you're stupid or because you've got balls?"

"Mr. Haskins," the stranger said, looking at him levelly and speaking with what struck George as bone-deep conviction, "I don't believe any government's got the right to tax what a working man earns with the sweat of his brow."

"Couldn't of said it better myself!" George cried. He thought his heart was going to burst. This boy was talking like he'd have wanted his son to talk, if he'd ever had one. "The sonsabitches'll bleed you dry if you let 'em! Look what they've been doin' to me!"

The young stranger stared at the floor. "I was hoping you'd understand."

"Understand? Of course I understand! I've been fighting the IRS for years but never had the guts to actually *resist*! My hat's off to you!"

"Can I stay the night?"

That brought George up short. He wanted to help this courageous young man, but what was he going to do about the tenants?

"What's going to happen to you if they catch you? What kind of sentence you facing?"

"Twenty."

George's stomach turned. A young guy like this in the hole for twenty years just for not paying taxes. He felt his blood begin to boil.

"Bastards!"

He'd have to chance it. Tenants or not, he felt obligated to give this guy a place to stay for the night. It would be okay. The tenants could take the day off and just rest up. They'd been working hard lately. He'd just have to watch his mouth so he didn't make another slip about them.

"Well, George? What do you say?"

"I can let you stay one night and one night only," George said. "After that—"

The young fellow leaped forward and shook his head. "Thanks a million, George!"

"Hear me out now. Only tonight. Come tomorrow morning, I'll drive you down to the train station, get you a ticket, and put you on board for New York with all the commuters. Once in the city, you can get lost real easy."

George thought he saw tears in the young man's eyes. "I don't know how to thank you."

"Never mind that. You just hit the sack in my room. You look bushed. Get some rest. No one'll know you're here."

He nodded, then went to the window and gazed out at the land. "Beautiful here," he said.

George realized it would probably look even more beautiful if the window were cleaner, but his eyes weren't good enough to notice much difference.

"If this were mine," the young fellow said passionately, "I'd sure as hell find a way to keep it out of the hands of the developers *and* the tax men. Maybe make it into a wildlife preserve or bird sanctuary or something. *Anything* to keep it wild and free."

Shaking his head, he turned and headed for the back room. George watched him in wonder. *A wildlife preserve!* Why hadn't he thought of that? It would be untaxable and unsubdividable! What a perfect solution!

But it was too late to start the wheels turning on something like that now. It would take years to submit all the proposals and wade through all the red tape to get it approved. And he didn't have years. He didn't need a doctor to tell him that his body was breaking down. He couldn't see right, he couldn't breathe right, and Christ Almighty, he couldn't even pee right. The parts were wearing out and there were no replacements available.

And what would happen when he finally cashed in his chips? What would happen to his land? And the tenants? Where would *they* go?

Maybe this young fellow was the answer. Maybe George could find a way to leave the land to him. He'd respect it, preserve it, just as George would if he could go on living. Maybe that was the solution.

But that meant he'd have to tell him the real truth about the tenants. He didn't know if the guy was ready for that.

He sat down in the sun on the front steps and lit another cigarette. He had a lot of thinking to do.

The five o'clock news was on.

George had kept himself busy all day, what with tending to the carrot patch outside and cleaning up a bit inside. Having company made him realize how long it had been since he'd given the place a good sweeping.

But before he'd done any of that, he'd waited until the young fellow had fallen asleep, then he'd lifted the trapdoor under the rug in the corner of the main room and told the tenants to lay low for the day. They'd understood and said they'd be quiet.

Now he was sitting in front of the TV watching *Eyewitness News* and going through today's mail: Three small checks from the greeting card companies—not much, but it would help pay this quarter's taxes. He looked up at the screen when he heard "the Long Island town of Monroe" mentioned. Some pretty Oriental girl was sitting across from a scholarly looking fellow in a blue suit. She was saying, ". . . explain to our viewers just what it is that makes Gilroy Connors so dangerous, Dr. Kline."

"He's a sociopath."

"And just what is that?"

"Simply put, it is a personality disorder in which the individual has no sense of 'mine' and 'not mine,' no sense of right or wrong in the traditional sense."

"No conscience, so to speak."

"Exactly."

"Are they all murderers like Connors?"

"No. History's most notorious criminals and serial killers are sociopaths, but violence isn't a necessary facet of their makeup. The confidence men who rip off the pensions of widows or steal from a handicapped person are just as sociopathic as the Charles Mansons of the world. The key element in the sociopathic character is his or her complete lack of guilt. They will do whatever is necessary to get what they want and will feel no remorse over anyone they have to harm along the way."

"Gilroy Connors was convicted in the Dorothy Akers murder. Do you think he'll kill again?"

"He has to be considered dangerous. He's a sociopathic personality with a particularly low frustration threshold. But he is also a very glib liar. Since the truth means nothing to him, he can take any side of a question, any moral stance, and speak on it with utter conviction."

A voice—George recognized it as belonging to one of the anchormen—called from off-camera: "Sounds like he'd make a great politician!"

Everyone had a good laugh, and then the Oriental woman said, "But all kidding aside, what should our viewers do if one of them should spot him?"

Dr. Kline's expression was suddenly grim. "Lock the doors and call the police immediately."

The camera closed in on the Oriental girl. "There you have it. We've been speaking to Dr. Edward Kline, a Long Island psychiatrist who examined Gilroy Connors and testified for the state at the Dorothy Akers murder trial.

"In case you've been asleep or out of the country during the last twenty-four hours, all of Long Island is being combed for Gilroy Connors, convicted killer of nineteen-year-old college coed Dorothy Akers. Connors escaped custody last night when, due to an error in paperwork, he was accidently transferred to the Monroe Neuropsychiatric Institute instead of a maximum security facility as ordered by the court. The victim's father, publisher Jeffrey Akers, is offering a fifty thousand dollar reward for information leading to his recapture."

Fifty thousand! George thought. *What I could do with that!*

"You've heard Dr. Kline," she continued. "If you see this man, call the police immediately."

A blow-up of a mug shot appeared on the screen. George gasped. He knew that man! Even with his rotten vision, he could see that the face on the TV belonged to the man now sleeping in his bed! He turned around to look toward the bedroom and saw his house guest standing behind him, a knife in his hand.

"Don't even think about that reward, old man," Connors said in a chillingly soft voice. "Don't even *dream* about it."

"You're hurtin' my hands!" the old fart whined as Gil knotted the cord around his wrists.

"I'm putting you down for the night, old man, and you're *staying* down!"

He pulled the rope tighter and the old man yelped.

Gil said, "There—that ought to hold you."

George rolled over onto his back and stared up at him. "What are you going to do with me?"

"Haven't figured that out yet."

"You're gonna kill me, aren't you?" There was more concern than fear in his eyes.

"Maybe. Maybe not. Depends on how you behave."

Truthfully, he didn't know what to do. It would be less of a hassle to kill him now and get it over with, but there was the problem of the mailman. If George wasn't waiting curbside at the box tomorrow morning, the USPS might come knocking on the door. So Gil had to figure out a way to pressure George into acting as if everything was nice and normal tomorrow. Maybe he'd have George stand at the door and wave to the mailman. That might work. He'd have to spend some time figuring this out.

"All that stuff you said about dodging the tax man was just lies, wasn't it?"

Gil smiled at the memory. "Yeah. Pretty good, wasn't it? I mean, I made that up right off the top of my head. Sucked you in like smoke, didn't I?"

"Nothing to be proud of."

"Why not?"

"You heard what they called you on the TV: a 'socialpath.' Means you're crazy."

"You watch your mouth, old man!" Gil could feel the rage surging up in him like a giant wave. He hated that word. "I'm *not* crazy! And I don't ever want to hear that word out of your mouth again!"

"Doesn't matter anyway," George said. "Soon as you're out of here, my tenants will untie me."

Gil laughed. "*Now* who's crazy!"

"It's true. They'll free me."

"That's enough of that," Gil said. It wasn't funny any more. He didn't like being called crazy any more than he liked being near crazy people. And this old man was talking crazy now. "No more of that kind of talk out of you!"

"You'll see. I'm their protector. Soon as you're—"

"Stop that!" Gil yanked George off the bed by his shirt front. He was losing it—he could feel it going. "God *damn* that makes me mad!"

He shoved the old man back against the wall with force enough to rattle the whole house. George's eyes rolled up as he slumped back onto the bed. A small red trickle crawled along his scalp and mixed with the gray of his hair at the back of his head.

"Sleep tight, Pops," Gil said.

He left George on the bed and returned to the other room. He turned the antique TV back on. After what seemed like an inordinately long warm-up time, the picture came in, flipped a few times, then held steady. He hoped there wasn't another psychiatrist on talking about him.

He hated psychiatrists. *Hated* them! Since he'd been picked up for killing that college chick, he'd seen enough of their kind to last a couple of lifetimes. Why'd she have to go and die? It wasn't fair. He hadn't meant to kill her. If only she'd been a little more cooperative. But no—she'd had to go and laugh in his face. He'd just got mad, that was all. He wasn't crazy. He just had a bad temper.

Psychiatrists! What'd they know about him? Labeling him, pigeon-holing him, saying he had no conscience and never felt sorry for anything he did. What'd they know? Did they know how he'd cried after Mom had burnt up in that fire in Dad's car? He'd cried for *days*. Mom wasn't supposed to be anywhere near that car when it caught fire. Only Dad.

He had *loads* of feelings, and nobody had better tell him any different!

He watched the tube for a while, caught a couple of news broadcasts, but there was only passing mention of his escape and the reward the girl's old man had posted for him. Then came a report that he had been sighted on Staten Island and the search was being concentrated there.

He smiled. They were getting farther and farther away from where he really was.

He shut off the set at eleven-thirty. Time for some more sleep. Before he made himself comfortable on the couch, he checked out the old man's room. He was there, snoring comfortably under the covers. Gil turned away and then spun back again.

How'd he get under the covers?

Two strides took him to the bedside. His foot kicked against something that skittered across the floor. He found what it was: the old guy's shoes. They'd been on his feet when he'd tied him up! He yanked back the covers and stared in open-mouthed shock at the old man.

George's hands and feet were free. The cords were nowhere in sight.

Just then he thought he caught a blur of movement by the doorway. He swung around but there was nothing there. He turned back to George.

"Hey, you old fart!" He shook George's shoulder roughly until his eyes opened. "Wake up!"

George's eyes slowly came into focus. "Wha—?"

"How'd you do it?"

"Go way!"

George rolled onto his other side and Gil saw a patch of white gauze where he had been bleeding earlier. He flipped him onto his back again.

"How'd you untie yourself, goddammit?"

"Didn't. My tenants—"

"You stop talking that shit to me, old man!" Gil said, cocking his right arm.

George flinched away but kept his mouth shut. Maybe he was finally learning.

"You stay right there!"

Gil tore through the drawers and piles of junk in the other room until he found some more cord. During the course of the search he came across a checkbook and some uncashed checks. He returned to the bedroom and began tying up George again.

"Don't know how you did it the first time, but you ain't doing it again!"

He spread-eagled George on the sheet and tied each skinny limb to a separate corner of the bed, looping the cord down and around on the legs of the frame. Each knot was triple-tied.

"There! See if you can get out of that!"

As George opened his mouth to speak, Gil glared at him and the old man shut it with an almost audible snap.

"That's the spirit," Gil said softly.

He pulled the knife out of his shirt and held its six-inch blade up before George. The old man's eyes widened.

"Nice, isn't it? I snatched it from the kitchen of that wimpy Monroe Neuropsychiatric Institute. Would've preferred getting myself a gun, but none of the guards there were armed. Still, I can do a whole lot of damage with something like this and still not kill you. Understand what I'm saying to you, old man?"

George nodded vigorously.

"Good. Now what we're going to have here tonight is a nice quiet little house. No noise, no talk. Just a good night's sleep for both of us. Then we'll see what tomorrow brings."

He gave George one last hard look straight in the eye, then turned and headed back to the couch.

Before sacking out for the night, Gil went through George's checkbook. Not a whole lot of money in it. Most of the checks went out to cash or to the township for quarterly taxes. He noticed one good-sized regular monthly deposit that was probably his Social Security check, and lots of smaller sporadic additions.

He looked through the three undeposited checks. They were all made out to George Haskins, each from a different greeting card company. The attached invoices indicated they were in payment for varying numbers of verses.

Verses?

You mean old George back there tied up to the bed was a poet? He wrote greeting card verse?

Gil looked around the room. Where? There was no desk in the shack. Hell, he hadn't seen a piece of paper since he got here! Where did George write this stuff?

He went back to the bedroom. He did his best not to show the relief he felt when he saw that old George was still tied up nice and tight.

"Hey, old man," he said, waving the checks in the air. "How come you never told me you were a poet?"

George glared at him. "Those checks are mine! I need them to pay my taxes!"

"Yeah? Well, right now I need them a lot more than you do. I think tomorrow morning we'll take a little trip down to the bank so you can cash these." He checked the balance in the account. "And I think you just might make a cash withdrawal, too."

"I'll lose my land if I don't pay those taxes on time!"

"Well then, I guess you'll just have to come up with some more romantic 'verses' for these card companies. Like, 'George is a poet/And nobody know it.' See? It's easy!"

Gil laughed as he thought of all the broads who get those flowery, syrupy birthday and anniversary cards and sit mooning over the romantic poems inside, never knowing they were written by this dirty old man in a falling-down shack on Long Island!

"I love it!" he said, heading back to the couch. "I just love it!"

He turned out all the lights, shoved the knife between two of the cushions, and bedded down on the dusty old couch for the night. As he drifted off to sleep, he thought he heard rustling movements from under the floorboards. George's 'tenants,' no doubt. He shuddered at the thought. The sooner he was out of here, the better.

What time is it?

Gil was rubbing the sleep from his eyes and peering around in the mineshaft blackness that surrounded him. Something had awakened him. But what? He sat perfectly still and listened.

A few crickets, maybe a frog—the noises seemed to come from outside instead of from the crawl space—but nothing more than that.

Still, his senses were tingling with the feeling that something was wrong. He stood up and stepped over toward the light switch. As he moved, his foot caught on something and he fell forward. On the way down his ribs slammed against something else, something hard, like a chair. He hit the floor with his left shoulder. Groaning, he got to his knees and crawled until his fingers found the wall. He fumbled around for the light switch and flipped it.

When his eyes had adjusted to the glare, he glanced at the clock over the kitchen sink—going on 4:00 A.M. He thought he saw something move by the sink, but when he squinted for a better look, it was just some junk George had left there. Then he turned back toward the couch to see what had tripped him up.

It was the little hassock that had been over by the rocking chair when he had turned the lights out. At least he was pretty sure it had been there. He *knew* it hadn't been next to the couch where it was now. And the chair he had hit on his way down—that had been over against the wall.

In fact, as he looked around he noticed that not a single piece of furniture in the whole room was where it had been when he had turned out the lights and gone to sleep three or four hours ago. It had all been moved closer to the couch.

Someone was playing games. And Gil only knew of one possible someone.

Retrieving his knife from the couch, he hurried to the bedroom and stopped dead at the door. George was tied hand and foot to the corners of the bed, snoring loudly.

A chill rippled over Gil's skin.

"How the hell . . . ?"

He went back to the main room and checked the door and windows—all were locked from the inside. He looked again at the furniture, clustered around the couch as if the pieces had crept up and watched him as he slept.

Gil didn't believe in ghosts but he was beginning to believe this little shack was haunted.

And he wanted out.

He had seen the keys to the old Torino in one of the drawers. He found them again and hurried outside to the car. He hoped the damn thing started. He wasn't happy about hitting the road so soon, but he preferred taking his chances with the cops out in the open to being cooped up with whatever was haunting that shack.

As he slipped behind the wheel, he noticed a sliver of light shining out from inside the shack's foundation. That was weird. *Really* weird. Nobody kept a light on in a crawl space. He was about to turn the ignition key but held up. He knew it was going to drive him nuts if he left without seeing what was down there.

Cursing himself for a jerk, he turned on the Ford's headlamps and got out for a closer look.

The light was leaking around a piece of plywood fitted into an opening in the foundation cinder blocks. It was hinged at the bottom and held closed by a short length of one-by-two shoved through the handle at the top. He pulled out the one-by-two and hesitated.

Connors, you are an asshole, he told himself, but he had to see what was in there. If it was snakes and snapping turtles, fine. That would be bad enough. But if it was something worse, he had to know.

Gripping the knife tightly in one hand, he yanked the board toward him with the other and quickly peered in, readying himself to slam it shut in an instant. But what he saw within so shocked him he almost dropped the knife.

There was a furnished apartment inside.

The floor of the crawl space was carpeted. It was worn, industrial grade carpet, but it was *carpet*. There were chairs, tables, bunk beds, the works. A fully furnished apartment . . . with a ceiling two feet high.

Everything was doll size except the typewriter. That was a portable electric model that looked huge in contrast to everything else.

Maybe George wasn't really crazy after all. One thing was certain: The old fart had been lying to him. There were no snakes and snapping turtles living down here in his crawl space.

But just what the hell *was* living down here?

Gil headed back inside to ask the only man who really knew.

As he strode through the big room, his foot caught on something and he went down again, landing square on his belly. It took him a moment to catch his breath, then he rolled over and looked to see what had tripped him.

It wasn't the hassock this time. A length of slim cord was stretched between the leg of the couch and an eye-hook that had been screwed into the wall.

He got up and continued on his way—carefully now, scanning the path for more trip ropes. There were none. He made it to the bedroom without falling again—

—and found George sitting on the edge of the bed, massaging his wrists.

Dammit! Every time he turned around it was something else! He could feel the anger and frustration begin to bubble up toward the overflow levels.

"Who the hell untied you?"

"I ain't talking to you."

Gil pointed the knife at him. "You'll talk, old man, or I'll skin you alive!"

"Leave him alone and leave our home!"

It was a little voice, high-pitched without being squeaky, and it came from directly behind him. Gil whirled and saw a fully dressed little man—or something squat, hairy, and bullnecked that came pretty close to looking like a little man—no more than a foot and a half high, standing outside the bedroom door. By the time Gil realized what he was looking at, the creature had started to run.

Gil's first thought was, *I'm going crazy!* But suddenly he had an explanation for that two-foot high furnished apartment in the crawl space, and for the moving furniture and trip cords.

He bolted after it. Here was what had been tormenting him tonight! He'd get the little sucker and—

He tripped again. A cord that hadn't been there a moment ago was stretched across the narrow hall. Gil went down on one knee and bounded up again. He'd been half ready for that one. They weren't going to—

Something caught him across the chin and his feet went out from under him. He landed flat on his back and felt a sharp, searing pain in his right thigh. He looked down and saw he had jabbed himself in the leg with his own knife during the fall.

Gil leaped to his feet, the pain a distant cry amid the blood rage that hammered through his brain. He roared and slashed at the rope that had damn near taken his head off and charged into the big room. There he saw not one but two of the little bastards. A chant filled the air:

"Leave him alone and leave our home! Leave him alone and leave our home!"

Over and over, from a good deal more than two voices. He couldn't see any others. How many of the little runts were there? No matter. He'd deal with these two first, then hunt down the others and get to the bottom of this.

The pair split, one darting to the left, the other to the right. Gil wasn't going to let them both escape. He took a single step and launched himself through the air at the one fleeing leftward. He landed with a bone-jarring crash on the floor but his outstretched free hand caught the leg of the fleeing creature. It was hairier than he had realized—furry, really—and it struggled in his grasp, screeching and thrashing like a wild animal as he pulled it toward him. He squeezed it harder and it bit his thumb. Hard. He howled with the pain, hauled the thing back, and flung it against the nearest wall.

Its screeching stopped as it landed against the wall with an audible crunch and fell to the floor, but the chant went on:

". . . our home! Leave him alone and leave our home! Leave him . . ."

"God *damn* it!" Gil said, sucking on his bleeding thumb. It hurt like hell.

Then he saw the thing start to move. Mewling in pain, it had begun a slow crawl toward one of the piles of junk in the corner.

"No, you don't!" Gil shouted.

The pain, the rage, that goddamn chant, they all came together in a black cloud of fury that engulfed him. No way he was going to let that little shit get away and set more booby traps for him. Through that cloud, he charged across the room, lifted the thing up with his left hand, and raised the knife in his right. Dimly he heard a voice shouting somewhere behind him but he ignored it.

He rammed the knife through the damned thing, pinning it to the wall.

The chant stopped abruptly, cut off in mid verse. All he could hear was George's wail.

"Oh, no! Oh, Lord, *no!*"

George stood in the hall and stared at the tiny figure impaled on the wall, watched it squirm as dark fluid flowed down the peeling wallpaper. Then it went slack. He didn't know the little guy's name—they all looked pretty much the same through his cataracts—but he felt like he'd lost an old friend. His anguish was a knife lodged in his own chest.

"You've killed him! Oh, God!"

Gil glared at him, his eyes wild, his breathing ragged. Saliva dripped from a corner of his mouth. He was far over the edge.

"Right, old man. And I'm gonna get the other one and do the same to him!"

George couldn't let that happen. The little guys were his responsibility. He was their protector. He couldn't just stand here like a useless scarecrow.

He launched himself at Gil, his long, nicotine-stained fingernails extended like claws, raking for the younger man's eyes. But Gil pushed him aside easily, knocking him to the floor with a casual swipe of his arm. Pain blazed through George's left hip as he landed, shooting down his leg like a bolt of white hot lightning.

"You're next, you worthless old shit!" Gil screamed. "Soon as I finish with the other little squirt!"

George sobbed as he lay on the floor. If only he were younger, stronger. Even ten years ago he probably could have kicked this punk out on his ass. Now all he could do was lie here on the floor like the worthless old half-blind cripple he was. He pounded the floor helplessly. Might as well be dead!

Suddenly he saw another of the little guys dash across the floor toward the couch, saw the punk spot him and leap after him.

"Run!" George screamed. *"Run!"*

Gil rammed his shoulder against the back of the couch as he shoved his arm far beneath it, slashing back and forth with the knife, trying to get a piece of the second runt. But the blade cut only air and dust bunnies.

As he began to withdraw his arm, he felt something snake over his hand

and tighten on his wrist. He tried to yank away but the cord—he was sure it was a cord like the one he had used to truss George—tightened viciously.

A slip knot!

The other end must have been tied to one of the couch legs. He tried to slash at the cord with the knife but he couldn't get the right angle. He reached under with his free left hand to get the knife and realized too late that they must have been waiting for him to do that very thing. He felt another noose tighten over that wrist—

—and still another over his right ankle.

The first cold trickles of fear ran down Gil's spine.

In desperation he tried to tip the couch over to give him some room to manuever but it wouldn't budge. Just then something bit deeply into his right hand. He tried to shake it off and in doing so he loosened his grip on the knife. It was immediately snatched from his grasp.

At that moment the fourth noose tightened around his left ankle, and he knew he was in deep shit.

They let him lie there for what must have been an hour. He strained at the ropes, trying to break them, trying to untie the knots. All he accomplished was to sink their coils more deeply into his flesh. He wanted to scream out his rage—and his fear—but he wouldn't give them the satisfaction. He heard George moving around somewhere behind him, groaning with pain, heard little voices—How many of the little fuckers were there, anyway?—talking in high-pitched whispers. There seemed to be an argument going on. Finally, it was resolved.

Then came a tugging on the cords as new ones were tied around his wrists and ankles and old ones released. Suddenly he was flipped over onto his back.

He saw George sitting in the rocker holding an ice pack to his left hip. And on the floor there were ten—*Jesus, ten of them!*—foot-and-a-half tall furry little men standing in a semicircle, staring at him.

One of them stepped forward. He was dressed in doll clothes: a dark blue pullover—it even had an Izod alligator on the left breast—and tan slacks. He had the face of a sixty-year-old man with a barrel chest and furry arms and legs. He pointed at Gil's face and spoke in a high-pitched voice:

"C'ham is dead and it's on your head."

Gil started to laugh. It was like landing in Munchkinland, but then he saw the look in the little man's eyes and knew this was not one of the Lollipop Kids. The laugh died in his throat.

He glanced up at the wall where he'd pinned the first little runt like a bug on a board and saw only a dark stain.

The talking runt gestured two others forward and they approached Gil, dragging his knife. He tried to squirm away from them but the ropes didn't allow for much movement.

"Hey, now, wait a minute! What're you—?"

"The decision's made: You'll make the trade."

Gil was beginning to know terror. "Forget the goddamn rhymes! What's going on here?"

"Hold your nose," the talking runt said to the pair with the knife, "and cut off his clothes. Best be cautious lest he make you nauseous."

Gil winced as the blade began to slice along the seams of his shirt, waiting for the sharp edge to cut him. But it never touched him.

George watched as the little guys stripped Connors. He had no idea what they were up to and he didn't care. He felt like more of a failure than ever. He'd never done much with his life, but at least since the end of the sixties he had been able to tell himself that he had provided a safe harbor for the last of the world's Little People.

When had it been—sixty-nine, maybe—when all eleven of them had first shown up at his door looking for shelter. They'd said they were waiting for "when time is unfurled and we're called by the world." He hadn't the vaguest notion what that meant but he'd experienced an immediate rapport with them. They were Outsiders, just like he was. And when they offered to pay rent, the deal was sealed.

He smiled. That rhymed. If you listened to them enough, you began to sound like them. Since they spoke in rhyme all the time—there was another one—it was nothing for them to crank out verse for the greeting card companies. Some of the stuff was pretty sappy, but it paid the taxes.

But what next? One of the little guys had been murdered by this psycho who now knew their secret. Soon all the world would know about these Little People. George had doubly failed at his job: He hadn't protected them and hadn't kept their secret. He was just what the punk had called him: a worthless old shit.

He heard Connors groan and looked up. He was nude as a jaybird and the little guys had tied him with new ropes looped through rings fastened high on the walls at each end of the room. They were hauling him off the floor, stringing him across the room like laundry hung out to dry.

George suddenly realized that although he wasn't too pleased with being George Haskins, at this particular moment he preferred it by far to being Gilroy Connors.

Gil felt as if his arms and legs were going to come out of their sockets as the runts hauled him off the floor and stretched him out in the air. For a moment he feared that might be their plan, but when he got halfway between the floor and the ceiling, they stopped pulling on the ropes.

He couldn't ever remember feeling so damn helpless in all his life.

The lights went out and he heard a lot of shuffling below him but he couldn't see what they were doing. Then came the sound, a new chant, high-pitched and staccato in a language he had never heard before, a language that didn't seem at home on the human tongue.

A soft glow began to rise from below him. He wished he could see what they were doing. All he could do was watch their weird shadows on the ceiling. So far they hadn't caused him too much pain, but he was beginning to feel weak and dizzy. His back got warm while his front grew cold and numb, like there was a cool wind coming from the ceiling and passing right through him, carrying his energy with it. All of his juice seemed to be flowing downward and collecting in his back.

So tired . . . and his back felt so heavy. What were they doing below him?

They were glowing.

George had watched them carry C'ham, their dead member, to a spot directly below Connor's suspended body. They had placed one of George's coffee mugs at C'ham's feet, then they stripped off their clothes and gathered in a circle around him. They had started to chant. After a while, a faint yellow light began to shimmer around their furry little bodies.

George found the ceremony fascinating in a weird sort of way—until the glow brightened and flowed up to illuminate the suspended punk. Then even George's lousy eyes could see the horror of what was happening to Gilroy Connors.

His legs, arms, and belly were a cold dead white, but his back was a deep red-purple color, like a gigantic bruise, and it bulged like the belly of a mother-to-be carrying triplets. George could not imagine how the skin was holding together, it was stretched so tight. Looked like it would rupture any minute. George shielded his face, waiting for the splatter. But when it didn't come, he chanced another peek.

It was raining on the Little People.

The skin hadn't ruptured as George had feared. No, a fine red mist was falling from Connors' body. Red microdroplets were slipping from the pores in the purpled swelling on his back and falling through the yellow glow, turning it orange. The scene was as beautiful as it was horrifying.

The bloody dew fell for something like half an hour, then the glow faded and one of the little guys boosted another up to the wall switch and the lights came on. George did not have to strain his eyes to know that Gilroy Connors was dead.

As the circle dissolved, he noticed that the dead little guy was gone. Only the mug remained under Connors.

George found his mouth dry when he tried to speak.

"What happened to . . . to the one he stabbed?"

"C'ham?" said the leader. George knew this one; his name was Kob. "He's over there." He wasn't rhyming now.

Sure enough. There were ten little guys standing over by the couch, one of them looking weak and being supported by the others.

"But I thought—"

"Yes. C'ham was dead, but now he's back because of the Crimson Dew."

"And the other one?"

Kob glanced over his shoulder at Connors. "I understand there's a re-ward for his capture. You should have it. And there's something else you should have."

The little man stepped under Connors' suspended body and returned with the coffee mug.

"This is for you," he said, holding it up.

George took the mug and saw that it was half-filled with a thin reddish liquid.

"What am I supposed to do with this?"

"Drink it."

George's stomach turned. "But it's . . . from him."

"Of course. From him to you." Kob gave George's calf a gentle slap. "We need you George. You're our shield from the world—"

"Some shield!" George said.

"It's true. You've protected us from prying eyes and we need you to go on doing that for some time to come."

"I don't think I've got much time left."

"That's why you should drain that cup."

"What do you mean?"

"Think of it as extending your lease," Kob said.

George looked over at C'ham, who'd surely been dead half an hour ago and now was up and walking about. He looked down into the cup again.

. . . extending your lease.

Well, after what he'd just seen, he guessed anything might be possible.

Tightening his throat against an incipient gag, George raised the cup to his lips and sipped. The fluid was lukewarm and salty—like a bouillon that had been allowed to cool too long. Not good, but not awful, either. He squeezed his eyes shut and chugged the rest. It went down and stayed down, thank the Lord.

"Good!" Kob shouted, and the ten other Little People applauded.

"Now you can help us cut him down and carry him outside."

"So what're you going to do with all that money, George?" Bill said as he handed George the day's mail.

"I ain't got it yet."

George leaned against the roof of the mail truck and dragged on his cigarette. He felt good. His morning backache was pretty much a thing of the past, and he could pee with the best of them—hit a wall from six feet away, he bet. His breathing was better than it had been in thirty years. And best of all, he could stand here and see all the way south along the length of the harbor to downtown Monroe. He didn't like to think about what had been in that mug Kob had handed him, but in the ten days since he had swallowed it down he had come to feel decades younger.

He wished he had some more of it.

"Still can't get over how lucky you were to find him laying in the grass over there," Bill said, glancing across the road. "Especially lucky he wasn't alive from what I heard about him."

"Guess so," George said.

"I understand they still can't explain how he died or why he was all dried up like a mummy."

"Yeah, it's a mystery, all right."

"So when you *do* get the fifty thou—what are you going to spend it on?"

"Make a few improvements on the old place, I guess. Get me some legal help to see if somehow I can get this area declared off-limits to developers. But mostly set up some sort of fund to keep paying the taxes until that comes to pass."

Bill laughed and let up on the mail truck's brake. "Not ready for the old folks' home yet?" he said as he lurched away.

"Not by a long shot!"

I've got responsibilities, he thought. *And tenants to keep happy.*
He shuddered.

Yes, he certainly wanted to keep those little fellows happy.

I'd planned on writing three ten-thousand word novelettes for *Night Visions 6*. I wound up doing four.

It was sometime in November when I sent Paul Mikol the thirty thousand words of new fiction I'd promised. He called back a few weeks later to say that the third story, "Ethics," was a little too lighthearted and too much like "Feelings." Could I do another in its place? My immediate reaction was, He's nuts. But I said I'd think about it. I went back to the two stories in question and reread them back-to-back.

He was right. I'd written "Feelings" and the other piece months apart and hadn't seen the similarities.

So here it was almost December and I needed ten thousand words of new fiction. I'd been perking a story about a serial killer (this was 1987, before *The Silence of the Lambs* and the serial killer glut) but one with a difference. This one would be female (they're almost always male), hideously deformed, and sympathetic. I felt if I could tell you about the forces driving Carly to these murderous acts—her childhood, her needs, her emotional hungers—you might understand her. You might even find some sort of love for her.

The result was "Faces" (yes, another plural noun). Paul Mikol loved it.

And he wasn't alone. This is my most reprinted story. So far it has appeared in two best-of-the-year anthologies and a host of others.

"Faces" remains one of my favorite stories. And it too has a tenuous link to *The Adversary Cycle*. You see, Carly was conceived just about the same time Carol Stevens conceived her child in *Reborn*.

FACES

Bite her face off.

No pain. Her dead already. Kill her quick like others. Not want make pain. Not her fault.

The boyfriend groan but not move. Face way on ground now. Got from behind. Got quick. Never see. He can live.

Girl look me after the boyfriend go down. Gasp first. When see face start scream. Two claws not cut short rip her throat before sound get loud.

Her sick-scared look just like all others. Hate that look. Hate it terrible.

Sorry, girl. Not your fault.

Chew her face skin. Chew all. Chew hard and swallow. Warm wet redness make sickish but chew and chew. Must eat face. Must get all down. Keep down.

Leave the eyes.

The boyfriend groan again. Move arm. Must leave quick. Take last look blood and teeth and stare-eyes that once pretty girlface.

Sorry, girl. Not your fault.

Got go. Get way hurry. First take money. Girl money. Take the boyfriend wallet, also too. Always take money. Need money.

Go now. Not too far. Climb wall of near building. Find dark spot where can see and not be seen. Where can wait. Soon the Detective Harrison arrive.

In downbelow can see the boyfriend roll over. Get to knees. Sway. See him look the girlfriend.

The boyfriend scream terrible. Bad to hear. Make so sad. Make cry.

Kevin Harrison heard Jacobi's voice on the other end of the line and wanted to be sick.

"Don't say it," he groaned.

"Sorry," said Jacobi. "It's another one."

"Where?"

"West Forty-ninth, right near—"

"I'll find it." All he had to do was look for the flashing red lights. "I'm on my way. Shouldn't take me too long to get in from Monroe at this hour."

"We've got all night, lieutenant." Unsaid but well understood was an admonishing, *You're the one who wants to live on Long Island.*

Beside him in the bed, Martha spoke from deep in her pillow as he hung up.

"Not another one?"

"Yeah."

"Oh, God! When is it going to stop?"

"When I catch the guy."

Her hand touched his arm, gently. "I know all this responsibility's not easy. I'm here when you need me."

"I know." He leaned over and kissed her. "Thanks."

He left the warm bed and skipped the shower. No time for that. A fresh shirt, yesterday's rumpled suit, a tie shoved into his pocket, and he was off into the winter night.

With his secure little ranch house falling away behind him, Harrison felt naked and vulnerable out here in the dark. As he headed south on Glen Cove Road toward the LIE, he realized that Martha and the kids were all that were holding him together these days. His family had become an island of sanity and stability in a world gone mad.

Everything else was in flux. For reasons he still could not comprehend, he had volunteered to head up the search for this killer. Now his whole future in the department had come to hinge on his success in finding him.

The papers had named the maniac "the Facelift Killer." As apt a name as the tabloids could want, but Harrison resented it. The moniker was callous, trivializing the mutilations perpetrated on the victims. But it had caught on with the public and they were stuck with it, especially with all the ink the story was getting.

Six killings, one a week for six weeks in a row, and eight million people in a panic. Then, for almost two weeks, the city had gone without a new slaying.

Until tonight.

Harrison's stomach pitched and rolled at the thought of having to look at one of those corpses again.

"That's enough," Harrison said, averting his eyes from the faceless thing.

The raw, gouged, bloody flesh, the exposed muscle and bone were bad enough, but it was the eyes—those naked, lidless, staring eyes were the worst.

"This makes seven," Jacobi said at his side. Squat, dark, jowly, the sergeant was chewing a big wad of gum, noisily, aggressively, as if he had a grudge against it.

"I can count. Anything new?"

"Nah. Same m.o. as ever—throat slashed, money stolen, face gnawed off."

Harrison shuddered. He had come in as Special Investigator after the third Facelift killing. He had inspected the first three via coroners' photos. Those had been awful. But nothing could match the effect of the real thing up close and still warm and oozing. This was the fourth fresh victim he had seen. There was no getting used to this kind of mutilation, no matter how many he saw. Jacobi put on a good show, but Harrison sensed the revulsion under the sergeant's armor.

And yet . . .

Beneath all the horror, Harrison sensed something. There was anger here, sick anger and hatred of spectacular proportions. But beyond that, something else, an indefinable something that had drawn him to this case. Whatever it was, that something called to him, and still held him captive.

If he could identify it, maybe he could solve this case and wrap it up. And save his ass.

If he did solve it, it would be all on his own. Because he wasn't getting much help from Jacobi, and even less from his assigned staff. He knew what they all thought—that he had taken the job as a glory grab, a short-cut to the top. Sure, they wanted to see this thing wrapped up, too, but they weren't shedding any tears over the shit he was taking in the press and on TV and from City Hall.

Their attitude was clear: *If you want the spotlight, Harrison, you gotta take the heat that goes with it.*

They were right, of course. He could have been working on a quieter case, like where all the winos were disappearing to. He'd chosen this instead. But he wasn't after the spotlight, dammit! It was this case—something about this case!

He suddenly realized that there was no one around him. The body had been carted off, Jacobi had wandered back to his car. He had been left standing alone at the far end of the alley.

And yet not alone.

Someone was watching him. He could feel it. The realization sent a little chill—one completely unrelated to the cold February wind—trickling down his back. A quick glance around showed no one paying him the slightest bit of attention. He looked up.

There!

Somewhere in the darkness above, someone was watching him. Probably from the roof. He could sense the piercing scrutiny and it made him a little weak. That was no ghoulish neighborhood voyeur, up there. That was the Facelift Killer.

He had to get to Jacobi, have him seal off the building. But he couldn't act spooked. He had to act calm, casual.

See the Detective Harrison's eyes. See from way up in dark. Tall-thin. Hair brown. Nice eyes. Soft brown eyes. Not hard like many-many eyes. Look here. Even from here see eyes make wide. Him know it me.

Watch the Detective Harrison turn slow. Walk slow. Tell inside him want to run. Must leave here. Leave quick.

Bend low. Run cross roof. Jump to next. And next. Again till most block away. Then down wall. Wrap scarf round head. Hide bad-face. Hunch inside big-big coat. Walk through lighted spots.

Hate light. Hate crowds. Theaters here. Movies and plays. Like them. Some night sneak in and see. See one with man in mask. Hang from wall behind big drapes. Make cry.

Wish there mask for me.

Follow street long way to river. See many lights across river. Far past there is place where grew. Never want go back to there. Never.

Catch back of truck. Ride home.

Home. Bright bulb hang ceiling. Not care. The Old Jessi waiting. The Jessi friend. Only friend. The Jessi's eyes not see. Ever. When the Jessi look me, her face not wear sick-scared look. Hate that look.

Come in kitchen window. The Jessi's face wrinkle-black. Smile when hear me come. TV on. Always on. The Jessi can not watch. Say it company for her.

"You're so late tonight."

"Hard work. Get moneys tonight."

Feel sick. Want cry. Hate kill. Wish stop.

"That's nice. Are you going to put it in the drawer?"

"Doing now."

Empty wallets. Put moneys in slots. Ones first slot. Fives next slot. Then tens and twenties. So the Jessi can pay when boy bring foods. Sometimes eat stolen foods. Mostly the Jessi call for foods.

The Old Jessi hardly walk. Good. Do not want her go out. Bad peoples round here. Many. Hurt one who not see. One bad man try hurt Jessi once. Push through door. Thought only the blind Old Jessi live here.

Lucky the Jessi not alone that day.

Not lucky bad man. Hit the Jessi. Laugh hard. Then look me. Get sick-scared look. Hate that look. Kill him quick. Put in tub. Bleed there. Bad man friend come soon after. Kill him also too. Late at night take both dead bad men out. Go through window. Carry down wall. Throw in river.

No bad men come again. Ever.

"I've been waiting all night for my bath. Do you think you can help me a little?"

Always help. But the Old Jessi always ask. The Jessi very polite.

Sponge the Old Jessi back in tub. Rinse her hair. Think of the Detective Harrison. His kind eyes. Must talk him. Want stop this. Stop now. Maybe will understand. Will. Can feel

Seven grisly murders in eight weeks.

Kevin Harrison studied a photo of the latest victim, taken before she was mutilated. A nice eight by ten glossy furnished by her agent. A real beauty. A dancer with Broadway dreams.

He tossed the photo aside and pulled the stack of files toward him. The remnants of six lives in this pile. Somewhere within had to be an answer, the thread that linked each of them to the Facelift Killer.

But what if there was no common link? What if all the killings were at random, linked only by the fact that they were beautiful? Seven deaths, all over the city. All with their faces gnawed off. *Gnawed.*

He flipped through the victims one by one and studied their photos. He had begun to feel he knew each one of them personally:

Mary Detrick, twenty, a junior at N.Y.U., killed in Washington Square Park on January 5. She was the first.

Mia Chandler, twenty-five, a secretary at Merrill Lynch, killed January 13 in Battery Park.

Ellen Beasley, twenty-two, a photographer's assistant, killed in an alley in Chelsea on January 22.

Hazel Hauge, thirty, artist agent, killed in her SoHo loft on January 27.

Elisabeth Paine, twenty-eight, housewife, killed on February 2 while jogging late in Central Park.

Joan Perrin, twenty-five, a model from Brooklyn, pulled from her car while stopped at a light on the Upper East Side on February 8.

He picked up the eight by ten again. And the last: Liza Lee, twenty-one, a dancer. Lived across the river in Jersey City. Ducked into an alley for a toot with her boyfriend tonight and never came out.

Three blondes, three brunettes, one redhead. Some stacked, some on the flat side. All caucs except for Perrin. All lookers. But besides that, how in the world could these women be linked? They came from all over town, and they met their respective ends all over town. What could—

"Well, you sure hit the bullseye about that roof!" Jacobi said as he burst into the office.

Harrison straightened in his chair. "What did you find?"

"Blood."

"Whose?"

"The victim's."

"No prints? No hairs? No fibers?"

"We're working on it. But how'd you figure to check the rooftop?"

"Lucky guess."

Harrison didn't want to provide Jacobi with more grist for the departmental gossip mill by mentioning his feeling of being watched from up there.

But the killer *had* been watching, hadn't he?

"Any prelims from pathology?"

Jacobi shrugged and stuffed three sticks of gum into his mouth. Then he tried to talk.

"Same as ever. Money gone, throat ripped open by a pair of sharp pointed instruments, not knives, the bite marks on the face are the usual: the teeth that made them aren't human, but the saliva is."

The "nonhuman" teeth part—more teeth, bigger and sharper than found in any human mouth—had baffled them all from the start. Early on someone remembered a horror novel or movie where the killer used some weird sort of false teeth to bite his victims. That had sent them off on a wild goose chase to all the dental labs looking for records of bizarre bite prostheses. No dice. No one had seen or even heard of teeth that could gnaw off a person's face.

Harrison shuddered. What could explain wounds like that? What were they dealing with here?

The irritating pops, snaps, and cracks of Jacobi's gum filled the office.

"I liked you better when you smoked."

Jacobi's reply was cut off by the phone. The sergeant picked it up.

"Detective Harrison's office!" he said, listened a moment, then, with his hand over the mouthpiece, passed the receiver to Harrison. "Some fairy wantsh to shpeak to you," he said with an evil grin.

"Fairy?"

"Hey," he said, getting up and walking toward the door. "I don't mind. I'm a liberal kinda guy, y'know?"

Harrison shook his head with disgust. Jacobi was getting less likable every day.

"Hello. Harrison here."

"Shorry dishturb you, Detective Harrishon."

The voice was soft, pitched somewhere between a man's and a woman's, and sounded as if the speaker had half a mouthful of saliva. Harrison had never heard anything like it. Who could be—?

And then it struck him: It was three A.M. Only a handful of people knew he was here.

"Do I know you?"

"No. Watch you tonight. You almosht shee me in dark."

That same chill from earlier tonight ran down Harrison's back again.

"Are . . . are you who I think you are?"

There was a pause, then one soft word, more sobbed than spoken: "Yesh."

If the reply had been cocky, something along the line of *And just who do you think I am?*, Harrison would have looked for much more in the way of corroboration. But that single word, and the soul-deep heartbreak that propelled it, banished all doubt.

My God! He looked around frantically. No one in sight. Where the fuck was Jacobi now when he needed him? This was the Facelift Killer! He needed a trace!

Got to keep him on the line!

"I have to ask you something to be sure you are who you say you are."

"Yesh?"

"Do you take anything from the victims—I mean, besides their faces?"

"Money. Take money."

This is him! The department had withheld the money part from the papers. Only the real Facelift Killer could know!

"Can I ask you something else?"

"Yesh."

Harrison was asking this one for himself.

"What do you do with the faces?"

He had to know. The question drove him crazy at night. He dreamed about those faces. Did the killer tack them on the wall, or press them in a book, or freeze them, or did he wear them around the house like that Leatherface character from the chainsaw movie?

On the other end of the line he sensed sudden agitation and panic: "No! Can not shay! Can *not*!"

"Okay, okay. Take it easy."

"You will help shtop?"

"Oh, yes! Oh, God, yes, I'll help you stop!" He prayed his genuine heartfelt desire to end this was coming through. "I'll help you any way I can!"

There was a long pause, then:

"You hate? Hate me?"

Harrison didn't trust himself to answer that right away. He searched his feelings quickly, but carefully.

"No," he said finally. "I think you have done some awful, horrible things but, strangely enough, I don't hate you."

And that was true. Why didn't he hate this murdering maniac? Oh, he wanted to stop him more than anything in the world, and wouldn't hesitate to shoot him dead if the situation required it, but there was no personal hatred for the Facelift Killer.

What is it in you that speaks to me? he wondered.

"Shank you," said the voice, couched once more in a sob.

And then the killer hung up.

Harrison shouted into the dead phone, banged it on his desk, but the line was dead.

"What's the hell's the matter with you?" Jacobi said from the office door.

"That so-called fairy on the phone was the Facelift Killer, you idiot! We could have had a trace if you'd stuck around!"

"Bullshit!"

"He knew about taking the money!"

"So why'd he talk like that? That's a dumb-ass way to try to disguise your voice."

And then it suddenly hit Harrison like a sucker punch to the gut. He swallowed hard and said:

"Jacobi, how do you think your voice would sound if you had a jaw crammed full of teeth much larger and sharper than the kind found in the typical human mouth?"

Harrison took genuine pleasure in the way Jacobi's face blanched slowly to yellow-white.

He didn't get home again until after seven the following night. The whole department had been in an uproar all day. This was the first break they had had in the case. It wasn't much, but contact had been made. That was the important part. And although Harrison had done nothing he could think of to deserve any credit, he had accepted the commissioner's compliments and encouragement on the phone shortly before he had left the office tonight.

But what was most important to Harrison was the evidence from the call—*Damn!* he wished it had been taped—that the killer wanted to stop. They didn't have one more goddamn clue tonight than they'd had yesterday, but the call offered hope that soon there might be an end to this horror.

Martha had dinner waiting. The kids were scrubbed and pajamaed and waiting for their goodnight kiss. He gave them each a hug and poured himself a stiff scotch while Martha put them in the sack.

"Do you feel as tired as you look?" she said as she returned from the bedroom wing.

She was a big woman with bright blue eyes and natural dark blond hair. Harrison toasted her with his glass.

"The expression 'dead on his feet' has taken on a whole new meaning for me."

She kissed him, then they sat down to eat.

He had spoken to Martha a couple of times since he had left the house twenty hours ago. She knew about the phone call from the Facelift Killer, about the new hope in the department about the case, but he was glad she didn't bring it up now. He was sick of talking about it. Instead, he sat in front of his cooling meat loaf and wrestled with the images that had been nibbling at the edges of his consciousness all day.

"What are you daydreaming about?" Martha said.

Without thinking, Harrison said, "Annie."

"Annie who?"

"My sister."

Martha put her fork down. "Your sister? Kevin, you don't have a sister."

"Not anymore. But I did."

Her expression was alarmed now. "Kevin, are you all right? I've known your family for ten years. Your mother has never once mentioned—"

"We don't talk about Annie, Mar. We try not to even think about her. She died when she was five."

"Oh. I'm sorry."

"Don't be. Annie was . . . deformed. Terribly deformed. She never really had a chance."

Open trunk from inside. Get out. The Detective Harrison's house here. Cold night. Cold feel good. Trunk air make sick, dizzy.

Light here. Hurry round side of house.

Darker here. No one see. Look in window. Dark but see good. Two little ones there. Sleeping. Move away. Not want them cry.

Go more round. The Detective Harrison with lady. Sit table near window. Must be wife. Pretty but not oh-so-beauty. Not have mom-face. Not like ones who die.

Watch behind tree. Hungry. They not eat food. Talk-talk-talk. Can not hear.

The Detective Harrison do most talk. Kind face. Kind eyes. Some terrible sad there. Hides. Him understands. Heard in phone voice. Understands. Him one can stop kills.

Spent day watch the Detective Harrison car. All day watch at police house. Saw him come-go many times. Soon dark, open trunk with claw. Ride with him. Ride long. Wonder what town this?

The Detective Harrison look this way. Stare like last night. Must not see me! Must *not*!

Harrison stopped in mid-sentence and stared out the window as his skin prickled.

That *watched* feeling again.

It was the same as last night. Something was out in the backyard watching them. He strained to see through the wooded darkness outside the window but saw only shadows within shadows.

But something was *there*! He could feel it!

He got up and turned on the outside spotlights, hoping, *praying* that the backyard would be empty.

It was.

He smiled to hide his relief and glanced at Martha.

"Thought that raccoon was back."

He left the spots on and settled back into his place at the table. But the thoughts racing through his mind made eating unthinkable.

What if that maniac had followed him out here? What if the call had been a ploy to get him off-guard so the Facelift Killer could do to Martha what he had done to the other women?

My God . . .

First thing tomorrow morning he was going to call the local alarm boys and put in a security system. Cost be damned, he had to have it. Immediately!

As for tonight . . .

Tonight he'd keep the .38 under the pillow.

*　*　*

Run way. Run low and fast. Get bushes before light come. Must stay way now. Not come back.

The Detective Harrison *feel* me. Know when watched. Him the one, sure.

Walk in dark, in woods. See back many houses. Come park. Feel strange. See this park before. Can not be—

Then know.

Monroe! This Monroe! Born here! Live here! Hate Monroe! Monroe bad place, bad people! House, home, old home near here! There! Cross park! Old home! New color but same house.

Hate house!

Sit on froze park grass. Cry. Why Monroe? Do not want be in Monroe. The Mom gone. The Sissy gone. The Jimmy very gone. House here.

Dry tears. Watch old home long time till light go out. Wait more. Go to windows. See new folks inside. The Mom took the Sissy and go. Where? Don't know.

Go to back. Push cellar window. Crawl in. See good in dark. New folks make nice cellar. Wood on walls. Rug on floor. No chain.

Sit floor. Remember . . .

Remember hanging on wall. Look little window near ceiling. Watch kids play in park cross street. Want go with kids. Want play there with kids. Want have friends.

But the Mom won't let. Never leave basement. Too strong. Break everything. Have TV. Broke it. Have toys. Broke them. Stay in basement. Chain round waist hold to center pole. Can not leave.

Remember terrible bad things happen.

Run. Run way Monroe. Never come back.

Till now.

Now back. Still hate house! Want hurt house. See cigarettes. With matches. Light all. Burn now!

Watch rug burn. Chair burn. So hot. Run back to cold park. Watch house burn. See new folks run out. Trucks come throw water. House burn and burn.

Glad but tears come anyway.

Hate house. Now house gone. Hate Monroe.

Wonder where the Mom and the Sissy live now.

Leave Monroe for new home and the Old Jessi.

*   *   *

The second call came the next day. And this time they were ready for it. The tape recorders were set, the computers were waiting to begin the tracing protocol. As soon as Harrison recognized the voice, he gave the signal. On the other side of the desk, Jacobi put on a headset and people started running in all directions. Off to the races.

"I'm glad you called," Harrison said. "I've been thinking about you."

"You undershtand?" said the soft voice.

"I'm not sure."

"Musht help shtop."

"I will! I will! Tell me how!"

"Not know."

There was a pause. Harrison wasn't sure what to say next. He didn't want to push, but he had to keep him on the line.

"Did you . . . hurt anyone last night."

"No. Shaw houshes. Your houshe. Your wife."

Harrison's blood froze. Last night—in the backyard. That had been the Facelift Killer in the dark. He looked up and saw genuine concern in Jacobi's eyes. He forced himself to speak.

"You were at my house? Why didn't you talk to me?"

"No-no! Can not let shee! Run way your house. Go mine!"

"*Yours?* You live in Monroe?"

"No! Hate Monroe! Once lived. Gone long! Burn old houshe. Never go back!"

This could be important. Harrison phrased the next question carefully.

"You burned your old house? When was that?"

If he could just get a date, a year . . .

"Lasht night."

"*Last night?*" Harrison remembered hearing the sirens and fire horns in the early morning darkness.

"Yesh! Hate houshe!"

And then the line went dead.

He looked at Jacobi who had picked up another line.

"Did we get the trace?"

"Waiting to hear. Christ, he sounds retarded, doesn't he?"

Retarded. The word sent ripples across the surface of his brain. Non-

human teeth . . . Monroe . . . retarded . . . a picture was forming in the set-
tling sediment, a picture he felt he should avoid.

"Maybe he is."

"You'd think that would make him easy to—"

Jacobi stopped, listened to the receiver, then shook his head disgustedly.

"What?"

"Got as far as the Lower East Side. He was probably calling from somewhere in one of the projects. If we'd had another thirty seconds—"

"We've got something better than a trace to some lousy pay phone,"
Harrison said. "We've got his old address!" He picked up his suit coat and
headed for the door.

"Where we goin'?"

"Not 'we.' Me. I'm going out to Monroe."

Once he reached the town, it took Harrison less than an hour to find the
Facelift Killer's last name.

He first checked with the Monroe Fire Department to find the address
of last night's house fire. Then he went down to the brick-fronted Town
Hall and found the lot and block number. After that it was easy to look up
its history of ownership. Mr. and Mrs. Elwood Scott were the current owners of the land and the charred shell of a three-bedroom ranch that sat
upon it.

There had only been one other set of owners: Mr. and Mrs. Thomas
Baker. He had lived most of his life in Monroe but knew nothing about the
Baker family. But he knew where to find out: Captain Jeremy Hall, Chief
of Police in the Incorporated Village of Monroe.

Captain Hall hadn't changed much over the years. Still had a big belly,
long sideburns, and hair cut bristly short on the sides. That was the "in"
look these days, but Hall had been wearing his hair like that for at least
thirty years. If not for his Bronx accent, he could have played a redneck
sheriff in any one of those southern chain gang movies.

After pleasantries and local-boy-leaves-home-to-become-big-city-cop-
and-now-comes-to-question-small-town-cop banter, they got down to
business.

"The Bakers from North Park Drive?" Hall said after he had noisily
sucked the top layer off his steaming coffee. "Who could forget them?

There was the mother, divorced, I believe, and the three kids—two girls and the boy."

Harrison pulled out his note pad. "The boy's name—what was it?"

"Tommy, I believe. Yeah—Tommy. I'm sure of it."

"He's the one I want."

Hall's eyes narrowed. "He is, is he? You're working on that Facelift case aren't you?"

"Right."

"And you think Tommy Baker might be your man?"

"It's a possibility. What do you know about him?"

"I know he's dead."

Harrison froze. "Dead? That can't be!"

"It sure as hell *can* be!" Without rising from his seat, he shouted through his office door. "Murph! Pull out that old file on the Baker case! Nineteen eighty-four, I believe!"

"Eighty-four?" Harrison said. He and Martha had been living in Queens then. They hadn't moved back to Monroe yet.

"Right. A real messy affair. Tommy Baker was thirteen years old when he bought it. And he bought it. *Believe* me, he bought it!"

Harrison sat in glum silence, watching his whole theory go up in smoke.

The Old Jessi sleeps. Stand by mirror near tub. Only mirror have. No like them. The Jessi not need one.

Stare face. Bad face. Teeth, teeth, teeth. And hair. Arms too thin, too long. Claws. None have claws like my. None have face like my.

Face not better. Ate pretty faces but face still same. Still cause sick-scared look. Just like at home.

Remember home. Do not want but thoughts will not go.

Faces.

The Sissy get the Mom-face. Beauty face. The Tommy get the Dad-face. Not see the Dad. Never come home anymore. Who my face? Never see where come. Where my face come? My hands come?

Remember home cellar. Hate home! Hate cellar more! Pull on chain round waist. Pull and pull. Want out. Want play. *Please.* No one let.

One day when the Mom and the Sissy go, the Tommy bring friends.

Come down cellar. Bunch on stairs. Stare. First time see sick-scared look. Not understand.

Friends! Play! Throw ball them. They run. Come back with rocks and sticks. Still sick-scared look. Throw me, hit me.

Make cry. Make the Tommy laugh.

Whenever the Mom and the Sissy go, the Tommy come with boys and sticks. Poke and hit. Hurt. Little hurt on skin. Big hurt inside. Sick-scared look hurt most of all. Hate look. Hate hurt. Hate them.

Most hate the Tommy.

One night chain breaks. Wait on wall for the Tommy. Hurt him. Hurt the Tommy outside. Hurt the Tommy inside. Know because pull inside outside. The Tommy quiet. Quiet, wet, red. The Mom and the Sissy get sick-scared look and scream.

Hate that look. Run way. Hide. Never come back. Till last night.

Cry more now. Cry quiet. In tub. So the Jessi not hear.

Harrison flipped through the slim file on the Tommy Baker murder.

"This is it?"

"We didn't need to collect much paper," Captain Hall said. "I mean, the mother and sister were witnesses. There's some photos in that manila envelope at the back."

Harrison pulled it free and slipped out some large black and whites. His stomach lurched immediately.

"My *God*!"

"Yeah, he was a mess. Gutted by his older sister."

"His *sister*?"

"Yeah. Apparently she was some sort of freak of nature."

Harrison felt the floor tilt under him, felt as if he were going to slide off the chair.

"Freak?" he said, hoping Hall wouldn't notice the tremor in his voice. "What did she look like?"

"Never saw her. She took off after she killed the brother. No one's seen hide nor hair of her since. But there's a picture of the rest of the family in there."

Harrison shuffled through the file until he came to a large color family portrait. He held it up. Four people: two adults seated in chairs; a boy and a girl, about ten and eight, kneeling on the floor in front of them. A perfectly normal American family. Four smiling faces.

But where's your oldest child? Where's your big sister? Where did you hide that fifth face while posing for this?

"What was her name? The one who's not here?"

"Not sure. Carla, maybe? Look at the front sheet under *Suspect*."

Harrison did. "Carla Baker—called 'Carly,' " he said.

Hall grinned. "Right. Carly. Not bad for a guy getting close to retirement."

Harrison didn't answer. An ineluctable sadness filled him as he stared at the incomplete family portrait.

Carly Baker . . . poor Carly . . . where did they hide you away? In the cellar? Locked in the attic? How did your brother treat you? Bad enough to deserve killing?

Probably.

"No pictures of Carly, I suppose."

"Not a one."

That figures.

"How about a description?"

"The mother gave us one but it sounded so weird, we threw it out. I mean, the girl sounded like she was half spider or something!" He drained his cup. "Then later on I got into a discussion with Doc Alberts about it. He told me he was doing deliveries back about the time this kid was born. Said they had a whole rash of monsters, all delivered within a few weeks of each other."

The room started to tilt under Harrison again.

"Early December, 1968, by chance?"

"Yeah! How'd you know?"

He felt queasy. "Lucky guess."

"Huh. Anyway, Doc Alberts said they kept it quiet while they looked into a cause, but that little group of freaks—'cluster,' he called them—was all there was. They figured that a bunch of mothers had been exposed to something nine months before, but whatever it had been was long gone. No monsters since. I understand most of them died shortly after birth, anyway."

"Not all of them."

"Not that it matters," Hall said, getting up and pouring himself a refill from the coffeepot. "Someday someone will find her skeleton, probably somewhere out in Haskins's marshes."

"Maybe." *But I wouldn't count on it.* He held up the file. "Can I get a Xerox of this?"

"You mean the Facelift Killer is a twenty-year-old girl?"

Martha's face clearly registered her disbelief.

"Not just any girl. A freak. Someone so deformed she really doesn't look human. Completely uneducated and probably mentally retarded to boot."

Harrison hadn't returned to Manhattan. Instead, he'd headed straight for home, less than a mile from Town Hall. He knew the kids were at school and that Martha would be there alone. That was what he had wanted. He needed to talk this out with someone a lot more sensitive than Jacobi.

Besides, what he had learned from Captain Hall and the Baker file had dredged up the most painful memories of his life.

"A monster," Martha said.

"Yeah. Born one on the outside, *made* one on the inside. But there's another child monster I want to talk about. Not Carly Baker. Annie . . . Ann Harrison."

Martha gasped. "That sister you told me about last night?"

Harrison nodded. He knew this was going to hurt, but he had to do it, had to get it out. He was going to explode into a thousand twitching bloody pieces if he didn't.

"I was nine when she was born. December 2, 1968—a week after Carly Baker. Seven pounds, four ounces of horror. She looked more fish than human."

His sister's image was imprinted on the rear wall of his brain. And it should have been after all those hours he had spent studying her loathsome face. Only her eyes looked human. The rest of her was awful. A lipless mouth, flattened nose, sloping forehead, fingers and toes fused so that they looked more like flippers than hands and feet, a bloated body covered with shiny skin that was a dusky gray-blue. The doctors said she was that color because her heart was bad, had a defect that caused mixing of blue blood and red blood.

A repulsed nine-year-old Kevin Harrison had dubbed her The Tuna—but never within earshot of his parents.

"She wasn't supposed to live long. A few months, they said, and she'd be dead. But she didn't die. Annie lived on and on. One year. Two. My father and the doctors tried to get my mother to put her into some sort of institution, but Mom wouldn't hear of it. She kept Annie in the third bedroom and talked to her and cooed over her and cleaned up her shit and just hung over her all the time. *All* the time, Martha!"

Martha gripped his hand and nodded for him to go on.

"After a while, it got so there was nothing else in Mom's life. She wouldn't leave Annie. Family trips became a thing of the past. Christ, if she and Dad went out to a movie, *I* had to stay with Annie. No babysitter was trustworthy enough. Our whole lives seemed to center around that freak in the back bedroom. And me? I was forgotten.

"After a while I began to hate my sister."

"Kevin, you don't have to—"

"Yes, I do! I've got to tell you how it was! By the time I was fourteen—just about Tommy Baker's age when he bought it—I thought I was going to go crazy. I was getting all Bs in school but did that matter? Hell, no! 'Annie rolled halfway over today. Isn't that wonderful?' Big deal! She was five years old, for Christ sake! I was starting point guard on the high school junior varsity basketball team as a goddamn freshman, but did anyone come to my games? Hell no!

"I tell you, Martha, after five years of caring for Annie, our house was a powder keg. Looking back now I can see it was my mother's fault for becoming so obsessed. But back then, at age fourteen, I blamed it all on Annie. I really hated her for being born a freak."

He paused before going on. This was the really hard part.

"One night, when my dad had managed to drag my mother out to some company banquet that he had to attend, I was left alone to babysit Annie. On those rare occasions, my mother would always tell me to keep Annie company—you know, read her stories and such. But I never did. I'd let her lie back there alone with our old black-and-white TV while I sat in the living room watching the family set. This time, however, I went into her room."

He remembered the sight of her, lying there with the covers halfway up her fat little tuna body that couldn't have been much more than a yard in length. It was winter, like now, and his mother had dressed her in a flannel nightshirt. The coarse hair that grew off the back of her head had been wound into two braids and fastened with pink bows.

"Annie's eyes brightened as I came into the room. She had never spoken. Couldn't, it seemed. Her face could do virtually nothing in the way of expression, and her flipperlike arms weren't good for much, either. You had to read her eyes, and that wasn't easy. None of us knew how much of a brain Annie had, or how much she understood of what was going on around her. My mother said she was bright, but I think Mom was a little whacko on the subject of Annie.

"Anyway, I stood over her crib and started shouting at her. She quivered at the sound. I called her every dirty name in the book. And as I said each one, I poked her with my fingers—not enough to leave a bruise, but enough to let out some of the violence in me. I called her a lousy goddamn tuna fish with feet. I told her how much I hated her and how I wished she had never been born. I told her everybody hated her and the only thing she was good for was a freak show. Then I said, 'I wish you were dead! Why don't you die? You were supposed to die years ago! Why don't you do everyone a favor and do it now!'

"When I ran out of breath, she looked at me with those big eyes of hers and I could see the tears in them and I knew she had understood me. She rolled over and faced the wall. I ran from the room.

"I cried myself to sleep that night. I'd thought I'd feel good telling her off, but all I kept seeing in my mind's eye was this fourteen-year-old bully shouting at a helpless five-year-old. I felt awful. I promised myself that the first opportunity I had to be alone with her the next day I'd apologize, tell her I really didn't mean the hateful things I'd said, promise to read to her and be her best friend, anything to make it up to her.

"I awoke next morning to the sound of my mother screaming. Annie was dead."

"Oh, my God!" Martha said, her fingers digging into his arm.

"Naturally, I blamed myself."

"But you said she had a heart defect!"

"Yeah. I know. And the autopsy showed that's what killed her—her heart finally gave out. But I've never been able to get it out of my head that my words were what made her heart give up. Sounds sappy and melodramatic, I know, but I've always felt that she was just hanging on to life by the slimmest margin and that I pushed her over the edge."

"Kevin, you shouldn't have to carry that around with you! Nobody should!"

The old grief and guilt were like a slowly expanding balloon in his chest. It was getting hard to breathe.

"In my coolest, calmest, most dispassionate moments I convince myself that it was all a terrible coincidence, that she would have died that night anyway and that I had nothing to do with it."

"That's probably true, so—"

"But that doesn't change the fact that the last memory of her life was of her big brother—the guy she probably thought was the neatest kid on earth, who could run and play basketball, one of the three human beings who made up her whole world, who should have been her champion, her defender against a world that could only greet her with revulsion and rejection—standing over her crib telling her how much he hated her and how he wished she was dead!"

He felt the sobs begin to quake in his chest. He hadn't cried in over a dozen years and he had no intention of allowing himself to start now, but there didn't seem to be any stopping it. It was like running down hill at top speed—if he tried to stop before he reached bottom, he'd go head over heels and break his neck.

"Kevin, you were only fourteen," Martha said soothingly.

"Yeah, I know. But if I could go back in time for just a few seconds, I'd go back to that night and rap that rotten hateful fourteen-year-old in the mouth before he got a chance to say a single word. But I can't. I can't even say I'm sorry to Annie! I never got a chance to take it back, Martha! I never got a chance to make it up to her!"

And then he was blubbering like a goddamn wimp, letting loose half a lifetime's worth of grief and guilt, and Martha's arms were around him and she was telling him everything would be all right, all right, all right . . .

The Detective Harrison understand. Can tell. Want to go kill another face now. Must not. The Detective Harrison not like. Must stop. The Detective Harrison help stop.

Stop for good.

Best way. Only one way stop for good. Not jail. No chain, no little window. Not ever again. Never!

Only one way stop for good. The Detective Harrison will know. Will understand. Will do.

Must call. Call now. Before dark. Before pretty faces come out in night.

* * *

Harrison had pulled himself together by the time the kids came home from school. He felt strangely buoyant inside, like he'd been purged in some way. Maybe all those shrinks were right after all: Sharing old hurts did help.

He played with the kids for a while, then went into the kitchen to see if Martha needed any help with slicing and dicing. He felt as close to her now as he ever had.

"You okay?" she said with a smile.

"Fine."

She had just started slicing a red pepper for the salad. He took over for her.

"Have you decided what to do?" she asked.

He had been thinking about it a lot, and had come to a decision.

"Well, I've got to inform the department about Carly Baker, but I'm going to keep her out of the papers for a while."

"Why? I'd think if she's that freakish looking, the publicity might turn up someone who's seen her."

"Possibly it will come to that. But this case is sensational enough without tabloids like the *Post* and *The Light* turning it into a circus. Besides, I'm afraid of panic leading to some poor deformed innocent getting lynched. I think I can bring her in. She *wants* to come in."

"You're sure of that?"

"She so much as told me so. Besides, I can sense it in her." He saw Martha giving him a dubious look. "I'm serious. We're somehow connected, like there's an invisible wire between us. Maybe it's because the same thing that deformed her and those other kids deformed Annie, too. And Annie was my sister. Maybe that link is why I volunteered for this case in the first place."

He finished slicing the pepper, then moved on to the mushrooms.

"And after I bring her in, I'm going to track down her mother and start prying into what went on in Monroe in February and March of sixty-eight to cause that so-called 'cluster' of freaks nine months later."

He would do that for Annie. It would be his way of saying good-bye and *I'm sorry* to his sister.

"But why does she take their faces?" Martha said.

"I don't know. Maybe because theirs were beautiful and hers is no doubt hideous."

"But what does she *do* with them?"

"Who knows? I'm not all that sure I *want* to know. But right now—"

The phone rang. Even before he picked it up, he had an inkling of who it was. The first sibilant syllable left no doubt.

"Ish thish the Detective Harrishon?"

"Yes."

Harrison stretched the coiled cord around the corner from the kitchen into the dining room, out of Martha's hearing.

"Will you shtop me tonight?"

"You want to give yourself up?"

"Yesh. Pleashe, yesh."

"Can you meet me at the precinct house?"

"No!"

"Okay! Okay!" God, he didn't want to spook her now. "Where? Anywhere you say."

"Jusht you."

"All right."

"Midnight. Plashe where lasht fashe took. Bring gun but not more cop."

"All right."

He was automatically agreeing to everything. He'd work out the details later.

"You undershtand, Detective Harrison?"

"Oh, Carly, Carly, I understand more than you know!"

There was a sharp intake of breath and then silence at the other end of the line. Finally:

"You know Carly?"

"Yes, Carly. I know you." The sadness welled up in him again and it was all he could do to keep his voice from breaking. "I had a sister like you once. And you . . . you had a brother like me."

"Yesh," said that soft, breathy voice. "You undershtand. Come tonight, Detective Harrishon."

The line went dead.

Wait in shadows. The Detective Harrison will come. Will bring lots cop. Always see on TV show. Always bring lots. Protect him. Many guns.

No need. Only one gun. The Detective Harrison's gun. Him's will shoot. Stop kills. Stop forever.

The Detective Harrison must do. No one else. The Carly can not. Must be the Detective Harrison. Smart. Know the Carly. Understand.

After stop, no more ugly Carly. No more sick-scared look. Bad face will go away. Forever and ever.

Harrison had decided to go it alone.

Not completely alone. He had a van waiting a block and a half away on Seventh Avenue and a walkie-talkie clipped to his belt, but he hadn't told anyone who he was meeting or why. He knew if he did, they'd swarm all over the area and scare Carly off completely. So he had told Jacobi he was meeting an informant and that the van was just a safety measure.

He was on his own here and wanted it that way. Carly Baker wanted to surrender to him and him alone. He understood that. It was part of that strange tenuous bond between them. No one else would do. After he had cuffed her, he would call in the wagon.

After that he would be a hero for a while. He didn't want to be a hero. All he wanted was to end this thing, end the nightmare for the city and for poor Carly Baker. She'd get help, the kind she needed, and he'd use the publicity to springboard an investigation into what had made Annie and Carly and the others in their 'cluster' what they were.

It's all going to work out fine, he told himself as he entered the alley.

He walked half its length and stood in the darkness. The brick walls of the building on either side soared up into the night. The ceaseless roar of the city echoed dimly behind him. The alley itself was quiet—no sound, no movement. He took out his flashlight and flicked it on.

"Carly?"

No answer.

"Carly Baker—are you here?"

More silence, then, ahead to his left, the sound of a garbage can scraping along the stony floor of the alley. He swung the light that way, and gasped.

A looming figure stood a dozen feet in front of him. It could only be Carly Baker. She stood easily as tall as he—a good six foot two—and looked like a homeless street person, one of those animated rag piles that live on subway grates in the winter. Her head was wrapped in a dirty scarf, leaving only her glittery dark eyes showing. The rest of her was muffled in a huge, shapeless overcoat, baggy old polyester slacks with dragging cuffs, and torn sneakers.

"Where the Detective Harrishon's gun?" said the voice.

Harrison's mouth was dry but he managed to get his tongue working. "In its holster."

"Take out. Pleashe."

Harrison didn't argue with her. The grip of his heavy Chief Special felt damn good in his hand.

The figure spread its arms; within the folds of her coat those arms seem to bend the wrong way. And were those black hooked claws protruding from the cuffs of the sleeves?

She said, "Shoot."

Harrison gaped in shock.

The Detective Harrison not shoot. Eyes wide. Hands with gun and light shake.

Say again: "Shoot!"

"Carly, no! I'm not here to kill you. I'm here to take you in, just as we agreed."

"No!"

Wrong! The Detective Harrison not understand! Must shoot the Carly! Kill the Carly!

"Not jail! Shoot! Shtop the kills! Shtop the Carly!"

"No! I can get you help, Carly. Really, I can! You'll go to a place where no one will hurt you. You'll get medicine to make you feel better!"

Thought him understand! Not understand! Move closer. Put claw out. Him back way. Back to wall.

"Shoot! Kill! Now!"

"No, Annie, please!"

"Not Annie! Carly! Carly!"

"Right. Carly! Don't make me do this!"

Only inches way now. Still not shoot. Other cops hiding not shoot. Why not protect?

"Shoot!" Pull scarf off face. Point claw at face. "End! End! *Pleashe!*"

The Detective Harrison face go white. Mouth hang open. Say, "Oh, my *God!*"

Get sick-scared look. Hate that look! Thought him understand! Say he know the Carly! Not! Stop look! *Stop!*

Not think. Claw go out. Rip throat of the Detective Harrison. Blood fly just like others.

No-No-No! Not want hurt!

The Detective Harrison gurgle. Drop gun and light. Fall. Stare.

Wait other cops shoot. Please kill the Carly. Wait.

No shoot. Then know. No cops. Only the poor Detective Harrison. Cry for the Detective Harrison. Then run. Run and climb. Up and down. Back to new home with the Old Jessi.

The Jessi glad hear Carly come. The Jessi try talk. Carly go sit tub. Close door. Cry for the Detective Harrison. Cry long time. Break mirror million piece. Not see face again. Not ever. Never.

The Jessi say, "Carly, I want my bath. Will you scrub my back?"

Stop cry. Do the Old Jessi's black back. Comb the Jessi's hair.

Feel very sad. None ever comb the Carly's hair. Ever.

1988

Another bridesmaid year—twice this time. Both "Traps" and "Dat-Tay-Vao" made the final ballot for the Bram Stoker short story award from the Horror Writers of America. The kiss of death. The vote was split and I lost. A neat little trophy, the Stoker. I would have loved one.

Nineteen eighty-eight was a strange year. I rarely do nonfiction, but I started off the year writing a short essay for *Horror: The 100 Best Books*. Stephen Jones and Kim Newman wrote from England and asked me to name horror books I'd like to write about. I offered only one: *The Exorcist*. As far as I'm concerned, this is the most effective horror novel ever written, wrenching on both the visceral and metaphysical levels. They said go ahead, and I knocked it out in an evening.

After that, I plunged back into *Reborn*. Later in the year I finished "Kids," the final novella in the saga of Sigmundo Dreyer, which when cobbled together would become the novel *Dydeetown World*.

In the spring of 1988 I was introduced to the world of television screenwriting (see the Appendix for more on that), and a few months later I was offered an opportunity to bring back Repairman Jack.

One of my phone friends, Ed Gorman (with whom I've spent countless hours in conversation but never have met) mentioned that he and Marty Greenberg were co-editing an anthology called *Stalkers* for Dark Harvest/NAL. Would I care to contribute? I said I'd been itching to revive Repairman Jack, the lead character from *The Tomb*. How about a Jack story? Ed, a Repairman Jack fan since the git-go, told me I *had* to do it.

The Tomb had been published five years earlier. It hit the best-seller lists, won the Porgie Award from *The West Coast Review of Books*, and the mail began pouring in. I'd closed the novel with Jack's life hanging by a thread, and readers wanted to know: What happened to Repairman Jack? When are you going to do another Repairman Jack novel? I didn't want to get involved in a series character, but the book kept selling, and the letters were still coming in.

Then there was the Hollywood interest. New World Pictures had optioned the novel, but a combination of low-rent antics by Fred Olen Ray and a lousy screenplay (they moved the action to Pasadena!) had the project dead in the water. I dashed off a spec script in an eleventh-hour attempt to save it, but too late.

The Tomb has been optioned a total of four times. Everyone loves the idea of Repairman Jack as a continuing character; but the rakoshi, the Bengali temple demons who provide the horror, have sunk all attempts to adapt it to film. How do you make them look real? The line between horror and hilarity is a couple of nanometers thick. A rakosh is scary; a guy in a rubber suit is dumb.

As I write this, Beacon Films (who brought us *Air Force One*) and First Street Films are earnestly trying to bring *The Tomb* to the screen. They think that with digital effects they can create believable rakoshi. We'll see.

The Hollywood connection provided an ulterior motive for writing a new Repairman Jack story. I had created a number of original action sequences for the Repairman Jack screenplay I sent to New World, and I wanted to protect them. The best way to do that was to copyright them in a story. They're all in "A Day in the Life."

I called Marty Greenberg (the world's most prolific anthologist—I doubt even he knows how many anthologies he's edited) for more details on the anthology, and during that conversation (the first of many) he managed to tap me to edit one of the anthologies the Horror Writers of America was shopping around. That was how *Freak Show* began, but that's a whole other story . . .

Stalkers turned out to be a hugely successful anthology—book clubs, audio version, and multiple foreign editions. But by contributing to that anthology I opened the door to the insidious influence of Martin H. Greenberg. Little did I know then what effect that seemingly innocent act would have on my short story output.

More on Marty as we go. And for those who care, the Tram character previously appeared in "Dat-Tay-Vao."

A DAY IN THE LIFE

When the cockroach made a right turn up the wall, Jack flipped another *shuriken* across the room. The steel points of the throwing star drove into the wallboard just above the bug's long antennae. It backed up and found itself hemmed in on all sides now by four of the stars.

"Did it!" Jack said from where he lay across the still-made hotel bed.

He counted the *shuriken* protruding from the wall. A dozen of them traveled upward in a gentle arc above and behind the barely functioning TV, ending in a tiny square where the roach was trapped.

Check that. It was free again. Crawled over one of the *shuriken* and was now continuing on its journey to wherever. Jack let it go and rolled onto his back on the bedspread.

Bored.

And hot. He was dressed in jeans and a loose, heavy sweater under an oversize lightweight jacket, both dark blue; a black-and-orange knitted cap was jammed on the top of his head. He'd turned the thermostat all the way down but the room remained an oven. He didn't want to risk taking anything off because, when the buzzer sounded, he had to hit the ground running.

He glanced over at the dusty end table where the little Walkman-sized box with the antenna sat in silence.

"Come on, already," he mumbled to it. "Let's do it."

Reilly and his sleazos were due to make their move tonight. What was taking them so long to get started? Almost one A.M. already—three hours here in this fleabag. He was starting to itch. He could handle only so much TV without getting drowsy. Even without the lulling drone of some host interviewing some actor he'd never heard of, the heat was draining him.

Fresh air. Maybe that would work.

Jack got up, stretched, and stepped to the window. A clear almost-Halloween night out there, with a big moon rising over the city. He gripped the handles and pulled. Nothing. The damn thing wouldn't budge. He was checking the edges of the sash when he heard the faint crack of a rifle. The bullet came through the glass two inches to the left of his head, peppering his face with tiny sharp fragments as it whistled past his ear.

Jack collapsed his legs and dropped to the floor. He waited. No more shots. Keeping his head below the level of the windowsill, he rose to a crouch, then leaped for the lamp on the end table at the far side of the bed, grabbed it, and rolled to the floor with it. Another shot spat through the glass and whistled through the room as his back thudded against the floor. He turned off the lamp.

The other lamp, the one next to the TV, was still on—sixty watts of help for the shooter. And whoever was shooting had to know Jack would be going for it next. He'd be ready.

On his belly, Jack slid along the industrial grade carpet toward the end of the bed until he had an angle where the bulb was visible under the shade. He pulled out his next to last *shuriken* and spun it toward the bulb. With an electric pop it flared blue-white and left the room dark except for the flickering glow from the TV.

Immediately Jack popped his head above the bed and looked out the window. Through the spider-webbed glass he caught sight of a bundled figure turning and darting away across the neighboring rooftop. Moonlight glinted off the long barrel of a high-powered rifle, flashed off the lens of a telescopic sight, then he was gone.

A high-pitched beep made him jump. The red light on the signal box was blinking like mad. Kuropolis wanted help. Which meant Reilly had struck.

"Swell."

* * *

Not a bad night," George Kuropolis thought, wiping down the counter in front of the slim young brunette as she seated herself. Not a great night, but still to have half a dozen customers at this hour was good. And better yet, Reilly and his creeps hadn't shown up.

Maybe they'd bother somebody else tonight.

"What'll it be?" he asked the brunette.

"Tea, please," she said with a smile. A nice smile. She was dressed nice and had decent jewelry on. Not exactly overdressed for the neighborhood, but better than the usual.

George wished he had more customers of her caliber. And he *should* have them. Why the hell not? Didn't the chrome inside and out sparkle? Couldn't you eat off the floor? Wasn't everything he served made right here on the premises?

"Sure. Want some pie?"

"No, thank you."

"It's good. Blueberry. Made it myself."

The smile again. "No, thanks. I'm on a diet."

"Sure," he mumbled as he turned away to get her some hot water. "Everyone's on a goddamn diet. Diets are gettin' hazardous to my health."

Just then the front door burst open and a white-haired man in his midtwenties leaped in with a sawed-off shotgun in his hands. He pointed it at the ceiling and let loose a round at the fixture over the cash register. The *boom* of the blast was deafening as glass showered everything.

Matt Reilly was here.

Four more of his gang crowded in behind him. George recognized them: Reece was the black with the white fringe leather jacket; Rafe had the blue Mohican, Tony had the white; and Cheeks was the baby-faced skinhead.

"Aw*right*!" Reilly said, grinning fiercely under his bent nose, mean little eyes, dark brows, and bleached crewcut. "It's ass-kickin' time!"

George reached into his pocket and pressed the button on the beeper there, then raised his hands and backed up against the wall.

"Hey, Matt!" he called. "C'mon! What's the problem?"

"You know the problem, George!" Reilly said.

He tossed the shotgun to Reece and stepped around the counter. Smiling, he closed with George. The smile only heightened the sick knot of fear coiling in George's belly. He was so fixed on that empty smile that he didn't see the sucker punch coming. It caught him in the gut. He doubled over in agony. His last cup of coffee heaved but stayed down.

He groaned. *"Christ!"*

"You're late again, George!" Reilly said through his teeth. "I told you last time what would happen if you didn't stick to the schedule!"

George struggled to remember his lines.

"I can't pay two protections! I can't afford it!"

"You can't afford *not* to afford it! And you don't have to pay two. Just pay me!"

"Sure! That's what the other guy says when *he* wants *his*! And where are *you* then?"

"Don't worry about the other guy! I'm taking care of him tonight! But *you*!" Reilly rammed George back against the wall. "I'm gonna hafta make a example outta you, George! People saw what happened to Wolansky when he turned pigeon. Now they're gonna see what happens to a shit who don't pay!"

Just then came a scream from off to George's right. He looked and saw Reece covering the five male customers in booths two and four, making them empty their pockets onto one of the tables. Further down the counter, Cheeks was waving a big knife with a mean-looking curved blade at the girl who'd wanted the tea.

"The ring, babe," he was saying. "Let's have it."

"It's my engagement ring!" she said.

"You wanna look nice at your wedding, you better give it quick."

He reached for it and she slapped his hand away.

"No!"

Cheeks straightened up and slipped the knife into a sheath tucked into the small of his back.

"Ooooh, you should'na done that, bitch," said Reece in oily tones.

George wished he were a twenty-five-year-old with a Schwarzenegger build instead of a wheezy fifty with pencil arms. He'd wipe the floor with these creeps.

"Stop him," he said to Reilly. "Please. I'll pay you."

"Couldn't stop him now if I wanted to," Reilly said, grinning. "Cheeks *likes* it when they play rough."

In a single smooth motion, the skinhead's hand snaked out, grabbed the front of the woman's blouse, and ripped. The whole front came away. Her breasts were visible through a semitransparent bra. She screamed and swatted at him. Cheeks shrugged off the blow and grappled with her, dragging her to the floor.

One of the men in the booth near Reece leaped to his feet and started toward the pair, yelling, "Hey! Whatta y'think you're doin'?"

Reece slammed the shotgun barrel across his face. Blood spurted from the guy's forehead as he dropped back into his seat.

"Tony!" Reilly said to the Mohican standing by the cash register. "Where's Rafe?"

"Inna back."

George suddenly felt his scalp turn to fire as Reilly grabbed him by the hair and shoved him toward Tony.

"Take George in the back. You and Rafe give him some memory lessons so he won't be late again."

George felt his sphincters loosening. Where was Jack?

"I'll pay! I told you I'll pay!"

"It's not the same, George," Reilly said with a slow shake of his head. "If I gotta come here and kick ass every month just to get what's mine, I got better things to do, y'know?"

As George watched, Reilly hit the No Sale button on the cash register and started digging into the bills.

Thick, pincerlike fingers closed on the back of George's neck as he was propelled into the rear of the diner. He saw Rafe off to the side, playing with the electric meat grinder where George mixed his homemade sausage.

"Rafe!" said Tony. "Matt wants us to teach Mr. Greasyspoon some manners!"

Rafe didn't look up. He had a raw chicken leg in his hand. He shoved it into the top of the meat grinder. The sickening crunch of bone and cartilage being pulverized rose over the whir of the motor, then ground chicken leg began to extrude through the grate at the bottom.

"Hey, Tone!" Rafe said, looking up and grinning. "I got a great idea!"

Jack pounded along the second floor hallway. He double-timed down the flight of stairs to the lobby, sprinted across the carpet tiles that spelled out "The Lucky Hotel" in bright yellow on dark blue, and pushed through the smudged glass doors of the entrance. One of the letters on the neon sign above the door was out. *The ucky Hotel* flashed fitfully in hot red.

Jack leaped down the three front steps and hit the pavement running. Half a block to the left, then another left down an alley, leaping puddles and dodging garbage cans until he came to the rear of the Highwater Diner. He had his key ready and shoved it into the deadbolt on the delivery door. He paused there long enough to draw his .45 automatic, a Colt Mark IV, and to stretch the knitted cap down over his face. It then became a Halloween decorated ski mask, and he was looking out through a bright orange jack-o'-lantern. He pulled the door open and slipped into the storage area at the rear of the kitchen.

Up ahead he heard the sound of a scuffle, and George's terrified voice crying, "No, don't! *Please* don't!"

He rounded the corner of the meat locker and found Tony and Rafe—he'd know those Mohicans anywhere—from Reilly's gang forcing George's hand into a meat grinder and George struggling like all hell to keep it out. But he was losing the battle. His fingers would soon be sausage meat.

Jack was just reaching for the slide on his automatic when he spotted a meat tenderizing hammer on a nearby counter. He picked it up and hefted it. Heavy—a good three pounds, most of it in the steel head. Pocketing the pistol, he stepped over to the trio and began a sidearm swing toward Tony's skull.

"Tony! Trick or treat!"

Tony looked up just in time to stop the full weight of the waffle-faced hammerhead with the center of his face. It made a noise like *smoonch!* as it buried itself in his nose. He was halfway to the floor before Rafe even noticed.

"Tone?"

Jack didn't wait for him to look up. He used the hammer to crunch a wide part in the center of Rafe's blue Mohican. Rafe joined Tony on the floor.

"God, am I glad to see you!" George said, gasping and fondling his fingers as if to reassure himself that they were all there. "What took you so long?"

"Can't've been more than two minutes," Jack said, slipping the handle of the hammer through his belt and pulling the automatic again.

"Seemed like a *year!*"

"The rest of them out front?"

"Just three—Reilly, the skinhead, and Reece."

Jack paused. "Where's the rest of them?"

"Don't know."

Jack thought he knew. The other three had probably been on that rooftop trying to plug him in his hotel room. But how had they found him? He hadn't even told George about staying at the Lucky.

One way to find out . . .

"Okay. You lock the back door and stay here. I'll take care of the rest."

"There's a girl out there—" George said.

Jack nodded. "I'm on my way."

He turned and almost bumped into Reilly coming through the swinging doors from the front. He was counting the fistful of cash in his hands.

"How we doin' back—?" Reilly said and then froze when the muzzle of Jack's automatic jammed up under his chin.

"Happy Halloween," Jack said.

"Shit! You again!"

"Right, Matt, old boy. Me again. And I see you've made my collection for me. How thoughtful. You can shove it in my left pocket."

Reilly's face was white with rage as he glanced over to where Tony writhed on the floor next to the unconscious Rafe.

"You're a dead man, pal. Worse than dead!"

Jack smiled through the ski mask and increased the pressure of the barrel on Reilly's throat.

"Just do as you're told."

"What's with you and these masks, anyway?" he said as he stuffed the money into Jack's pocket. "You that ugly? Or do you think you're Spider-man or something?"

"No, I'm Pumpkinman. And this way I know you but you don't know me. You see, Matt, I've been keeping close tabs on you. I know all your haunts. I stand in plain view and watch you. I've watched you play pool at Gus's. I've walked up behind you in a crowd and bumped you as I passed. I could have slipped an ice pick between your ribs a dozen times by now. But don't try to spot me. You won't. While you're trying too hard to look like Billy Idol, I'm trying even harder to look like nobody."

"You *are* nobody, man!" His voice was as tough as ever, but a haunted look had crept into his eyes.

Jack laughed. "Surprised to see me?"

"Not really," Reilly said, recovering. "I figured you'd show up."

"Yeah? What's the matter? No faith in your hit squad?"

"Hit squad?" There was genuine bafflement in his eyes. "What the fuck you talkin' about?"

Jack sensed that Reilly wasn't faking it. He was as baffled as Jack.

He let his mind wander an instant. *If not Reilly's bunch, then who?*

No time for that now. Especially with the muffled screams coming from the front. He turned Reilly around and shoved him back through the swinging doors to the front of the diner. Once there, he bellied Reilly up against the counter and put the .45 to his temple. He saw Reece covering half a dozen customers with a sawed off shotgun. But where was that psycho, Cheeks?

"Okay, turkeys!" Jack yelled. "Fun's over! Drop the hardware!"

Reece spun and faced them. His eyes widened and he raised the scattergun in their direction. Jack felt Reilly cringe back against him.

"Go ahead," Jack said, placing himself almost completely behind Reilly. "You can't make him any uglier."

"Don't, man!" Reilly said in a low voice.

Reece didn't move. He didn't seem to know what to do. So Jack told him.

"Put the piece on the counter or I'll blow his head off."

"No way," Reece said.

"Don't try me, pal. I'll do it just for fun."

Jack hoped Reece didn't think he was bluffing, because he wasn't. He'd already been shot at twice tonight and he was in a foul mood.

"Do what he says, man," Reilly told him.

"No *way*!" Reece said. "I'll get outta here, but no way I'm givin' that suckuh my piece!"

Jack wasn't going to allow that. As soon as Reece got outside he'd start peppering the big windows with shot. He was about to move Reilly out from behind the counter to block the aisle when one of the customers Reece had been covering stood up behind him and grabbed the pump handle of the scattergun. A second man leaped to his side to help. One round blasted into the ceiling, and then the gun was useless—with all those hands on it, Reece couldn't pump another round into the chamber. Two more customers jumped up and overpowered him. The shotgun came free as a fifth man with a deep cut in his forehead shoved Reece back onto the seat of the booth and began pounding his face. More fists began to fly. These were *very* angry men.

Jack guided Reilly toward the group. He saw two pairs of legs—male and female, struggling on the floor around the far end of the counter. He shoved Reilly toward the cluster of male customers.

"Here's another one for you. Have fun. Just don't do anything to them they wouldn't do to you."

Two of the men smiled and slammed Reilly down face first on the booth's table. They began pummeling his kidneys as Jack hurried down to where Cheek's was doing his dirty work.

He looked over the edge of the counter and saw that the skinhead held the woman's arms pinned between them with his left hand and had his right thrust up under her bra, twisting her nipple, oblivious to everything else. Her right eye was bruised and swollen. She was crying and writhing under him, even snapping at him with her teeth. A real fighter. She must have put up quite a struggle. Cheeks's face was bleeding from several scratches.

Jack was tempted to put a slug into the base of Cheeks's spine so he'd not only never walk again, he'd never get it up again, either. But Cheeks's knife was in the way, and besides, the bullet might pass right through him and into the woman. So he pocketed the .45, grabbed Cheeks's right ear, and ripped upward.

Cheeks came off the floor with a howl. Jack lifted him by the ear and stretched his upper body across the counter. He could barely speak. He really wanted to hurt this son of a bitch.

"Naughty, naughty!" he managed to say. "Didn't you ever go to Catholic school? Didn't the nuns tell you that bad things would happen to you if you ever did that to a girl?"

He stretched Cheeks's right hand out on the counter, palm down.

"Like you might get warts?"

He pulled the meat hammer from his belt and raised it over his head.

"Or worse?"

He put everything he had into the shot. Bones crunched like breadsticks. Cheeks screamed and slipped off the counter. He rolled on the floor, moaning and crying, cradling his injured hand like a mother with a newborn baby.

"Never hassle a paying customer," Jack said. "George can't pay his protection without them."

He grabbed Reece's scattergun and pulled him and Reilly free from the customers. Both were battered and bloody. He shoved them toward the front door.

"I told you clowns about trying to cut in on my turf! How many times we have to do this dance?"

Reilly whirled on him, rage in his eyes. He probably would have leaped at Jack's throat if not for the shotgun.

"We was here *first*, asshole!"

"Maybe. But *I'm* here now, so scrape up your two wimps from the back room and get them out of here."

He oversaw the pair as they dragged Rafe and Tony out the front door. Cheeks was on his feet by then. Jack waved him forward.

"C'mon, loverboy. Party's over."

"He's got my ring!" the brunette cried from the far end of the counter. She held her torn dress up over her breasts. There was blood at the corner of her mouth. "My engagement ring."

"Really?" Jack said. "That ought to be worth something! Let's see it."

Cheeks glared at Jack and reached into his back pocket with his good hand.

"You wanna see it?" he said. Suddenly he was swinging a big Gurkha *kukri* knife through the air, slashing at Jack's eyes. "Here! Get a close look!"

Jack blocked the curved blade with the short barrel of the sawed-off, then grabbed Cheeks's wrist and twisted. As Cheeks instinctively brought his broken hand up, Jack dropped the shotgun. He grabbed the injured hand and squeezed. Cheeks screamed and went to his knees.

"Drop the blade," Jack said softly.

It clattered to the counter.

"Good. Now find that ring and put it on the counter."

Cheeks dug into the left front pocket of his jeans and pulled out a tiny diamond on a gold band. Jack's throat tightened when he saw the light in the brunette's eyes at the sight of it. Such a little thing . . . yet so important.

Still gripping Cheeks's crushed hand, he picked up the ring and pretended to examine it.

"You went to all that trouble for this itty-bitty thing?" Jack slid it down the counter. "Here, babe. Compliments of the house."

She had to let the front of her dress drop to grab it. She clutched the tiny ring against her with both hands and began to cry. Jack felt a black fury crowd the edges of his vision. He looked at Cheeks's round baby face, glaring up at him from seat level by the counter top, and picked up the *kukri*. He held it before Cheeks's eyes. The pupils dilated with terror.

Releasing the broken hand, Jack immediately grabbed Cheeks's throat and jaw, twisted him up and around, and slammed the back of his head down on the counter, pinning him there. With two quick strokes he carved a crude *X* in the center of Cheeks's forehead. He howled and Jack let go. He grabbed the shotgun again and shoved Cheeks toward the door.

"Don't worry, Cheeks. It's nothing embarrassing—just your signature."

Once he had them all outside, he used the shotgun to prod them into the alley between the diner and the vacant three-story Borden building next door. They were a pitiful bunch, what with Tony and Rafe barely able to stand, Cheeks with a bloody forehead and a hand swollen to twice normal size, and Reece and Reilly nursing cracked ribs and swollen jaws.

"This is the last time I want to do this dance with you guys. It's bad for business around here. And besides, sooner or later one of you is really going to get hurt."

Jack was about to turn and leave them there when he heard tires squeal in the street. Headlights lit the alley and rushed toward him. Jack dove to his left to avoid being hit as the nose of a beat-up Chrysler rammed into the mouth of the alley. His foot slipped on some rubble and he went down. By the time he scrambled to his feet, he found himself looking into the business ends of a shotgun, a 9mm automatic, and a Tec-9 assault pistol.

He'd found the missing members of Reilly's gang.

Even though it made his ribs feel like they were breaking, Matt couldn't help laughing.

"Gotcha! *Gotcha,* scumbag!"

He picked up the fallen scattergun and jabbed the barrel at Ski mask's gut. The guy deflected the thrust and almost pulled it from his grasp. Fast hands. Better not leave this guy any openings.

"The gun," he said. "Take it out real slow and drop it."

The guy looked at all the guns pointed at him, then reached into his pocket and pulled out his own by the barrel; it fell to the alley floor with a thud.

"Turn around," Matt told him, "lean on the wall, and spread 'em, police style. And remember—one funny move and you're full of holes."

Matt patted down his torso and legs and told him, "You musta thought

I was a stupid jerk to hit this place without backup. These guys've been waiting the whole time for you to show. Never figured you'd come in the back, though. But that's okay. We gotcha now."

The frisk turned up nothing, not even a wallet. The blue jacket had nothing in the pockets except the cash from the register. He'd get that later. Right now, though, it was game time.

"All right. Turn around. Let's see what you look like."

When the guy turned, Matt reached up and pulled off the pumpkin-headed ski mask. He saw an average-looking guy about ten years older than he and his boys—midthirties, maybe—with dark brown hair. Nothing special. Matt shoved the mask back on the top of the guy's head where it perched at a stupid-looking angle.

"What's your name, asshole?"

"Jack."

"Jack what?"

"O'Lantern. It's an old Irish—"

Suddenly Cheeks was at Matt's shoulder, brandishing the special forces knife they kept in the car.

"He's *mine*!" he screeched. "Lemme make his face into a *permanent* jack-o'-lantern!"

"Cool it, man."

"Look what he did to me! Look at my fuckin' hand! And look at this!" He pointed the knife at the bloody *X* on his forehead. "Look what he did to my face! He's *mine*, man!"

"You get firsts, okay? But not here, man. We're gonna take Mr. Jack here for a ride, and then we're *all* gonna get a turn with him." He held the shotgun out to Cheeks. "Here. Trade ya."

Matt took the heavy, slotted blade and placed the point against one of the guy's lower eyelids. He wanted to see him squirm.

"Some knife, huh? Just like the one Rambo uses. Even cuts through *bone*!"

The guy winced. His tough guy act was gone. He was almost whining now.

"Wha . . . what are you going to do?"

"Not sure yet, Mr. Jack. But I'm sure Cheeks and me can think up a thousand ways to make you wish you'd never been born."

The guy slid along the wall a little, pressing back like he was trying to seep into it. His right hand crept up and covered his mouth.

"You're not gonna t-torture me, are you?"

Behind him, Cheeks laughed. Matt had to smile. Yeah, this was more like it. This was going to be *fun*.

"Who? Us? Torture? Nah! Just a little sport. 'Creative playtime,' as my teachers used to call it. I've got this *great* imagination. I can think of all sorts of—"

Matt saw the guy twist his arm funny. He heard a *snikt!* and suddenly this tiny pistol was in the guy's hand and the big bore of the stubby barrel was staring into his left eye from about an inch away. And the guy wasn't whining anymore.

"Imagine *this*, Matt!" he said through his teeth. "You do a lousy frisk."

Matt heard his boys crowding in behind him, heard somebody work the slide on an automatic.

"You got no way out of this," he told the guy.

"Neither do you," the guy said. "You want to play Rambo? Fine. You've got your oversized fishing knife? I've got this Semmerling LM-4, the worlds smallest .45. It holds four three-hundred-grain hollowpoints. You know about hollowpoints, Matt? Imagine one of those going into your skull. It makes a little hole going in but then it starts to break up into thousands of tiny pieces that fan out as they go through your brain. When those pieces leave your head they'll take most of your brain—not a heavy load in your case—and the back half of your skull with them, spraying the whole alley behind you."

Without turning, Matt could sense his boys moving away from directly behind him.

He dropped the knife. "Okay. We call this one a draw."

The guy grabbed the front of his shirt and dragged him deeper into the alley, to an empty doorway. Then he shoved Matt back and dove inside.

Matt didn't have to tell the others what to do. They charged up and began blasting away into the doorway. Jerry, one of the new arrivals, stood right in front of the opening and emptied his Tec-9's thirty-six-round clip in one long, wild, jittery burst. He stopped and was grinning at Matt when a single shot came from inside. Jerry flew back like someone had jerked a wire. His assault pistol went flying as he spun and landed on his face. This big wet red hole gaped where the middle of his back used to be.

"Shit!" Matt said. He turned to Cheeks. "Go around the other side and make sure he doesn't sneak out."

Reece nudged him, making climbing motions as he pointed up at the rusty fire escape. Matt nodded and boosted him up. It creaked and groaned as Reece, his scattergun clamped under his arm, headed for the second floor like a ghost in white fringed leather. Matt hoped he got real close to the bastard before firing—close enough to make hamburger out of his head with the first shot.

Everybody waited. Even Rafe and Tony had come around enough to get their pieces out and ready. Tony was in bad shape, though. His nose was all squished in and he made weird noises when he breathed. His face looked *awful*, man.

They waited some more. Reece should have found him by now.

Then a shotgun boomed inside.

"Awright *Reece*!" Rafe shouted.

Matt listened to the quiet inside. "Reece! Y'get him?"

Suddenly someone came flying out the door, dark blue jacket and jack-o'-lantern ski mask, stumbling like he was wounded.

"Shit, it's *him*!"

Matt opened up and so did everyone else. They pumped that bastard so full of holes a whole goddamn medical center couldn't patch him up even if they got the chance. And they kept on blasting as he fell to the rubble-strewn ground and twisted and writhed and jolted with the slugs. Finally he lay still.

Cheeks came running back from the other side of the building.

"Y'get 'im?" he said. "Y'get 'im?"

"Got him, Cheeks!" Rafe said. "Got him *good*!"

Matt pointed the guy's own .45 at him as he approached the body. No way he could be alive, but no sense in taking chances. That was when he noticed that the guy's hands were tied behind his back. Matt suddenly had a sick feeling that he'd been had again. He pulled off the ski mask, knowing he'd see Reece's face.

He was right. And he had a sock shoved in his mouth.

Behind Matt, Cheeks howled with rage.

Abe ran his fingers through the shoulder fringe of the white leather jacket.

"So, Jack. Who's your new tailor? Now that Liberace's gone, you're thinking maybe of filling his sartorial niche? Or is this Elvis you're trying to look like?"

Jack couldn't help smiling. "Could be either. But since I don't play piano, it'll have to be Elvis. You can open for me, seeing as you've got the Jackie Mason patter down perfect. You write for him?"

"What can I say?" Abe said with an elaborate shrug. "He comes to me, I give him material."

Jack pulled off the jacket. He'd known he'd get heat from Abe for it, but it was a little too cold out tonight for just a sweater. But he was glad Abe was still in his store. He kept much the same hours as Jack.

Jack rolled up the right sleeve of his sweater and set the little Semmerling back into the spring holster strapped to his forearm. Not the most comfortable rig, but after tonight he ranked it as one of the best investments he'd ever made.

"You had to use that tonight?"

"Yeah. Not one of my better nights."

"*Nu?* You're not going to tell me how such a beautiful and stylish leather coat fits in?"

"Sure. I'll tell you downstairs. I need some supplies."

"Ah! So this is a for-buying visit and not just a social call. Good! I'm having a special on Claymores this week."

Abe stepped to the front door of the Isher Sports Shop, locked it, making sure the "SORRY, WE ARE CLOSED" sign faced toward the street. Jack waited as he unlocked the heavy steel door that led to the basement. Below, light from overhead lamps gleamed off the rows and stacks of pistols, rifles, machine guns, bazookas, grenades, knives, mines, and other miscellaneous tools of destruction.

"What'll it be?"

"I lost my .45, so I'll need a replacement for that."

"Swishy leather jackets and losing guns. A change of life, maybe? How about a nine millimeter parabellum instead? I can give you something nice in a Tokarev M213, or a TT9, or a Beretta 92F. How about a Glock 17, or a Llama Commander?"

"Nah."

" 'Nah.' You never want to change."

"I'm loyal."

"To a person you can be loyal. To a country maybe you're loyal. But loyal to a caliber? *Feh!*"

"Just give me another Colt like the last."

"I'm out of the Mark IV. How about a Combat Stallion. Cost you fifty-fifty."

"Deal. And maybe I should look into one of those Kevlar vests," Jack said, glancing at a rack of them at the far end of the basement.

"For years I've been telling you that. What makes a change of mind now?"

"Somebody tried to kill me tonight."

"So? This is new?"

"I mean a sniper. Right through the hotel room window. Where nobody but me knew I was staying. I didn't even use Jack in the name when I called in the reservation."

"So maybe it wasn't you they were after. Maybe it was meant for somebody who happened to walk by a window."

"Maybe," Jack said, but he couldn't quite buy it. "Lousy shot, too. I spotted a telescopic sight on it and still he managed to miss me."

Abe made a disgusted noise. "They sell guns to anybody these days."

"Maybe I'll take a raincheck on the vest," Jack said, then quickly added, "Oh, and I need another dozen *shuriken*."

Abe whirled on him. "Don't tell me! Don't *tell* me! You've been spiking cockroaches with my *shuriken* again, haven't you? Jack, you promised!"

Jack cringed away. "Not exactly spiking them. Hey, Abe, I get bored."

Abe reached into a square crate and pulled out one of the six-pointed models, wrapped in oiled paper. He held it up and spoke to heaven.

"Oy! Precision weapons made of the finest steel! Honed to a razor's edge! But does Mr. *macher* Repairman Jack appreciate? Does he show respect? Reverence? Of course not! For pest control he uses them!"

"Uh, I'll need about a dozen."

Muttering Yiddish curses under his breath, Abe began pulling the *shuriken* out of the crate and slamming them down on the table one by one.

"Better make that a dozen and a half," Jack said.

First thing the next morning, Jack called George at the diner and told him to meet him at Julio's at ten. Then he went for his morning run. From a booth on the rim of Central Park, he called the answering machine that sat alone in the fourth-floor office he rented on Tenth Avenue. He fast-forwarded through a couple of requests for appliance repairs, then came to a tentative Asian voice, Chinese maybe:

"Mistah Jack, this is Tram. Please call. Have bad problem. People say you can help." He gave a phone number, a downtown exchange.

Tram. Jack had never heard of him. He was the last on the tape. Jack re-set it, then called this Tram guy. He was hard to understand, but Jack de-cided to see him. He told him where Julio's was and to be there at ten-thirty.

After a shave and a shower, he headed to Julio's for some breakfast. He was on the sidewalk, maybe half a block away, when he heard someone shout a warning. He glanced left, saw a man halfway across the street, pointing above him. Something in his expression made Jack dive for the nearest doorway. He was halfway there when something brushed his ankle and thudded against the pavement in an explosion of white.

When the dust finally cleared, Jack was staring at what was left of a fifty-pound bag of cement. The man who had shouted the warning was stand-ing on the other side of the mess.

"That maniac could've killed you!"

"Maniac?" Jack said, brushing the white powder off his coat and jeans.

"Yeah. That didn't fall. Somebody dropped it. Looked like he was aim-ing for your head!"

Jack spun and raced around the corner to the other side of the building. This was the second time since midnight someone had tried to off him. Or maim him. The cement bag probably wouldn't have killed him, but it easily could have broken his neck or his back.

Maybe he had a chance to catch this guy.

He found the stairs to the upper floors and pounded up a dozen flights, but by the time he reached the roof it was empty. Another bag of cement sat on the black tar surface next to a pile of bricks. Someone was planning to repair a chimney.

Warily, he hurried the rest of the way to Julio's. He didn't like this at all. Because of the nature of his business, he had carefully structured it for ano-nymity. He did things to people that they didn't like, so it was best that they not know who was doing it to them. He did a cash business and worked hard at being an average-looking Joe. No trails. Most of the time he worked behind the scenes. His customers knew his face, but their only contact with him was over the phone or in brief meeting in places like Julio's. And he never called his answering machine from home.

But somebody seemed to know his every move. How?

"Yo, Jack!" said Julio, the muscular little man who ran the tavern. "Long time no see." He began slapping at Jack's jacket, sending white clouds into the air. "What's all this white stuff?"

He told Julio about the two near misses.

"Y'know," Julio said, "I seem to remember hearing about some guy asking aroun' for you a coupla weeks ago. I'll fine out who he was."

"Yeah. Give it a shot."

Probably wouldn't pan out to anything, but it was worth a try.

Jack scanned the tavern. It was dustier than usual. The hanging plants in the window were withered and brown.

"Your cleaning man die, Julio?"

"Nah. It's the yuppies. They keep comin' here. So I let the place get rundown and dirty, an' they *still* come."

"Déclassé must be in."

"They make me crazy, Jack."

"Yeah, well, we've all got our crosses to bear, Julio."

Jack had finished his roll and was on his second coffee when George Kuropolis came in. He handed George a wad of cash.

"Here's what Reilly's boys took from you last night—minus your portion of the next installment on my fee. Tell the rest of your merchants association to ante up their shares."

George avoided his eyes.

"Some of them are saying you cost as much as Reilly."

Jack felt the beginnings of a surge of anger but if flattened out quickly. He was used to this. It always had happened with a number of his customers, but more often since *The Neutralizer* hit the air. Before that, people who called him never expected him to work for free. Now because of some damn stupid goody-two-shoes TV vigilante, more and more of his customers had the idea it was Jack's civic duty to get them out of jams. He'd been expecting some bitching from the group.

This particular merchants association had had it rough lately. They ran a cluster of shops on the lower west side. With the Westies out of the picture, they'd thought they'd have some peace. Then Reilly's gang came along and began bleeding them dry. Finally one of them, Wolansky, went to the police. Not too long after, a Molotov cocktail came through the front door of his greengrocery, blackening most of his store; and shortly after that his son was crippled in a hit-and-run accident outside their apartment building. As a result, Wolansky developed acute Alzheimer's when the police asked him to identify Reilly.

That was when George and the others got together and called Repairman Jack.

"You going to tell me you don't see the difference?"

"No, of course not," George said hurriedly.

"Well, let me refresh your memory," Jack said. "*You* came to *me*, not the other way round. This isn't television and I'm not The Neutralizer. Don't get reality and make-believe confused here. This is my work. I get paid for what I do. I was around before that do-gooder came on the air and I'll be around after he's off. Those knives Reilly and his bunch carry aren't props. Their guns aren't loaded with blanks. This is the real thing. I don't risk my neck for kicks."

"All right, all right," George said. "I'm sorry—"

"And another thing. I may be costing you, but I'm just temporary, George. Like purgatory. Reilly is hell, and hell is forever. He'll bleed you until he's stopped."

"I know. I just wish it was over. I don't know if I can take another night like last night," George began rubbing his right hand. "They were gonna—"

"But they didn't. And as long as they see me as a competitor, they'll save their worst for me."

George shuddered and looked at his fingers. "I sure hope so."

Shortly after George left, an Asian man who looked to be on the far side of fifty showed up at the door. His face was bruised and scraped, his left eye swollen half shut. Julio intercepted him, shook his hand, welcomed him to his place, clapped him on the back, and led him toward the rear of the tavern. Jack noticed that he walked with a limp. A bum right leg. By the time he reached Jack's table, he had been thoroughly frisked. If Julio found anything, he would lead him right past Jack and out the back door.

"Tram," Julio said, stopping at Jack's table, "this is the man you're looking for. Jack, this is Tram."

They had coffee and made small talk while Tram smoked unfiltered Pall Malls back-to-back. Jack led the conversation around to Tram's background. His fractured English was hard to follow but Jack managed to piece together the story.

Tram was from Vietnam, from Quang Ngai, he said. He had fought in a string of wars for most of his life, from battling the French with the Viet Minh at Dien Bien Phu through the final civil war that had ravaged what was left of his country. It was during the last one that a Cong finger charge finished his right leg. Along with so many others who had fought on the losing side, Tram became a refugee after the war. But things improved after he made it to the States. Now an American-made prosthesis of metal and plastic took up where his own flesh left off below the knee. And he now ran a tiny laundry just off Canal Street, on the interface between Little Italy and Chinatown.

Finally he got around to the reason he had called Jack.

His laundry had been used for years as a drop between the local mob and some drug runners from Phnom Penh. The setup was simple. The "importers" left a package of Cambodian brown on a given morning; that afternoon it was picked up by one of the local Italian guys who would leave a package of cash in its place. No one watching would see anything unusual. The laundry's customers ran the ethnic gamut of the area—white, black, yellow, and all the shades between; the bad guys walked in with bundles of dirty clothes and walked out with packages wrapped in brown paper, just like everyone else.

"How'd you get involved in this?" Jack asked.

"Mr. Tony," Tram said, lighting still another cigarette.

Sounded like a hairdresser. "Mr. Tony who?"

"Campisi."

"*Tony Campisi?*" That was no hairdresser.

Tram nodded. "Yes, yes. Knew very good Mr. Tony nephew Patsy in Quang Ngai. We call him 'Fatman' there. Was with Patsy when he die. Call medic for him but too late."

Jack had heard of Tony "the Cannon" Campisi. Who hadn't? A big shot in the dope end of the Gambino family. Tram went on to say that "Fatman" Pasquale had been one of Tony's favorite nephews. Tony learned of Tram's friendship with Patsy and helped Tram get into the States after the U. S. bailed out of Nam. Tony even set him up in the laundry business.

But there was a price to pay. Natch.

"So he put you in business and used your place as a drop."

"Yes. Make promise to do for him."

"Seems like small time for a guy like Campisi."

"Mr. Tony have many place to drop. Not put all egg in one basket, he say."

Smart. If the narcs raided a drop, they never got much and didn't affect the flow through all the other drops around the city. Campisi had a slick rep. Which was probably why he had rarely seen the inside of a federal courtroom.

"So why the change of heart?"

Tram shrugged. "Mr. Tony dead."

Right. The Gambino family had pretty much fallen apart after old Carlo's death and a deluge of federal indictments. And Tony "the Cannon" Campisi had succumbed to the Big Casino of the lung last summer.

"You don't like the new man?"

"No like dope. Bad."

"Then why'd you act as middle man for Campisi?"

"Make promise."

Jack's gaze locked with Tram's for an instant. The brown eyes stared back placidly. Not much more needed in the way of explanation.

"Right. So what's the present situation?"

The present situation was that the hard guy who had made the drops and pickups for Campisi over the years was now running that corner of the operation himself. Tram had tried to tell him that the deal was off—"Mr. Tony dead . . . promise dead," as Tram put it. But Aldo D'Amico wasn't listening. He'd paid Tram a personal visit the other day. The result was Tram's battered face.

"He belted you around *himself*?"

A nod. "He like that."

Jack knew the type—you could take the guy off the street, but you couldn't take the street out of the guy.

Obviously, Tram couldn't go to the police or the DEA about Aldo. He'd had to find some unofficial help.

"So you want me to get him off your back."

Another nod. "Have heard you can do."

"Maybe. Don't you have an Vietnamese friends who can help you?"

"Mr. Aldo will know is me. Will break my store, hurt my family."

And Jack could imagine how. The Reillys and the D'Amicos . . . bully boys, pure and simple. The only difference between them was the size of their bank accounts. And the size of their organizations.

That last part bothered Jack. He did *not* want to get into any rough-and-tumble with the mob. But he didn't like to turn down a customer just because the bad guys were too tough.

Maybe he could find a way.

Central to the Repairman Jack method was shielding himself and the customer by making the target's sudden run of bad luck appear unrelated to the customer. The hardest part was coming up with a way to do that.

"You know my price?"

"Have been saving."

"Good." Jack had a feeling he was going to earn every penny of this one. The brown eyes lit with hope. "You will help?"

"I'll see. When's the next pickup?"

"This day. At four."

"Okay. I'll be there."

"It will not be good to shoot him dead. He has many friends."

Jack had to smile at Tram's matter-of-fact manner.

"I know. Besides, that's only a last resort. I'll just be there to research."

"Good. Want peace. Very tired of fight. Too much fight in my life."

Jack looked at Tram's battered face, thought of his missing leg below the knee, of the succession of wars he had fought in since age fifteen. The man deserved a little peace.

"I read you."

Tram gave him the address of his laundry and a down payment in twenty-dollar bills that were old yet clean and crisp—like he had washed, starched, and pressed them. Jack in return gave him his customary promise to deduct from his fee the worth of any currency or valuables he happened to recover from D'Amico & Co. during the course of the job.

After bowing three times, Tram left him alone at the table. Julio took his place.

"The name *Cirlot* mean anything to you?" he asked.

Jack thought a moment. "Sure. Ed Cirlot. The blackmailer."

A customer named Levinson—Tom Levinson—had come to Jack a few years ago asking to get Cirlot off his back. Levinson was a high-end dealer in identities. *Primo* quality. Jack had used him twice in the past himself. So Levinson had called him when Cirlot had found a screw and began turning it.

Cirlot, it seemed, had learned of a few high-placed foreign mobsters who had availed themselves of Levinson's services. He threatened to tip the Feds to their ersatz ID the next time they came Stateside. Levinson knew that if that ever happened, their boys would come looking for him.

Cirlot had made a career out of blackmail, it seemed. He was always looking for new pigeons. So Jack set himself up as a mark—supposedly a crooked coin dealer running a nationwide scam from a local boiler room. Cirlot wanted ten large down and one a month to keep quiet. If he didn't get it, the FTC would come a-knockin' and not only close Jack down but take him to court.

Jack had paid him—in bogus twenties. Cirlot had been caught with the counterfeit—enough of it to make a charge of conspiracy to distribute stick. When he'd named Jack's coin operation as his source, no such operation could be found. He got ten years soft Fed time.

"Don't tell me he's out already."

"*Si*. Good behavior. And he was asking around about you."

Jack didn't like that. Cirlot wasn't supposed to know anything about Repairman Jack. The coin dealer who had stiffed the blackmailer with bogus was gone like he had never existed. Because he hadn't.

So why was Cirlot looking for Repairman Jack? There was no connection.

Except for Tom Levinson.

"I think I'll go visit a certain ID dealer."

Jack spotted Levinson up on East 92nd Street, approaching his apartment house from the other side. Levinson spotted him at the same time. Instead of waving, he turned and started to run. But he couldn't move too fast because his foot was all bandaged up. He did a quick hop-skip-limp combination that made him look like a fleeing Walter Brennan. Jack caught up to him easily.

"What's the story, Tom?" he said, grabbing Levinson's shoulder.

He looked frightened, and his spiked black hair only heightened the effect. He was a thin, weasely man trying to look younger than his forty-something years. He was panting, and his eyes were darting left and right like a cornered animal.

"I couldn't help it, Jack! I had to tell him!"

"Tell him what?"

"About you!" His mouth began running at breakneck speed. "Somehow he connected me and that coin dealer you played. Maybe he had lots of time to think while he was inside. Maybe he remembered that he first heard about a certain coin dealer from me. Anyway, the first thing he does when he gets out is come to me. I was scared shitless, but he doesn't want me. He wants you. Said you set him up for a fall and made him look like a jerk."

Jack turned away from Levinson and walked in a small circle. He was angry at Levinson, and disappointed as well. He had thought the forger was a stand-up guy.

"We had a deal," Jack said. "When I took you on, you were to keep quiet about it. You don't know Repairman Jack—never heard of him. That's part of the deal. Why didn't you play dumb?"

"I did, but he wasn't having any."

"So tell him to go squat."

"I did." Levinson sighed. "Jack . . . he started cutting off my toes."

The words stunned Jack. "He *what*?"

"My toes!" Levinson pointed to his bandaged left foot. "He tied me up and cut off my fucking little toe! And he was going to cut off another and another and keep on cutting until I told him how to find you!"

Jack felt his jaw muscles tighten. "Jesus!"

"So I told him all I knew, Jack. Which ain't much. I gave him the White Pages number and told him we met at Julio's. I don't know any more so I couldn't tell him any more. He didn't believe me, so he cut off the next one."

"He cut off *two* toes?" Jack felt his gut knot.

"With a big shiny meat cleaver. You want to see?"

"Hell no." He shook off the revulsion. "I took Cirlot for the white-collar type. He never seemed the kind to mix it up."

"Maybe he used to be, but he ain't that way now. He's *crazed*, Jack. And he wants to bring you down real bad. Says he's gonna make you look like shit, then he's gonna ice you. And I guess he's already tried, otherwise you wouldn't be here."

Jack thought of the shot through the hotel window and the falling cement bag.

"Yeah. Twice."

"I'm sorry, Jack, but he really *hurt* me."

"Christ, Tom. Don't give it another thought. I mean, your toes . . . *damn!*"

He told Levinson he'd take care of things and left him there. As he walked away, he wondered how many toes he'd have given up for Levinson.

He decided he could muddle through life without ever knowing the answer to that one.

As soon as the car pulled to a stop in front of the laundry, Aldo reached for the door handle. He felt Joey grab his arm.

"Mr. D. Let me go in. You stay out here."

Aldo shrugged off the hand. "I know where you're comin' from, Joey, but don't keep buggin' my ass about this."

Joey spread his hands and shrugged. "Ay. You're the boss. But I still don't think it's right, know what I mean?"

Joey was okay. Aldo knew how he felt: He was Aldo D'Amico's driver and bodyguard, so *he* should be doing all the rough stuff. And as far as Aldo was concerned, Joey could have most of it. But not all of it. Aldo wasn't going to hide in the background all the time like Tony C. Hell, in his day Tony could walk through areas like this and hardly anyone would know him. He was just another *paisan* to these people. Well, that wasn't going to be Aldo's way. *Everybody* was going to know who he was. And when he walked through it was going to be, "Good morning, Mr. D'Amico!" "Would you like a nice apple, Mr. D'Amico?" "Have some coffee, Mr. D'Amico!" "Right this way, Mr. D'Amico!" People were going to know him, were going to treat him with respect. He deserved a little goddamn respect by now. He'd be forty-five next month. He'd done Tony the Cannon's scut work forever. Knew all the ins and outs of the operation. Now it was *his*. And everybody was going to know that.

"I'll handle this like I did yesterday," he told Joey. "Like I told you: I believe in giving certain matters the *personal* touch."

What he didn't tell Joey was that he *liked* the rough stuff. That was the only bad thing about moving up in the organization—you never got a chance for hands-on communication with jerks like the gook who owned this laundry. Never a peep out of the little yellow bastard all the years Tony C. was running things, but as soon as he's gone, the gook thinks he's gonna get independent with the new guy. Not here, babe. Not when the new guy's Aldo D'Amico.

He was hoping the gook gave him some more bullshit about not using his place for a drop anymore. Any excuse to work him over again like the other day.

"Awright," Joey said, shaking his head with frustration, "but I'm comin' in to back you up. Just in case."

"Sure, Joey. You can carry the laundry."

Aldo laughed, and Joey laughed with him.

Jack had arrived at Tram's with a couple of dirty shirts at about three-thirty. Dressed in jeans, an army fatigue jacket, and a baseball cap pulled low on his forehead, he now sat in one of the three chairs and read the *Post* while Tram ran the shirts through the machine. It was a tiny hole-in-the-wall shop that probably cost the little man most of his good leg in rent. A one-man operation except for some after-school counter help, which Tram always sent on an errand when a pickup or delivery was due.

Jack watched the customers, a motley group of mostly lower-middle-class downtowners, flow in and out. Aldo D'Amico and his bodyguard were instantly identifiable by their expensive topcoats when they arrived at four on the button. Aldo's was dark gray with a black felt collar, a style Jack hadn't seen since the Beatles' heyday. He was mid-forties with a winter tan and wavy blow-dried hair receding on both sides. Jack knew he had to be Aldo because the other guy was a side of beef and was carrying a wad of dirty laundry.

Jack noticed the second guy giving him a close inspection. He might as well have had Bodyguard stenciled on his back. Jack glanced up, gave the two of them a disinterested up-and-down, then went back to the sports page.

"Got something for me, gook?" Aldo said, grinning like a shark as he slapped the knuckles of his right fist into his left palm.

Jack sighed. He knew the type. Most tough guys he knew wouldn't hesitate to hurt somebody, even ice them if necessary, but to them it was like driving a car through downtown traffic in the rain: You didn't particularly like it but you did it because you had to get someplace; and if you had the means, you preferred to have somebody else do it for you.

Not this Aldo. Jack could tell that mixing it up was some kind of fix for him.

Maybe that could be turned around. Jack didn't have a real plan here. His old Corvair was parked outside. He intended to pick up Aldo and follow him around, follow him home if he could. He'd do that for a couple of days. Eventually, he'd get an idea of how to stick him. Then he'd have to find a way to work that idea to Tram's benefit. This was going to be long, drawn out, and touchy.

At the counter, Tram sullenly placed a brown paper–wrapped bundle on the counter. The bodyguard picked it up and plopped the dirty laundry down in its place. Tram ignored it.

"Please, Mr. Aldo," he said. "Will not do this any more."

"Boy, you're one stupid gook, y'know that?" He turned to his bodyguard. "Joey, take the customer for a walk while I discuss business with our Vietnamese friend here."

Jack felt a tap on his shoulder and looked up from his paper into Joey's surprisingly mild eyes.

"C'mon. I'll buy you a cup of coffee."

"I got shirts coming," Jack said.

"They'll wait. My friend wants a little private talk with the owner."

Jack wasn't sure how to play this. He wasn't prepared for any rough-and-tumble here, but he didn't want to leave Tram to Aldo's tender mercies again.

"Then let him talk in the back. I ain't goin' nowhere."

Joey grabbed him under the arm and pulled him out of the chair. "Yeah. You are."

Jack came out of the chair quickly and knocked Joe's arm away.

"Hands off, man!"

He decided that the only way to get out of this scene on his terms was to pull a psycho number. He looked at Joey's beefy frame and heavy over-coat and knew attacking his body would be a waste of time. That left his face.

"Just stay away!" Jack shouted. "I don't like people touching me. Makes me mad! *Real* mad!"

Joey dropped the brown paper bundle onto a chair. "All right. Enough of this shit." He stepped in close, gripped Jack's shoulders, and tried to turn him around.

Jack reached up between Joey's arms, grabbed his ears, and yanked the bodyguard's head forward. As he lowered his head and butted, he had a fleeting glimpse of the sick look on Joey's startled face. He hadn't been ex-pecting anything like this, but he knew what was coming.

When Jack heard Joey's nose crunch against the top of his skull, he pushed him away and kicked him hard in the balls. Joey dropped to his knees and groaned. His bloody face was slack with pain and nausea.

Jack next leapt on Aldo who was gaping at him with a stunned expres-sion.

"You want some of me, too?" he shouted.

Aldo's overcoat was unbuttoned and he was leaner than Joe. Jack went for the breadbasket: right-left combination jabs to the solar plexus, then a knee to the face when he doubled over. Aldo went down in a heap.

But it wasn't over. Joey was reaching a hand into his overcoat pocket. Jack jumped on him and wrestled a short-barreled Cobra .357 revolver away from him.

"A gun? You pulled a fucking *gun* on me, man?" He slammed the barrel and trigger guard across the side of Joey's head. "*Shit* that makes me mad!"

Then he spun and pointed the pistol at the tip of Aldo's swelling nose.

"You!" he screamed. "You started this! You didn't want me to get my shirts! Well, you can have them! They're old anyway! I'll take *yours*! All of them!"

He grabbed the bundle of dirty shirts from the counter and then went for the brown paper package on the chair.

"Jesus, no!" Aldo said. "No! You don't know what—"

Jack leapt on him and began pistol-whipping him, screaming, "Don't tell me what I don't know!"

As Aldo covered his head with his arms, Jack glanced at Tram and motioned him over. Tram got the idea. He came out from behind the counter and shoved Jack away, but not before Jack had managed to open Aldos' scalp in a couple of places.

"You get out!" Tram cried. "Get out or I call police!"

"Yeah, I'll get out, but not before I put a couple of holes in this rich pig here!"

Tram stood between him and Aldo. "No! You go! You cause enough trouble!"

Jack made a disgusted noise and ran out with both bundles. Outside he found an empty Mercedes 350 SEL idling at the curb by a fire hydrant. *Why not?*

As he gunned the heavy car toward Canal Street, he wondered at his screaming psycho performance. Pretty convincing. And easy, too. He'd hardly stretched at all to take the part and really get into it.

That bothered him a little.

"Fifty thousand in small bills," Abe said after he'd finished counting the money that had been wrapped inside the dirty laundry. He had it spread out in neat piles on a crate in the basement of his store. "If I were you, I shouldn't complain. Not so bad for an afternoon's work."

"Yeah. But it's the ten keys of cocaine and the thirty of Cambodian brown." The wrapped package had housed some of the heroin. The cocaine and the rest of the heroin had been in a duffel bag in the trunk. "What am I going to do with *that*?"

"There's a storm drain outside. Next time it rains . . ."

Jack thought about that. The heroin would definitely go down the drain. Any alligators or crocs living down in the sewers would be stoned for life. But the cocaine . . . that might come in handy in the future, just like the bogus twenties had come in handy against Cirlot.

Cirlot. Something about him was perking in the back of Jack's mind.

"I've always wanted a Mercedes," Abe said.

"What for? You haven't been further east than Queens and further west than Columbus Avenue in a quarter century."

"Someday I might like maybe to travel. See New Jersey."

"Yeah. Well, that's not a bad idea. No doubt about it, the best way to see New Jersey is from the inside of a Mercedes. But it's too late. I gave the car to Julio to dispose of."

Abe sagged. "Chop shop?"

Jack nodded. "He's going to shop it around for quick cash. Figures another ten grand, minimum, maybe twenty."

A take of sixty-seventy K so far from one visit to Tram's laundry. Which meant that Jack would be returning Tram's down payment and giving him a free ride on this job. Which was fine for Tram's bank account, but Jack didn't know what his next step was. He'd shaken things up down there. Now maybe it would be best to sit back and watch what fell out of the trees.

He headed for Gia's. He kept to the windy shadows as he walked along, kept looking over his shoulder. Cirlot had seemed to know where he was going, and when he'd be there. Was he watching him now?

Jack didn't like being on this end of the game.

But how did Cirlot know? That was what ate him. Jack knew his apartment wasn't bugged—the place was like a fortress. Besides, Cirlot didn't know where he lived. And even if he did, he couldn't get inside to place a bug. Yet he seemed to know Jack's moves. How, dammit?

Jack made a full circuit of Gia's block and cut through an alley before he felt it was safe to enter her apartment house.

Two fish-eye peepholes nippled Gia's door. Jack had installed them himself. One was the usual height, and one was Vicky-height. He knocked and stood there, pressing his thumb over the lower peephole as he waited.

"Jack, is that you?" said a child's voice from the other side.

He pulled his thumb away and grinned into the convex glass.

"Ta-daaa!"

The deadbolt slid back, the door swung inward, and suddenly he was holding a bony seven-year-old girl in his arms. She had long dark hair, blue eyes, and a blinding smile.

"Jack! Whatcha bring me?"

He pointed to the breast pocket of his fatigue jacket. Vicky reached inside and pulled out a pack of bubblegum cards.

"Football cards! Neat! You think there's any Jets in this one?"

"Only one way to find out."

He carried her inside and put her down. He locked the door behind them as she fumbled with the wrapper.

"Jack!" she said, her voice hushed with wonder. "They're all Jets! *All* Jets! Oh, this is *so* neat!"

Gia stepped into the living room. "The only eight-year-old in New York who says 'neat.' Wonder where she got that from?"

She kissed him lightly and he slid an arm around her waist, pulling her close to him. She shared her daughter's blue eyes and bright smile, but her hair was blond. She brightened up the whole room for Jack.

"I don't know about you," he said, "but I think it's pretty neat to get five—*five*—members of your favorite team in a single pack of bubblegum. I don't know anybody else who's got that kind of luck."

Jack had gone through a dozen packs of cards before coming up with those five Jets, then he had slipped them into a single wrapper and glued the flaps back in place. Vicky had developed a thing for the Jets, simply because she liked their green-and-white jerseys. Which, until Parcells had taken over, had been as good a reason as any to be a Jets fan.

"Start dinner yet?" he asked.

Gia shook her head. "Just getting ready to. Why?"

"Have to take a raincheck. I've got a few things I've got to do tonight."

She frowned. "Nothing dangerous, I hope."

"Nah."

"That's what you always say."

"Well, sure. I mean, after surviving the blue meanies last year, everything else is a piece of cake."

"Don't mention those things!" Gia shuddered and hugged him. "Promise you'll call me when you're back home?"

"Yes, mother."

"I'm serious. I worry about you."

"You just made my day."

She broke away and picked up a slim cardboard box from the couch. "Land's End" was written across one end.

"Your order arrived today."

"Neat." He pulled out a bright red jacket with navy blue lining. He pulled off the fatigue jacket and tried it on. "Perfect. How do I look?"

"Like every third person in Manhattan," Gia said.

"Great!"

"All you need is a Hard Rock Cafe sweatshirt and the picture will be complete."

Jack worked at being ordinary, at being indistinguishable from everybody else, just another face in the crowd. To do that, he had to keep up with what the crowd was wearing. Since he didn't have a charge card, Gia had ordered the jacket for him on hers.

"I'd better turn off the oven," Gia said.

"I'll treat tomorrow night. Chinese. For sure."

"Sure," she said. "I'll believe it when I smell it."

Jack stood there in the tiny living room, watching Vicky spread out her football cards, listening to Gia move about the kitchen over the drone of *Eyewitness News*, drinking in the rustle and bustle and noises and silences of a *home*. The domestic feel of this tiny apartment—he wanted it. But it seemed so out of reach. He could come and visit and warm himself by the fire, but he couldn't stay. As much as he wanted to, he couldn't gather it up and take it with him.

His work was the problem. He had never asked Gia to marry him because he knew the answer would be no. Because of what he did for a living. And he *wouldn't* ask her for the same reason. Because of what he did for a living. Marriage would make him vulnerable. He couldn't expose Gia and Vicky to risk like that. He'd have to retire first. But he wasn't even forty. Besides go crazy, what would he do for the next thirty or forty years?

Become a citizen? Get a day job? How would he do that? How would he explain why there was no record of his existence up till now? No job history, no Social Security hours, no file of 1040s. The IRS would want to know if he was an illegal alien or a Gulag refugee or something. And if he wasn't, they'd ask a lot of questions he wouldn't want to answer.

He wondered if he had started something he couldn't stop.

And then he was looking out through the picture window in Gia's dining room at the roof of the apartment house across the street and remembering the bullets tearing through the hotel room less than twenty-four hours ago. His skin tingled with alarm. He felt vulnerable here. And worse, he was exposing Gia and Vicky to his own danger. Quickly he made his apologies and good-byes, kissed them both, and hurried back to the street.

He stood outside the apartment house, slowly walking back and forth before the front door.

Come on, you son of a bitch! Do you know I'm here? Take a shot! Let me know!

No shot. Nothing fell from the roof.

Jack stretched his cramped fingers out from the tight fists he had made. He imagined some vicious bastard like Cirlot finding out about Gia and Vicky, threatening them, maybe hurting them . . . it almost put him over the edge.

He began walking back toward his own apartment. He moved quickly along the pavement, then broke into a run, trying to work off the anger, the mounting frustration.

This had to stop. And it was going to stop. Tonight, if he had anything to say about it.

Jack stopped at a pay phone and called Tram. The Vietnamese told him that Aldo and his bodyguard had limped out and found a cab, swearing vengeance on the punk who had busted them up. Tram was worried that Aldo might take his wrath out on him if he couldn't find Jack. That worried Jack, too. He called his answering machine but found nothing of interest on it.

As he hung up he remembered something: Cirlot and phones. *Yes.* That was how the blackmailer had got his hooks into his victims. The guy was an ace wiretapper.

Jack trotted back to his brownstone. But instead of going up to his apartment, he slipped down to the utility closet. He pulled open the phone box and spotted the tap immediately: jumper wires attached to a tiny high-frequency transmitter. Cirlot probably had a voice-activated recorder stashed not too far from here.

Now things were starting to make sense. Cirlot had learned from Levinson that Jack met customers at Julio's. He'd hung around outside until he spotted Jack, then tailed him home.

Jack clucked to himself. He was getting careless in his old age.

Soon after that, Cirlot had shown up, probably as a phone man, inserted the tap, and sat back and listened. Jack had used his apartment phone to reserve the room at the Lucky Hotel . . . and he had called Julio this morning to tell him he'd be over by ten-thirty. It all fit.

Jack closed the phone box, leaving the tap in place.

Two could play this game.

Jack sprawled amid the clutter of Victorian oak and bric-a-brac that filled the front room of his apartment and called George at the diner. This was his second such call in half an hour, except that the first had been made from a public phone. He had told George to expect this call, and had told him what to say.

"Hello, George," he said when the Greek picked up the other end. "You got the next payment together from your merchants association?"

"Yeah. We got it. In cash like usual."

"Good deal. I'll be by around midnight to pick it up."

"I'll be here," George said.

Jack hung up and sat there, thinking. The bait was out. If Cirlot was listening, chances were good he'd set up another ambush somewhere in the neighborhood of the Highwater Diner at around midnight. But Jack planned to be there first to see if he could catch Cirlot setting up. And then they would settle things. For good. Jack wasn't going to have anybody dogging his steps back to Gia and Vicky, especially someone who had chopped a couple of toes off a former customer.

On his way downtown an hour later, Jack called his answering machine again. He heard a message from George asking him to call right away. When he did, he heard a strange story.

"I asked you to *what?*" Jack said.

"Meet you in the old Borden building next door. You said there'd been a change of plans and it was probably safer if you didn't show up at the diner. So I was to meet you next door at ten-thirty and hand over the money."

Jack had to smile. This Cirlot was slicker than he'd thought.

"Did it sound like me?"

"Hard to say. The connection was bad."

"What did you say?"

"I agreed, but I thought it was fishy because it wasn't the way we had set it up before. And because you said you'd be wearing a ski mask like last night. That sounded fishy, too."

"Good man. I appreciate the call. Call me again if you hear from anyone who says he's me."

"Will do."

Jack hung up. Instead of hailing a cab to go downtown, he ducked into a nearby tavern and ordered a draft of Amsterdam.

Curiouser and curiouser.

Cirlot seemed more interested in ripping him off than knocking him off—at least tonight. Tom Levinson's words came back: *Gonna make you look like shit, then he's gonna ice you.*

So that was it. Another piece fell into place. The bag of cement had missed him. Okay—no one could expect much accuracy against a moving target with a heavy, cumbersome object like that. But the shooter outside the Lucky Hotel had had a telescopic sight. Jack had been a sitting duck. The guy shouldn't have missed.

Unless he'd wanted to. That had to be it. Cirlot was playing head games with him, getting him off balance until he had a chance to humiliate him, expose him, make him look like a jerk. He wanted payback in kind before he killed Jack.

Ripping off one of his fees would be a good start.

Jack's anger was tinged with amusement.

He's playing my own game against me.

But not for long. Jack was the old hand here. It was his game. He'd invented it, and he'd be damned if he'd let Cirlot outplay him. The simplest thing to do was to confront Cirlot in that old wreck of a building and have a showdown.

Simple, direct, effective, but lacking in style. He needed to come up with something very neat here. A masterstroke, even.

And then, as he lifted his glass to drain the final ounces of his draft, he had it.

Reilly was waiting his turn at the pool table. He didn't feel like shooting much. With Reece and Jerry dead, everybody was down and pissed. All they'd talked about since last night was finding that jack-o'-lantern guy. The only laugh they'd had all day was when they learned that Reece's real name was *Mau*rice.

Just then Gus called over from the bar. He was holding the phone receiver in the air.

"Yo! Reilly! You're wanted!"

"Yeah? Who?"

"Said to tell you it's Pumpkinhead."

Reilly nearly tripped over his stick getting to the phone. Cheeks and the others were right behind him.

"Gonna find you, fucker!" he said as soon as he got the receiver to his head.

"I know you are," said the voice on the other end. "Because I'm gonna tell you where I am. We need a meet. Tonight. You lost two men and I almost got killed last time we tangled. What do you say to a truce? We can find some way to divide things up so we both come out ahead."

Reilly was silent while he controlled himself. Was this fucker crazy? A *truce*? After what he did last night?

"Sure," he managed to say. "We can talk."

"Good. Just you and me."

"Okay." *Riiiiight.* "Where?"

"The old place we were in last night—next to the Highwater. Ten-thirty okay?"

Reilly looked at his watch. That gave him an hour and a half. Plenty of time.

"Sure."

"Good. And remember, Reilly: Come alone or the truce is off."

"Yeah."

He hung up and turned to his battered boys. They didn't look like much, what with Rafe, Tony, and Cheeks all bandaged up, and Cheeks's hand in a cast. Hard to believe only one guy had done all this. But that one guy was a mean dude, full of tricks. So they weren't going to take any chances this time. No talk. No deals. No hesitation. No reprieve. They were going to throw everything they had at him tonight.

"That really him?" Cheeks asked.

"Yeah," said Reilly, smiling. "And tonight we're gonna have us some punkin pie!"

"Aldo, this man insists on speaking to you!"

Aldo D'Amico glared at his wife and removed the ice pack from his face. He had a brutal headache from the bruises and stitches in his scalp. His nose was killing him. Broken in two places. The swelling made him sound like he had a bad cold.

He wondered for the hundredth time about that punk in the laundry. Had this gook set them up? Aldo wanted to believe it, but it just didn't wash. If he'd been laying for Aldo, he'd have had his store filled with some sort of gook army, not one white guy. But Christ the way that one guy moved! *Fast.* Like liquid lightning. A butt and a kick and Joey was down and then he'd been on Aldo, his face crazy. No. It hadn't been a setup. Just some *stunad* punk. But that didn't make it any easier to take.

"I told you, Maria, no calls!"

Bad enough he'd be laughed at all over town for being such a *gavone* to allow some nobody to bust him up and steal his car, and even worse that his balls were on the line for the missing money and shit, so why couldn't Maria follow a simple order. He never should have come home tonight. He'd have been better off at Franny's loft on Greene Street. Franny did what she was told. She damn well better. He paid her rent.

"But he says he has information on your car."

Aldo's hand shot out. "Gimme that! Hello!"

"Mr. D'Amico, sir," said a very deferential voice on the other end. "I'm very sorry about what happened today at the laundry. If I'da known it was someone like you, I wouldn'a caused no trouble. But I didn't know, y'see, an I got this real bad temper, so like I'm sorry—"

"Where's the car?" Aldo said in a low voice.

"I got it safe and I wanna return it to you along with the money I took and the, uh, other laundry and the, uh, stuff in the trunk, if you know what I mean and I think you do."

The little shit was scared. Good. Scared enough to want to give everything back. Even better. Aldo sighed with relief.

"Where is it?"

"I'm in it now. Like I'm talkin' on your car phone. But I'm gonna leave it somewhere and tell you where you can find it."

"Don't do that!" Aldo said quickly.

His mind raced. Getting the car back was number one priority, but he wanted to get this punk, too. If he didn't even the score, it would be a damn long time before he could hold his head up on the street.

"Don't leave it *anywhere*! Someone might rip it off before I get there, and that'll be on your head! We'll meet—"

"Oh, no! I'm not getting plugged full of holes!"

Yes, you are, Aldo thought, remembering the punk pointing Joey's magnum in his face.

"Hey, don't worry about that," Aldo said softly. "You've apologized and you're returning the car. It was an accident. We'll call it even. As a matter of face, I like the way you move. You made Joey look like he was in slow motion. Actually, you did me a favor. Made me see how bad my security is."

"Really?"

"Yeah. I could use a guy like you. How'd you like to replace Joey?"

"Y'mean be your bodyguard? I don't know, Mr. D'Amico."

"Think about it. We'll talk about it when I see you tonight. Where we gonna meet?"

"Uuuuh, how about by the Highwater Diner. It's down on—"

"I know where it is."

"Yeah, well there's an old abandoned building right next door. How about if I meet you there?'

"Great. When?"

"Ten-thirty."

"That's kinda soon—"

"I know. But I'll feel safer."

"Hey, don't worry! When Aldo D'Amico gives his word, you can take it to the bank!"

And I promise you, punk, you're a dead man!

"Yeah, well, just in case we don't hit it off, I'll be wearing a ski mask. I figure you didn't get a real good look at me in that laundry and I don't want you getting a better one."

"Have it your way. See you at ten-thirty."

He hung up and called to his wife. "Maria! Get Joey on the phone. Tell him to get over here now!"

Aldo went to his desk drawer and pulled out his little Jennings .22 automatic. He hefted it. Small, light, and loaded with high-velocity longs. It did the job at close range. And Aldo intended to be real close when he used this.

A little before ten, Jack climbed up to the roof of the Highwater Diner and sat facing the old Borden building. He watched Reilly and five of his boys—the whole crew—arrive shortly afterward. They entered the building from the rear. Two of them carried large duffel bags. They appeared to have come loaded for bear. Nor too long after them came Aldo and three wiseguys. They took up positions outside in the alley below and out of sight on the far side.

No one, it seemed, wanted to be fashionably late.

At ten-thirty sharp, a lone figure in a dark coat, jeans, and what looked like a knit watch cap strolled along the sidewalk in front of the Highwater. He paused a moment to stare in through the front window. Jack hoped George was out of sight like he had told him to be. The dark figure continued on. When he reached the front of the Borden building, he glanced around, then started toward it. As he approached the gaping front entry, he stretched the cap down over his face. Jack couldn't see the design clearly but it appeared to be a crude copy of the one he'd worn last night. All it took was some orange paint . . .

Do you really want to play Repairman Jack tonight, pal?

For an instant he flirted with the idea of shouting out a warning and aborting the setup. But he called up thoughts of life in a wheelchair due to a falling cement bag, of Levinson's missing toes, of bullets screaming through Gia and Vicky's apartment.

He kept silent.

He watched the figure push in through the remains of the front door and disappear inside. In the alley, Aldo and Joey rose from their hiding places and shrugged to each other in the moonlight. Jack knew what Aldo was thinking: *Where's my car?*

But they leaped for cover when the gunfire began. It was a brief roar, but very loud and concentrated. Jack picked out the sound of single rounds, bursts from a pair of assault pistols, and at least two, maybe three shotguns, all blasting away simultaneously. Barely more than a single prolonged flash from within. Then silence.

Slowly, cautiously, Aldo and his boys came out of hiding, whispering, making baffled gestures. One of them was carrying an Uzi, another held a sawed-off. Jack watched them slip inside, heard shouts, even picked out the word "car."

Then all hell broke loose.

It looked as if a very small, very violent thunderstorm had got itself trapped on the first floor of the old Borden building. The racket was deafening, the flashes through the glassless windows like half a dozen strobe lights going at once. It went on full force for what seemed like twenty minutes but ticked out to slightly less than five on Jack's watch. Then it tapered and died. Finally . . . quiet. Nothing moved.

No. Check that. Someone was crawling out a side window and falling into the alley. Jack went to see.

Reilly. He was bleeding from his mouth, his nose, and his gut. And he was hurting. "Get me an ambulance, man!" he grunted as Jack crouched over him. His voice was barely audible.

"Right away, Matt," Jack said.

Reilly looked up at him. His eyes widened. "Am I dead? I mean . . . we offed you but good in there."

"You offed the wrong man, Reilly."

"Who cares . . . you can have this turf . . . I'm out of it . . . just get me a fucking ambulance! Please?"

Jack stared at him a moment. "Sure," he said.

Jack got his hands under Reilly's arms and lifted. The wounded man nearly passed out with the pain of being moved. But he was aware enough to notice that Jack wasn't dragging him toward the street.

"Hey . . . where y'takin' me?"

"Around back."

Jack could hear the sirens approaching. He quickened his pace toward the rear.

"Need a doc . . . need a ambulance."

"Don't worry," Jack said. "There's one coming now."

He dumped Reilly in the rearmost section of the Borden building's back alley and left him there.

"Wait here for your ambulance," he told him. "It's the same one you called for Wolansky's kid when you ran him down last month."

Then Jack headed for the Highwater Diner to call Tram and tell George that they didn't need him anymore.

1989

Bridesmaid again. *Black Wind* was a finalist for the Bram Stoker Award for novel that year. It lost, but who can grouse about finishing close behind *The Silence of the Lambs*? I almost voted for it over my own novel. (Yeah, right.)

In 1989 my writing switched into high gear. A novel and a half, one novella, a novelette, six short stories, and a comic book script.

Plus the introduction to John Lennon's "No Flies on Frank." Stephen Jones asked me to do it for his Pan anthology, *Dark Voices*. I slipped into a Lennonesque voice and knocked it off in about twenty minutes. I had to keep the reins tight or it easily would have run longer than the story. Steve paid me for it with a bottle of champagne.

I began and finished *Sibs* in the spring of '89. The genesis of that novel still amazes me. I was down in Baltimore at a geriatrics update at Johns Hopkins Medical Center; after dinner I sat in my room at the Tremont Plaza, going over the first sixty pages of *Reprisal* (working title: *Lisl*) that I'd written during the preceding month. I wasn't happy with them. The whole book needed restructuring. My mind wandered to a half-formed idea I'd been kicking around for years. Suddenly the final twist occurred to me and the entire novel was there, spread out before me. I started scribbling the outline.

When I got home I put *Reprisal* aside and jumped into the new book (the working title was *Gemini*). I finished in 62 days. I've never written like that before or since. Like taking dictation. A gift. Every writer deserves one of those.

In the spring I finished "Biosphere," a script for Marvel Graphic's *Open Space* series (it appeared in #2, superbly illustrated by John Ridgway).

The year also saw the publication of *Soft & Others*, a collection of sixteen stories from my first two decades as a professional writer, ordered chronologically like this book, from my very first sale onward. (Maybe I should have subtitled the collection, "Watch Wilson Learn How To Write.") A lot of readers told me how much they liked the introductory material; a few said they liked the intros better than some of the stories.

Baen published *Dydeetown World* (a melding of the novellas "Dydeetown World," "Wires," and "Kids") with a marvelous cover by Gary Ruddell in the summer. It had started in 1984 as an idea for a short story—five, maybe six thousand words, tops. A quiet little SF tribute to Raymond Chandler, whose work has given me such pleasure over the years. I was going to use all the clichés—the down-and-out private eye, his seedy friends, the tired, seamy city, the bar hangout, the ruthless mobster, the whore with the heart of gold. And I was going to set it in the far future, in a future I had developed for the LaNague Federation science fiction stories (four novels and a handful of shorts) written during the seventies.

But "Dydeetown Girl" was going to be different. Rather than bright and full of hope like its predecessors, this story was going to be set on the grimy, disillusioned underbelly of that future. I wanted to move through the LaNague future at ground level, take a hard look at the social fallout of the food shortages, the population-control measures, the wires into the pleasure centers of the brain—things I'd glossed over or mentioned only in passing before. But despite the downbeat milieu, the story would be about freedom, friendship, and self-esteem.

Beneath its hard-boiled voice, its seamy settings, and violent events (Cyber/p-i/sci-fi, as Forry Ackerman might call it) were characters trying to maintain—or reestablish—a human connection. The intended short story stretched to novella length by the time it was done, but I think it worked.

Apparently, a few other folks agreed. After the "Dydeetown Girl" novella snagged a finalist spot for the Nebula Award in 1987, Betsy Mitchell prodded me into writing the sequel novellas "Wires" and "Kids" (oh, those plural nouns) and splicing them together into a single story.

Although written for adults, the *Dydeetown World* novel wound up on the American Library Association's list of "Best Books for Young Adults" and on the New York Public Library's recommended list of "Books for the Teen Age."

One scene in "Dydeetown Girl" involves a *Tyrannosaurus rex* used as a guard animal. That's right: In a story written way back in 1985 I used a dinosaur cloned from reconstituted fossil DNA, but I tossed it off as background color.

If only I'd thought to stick a bunch of them in a park . . .

At last. A story without a plural noun for a title.

Remember "Ethics," the story I replaced with "Faces" for *Night Visions 6*? This is what happened to it. It became "The Tenth Toe."

The metamorphosis began on November 14, 1988, at the annual SFWA Editor-Publisher reception in New York (which I was overseeing for the fifth time) when Pat LoBrutto asked me if I'd be interested in contributing to this anthology he and Joe Lansdale were editing for Dark Harvest. They were calling it *Razored Saddles*. The story could be sf, horror, fantasy, alternate history, anything my little heart desired . . . as long as it had something to do with the West.

In a word, cowpunk.

I said, Seriously, Pat—what's it *really* about? He said it wasn't a joke. Could I contribute? I said something like, Gee, that sounds really neat, Pat, but I'm awfully busy. Thanks a million for asking, though.

Avoiding any sudden moves, I backed away, thinking somehow both Pat's and Joe's belts were no longer going through all the loops.

Cowpunk. Sheesh.

I forgot all about it, but Pat called me in February while I was working on "A Day in the Life" to prod me for that cowpunk story. Joe Lansdale called in March. Same (cattle) prod. I was going strong on *Sibs* then but promised to do my best to write them a story.

I was wrung out after finishing *Sibs*, but I started wondering if maybe some of the plot elements in "Ethics" could be transposed to the West. I've always found Doc Holliday a weird, wild, and enigmatic figure (this is long before Val Kilmer's portrayal in *Tombstone*). You can't make up a character like that. Why not use him as the protagonist? It would require a complete rewrite but, approached with tongue firmly in cheek, it just might work.

Pat and Joe agreed that it did.

THE TENTH TOE

(OR: THE BEGINNING OF MY END)

by Doc Holliday

(transcribed by F. Paul Wilson)

I am thirty-five years old and will not see thirty-six.

I was not always this weak, wheezing, crumbling sack of bones you see before you, a man whose days can be numbered on the fingers of one hand. Nor was I always the hard-drinking gambler and shootist you read of in the penny dreadfuls. I started out a much more genteel man, a professional man, even a bit of a milquetoast.

I attended medical school but did not succeed there, so I became a matriculant at a nearby dental school, from which I managed to graduate. I was then a professional man, and proud of it. But I remained flawed—cursed with a larcenous heart. No amount of schooling, be it of the medical, dental, or (I dare say) divinity sort, can extract that stubborn worm. You are born with it, and you die with it, if not from it.

I am dying from it. It was that young professional man with the larcenous heart who led me to notoriety, and to this premature death from consumption.

Allow me to explain . . .

The first inkling I had of the curse was in the spring of 1878 while I was examining Mrs. Duluth.

Mrs. Duluth's husband owned the Dodge City General Store and it was obvious (at least to me) that food was not in short supply on her supper table. She was fat. Truthfully, I have been in outhouses smaller than this woman. Everything about her was fat. Her face was fat and round like a huge honeydew melon. Her lips were thick and fat. Even her nose and ears were fat.

"Will this hurt?" she said as she lay back, overflowing my relatively new reclining dental chair. I hoped she wouldn't break its lift mechanism.

"Not a bit," I told her. "After all, this is 1878, not the Dark Ages. We are now blessed with the modern methods of painless dentistry."

"What do you plan to do?"

"I'm going to administer some sulfuric ether," I heard myself say. "And when you're unconscious, I'm going to rob you."

I saw her eyes widen and she must have seen mine do the same. I hadn't meant to say that. True, I had been thinking it, but I'd had no intention of verbalizing it.

"What . . . what did you say, Dr. Holliday?"

"I said I'm going to rob you. Just a little. I'll go through your purse and take some of your money. Not all of it. Just enough to make this exercise worth my while."

"I really don't think that's very funny, Doctor," she said.

I gulped and steadied myself with an effort. "Neither do I, Mrs. Duluth." And I meant it. What was coming over me? Why was I saying these things? "A joke. A dentist's joke. Sorry."

"I should hope so." She seemed somewhat mollified. "Now, about this tooth—"

"Who cares about that tooth. I'm interested in the third molar there with the big gold filling. I'm going to pop that beauty out and replace it with some garbage metal that looks like gold."

(What was I *saying*?)

"That is quite enough!" she said, rolling out of the chair. She straightened her enormous gingham dress and headed for the door.

"Mrs. Duluth! Wait! I—"

"Never mind! I'll find myself another dentist! One I can trust. Like that new fellow across the street!"

As she went down the steps, she slapped at my shingle, knocking it off one of its hooks. It swung and twisted at a crazy angle until I stepped out and rehung it.

JOHN HENRY HOLLIDAY, DDS
Painless Dentistry

I loved that sign. It was making me rich. I could have made a good living just from the usual drilling, filling, and pulling of my patients' teeth, but that was not enough for my larcenous heart. I had to be *rich*! And I was getting rich quickly from the gold I was mining—literally—from my patients' teeth. I'd found an excellent gold-like compound that I substituted for the real thing while they were out cold in the chair. It was nowhere near as good as gold, but no one had caught on yet. I had another couple of years before the replacement fillings started to fall apart.

Of course, my practice wouldn't last a couple of years if I treated all my patients like Mrs. Duluth. Luckily the waiting room had been empty. I closed the door behind her and stood there thinking. I admit I was somewhat shaken. What was wrong with me? I hadn't meant to say any of those things.

A short while later the widow Porter arrived with her daughter, Bonnie, who had a toothache.

Bonnie was sixteen and extremely buxom for her age. Her bosom was apparently growing at such a rate that the bodice of her dress could not keep pace. She was fairly bursting from it. The tortured seams appeared ready to split. From the way she carried herself, proudly erect with her bust thrust out at the world, I assumed that she was well aware of (and reveled in) the male gender's reaction to her proportions.

Bonnie had a cavity in her second lower left molar. As I leaned over her to examine the tooth more closely, she arched her back so that her breasts brushed against my arm. I straightened and looked at her. She stared back and smiled boldly. This was one of the most brazen young females I'd ever met! I was becoming (I hesitate to say it) aroused.

Teenaged girls were never my style. They tend to fall in love, which can be most inconvenient. But for a young thing of Bonnie's proportions, I realized that I might make an exception.

"She'll need a filling," I told her mother.

"Oh, dear!" the widow Porter said. "You mean you'll have to use the drill?"

"The drill?" Bonnie said, the simper suddenly gone out of her. "The *drill*?"

"Yes." I lifted the instrument from its hook and pumped the pedal to show her how the bit spun.

Her expression was horrified. "You're going to put *that* in my mouth?"

"Yes. But I'd really—"

I could feel my tongue starting to run off without me, but I refused to let it get away this time. I bit down to hold it in place but it broke free.

"—like to put something else in your mouth, if you know what I mean."

Not again! I seemed utterly helpless against this!

"Really?" Bonnie said, smiling again and thrusting her breasts out even further. "Like what?"

I wanted to shove my fist down my throat. Bonnie's mother, I could see, was thinking along similar lines.

The widow Porter shot to her feet and thrust her face to within an inch of mine.

"*What* did you say?"

I tried to pacify her.

"I'm sorry, Mrs. Porter. Perhaps you misunderstood me. Sometimes I don't make myself clear."

She backed off a little. Good. She was listening—even better. I knew I could smooth this over if my mouth would only let me. Just as her face began to soften, I felt my lips begin to move. I could do nothing but listen.

"What I really meant to say was that I'd like to drill her with a special tool I keep buttoned in my pants. As a matter of fact, I'd like to use it on both of you."

"Scoundrel!" she cried, and swung her heavy purse at me, missing my face by a fraction of an inch. "Bounder!"

She grabbed Bonnie by the hand and yanked her from the room. The girl flashed me a smile and a lascivious wink on the way out.

Sweating and gasping, I slumped against the door. I had lost control of my voice! Every thought that flashed into my brain was going straight out my mouth! What was wrong with me?

I was glad it was a slow day. I went to my office and poured two fingers of bourbon from the bottle I kept in the bottom drawer. I downed it in a single swallow. I looked at my framed degree from dental school hanging on the wall. I had counted on becoming wealthy here in Dodge. Now I was ruining it.

When I heard the front door open, I hesitated going out. It was frightening not to be able to control your words. But I had to defeat this malady. I had to overcome it by sheer force of will. I forced myself into the anteroom.

It was empty. I went into the drilling room and I found a familiar figure sitting in the chair. We played draw poker most nights over at the Forty-Niner Saloon. I wouldn't say we were friends in the truest sense of the word, but I was the closest thing he had to a friend besides his brother.

Wyatt Earp slouched in the chair, helping himself to my nitrous oxide. Wyatt giggled. "Got a toothache, Doc!"

"Don't overdue that sweet air, Wyatt," I said. "I have to send all the way to Chicago for more."

The smile wavered off and on again. "You'll be going to Chicago and staying there if you try anymore funny business with Miss Bonnie Porter."

I remembered then that Wyatt had been keeping company with the widow Porter lately.

"I never touched her!"

"But you said some lewd and obscene things that I'd jail you for if you weren't a friend. She's a fine example of young Kansas womanhood and should not be exposed to such behavior."

"She's a tease waiting to blossom into a tart," I said.

Wyatt looked at me with a strange expression. He wanted to frown but the nitrous oxide wouldn't let him.

"I won't have you speak that way about the daughter of a woman for whom I harbor deep feelings."

"You harbor deep feelings for the daughter and you don't want anyone to get to Bonnie before you! And as for the widow Porter, your only deep feelings are for her bank account!"

His half-smile finally disappeared. "Hey, now wait a minute, Doc. I really love that woman!"

I laughed. "You must think I'm as stupid as you are!"

(What was I *saying*? Wyatt had four inches and a good hundred pounds over me! I wanted to vomit!)

"I think you might be a stupid dead man, Doc, if you don't watch what you're saying," he said menacingly as he straightened up from the chair.

I tried to stop myself but couldn't. My mouth ran on.

"Come on, Wyatt. You're fleecing her."

"It's true that I'm allowing her to invest in a couple of the mines that I own, but as a peace officer, I resent your implication that I'm involved in anything illegal."

"You're a disgrace to the badge, Wyatt. People laugh at you—behind your back, of course, because they know if they get on your wrong side they'll wind up in jail on some trumped-up charge, or backshot by your brother Virgil!"

He was stepping toward me, his right hand balled into a fist. I broke out in cold sweat and felt my bladder try to empty. I probably could have stopped him there with a few rational words, or even a quick confession of abject fear. I actually felt the words forming in my mouth as he raised his arm to punch me—

—and that was when the odor hit me.

Standing helpless before him as he loomed over me, I listened in horror as my voice said:

"God! You smell, too! Did it ever occur to you to take a bath before—"

When I woke up on the floor, Wyatt was gone. I staggered to my feet. My jaw ached and my upper lip was swelling. When the room stopped tilting back and forth, I stumbled into the waiting room.

This was a nightmare! If I kept insulting everyone who came to my office, I'd have to close my practice. What would I do? I was already twenty-six and not good for much else besides gambling and shooting. I wasn't a bad shot. Maybe I could take over Earp's job when he left for Tombstone next year.

An odd-looking figure entered then. A skinny old squaw with a hooked nose and dark, piercing eyes set in a face wrinkled like a raisin. That was all I could see of her. The rest of her was swathed in a dusty serape. There was a small red kerchief around her head.

I knew her. Everybody in town knew her: Squaw Jones. She'd been married to an old white man, Aaron Jones, until he got drunk and trampled by a stagecoach a few years ago. Now she wandered in and out of town, selling charms and potions.

"I see Dr. Holliday has bad times," Squaw Jones said. "What is problem?"

"That's what *I'm* supposed to say!" I shouted. "*I'm* the doctor here!"

"Is your words? You say what wish to hide inside?"

I was shocked. "Yes! How did you know?"

"Squaw smell bad medicine when she pass."

"Bad medicine?"

"You have curse."

"I am well aware of that!"

"Squaw Jones can help. Know of these things. You victim of curse of Untethered Tongue. Very bad medicine."

"You're serious? You're talking about a *curse*, like the evil eye or something like that?"

"Much worse."

"I feel bad enough already. Don't try to make me feel stupid, too!"

"You will see, Dr. Holliday," she said, reaching for the door handle. "You will see. And then you will come to Squaw Jones."

"I sincerely doubt it."

"Remember these words. When find man with missing piece, you find enemy."

"I haven't *got* any enemies!"

"It could be friend."

"I haven't got any of those, either! At least not after this morning!"

"Remember Squaw Jones," she said as she shuffled out the door. "You will need her."

That'll be the day, I thought. I didn't need an Indian. I needed another drink.

The next few days recapitulated the events of that morning: I insulted and alienated each member of a steadily dwindling flow of patients. But at least no one punched me.

As I sat and looked out the front window of my empty waiting room, I noticed Mrs. Duluth waddling along the boardwalk. She turned into the doorway of the new dentist who had come into town a few months ago. Dr. James Elliot. He had been starving. Now he had Mrs. Duluth. Glumly, I wondered how many other patients I was driving to him.

The waiting room door opened and there was Squaw Jones again.

"Squaw can come in?"

I motioned her forward. Why not? I had plenty of time on my hands.

Squaw Jones looked the same as she had days ago—a stick figure swathed in a dirty serape. Her bright, beady eyes swept the barren waiting room. I thought I detected a hint of a smile at the corners of her mouth, but it was hard to be sure amid all her wrinkles.

"Curse of Untethered Tongue continue, yes?"

"It's not a curse," I said. "Just a little problem I have to resolve. I don't believe in curses."

She looked me in the eye. There was no doubt about the smile now.

"You could have sent squaw away," she said. "But you chose to see her."

I knew right then I was dealing with a sly old squaw.

"I'm a man of science," I told her. "A dentist. What do you want from me?"

"Squaw wants only to help."

"For a price, I'm sure."

Her shrug was elaborate. "Must clothe this body. Must eat."

"This wouldn't be blackmail, would it?"

"Dr. Holliday!" she said, puffing herself up. "Squaw is like you. Have medicine to sell—like you. Have honor."

"That's not the point. Even granting the existence of such a thing as a curse, I can't imagine anyone who dislikes me enough—before this week, that is—to place a curse on me."

"Unhappy patient, maybe?"

That was all too possible, what with all the gold fillings I'd yanked from people's mouths while they were unconscious in the chair. But someone like that would go to Wyatt first.

"I can't image what complaint a patient of mine could have." (I almost choked on that one.)

"Enemy?"

"None whatsoever."

"Someone want to steal your medicine?"

"You mean a competitor? Well, there is one of those. There seems to be an increasing flow of new dentists from the East."

"Who win from Dr. Holliday bad medicine?"

"Well, Dr. Elliot is benefiting now, but . . ." I laughed. "No. It's too absurd!"

"May be him."

"Jim Elliot? Putting a curse on me so I'll say things I don't want to? Ridiculous!"

"Curse of Untethered Tongue say what in heart. Perhaps Dr. Holliday not like his patients."

I said, "Look, I'm very busy right now—"

"Bad medicine always help someone."

I felt the first twinges of uneasiness. This whole idea was absurd! And yet . . .

I turned and found Squaw Jones grinning at me with crooked yellow teeth. She said, "Find man with missing piece."

"You could use a good dentist," I said.

Around supper time, I was at my usual table in the Forty-Niner, alone, nursing a whiskey, shuffling a deck of cards. I dared not play for fear that I would tell everyone what was in my hand at any moment. My fingers froze in mid-shuffle when Dr. Elliot walked in.

I watched him for a few moments. As much as my mind rebelled against the concept of such a thing as a curse, I couldn't get the thought out of my head. Could this mild-looking fellow dentist have actually placed a curse on my practice? The more I thought about it here amid the smells and laughter of the cowhands, the stage drivers, the gamblers, and the plain old riffraff, the more laughable it became.

I wandered over to where he stood. He had a round face made wider by bushy sideburns. He looked tired. Why not? He had been drilling the teeth of my former patients all day.

I was about to say hello when I noticed that he was missing a part of his left fifth digit—the terminal phalanx was gone! As I gaped at the shiny pink dome of fresh scar tissue where his first knuckle should have been, I heard Squaw Jones's voice in my head:

. . . *Find man with missing piece* . . .

I was too shocked for subtlety.

"Your finger! What happened to it?"

He jumped at the sound of my voice and his complexion faded a couple of shades as he looked at me.

"Hello, John. My finger? Why . . . why nothing happened to it. Why do you ask?"

"I never noticed that you had a . . . piece missing before now. When did it happen?"

He smiled, regaining his composure. "Oh, that. An old accident when I was in school back east. An industrial accident, you might say. I caught it in a defective drilling machine."

I couldn't take my eyes from that foreshortened digit. "The scar tissue doesn't look that old."

"An old injury, do you hear?" He was becoming agitated. "Very old. Very, *very* old!"

The obvious freshness of the scar and Dr. Elliot's overwrought behavior sent a stream of ice water running through my arteries.

. . . When find man with missing piece, you find enemy . . .

"Yes, of course," I said. "Very old. Of course."

He thrust his hand into his pocket.

I fled the saloon and ran to the stable. I saddled my horse and rode out to where Squaw Jones made her camp.

"So, now Dr. Holliday believe in curse of Untethered Tongue," she said, nodding and smiling with smug satisfaction.

"Not completely," I said. "Let's just say I disbelieve in it less than I did this afternoon."

Her tent was dim, the air inside steamy and layered with reminders of past meals, strangely spiced.

"But I just can't believe," I said, "that one of my colleagues, a fellow dental practitioner, would be so unethical as to use such scurrilous means to build his practice at my expense!"

"You would never do such thing?"

"Never! I am an ethical practitioner!"

"And what is your wish, Dr. Holliday?"

"To have the curse—if that's what it is—lifted."

"By this squaw?"

"Of course. That's why I'm here."

"Want thirteen ounces gold for ending Untethered Tongue."

"Thirteen oun—?"

"This squaw know it very small price for saving Dr. Holliday's honor, but her heart is touched by his misfortune." She cleared her throat. "Please pay in metal, not bills."

I'd hidden away significantly more than that amount of gold from the fillings I'd removed over the years. But thirteen ounces!

"I'd want a guarantee."

"Nothing sure in magic, Dr. Holliday."

I rose from my seat and started for the door. "I'm sorry. I can't allow myself to be made into a fool." I was bluffing. I bluffed well in poker, even back then, and had little doubt I could get her to back down. But she kept quiet, waiting until my hand closed on the doorknob before she spoke. She did not, however, say the words I was hoping for.

"For three more ounces, maybe this squaw can turn bad medicine back on one who start it."

As I said before: A sly old bird. I had taken the bait, now she set the hook. A gamble of sixteen ounces, but suddenly I didn't care. I wanted to get even.

I returned to my chair.

"Can you really do that?"

She nodded. "If Dr. Holliday make sacrifice."

"Sacrifice? Wait a second here. I—"

"Must have no fear."

"I'll have no fear as long as I have my revenge."

She smiled and rubbed her hands together. "This is good."

"What do I have to do?"

"Dr. Holliday must give three things. First thing closely touches maker of Untethered Tongue. You know who he is?"

"Dr. Elliot," I said. "No doubt about it. But just how 'closely' must this thing touch?"

"Very close. Underclothes. Pen."

I considered that for a moment. How on earth was I going to handle that? How was I going to get ahold of a pair of Elliot's underwear. Maybe a sock would do.

No matter. I'd find a way.

"What else do you need?"

"Need small amount of Dr. Holliday's liquid."

"Liquid?" This was getting more clichéd by the minute. "You mean blood?"

She shook her head. She seemed embarrassed. "Fluid that only man can give."

"I don't understand—" I began. And then I did. "What kind of magic is this?"

"Very, very old."

"Really. And what if I were a woman?"

"We wait for your time of month."

"I see." I found it difficult to believe that I was sitting here having a serious conversation about this.

She cleared her throat again. "The sample—you can give soon?"

I squared my shoulders. "Of course. And the third thing?"

"This squaw will tell you when you bring first two."

I wasn't sure I liked the sound of that, but I couldn't turn back now. I had stepped over the edge and had left the safe and sane world behind; I was now adrift in the world of the magical and the irrational. Squaw Jones's world. I had to trust her as a guide.

Early the next morning I was at the hotel next to my office eating eggs and potatoes. I've never liked eggs and potatoes, but I was there because Elliot was there. I raged silently as I watched him storing up on his nourishment before a busy day of drilling the teeth of my patients.

I was in a black mood. I had been by his rooming house earlier but had found none of his laundry around. I'd been tempted to break into his quarters but was afraid I'd get caught. I couldn't risk that, not with Wyatt still mad at me.

As I watched him, he stirred his coffee and licked the spoon dry before placing it on the tablecloth. A neat man. A fastidious man. I felt like running over and wringing his—

The spoon.

I almost shouted out loud. *That's it!* The spoon! It had been in his mouth! What contact could be more "close" than being in someone's mouth?

I waited until he finished his meal and departed, then hurried over to his table, just beating the serving girl to it. She gave me a strange look as I darted in front of her and grabbed his spoon off the tray, but I simply continued on my way without a backward glance, as if this were the most natural thing in the world.

The hard part was over. I headed across the street to the back rooms at the Forty-Niner. Miss Lily would be waking up just about now. For a nominal fee, she'd help me obtain the second ingredient. This was the easy part.

"Now what?" I said as I held out the spoon and a small cup of cloudy liquid to Squaw Jones.

She made no move to take them from me. "You have gold?"

"Yes." I pulled a leather pouch from my coat pocket. "Sixteen ounces, as agreed."

I held my breath as she loosened the draw string and looked inside. My larcenous heart had prevailed on me to cheat her of her payment. No gold for Squaw Jones. Instead I'd made nuggets of lead and coated them with the gold colored material I used for my fake gold fillings. They wouldn't stand close inspection.

She looked inside, gauged the weight of the bag in her hand, then nodded.

"Is good." The pouch disappeared inside her serape and then she took the two ingredients from me. "Now this squaw make mix. Dr. Holliday wait outside."

"What about the third ingredient?"

She smiled. "Soon, Dr. Holliday. Must be patient."

I stepped outside her tent. It was difficult to be patient knowing that Dr. Elliot was busy in his office working on my patients while my office door was locked.

After what seemed like hours, Squaw Jones called me back in. I found her sitting there with a cup of steaming liquid.

"Now time for third ingredient. The sacrifice."

"What sort of sacrifice?" I didn't like the sound of this one bit.

"Small part of you. Something Dr. Holliday will not miss, but something that will not grow back."

"Wait just a minute!" I said. I'd heard about deals like this where you make a trade for "something you'll never miss" and I didn't want to fall into *that* trap! "We're not talking about my soul, are we?"

She laughed. "No! Only small piece of flesh. Token for gods. Dr. Elliot gave finger."

"How did you know that?"

"You told this squaw last night."

"Did I? I don't remember."

"You did. Dr. Holliday must make same sacrifice if he wish bad medicine go away."

Something that won't grow back. That left out hair and fingernail clippings. I certainly didn't want to lose a part of a finger—I didn't approve of public deformity.

"Maybe this isn't such a good idea."

She shrugged. "Without sacrifice, Dr. Elliot will not feel curse of Unhindered Hands."

" 'Unhindered Hands?' Just what is that?"

"Like Untethered Tongue. As Dr. Holliday's lips now speak what he wish kept hidden in heart, Dr. Elliot's hands will do things he only wish to do."

The thought of Dr. Elliot's hands acting upon whatever physical desires occurred to him, to be no more able to restrain his hands than I had been able to restrain my tongue delighted me.

Then I thought of something neither I nor anyone else would miss—

"How about my little toe?"

"It is good," she said.

"How do we do this?"

Following her directions, I removed the boot and sock from my left food and held it over the steaming liquid.

"Dip toe."

Feeling like a fool for going through this hocus-pocus, yet hating myself for not having the nerve to call the whole thing off and take my chances with my unruly tongue, I dipped my little toe into the cup.

"Enough," she said after a moment. She withdrew the cup and handed me a dirty cloth. "Dry toe."

I scrutinized my left fifth toe. It looked just like the others, only wet.

"Something's wrong!" I said. "I thought I was supposed to 'sacrifice' this toe! Nothing happened!"

"Patience, Dr. Holliday. Patience."

I was convinced now that I was being hoodwinked. I quickly rubbed my toe dry and rose to my feet.

"This is a farce! I'm glad I didn't give you any real gold!"

Her head snapped around. She stared at me. "Gold not real?"

"No. So you can call off this whole charade."

"Too late. Medicine is made. Curse begins."

"But my toe—"

I looked down at my left foot. There were only four toes. All that remained of my tenth toe was a small pink bulge of fresh scar tissue.

"Where—?"

I opened the cloth and there was my toe. As I watched, it fumed and melted into a pink fluid that was absorbed by the cloth. The odor made me want to gag.

Squaw Jones was pawing through the bag of fake gold nuggets. "Dr. Holliday trick this squaw?"

"Why not? You're probably the one who got me in this fix in the first place. You're playing both sides of the street."

She approached me, menace in her eyes. I kept watch on her hands, making sure both were in sight. They were: clutching the pouch of fake gold. Her face came within inches of mine. She stared at me.

Then she coughed. Once.

"Return to your office, Dr. Holliday. Curse of Untethered Tongue is broken; curse of Unhampered Hands begin. Squaw Jones cannot change that now."

I glanced down at my four-toed foot again and realized I was rapidly become a believer. With boot and sock in hand, I hurried from Squaw Jones's tent.

"But you will pay another way!" she called after me.

The first patient to show up was Mr. O'Toole. My private name for him was "Mr. O'Stool"—he had a bowel fixation that he blamed on his bad teeth. He spent most office visits describing his movements. He was a bore but he came every two weeks for a new filling.

But I got through the visit with no problem. I'd had an urge to tell him that I thought he was suffering from a fecal impaction that had backed up to his brain but the remark remained within my mind while my mouth offered bland reassurances.

I drilled his latest imaginary cavity and fairly danced out of the examining room.

I've done it! I've broken the curse!

I went to the front window in my waiting room and looked across the street at Dr. Elliot's office. I whispered:

"I've beaten you, Elliot! Beaten you at your own game!"

As I watched, I saw Bonnie Porter come racing out of Dr. Elliot's office, trying to cover her bobbing, exposed breasts with one hand while holding up her ripped skirt with the other. In close pursuit, with a piece of Bonnie's torn bodice clutched in his teeth, was Dr. Elliot. And right behind the two of them was the widow Porter, swinging her handbag. She caught Dr. Elliot full force in the back of the head with a swing and he went down. Then she stood over him and began pounding him with her bag.

I watched until Wyatt ran up. He pulled his pistol and just stood there, his eyes captured by the pink-tipped whiteness of Bonnie's breasts. I knew though that as soon as she covered herself, Wyatt would be on Dr. Elliot like a lynch mob. He wasn't going to take at all kindly to someone going after Bonnie Porter before he'd had firsts.

Poor Dr. Elliot. Couldn't control his hands. Such a shame.

As I turned away I felt a twinge behind my sternum. I began to cough. I'd never coughed like this before in my life. Spasms racked my chest. I pulled out my handkerchief and buried my face in it, trying to muffle the coughs, perhaps suppress them by trapping them inside. Suddenly I felt something tear free in my chest and fill my throat. I gagged it out.

Blood stained my handkerchief.

Hemoptysis—a bloody cough. A sure sign of consumption, or what they were now calling tuberculosis.

But how could I have tuberculosis? I hadn't been visiting anyone in a sanitarium, and the only people in these parts who had any tuberculosis were . . .

. . . Indians.

Squaw Jones had coughed in my face, but only once, and that had been just a few hours ago. I couldn't have developed tuberculosis in that short of time. It was impossible.

I glanced out the window again. Wyatt was leading Dr. Elliot off toward the jail, and being none too gentle about it. In the crowd that had gathered, all heads were turned to watch them go. All except one. Squaw Jones was there, staring directly at me.

I coughed again.

This one's for Joe Lansdale.

Mainly because I borrowed one of the plot elements from his novel *Cold in July*. If you've never read *Cold in July*, do so immediately. (That's right—put this book down and go out and buy it.) It's a bloody, funny, sad, scary moral pretzel of a novel that will keep you flipping pages until three in the morning. As soon as I finished reading it, I called Joe to tell him what a great job he'd done. The only thing I wanted to know was where all the exclamation points had gone. I couldn't find a single one in the entire book. Joe said they're not necessary in a properly written scene. I begged to differ.

Thus began the ongoing Wilson-Lansdale Exclamation Point Debate. I admit I've used too many in the past, and as a result of the debate I've cut way back. I've got them under control now. (But Joe . . . a character screaming at the top of his lungs in red-faced rage deserves at least one "!", don't you think?)

Next he'll be dumping question marks.

But back to "Slasher." I liked *Cold in July* so much that when Ed Gorman and Marty Greenberg requested a story for *Stalkers II* (eventually published as *Predators*), I borrowed a piece of the *Cold in July* setup—the idea of a killer being kept in protective custody because he's a witness in an important case—and took off from there. (By the way, the setting is Monroe.)

"Slasher" is a twisted little piece of fiction without the slightest hint of the supernatural. As such it wound up in *The Year's 25 Finest Crime and Mystery Stories*.

The perfect kind of story to dedicate to Joe R. Lansdale.

SLASHER

I saved the rage.

I let them bury my grief with Jessica. It cocooned her in her coffin, cushioned her, pillowed her head. There it would stay, doing what little it could to protect her from the cold, the damp, the conqueror worm.

But I saved the rage. I nurtured it. I honed its edge until it was fine and tough and sharp. Sharp enough to cut one day through the darkness encrusting my soul.

Martha was on the far side of the grave, supported by her mother and father and two brothers—Jessie's grandparents and uncles. I stood alone on my side. A few friends from the office were there, standing behind me, but they weren't really with me. I was alone, in every sense of the word.

I stared at the top of the tiny coffin that had remained closed during the wake and the funeral mass because of the mutilated state of the little body within. I watched it disappear by tiny increments beneath a growing tangle of color as sobbing mourners each took a turn at tossing a flower on it. Jessica, my Jessica. Only five years old, cut to ribbons by some filthy rotten stinking lousy—

"Bastard!"

The grating voice wrenched my gaze away from the coffin. I knew that voice. Oh, how I knew that voice. I looked up and met Martha's hate-filled eyes. Her face was pale and drawn, her cheeks were black with eyeliner that had flowed with her tears. Her blond hair was masked by her black hat and veil.

"It's your fault! She's dead because of you! You had her only every other weekend and you couldn't even pay attention to her! It should be *you* in there!"

"Easy, Martha," one of her brothers told her in a low voice. "You'll only upset yourself more."

But I could see it in his eyes, too—in everybody's eyes. They all agreed with her. Even I agreed with her.

"*No!*" she screamed, shaking off her brother's hand and pointing at me. "You were a lousy husband and a lousier father. And now Jessie's dead because of you! *You!*"

Then she broke down into uncontrollable sobbing and was led off by her parents and brothers. Embarrassed, the rest of the mourners began to drift away, leaving me alone with my dead Jessie. Alone with my rage. Alone with my guilt.

I hadn't been the best father in the world. But who could be? Either you don't give them enough love or you overindulge them. You can't seem to win. But I do admit that there were too many times when something else seemed more important than being with Jessie, some deal, some account that needed attention right away, so Jessie would have to wait. I'd make it up to her later—that was the promise. I'd play catch-up next week. But now there wouldn't be any later. No more next weeks for Jessica Santos. No catching up on the hugs and the playing and the I-love-yous.

If only . . .

If only I hadn't left her on the curb to go get her that goddamn ice-cream cone.

We'd been watching the Fourth of July fireworks down at the harbor front. Jessie was thrilled and fascinated by the bright flashes blooming and booming in the sky. She'd wanted an ice cream, and being a divorced daddy who didn't get to see her very often, I couldn't say no. So I carried her back to the pushcart vendor near the entrance to Crosby's Marina. She couldn't see the fireworks from the end of the line so I let her stand back by the curb to watch while I queued up. While she kept her eyes on the sky, I kept an eye on her all the time I was on line. I wasn't worried about someone grabbing her—the thought never entered my mind. I just didn't want her wandering into the street for an even better view. The only time I looked away was when I placed the order and paid the guy.

When I turned around, a cone in each hand, Jessie was gone.

No one had seen anything. For two days the police and a horde of volunteers combed all of Monroe and most of northern Nassau county. They found her—what was left of her—on the edge of old man Haskins's marshes.

A manhunt was still on for the killer, but with each passing day, the trail got colder.

So now I stood by my Jessica's grave in Tall Oaks Cemetery, sweating in my dark suit under the obscenely bright sun as I fought my guilt and nurtured my hate, praying for the day they caught the scum who had slashed my Jessica to ribbons. I renewed the vow I had made before—the guy was never going to get to trial. I would find a way to get to him while he was out on bail, or even in jail, if it came to that, and I would do to him what he'd done to my Jessica. And then I would dare the courts to find a jury that would convict me.

When everyone was gone, I said my final good-bye to Jessie. I'd wanted to erect a huge angelic monument to her, but Tall Oaks didn't allow that sort of thing. A little plaque would have to suffice. It didn't seem right.

As I turned to go, I noticed a man leaning against a tree a hundred feet or so away. He was watching me. As I started down the grassy slope, he began walking, too. Our paths intersected at my car.

"Mr. Santos?" he said.

I turned. He was a big man, six-two at least, midforties, maybe two-fifty, with most of it settled around his gut. He wore a white shirt under a rumpled gray suit. His thinning brown hair was slick with sweat. I looked at him but said nothing. If he was another reporter—

"I'm Gerald Caskie, FBI. Can we talk a minute?"

"You found him?" I said, my spirits readying for a leap. I stepped closer and grabbed two fistfuls of his suit jacket. "You've got him?"

He pulled his jacket free of my grasp.

"We can talk in my car. It's cooler."

I followed about fifty yards along the curving asphalt path to where a monotone Ford two-door sedan waited in the shade of one of the cemetery's eponymous trees. The motor was running. He indicated the passenger side. I joined him in the front seat of the Ford. The air conditioner was blasting. It was freezing inside.

"That's better," he said, adjusting one of the vents to blow directly on his face.

"All right," I said, unable to contain my impatience any longer. "We're here. Tell me: Do you have him?"

He looked at me with basset hound brown eyes.

"What I'm about to tell you is off the record, agreed?"

"What are you—?"

"Agreed? You must never reveal what I'm about to tell you. Do I have your word as a man that what I tell you will never go beyond this car?"

"No. I have to know what it's about, first."

He shifted in his seat and put the Ford in gear.

"Forget it. I'll drive you back to your car."

"No. Wait. All right. I promise. But enough with the games, already."

He threw the gear shift back into Park.

"This isn't a game, Mr. Santos. I could lose my job, even be brought up on criminal charges for what I'm going to tell you. And if you do try to spill it, I'll deny we've ever met."

"What is it, goddamn it?"

"We know who killed your daughter."

The words hit me like a sledge to the gut. I felt almost sick with relief.

"Have you got him? Have you arrested him?"

"No. And we won't be. Not for some time to come."

It took a while for the words to sink in, probably because my mind didn't want to accept them. But when it did, I was ready to go for his throat. I reined in my fury, however. I didn't want to get hit with assault and battery on a federal officer. At least not yet.

"You'd better explain that," I said in a voice barely above a whisper.

"The killer is presently a protected witness in an immensely important federal trial. Can't be touched until all the testimony is in and we get our conviction."

"Why the hell not? My daughter's death has nothing to do with your trial!"

"The killer's a psycho—that's obvious. Think how a child-killing charge will taint the testimony. The jury will throw it out. We've got to wait."

"How long?"

"Less than a year if we lose the case. If we get a conviction, we'll have to wait out all the appeals. So we could be looking at five years, maybe more."

Cool as it was in the car, I felt a different kind of cold seep through me.

"Who is he?"

"Forget it. I can't tell you that."

I couldn't help it—I went for his throat.

"Tell me, goddamn it!"

He pushed me off. He was a lot bigger than I—I'm just a bantamweight accountant, one-fifty soaking wet.

"Back off, Santos! No way I'm going to give you a name. You'll have it in all the papers within hours."

I folded. I crumpled. I turned away and pressed my head against the cool of the side window. I thought I was going to cry, but I didn't. I'd left all my tears with Jessie.

"Why did you tell me any of this if you're not going to tell me his name?"

"Because I know you're hurting," he said in a soft voice. "I saw what you did to that reporter on TV."

Right. The reporter. Mel Padner. My claim to fame. As I walked out of the morgue after identifying Jessica's tattered body, I was greeted by an array of cameras and reporters. Most of them kept a respectful distance, but not Padner. He stuck a mike in my face and asked me how I felt about my daughter's death. I had the microphone halfway down his throat before they pulled me off him. His own station never ran the footage, but all the others did, including CNN. I was still getting cards and telegrams telling me how I should have shoved it up Padner's other end instead.

"And this is supposed to make me feel better?" I said to Caskie.

"I thought it would. Because otherwise the weeks and months would go on and on with no one finding the killer, and you'd sink deeper and deeper into depression. At least I know I would. I've got a daughter myself, and if anything ever happened to her like . . . well, if anything happened to her, that's the way I'd feel. I just thought I'd try to give you some peace of mind. I thought you'd be able to hang in there better knowing that we already have the killer in a custody of sorts, and that, as one father to another, justice will be done."

I turned and stared at him. It's a comment on our age, I suppose, that decency from a stranger is so shocking.

"Thanks," I said. "Maybe that will make a difference later when I think about it some. Right now all I'm thinking is how I want to take the biggest, sharpest carving knife I can find and chop this guy into hamburger."

He raised his right fist with the thumb stuck in the air.

"I hear you, Mr. Santos."

"Call me Pete."

"I'm Gerry. And if the government didn't need the testimony so desperately, I might be tempted to do it myself."

We shook hands, then I got out of the car and walked around to his side. He rolled the window down.

"Thanks again," I said. "You didn't have to do this."

"Yes, I did."

"Sure you won't tell me his name?"

He smiled. "These are some *bad* dudes we want to put away with this trial. But don't you worry. Once all the legal proceedings are over, justice will be done." Again, the thumbs-up sign. "We'll see to it that she gets what's coming to her."

And then he drove away, leaving me standing on the path, gaping.

Her?

It wasn't working.

The day after Jessica's body was found, I went back to my apartment—Martha got the house, so I've been living in a two-bedroom box at the Soundview condos—and trashed the place. All except Jessica's room. The second bedroom had been reserved exclusively for Jessie. I went in there and with a black magic marker drew the outline of a man on one of her walls. Then I took the biggest carving knife I could find and attacked that figure. I slashed at the wallboard, driving the blade through it again and again until I was exhausted. Only then was I able to get some sleep.

I'd done that every night since Jessica's death, but tonight it wasn't working.

Caskie's last words were driving me crazy.

My little Jessica had been slashed to ribbons by a woman? A *woman*? I couldn't believe it. It gnawed at my insides like some monstrous parasite. I couldn't work, couldn't eat, couldn't sleep. The FBI knew who'd killed my Jessica and they weren't telling. I had to know, too. I needed a name. A face. Somewhere to focus this rage that was coloring my blood and poisoning every cell in my body.

A woman! Caskie must have been mistaken. Jessica had been—I retched every time I thought of it—sodomized. A woman couldn't do that.

I lasted two days—and two nights of heartlessly attacking the male figure outlined on her wall. Then I acted.

First thing in the morning, I took a trip to the nearest FBI office. It was on Queens Boulevard in Rego Park. I knew I'd given agent Caskie my word, but . . . my daughter . . . her killer . . . no one could expect me to hold to that promise. No one!

I was in the lobby of the FBI building, searching the directory, when I heard a voice to my left.

"What the hell are you doing here?"

I turned. It was Caskie. I stepped toward him with my hand extended.

"Just the man I was looking—"

"Don't talk to me!" the hissed, staring across the lobby. "Get out of here!"

"No way, Caskie. Your people know who killed my daughter and they're going to tell me, or I'm going to the papers."

"You trying to ruin me?"

"No. I don't want that. But if I have to, I will."

He was silent for a moment, then he made a noise like a cross between a sigh and a growl.

"Shit! Meet me outside. Around the corner in the alley. Ten minutes."

He walked away without waiting for my reply.

The alley was long and narrow, blocked at the far end by a ten-foot cyclone fence. I waited near its mouth, keeping to the shady side. Midmorning and already it was getting hot. Caskie showed up a few minutes later. He walked by as if he hadn't noticed me, but he spoke out of the corner of his mouth.

"Follow me. I don't want to be seen with you."

I followed. He led me all the way back to the rear of the building. When we rounded a rancid smelling dumpster, he turned, grabbed me by the front of my shirt, and threw me against the wall. I was caught by surprise. The impact knocked the wind out of me.

"What the fuck do you think you're doing here?" he said through clenched teeth.

I was ready to take a shot at his jaw but the fury in his eyes made me hesitate. He looked ready to kill.

"I told you," I said. "I want to know who killed my daughter. And I'm going to find out."

"No way, Santos."

I looked him in the eye.

"What're you going to do? Kill me?"

He seemed to be considering it, and that made me a little nervous. But then his shoulders slumped.

"I'm so fucking *stupid*!" he said "I should have minded my own business and let you stew for a year or two. But no, I had to try to be Mr. Goodguy."

I felt for him. Actually, I felt like a shit, but I couldn't let that stop me.

"Hey, look," I said. "I appreciate what you tried to do, but it just didn't work the way you thought it would. Instead of easing my mind, it's done just the opposite. It's made me crazy."

Caskie's expression was as bleak as his voice.

"What do you want, Santos?"

"First off, I want to know why you said the killer was a 'she' the other day?"

"When did I say that? I never said that."

"Oh, yes you did. As you drove off. And don't tell me I misunderstood you, because I didn't. You said, 'We'll see to it that *she* gets what's coming to *her*.' So how could Jessie's killer have been a woman if they're tracing the killer through DNA analysis of the semen they found in . . ." My stomach lurched.

Caskie's smile was grim and sour.

"You think the Bureau can't get a local coroner to change his report for matters of security? Wake up, Santos. That was put in there to make sure no one ever has the slightest doubt that they're looking for a male."

I wanted to kill him. Here I'd spent nearly a week believing Jessica had been raped before she was slashed up. And it had never happened. But I kept calm.

"I want her name."

"No way."

"Then I go to the *Times*, the *Post*, and the *News*! Right now!"

I turned and began walking up the alley. I'd gone about ten feet when he spoke.

"Ciullo. Regina Ciullo."

I turned.

"Who is she?"

"Bruno Papillardi's ex-girlfriend."

That rocked me. Bruno Papillardi—New York City's number one crime boss. His racketeering trial had been in the papers for months.

"Is she that important to the case?"

"The way the judge is tossing out our evidence left and right, it looks like she's going to be the *whole* case. She may be a psycho, but she's not dumb. She made recordings while she and Bruno were in bed together. Seems that when all the grunting and groaning is done, Bruno tends to brag. There's one particularly juicy night where he talks about how he personally offed a Teamsters' local boss who wouldn't play ball. With Regina Ciullo's testimony, we might be able to nail him for more than racketeering. We might get him for murder-one."

I didn't care about Papillardi. I cared about only one person.

"But Jessica . . . why?"

Caskie shook his head.

"I don't know. I'm not a shrink. But I know your daughter wasn't the first. Regina Ciullo's done at least two others over the past two years. The others were just never found."

"Then how do you—?"

"She told us. She gave us the slip on the Fourth. She returned the following morning around three A.M. We found the knife in the back seat of the car. We made the connection, put the pressure on her, and she told us. We'd always known she was weird but . . ." He shuddered. "We never realized . . ."

I wanted to run from the alley, but I had to see this through.

"So you can see our dilemma," Caskie went on. "We can't turn her in. At least not yet. Papillardi's people are combing the whole Northeast for her. If she's arrested she won't survive her first night in jail. And if by some miracle she does, her lawyer will immediately enter an insanity plea, which will destroy the value of her testimony against Papillardi."

I swallowed. My throat was gritty.

"Where are you keeping her?"

"Are you kidding? I tell you so you can go out there and try to do a Rambo number on her? No way."

"I don't want to kill her."

"That's not what you said the other day at the cemetery."

I smiled. It must have been a hideous grimace because I saw Caskie flinch.

"I was upset then. A little crazy. I couldn't stick a knife in someone. Besides, I already have enough information now to kill her. If I want her dead. I can call Papillardi and tell him she's in Monroe. He'll do the rest. But I don't want that. I just want to know what she looks like. I want to see a picture of her. And I want to know where she lives so I can drive by every once in a while and make sure she's still there. If I can do that, I can survive the wait."

He was studying me. I hoped I'd been convincing. I prayed he'd buy it. But actually, I hadn't left him much choice.

"She's staying on Shore Drive in Monroe."

I couldn't restrain myself.

"In my hometown?" You brought a child killer to my hometown?"

"We didn't know about her then. But believe me, she won't get out of our sight again. She's hurt her last kid."

Damn right! I thought.

"I want to see her file."

"I can't get that—"

"You will," I said, turning. "And by tonight. Or I'll be on the phone. Bring it to my apartment."

I didn't give him my address. I was sure he already had it.

Back in my apartment, I took the Magic Marker and enhanced the drawing on Jessica's wall with a few details. I added a skirt. And long flowing hair styled in a flip. Then I picked up the knife and went to work with renewed vigor.

Caskie showed up around ten P.M., smelling like a leaky brewery, a buff folder under his arm. He brushed by me and tossed the folder onto the living room table.

"I'm dead!" he said, pulling off his wilted suit jacket and hurling it across the room. "Two more years till my pension and now I might as well kiss it all good-bye!"

"What's the matter?"

"*That's* what's the matter!" he said, pointing at the folder. "When that turns up missing, the Bureau will trace it to me and put my ass in a sling! Nice guys really do finish fucking last!"

"Just a minute, now," I said, approaching him but staying out of reach. He looked *very* upset. "Hold it down. If you return it first thing tomorrow morning, who's going to know it was ever missing?"

He stared at me, a blank look on his face.

"I thought you wanted it."

"I want to *look* at it. That's all. Like I told you: just to know where she lives and what she looks like. If the killer's got a name and a place and a face, I can stay sane until the Papillardi trial is over."

As I was speaking, my body had been gravitating toward the folder. I wasn't aware of my legs moving, but by the time I'd finished, I was standing over it. I reached down and flipped the cover open. An eight-by-ten black-and-white close-up of a woman's face stared back at me.

"That's . . . that's her?"

"Yeah. That's Regina Ciullo."

"She's so ordinary."

Caskie snickered.

"You think someone with Bruno Papillardi's bucks and pull is gonna waste his time with someone 'ordinary'? No way. Good-looking babes are falling all over that guy. But Ciullo's weirdness is one of a kind. She's *anything* but ordinary. That's what attracted him." His voice turned serious. "You really mean that about not wanting to take the file?"

"Of course."

I picked up the photo and stared at it. Her irises were dark, the lashes long. Her hair was wavy and long, and very black. Despite strategic angling of the camera, he nose appeared somewhat on the large side. Her lips were full and pouty. She looked thirty-five or so.

Caskie peered over my shoulder.

"That picture's a few years old, when she was going under the stage name of Bloody Mary. Doesn't show any of her body which is incredible."

"Stage name?"

"Yeah. She used to be a dancer in a specialty club down in SoHo called The Manacle. She'd do a strip while letting a white rat crawl all over her body, and when she was down to the buff, she'd slice its throat and squeeze its blood down her front as she finished her dance." Caskie's expression was sour. "A real sicko, but she sure as hell got to Papillardi. One show and he was hot for her ass. Say, you got any beer?"

I pointed the way to the kitchen as I continued to stare at the photo.

"In the fridge."

This was the killer of dear Jessica. Regina Ciullo. When she tired of slashing rats she went out and found a child. I felt my pulse quicken, my palms become moist. The photo trembled in my grasp, as if she knew I'd be coming for her.

"Where on Shore Drive is she staying?"

Caskie popped the top of a can of Bud as he returned to the living room.

"The Jensen place."

"Jensen! How'd you get her in there?"

The beer can paused inches from his lips.

"You know them?"

"I just know they're rich."

He took a long gulp.

"They are. And they're hardly ever home—at least in this home—except in the spring. They're on a world cruise now. And since Mr. Jensen is a friend of the present administration, and a personal friend of the Bureau's director, he's allowed us to stash her in his mansion. It's a perfect cover. She's posing as Mr. Jensen's niece." He shook his head slowly. "What a place. That's the way to live, I tell you."

The woman who murdered my daughter was living in luxury out on Shore Drive, guarded by the FBI. I wanted to scream. But I didn't. I closed the file and handed it back to Caskie.

"I'll keep the picture," I said. "The rest is all yours."

He snatched the folder away from me.

"You mean it?"

"Of course. You'll never hear from me again . . . *unless,* of course, Papillardi is convicted and she isn't indicted. *Then* you'll hear from me. Believe me, you'll hear from me."

I had put on a performance of Barrymore caliber. And Caskie bought it. He smiled like a death row prisoner who'd just got a last minute reprieve.

"Don't worry about that, Santos. As soon as Papillardi's case is through, we're on her. Don't you worry about that!" He turned at the door and gave me another of his thumps-up gestures. "You can take that to the bank!"

And then he was gone.

For a while I stood there in the living room and stared at the picture of Regina Ciullo. Then I took it into Jessica's room and tacked it over the head of the latest outline on the wall. Then I stabbed the figure so hard, so fast, and so many times that there was a football sized hole in the wall in less than a minute.

A week later the walls of Jessica's room were so Swiss-cheesed with holes that there was no space left for new outlines.

Time for the real thing.

I'd been driving by the Jensen place regularly, sometimes three times a day. I always kept the photo on the seat beside me, for quick reference in case I saw someone who resembled Regina Ciullo. I was sure I'd know her anywhere, but it's good to be prepared.

The houses on Shore Drive all qualified as mansions—all huge, all waterfront, facing Connecticut across the Long Island Sound. Although there was always a car or two in the driveway behind the electric steel gate—a Bentley or a Jag or a Porsche Carrera—I never saw anybody.

Until Thursday. I was in the midst of cruising past when I saw the front gate begin to slide open. I almost slammed on the brakes, then had the presence of mind to keep moving. But slow.

And who pulls out but the bitch herself, the slasher of my daughter, slayer of the last thing in my life that held any real meaning. She was driving the Mercedes. Speeding. She passed me doing at least fifty, and still accelerating. On a residential street. The bitch didn't care. The top was down. No question about it. It was her. And she was alone.

Had she given her FBI guardians the slip again? Was she on her way to find another innocent, helpless, trusting child to slaughter?

Not if I could help it.

I followed her to the local Gristedes, trailed her as she dawdled along the cosmetics aisle, touching, feeling, sniffing. Probably looking for the means to whore herself up. As ordinary as the photo had been, it had done her a service. In the light of day she was extremely plain. She needed all the help she could get. And her body. Caskie had described it as "incredible." It was anything but that from what I could see. I guess there's no accounting for tastes.

I caught up to her in the housewares aisle. That was where they sold the knives. When I saw a stainless steel carving set displayed on a shelf I got dizzy. Visions of Jessica's mutilated body lying on that cold, steel gurney in the morgue flashed before me. A knife like that had ripped her up. I saw Martha's face, the expressions on her brothers' faces—*Your fault! Your fault!*

That did it.

I ripped the biggest knife from the set and spun her around.

"Remember Jessica Santos?" I screamed.

Shock on her face. Sure! No one was supposed to know.

I pretended she was one of the outlines on Jessica's wall. A deep thrust to the abdomen, feeling the knife point hesitate against the fabric of her dress, and then rip through cloth and skin, into the tender innards. She screamed but I didn't let that stop me. I tugged the blade free and plunged it in again and again, each time screaming,

"This is for Jessica! This is for Jessica!"

Somebody pulled me free of her and I didn't resist. She'd been slashed like Jessica. The damage was irreparable. I knew my duty was done, knew I'd avenged my daughter.

But as I looked into her dying eyes, so hurt, so shocked, so bewildered, I had the first inkling that I had made a monstrous mistake.

I slammed my fist on the table.

"Call the FBI! Check it out with them!"

They'd had me in this interrogation room for hours. Against my lawyer's advice—who wanted me to plead insanity—I'd given them a full statement. I wasn't going to hide anything. This was an open and shut case of a man taking justifiable revenge against his daughter's murderer. I wasn't going to be coy about it. I did it and that was that. Now they could do their damnedest to convict me. All I needed was the FBI file to prove that she was the killer.

"We *have* called the FBI," said Captain Hall, chief of the Monroe police department. He adjusted his belt around his ample gut for the hundredth time since he'd stuck me in here. "And there's no such agent as Caskie assigned anywhere in New York."

"It's a deep cover thing! That woman posing as a Jensen is Regina Ciullo, a federal witness against Bruno Papillardi!"

"Who told you that?" Captain Hall said.

"Agent Caskie."

"The agent who doesn't exist. How convenient. When did you meet him?"

I described my encounters with Caskie, from the cemetery to my apartment.

"So you were never in his office—if he ever had one. Did anyone see you with him?"

I thought about that. The funeral had been over and everyone was gone when I'd met him in the cemetery. We'd stood side by side for less than a minute in the foyer of the FBI building, and then we'd been together in the alley and my apartment. A cold lump was growing in my gut.

"No. No one that I recall. But what about the picture? It's got to have Caskie's fingerprints on it!"

"We've searched your car three times now, Mr. Santos. No picture. Maybe you *should* plead insane. Maybe this FBI agent is all in your mind."

"I'm not crazy!"

Captain Hall's face got hard as he leaned toward me.

"Well then, maybe you should be. I know you've had a terrible thing happen to your family, but I've known Marla Jensen since she was a girl, back when she was still Marla Wainwright. That was poor Marla you sliced up. And what's more, we think we've found the killer—the *real* killer—out in Islip a few hours ago."

He had to be wrong! Please God, he had to be! If I did that to the woman—

"No! You got to listen to me!"

A disgusted growl rumbled from Captain Hall's throat.

"Enough of this bullshit. Get him out of here."

"No, wait! Please!"

"Out!"

Two uniformed cops yanked me out of the chair and dragged me into the hall. As they led me upstairs to a holding cell, I spotted Caskie walking in with two other cops.

"Thank God!" I shouted. "Where have you been?"

His face was drawn and haggard. He almost looked as if he had been crying. And he looked *different*. He looked trimmer and he held himself straighter. The rumpled suit was gone, replaced by white duck slacks, a white linen shirt, open at the collar, and a blue blazer with an emblem on the pocket. He looked like a wealthy yachtsman. He stared at me without the slightest hint of recognition.

One of the cops with him whispered in his ear and suddenly Caskie was bounding toward me, face white with rage, arms outstretched, fingers curved like an eagle's talons, ready to tear me to pieces. The cops managed to haul him back before he reached me.

"What's the matter with him?" I said to anyone who'd listen as my two cops hustled me up the stairs.

My attorney answered from behind me.

"That's Harold Jensen, the husband of the woman you cut up."

I felt my knees buckle.

"Her husband?"

"Yeah. I heard around the club that she started divorce proceedings against him, but I guess that's moot now. Her death leaves him sole heir to the entire Wainwright fortune."

With my insides tying themselves in a thousand tight little knots, I glanced back at the man I'd known as Caskie. He was being ushered through the door that led to the morgue. But on the threshold he turned and stole a look at me. As our eyes met, he winked and gave me a secret little thumbs-up.

John Betancourt wrote to me sometime in 1989 asking if I'd be interested in participating in a "Special F. Paul Wilson Issue" of *Weird Tales* magazine. Like I could say no? An entire issue of the world's first and greatest horror fiction magazine—where the classics of Lovecraft and Howard and Bloch and Bradbury first saw print—devoted to me? How could I *not* be interested? I was restarting *Reprisal* then but promised I'd send the requested twenty thousand words of new fiction just as soon as I got free.

"The Barrens" was intended to be those twenty thousand words. Because *Weird Tales* was the target market, I designed it to be Lovecraftian, but not without my own little twists. It was August, and I was cruising along on it when I got a letter from Bob Weinberg requesting a story for *Lovecraft's Legacy*, an anthology he and Marty Greenberg (see how that name keeps popping up?) were editing in honor of H. P. Lovecraft's centennial. I realized that "The Barrens" was perfect.

So now I had a dilemma. Which meant more: the ego stroke of an issue of *Weird Tales* devoted to me, or being part of a one-shot anthology dedicated to the work of one of the most influential dark fantasy writers of all time?

I chose the latter.

Why? Because HPL is special to me.

Donald A. Wollheim is to blame. He started me on Lovecraft. It was 1959. I was just a kid, a mere thirteen years old when he slipped me my first fix. I was a good kid up till then, reading Ace Doubles and clean, wholesome science fiction stories by the likes of Heinlein, E. E. Smith, Poul Anderson, Fred Pohl, and the rest. But he brought me down with one anthology. He knew what he was doing. He called it *The Macabre Reader* and slapped this lurid neato cool Ed Emshwiller cover on it. I couldn't resist. I bought it. I read it. And that was it. The beginning of my end.

The Macabre Reader is an excellent collection—Bloch, Wandrei, Smith, Bishop, Howard. Good stories—dark, eerie, intense, the emotions jumping right off the page—like nothing I'd ever read before. But the one that grabbed me by the throat was "The Thing on the Doorstep" by somebody named H. P. Lovecraft. I was dragged into the story by the opening line ("It is true I have sent six bullets through the head of my best friend, and yet I hope to show by this statement that I am not his murderer."), captivated by the setting (". . . witch-cursed, legend-haunted Arkham, whose huddled, sagging gambrel roofs and crumbling Georgian balustrades brood out the centuries beside the darkly muttering Miskatonic."), blown away by the dense prose that tossed off words like *eldritch* and *foetor* and *Cyclopean* and *nacreous*, that spoke of poets who die screaming in madhouses, that casually mentioned strange, forbidden books and towns like Innsmouth (where even Arkhamites fear to go) as if I should be familiar with them.

But it was the heart of the tale that lingered in my mind long after I'd finished it—the concept of another reality impinging on ours, knowledge of which could drive you stark raving mad; a dimension of perverse logic and bizarre geometry, full of godlike creatures with unpronounceable names, aloof and yet decidedly inimical.

My thirteen-year-old world did not seem quite so safe and sane, my reality seemed a tad less real.

"The Thing on the Doorstep" delivered on the up-close, breath-clogging horror that *The Macabre Reader* cover had promised, but it also served as my Cthulhu Mythos primer, my introduction to what is known as Cosmic Horror.

After that first fix, I started mainlining Lovecraft. The local pushers—excuse me, book dealers—introduced me to Arkham House books and I nearly died of an overdose. Eventually I went cold turkey and kicked the habit. (Well, not completely. Occasionally I'll reread a favorite story. I can handle it now. Really.) But the Cosmic Horror concept still fascinates me. I used it in *The Keep* and I've used it here in "The Barrens." I'll no doubt use it again.

So here's my official tribute to H. P. Lovecraft. I purposely avoided rereading any of his fiction before writing "The Barrens." I wasn't out to do a slavish pastiche; I wanted to capture the Lovecraft gestalt as I remembered it. The Jersey Pine Barrens, by the way, are real, a truly Lovecraftian setting; all the Piney history and lore in the story are true, every locale except Razorback Hill is real. (In fact, I liked Razorback Hill so much I returned there for the backstory of *Freak Show*.) The style is mine, but the Cosmic Horror is Lovecraft's.

The following year it wound up as a finalist for the World Fantasy Award for best novella. It lost (of course) but John Betancourt did get his chance to publish it through his own Wildside Press in a signed, limited hardcover edition in 1991. More recently it was revived for Arkham House's *Cthulhu 2000*.

I'm happy with "The Barrens," but it's nothing like "The Thing on the Doorstep." That's the real thing. Read it (or reread it) when you get a chance.

THE BARRENS

1. In Search of a Devil

I shot my answering machine today. Took out the old twelve gauge my father left me, and blew it to pieces. A silly, futile gesture, I know, but it illustrates my present state of mind, I think.

And it felt good. If not for an answering machine, my life would be completely different now. I would have missed Jonathan Creighton's call. I'd be less wise but far, far happier. And I'd still have some semblance of order and meaning in my life.

He left an innocent enough message:

"The office of Kathleen McKelston and Associates! Sounds like big business! How's it going, Mac? This is John Creighton calling. I'm going to be in the area later this week and I'd like to see you. Lunch or dinner—whatever's better. Give me a buzz." And he left a number with a 212 area code.

So simple, so forthright, giving no hint of where it would lead.

You work your way through life day by day, learning how to play the game, carving out your niche, making a place for yourself. You have some good luck, some bad luck, sometimes you make your own luck, and along the way you begin to think that you've figured out some of the answers—not all of them, of course, but enough to make you feel that you've learned something, that you've got a handle on life and just might be able to get a decent ride out of it. You start to think you're in control. Then along comes someone like Jonathan Creighton and he smashes everything. Not just your plans, your hopes, your dreams, but *everything*, up to and including your sense of what is real and what is not.

I'd heard nothing from or about him since college, and had thought of him only occasionally until that day in early August when he called my office. Intrigued, I returned his call and set a date for lunch.

That was my first mistake. If I'd had the slightest inkling of where that simple lunch with an old college lover would lead, I'd have slammed down the phone and fled to Europe, or the Orient, anywhere where Jonathan Creighton wasn't.

We'd met at a freshmen mixer at Rutgers University back in the sixties. Maybe we each picked up subliminal cues—we called them "vibes" in those days—that told us we shared a rural upbringing. We didn't dress like it, act like it, or feel like it, but we were a couple of Jersey hicks. I came from the Pemberton area, Jon came from another rural zone, but in North Jersey, near a place called Gilead. Despite that link, we were polar opposites in most other ways. I'm still amazed we hit it off. I was career-oriented while Jon was . . . well, he was a flake. He earned the name Crazy Creighton and he lived up to it every day. He never stayed with one thing long enough to allow anyone to pin him down. Always on to the Next New Thing before the crowd had tuned into it, *always* into the exotic and esoteric. Looking for the Truth, he'd say.

And as so often happens with people who are incompatible in so many ways, we found each other irresistible and fell madly in love.

Sophomore year we found an apartment off campus and moved in together. It was my first affair, and not at all a tranquil one. I read the strange books he'd find and I kept up with his strange hours, but I put my foot down when it came to the Pickman prints. There was something deeply disturbing about those paintings that went beyond their gruesome subject matter. Jon didn't fight me on it. He just smiled sadly in his condescending way, as if disappointed that I had missed the point, and rolled them up and put them away.

The thing that kept us together—at least for the year we were together—was our devotion to personal autonomy. We spent weeks of nights talking about how we had to take complete control of our own lives, and brainstorming how we were going to go about it. It seems so silly now, but that was the sixties, and we really discussed those sorts of things back then.

We lasted sophomore year and then we fell apart. It might have gone on longer if Creighton hadn't got in with the druggies. That was the path toward loss of *all* autonomy as far as I was concerned, but Creighton said you can't be free until you know what's real. And if drugs might reveal the Truth, he had to try them. Which was hippie bullshit as far as I was concerned. After that, we rarely ran into each other. He wound up living alone off campus in his senior year. Somehow he managed to graduate, with a degree in anthropology, and that was the last I'd heard of him.

But that doesn't mean he hadn't left his mark.

I suppose I'm what you might call a feminist. I don't belong to NOW and I don't march in the streets, but I don't let anyone leave footprints on my back simply because I'm a woman. I believe in myself and I guess I owe some of that to Jonathan Creighton. He always treated me as an equal. He never made an issue of it—it was simply implicit in his attitude that I was intelligent, competent, worthy of respect, able to stand on my own. It helped shape me. And I'll always revere him for that.

Lunch. I chose Rosario's on the Point Pleasant Beach side of the Manasquan Inlet, not so much for its food as for the view. Creighton was late and that didn't terribly surprise me. I didn't mind. I sipped a chablis spritzer and watched the party boats roll in from their half-day runs of bottom fishing. Then a voice with echoes of familiarity broke through my thoughts.

"Well, Mac, I see you haven't changed much."

I turned and was shocked at what I saw. I barely recognized Creighton. He'd always been thin to the point of emaciation. Could the plump, bearded, almost cherubic figure standing before me now be—?

"Jon? Is that you?"

"The one and only," he said and spread his arms.

We embraced briefly, then took our seats in a booth by the window. As he squeezed into the far side of the table, he called the waitress over and pointed to my glass.

"Two Lites for me and another of those for her."

At first glance I'd thought that Creighton's extra poundage made him look healthy for the first time in his life. His hair was still thick and dark brown, but despite his round, rosy cheeks, his eyes were sunken and too bright. He seemed jovial but I sensed a grim undertone. I wondered if he was still into drugs.

"Almost a quarter century since we were together," he said. "Hard to believe it's been that long. The years look as if they've been kind to you."

As far as looks go, I suppose that's true. I don't dye my hair, so there's a little gray tucked in with the red. But I've always had a young face. I don't wear makeup—with my high coloring and freckles, I don't need it.

"And you."

Which wasn't actually true. His open shirt collar was frayed and looked as if this might be the third time he'd worn it since it was last washed. His tweed sport coat was worn at the elbows and a good two sizes too small for him.

We spent the drinks, appetizers, and most of the entreées catching up on each other's lives. I told him about my small accounting firm, my marriage, my recent divorce.

"No children?"

I shook my head. The marriage had gone sour, the divorce had been a nightmare. I wanted off the subject.

"But enough about me," I said. "What have you been up to?"

"Would you believe clinical psychology?"

"No," I said, too shocked to lie. "I wouldn't."

The Jonathan Creighton I'd known had been so eccentric, so out of step, so self-absorbed, I couldn't imagine him as a psychotherapist. Jonathan Creighton helping other people get their lives together—it was almost laughable.

He was the one laughing, however—good-naturedly, too.

"Yeah. It *is* hard to believe, but I went on to get a Master's, and then a Ph.D. Actually went into practice."

His voice trailed off.

"You're using the past tense," I said.

"Right. It didn't work out. The practice never got off the ground. But the problem was really within myself. I was using a form of reality therapy but it never worked as it should. And finally I realized why: I don't know—really *know*—what reality is. Nobody does."

This had an all too familiar ring to it. I tried to lighten things up before they got too heavy.

"Didn't someone once say that reality is what trips you up whenever you walk around with your eyes closed?"

Creighton's smile showed a touch of the old condescension that so infuriated some people.

"Yes, I suppose someone would say something like that. Anyway, I decided to go off and see if I could find out what reality really was. Did a lot of traveling. Wound up in a place called Miskatonic University. Ever heard of it?"

"In Massachusetts, isn't it?"

"That's the one. In a small town called Arkham. I hooked up with the anthropology department there—that was my undergraduate major, after all. But now I've left academe to write a book."

"A book?"

This was beginning to sound like a pretty disjointed life. But that shouldn't have surprised me.

"What a deal!" he said, his eyes sparkling. "I've got grants from Rutgers, Princeton, the American Folklore Society, the New Jersey Historical Society, and half a dozen others, just to write a book!"

"What's it about?"

"The origins of folktales. I'm going to select a few and trace them back to their roots. That's where you come in."

"Oh?"

"I'm going to devote a significant chapter to the Jersey Devil."

"There've been whole books written about the Jersey Devil. Why don't you—"

"I want real sources for this, Mac. Primary all the way. Nothing second-hand. This is going to be definitive."

"What can I do for you?"

"You're a Piney, aren't you?"

Resentment flashed through me. Even though people nowadays described themselves as "Piney" with a certain amount of pride, and I'd even seen bumper stickers touting "Piney Power," some of us still couldn't help bristling when an outsider said it. When I was a kid it was always used as a pejorative. Like "clam-digger" here on the coast. Fighting words. Officially it referred to the multigenerational natives of the great Pine Barrens that ran south from Route 70 all the way down to the lower end of the state. I've always hated the term. To me it was the equivalent of calling someone a redneck.

Which, to be honest, wasn't so far from the truth. The true Pineys are poor rural folk, often working truck farms and doing menial labor in the berry fields and cranberry bogs—a lot of them do indeed have red necks. Many are uneducated, or at best undereducated. Those who can afford wheels drive the prototypical battered pickup with the gun rack in the rear window. They even speak with an accent that sounds southern. They're Jersey hillbillies. Country bumpkins in the very heart of the industrial Northeast. Anachronisms.

Pineys.

"Who told you that?" I said as levelly as I could.

"You did. Back in school."

"Did I?"

It shook me to see how far I'd traveled from my roots. As a scared, naive, self-deprecating frosh at Rutgers I probably had indeed referred to myself as a Piney. Now I never mentioned the word, not in reference to myself or anyone else. I was a college-educated woman; I was a respected professional who spoke with a colorless Northeast accent. No one in his right mind would consider me a Piney.

"Well, that was just a gag," I said. "My family roots are back in the Pine Barrens, but I am by no stretch of the imagination a Piney. So I doubt I can help you."

"Oh, but you can! The McKelston name is big in the Barrens. Everybody knows it. You've got plenty of relatives there."

"Really? How do you know?"

Suddenly he looked sheepish.

"Because I've been into the Barrens a few times now. No one will open up to me. I'm an outsider. They don't trust me. Instead of answering my questions, they play games with me. They say they don't know what I'm talking about but they know someone who might, then they send me driving in circles. I was lost out there for two solid days last month. And believe me, I was getting scared. I thought I'd never find my way out."

"You wouldn't be the first. Plenty of people, many of them experienced hunters, have gone into the Barrens and never been seen again. You'd better stay out."

His hand darted across the table and clutched mine.

"You've got to help me, Kathy. My whole future hinges on this."

I was shocked. He'd always called me "Mac." Even in bed back in our college days he'd never called me "Kathy." Gently, I pulled my hand free, saying, "Come on, Jon—"

He leaned back and stared out the window at the circling gulls.

The Barrens   195

"If I do this right, do something really definitive, it may get me back into Miskatonic where I can finish my doctoral thesis."

I was immediately suspicious.

"I thought you said you 'left' Miskatonic, Jon. Why can't you get back in without it?"

" 'Irregularities,' " he said, still not looking at me. "The old farts in the antiquities department didn't like where my research was leading me."

"This 'reality' business?"

"Yes."

"They told you that?"

Now he looked at me.

"Not in so many words, but I could tell." He leaned forward. His eyes were brighter than ever. "They've got books and manuscripts locked in huge safes there, one-of-a-kind volumes from times most scholars think of as prehistory. I managed to get a pass, a forgery, that got me into the vaults. It's incredible what they have there, Mac. *Incredible!* I've got to get back there. Will you help me?"

His intensity was startling. And tantalizing.

"What would I have to do?"

"Just accompany me into the Pine Barrens. Just for a few trips. If I can use you as a reference, I know they'll talk to me about the Jersey Devil. After that, I can take it on my own. All I need is some straight answers from these people and I'll have my primary sources. I may be able to track a folk myth to its very roots! I'll give you credit in the book, I'll pay you, anything, Mac, just don't leave me twisting in the wind!"

He was positively frantic by the time he finished speaking.

"Easy, Jon. Easy. Let me think."

Tax season was over and I had a loose schedule for the summer. And even if I was looking ahead to a tight schedule, so what? Frankly, the job wasn't anywhere near as satisfying as it once had been. The challenge of overcoming the business community's prejudice and doubts about a woman accountant, the thrill of building a string of clients, that was all over. Everything was mostly routine now. Plus, I no longer had a husband. No children to usher toward adulthood. I had to admit that my life was pretty empty at that moment. And so was I. Why not take a little time to inspect my roots and help Crazy Creighton put his life on track, if such a thing was possible? In the bargain maybe I could gain a little perspective on my own life.

"All right, Jon," I said. "I'll do it."

Creighton's eyes lit with true pleasure, a glow distinct from the feverish intensity since he'd sat down. He thrust both his hands toward me.

"I could kiss you, Mac! I can't tell you how much this means to me! You have no idea how important this is!"

He was right about that. No idea at all.

2. The Pine Barrens

Two days later we were ready to make our first foray into the woods.

Creighton was wearing a safari jacket when he picked me up in a slightly battered four-wheel-drive Jeep Wrangler.

"This isn't Africa we're headed for," I told him.

"I know. I like pockets. They hold all sorts of things."

I glanced in the rear compartment. He was surprisingly well equipped. I noticed a water cooler, a food chest, backpacks, and what looked like sleeping bags. I hoped he wasn't harboring any romantic ideas. I'd just split from one man and I wasn't looking for another, especially not Jonathan Creighton.

"I promised to help you look around. I didn't say anything about camping out."

He laughed. "I'm with you. Holiday Inn is my idea of roughing it. I was never a Boy Scout, but I do believe in being prepared. I've already been lost once in there."

"And we can do without that happening again. Got a compass?"

He nodded. "And maps. Even have a sextant."

"You actually know how to use one?"

"I learned."

I dimly remember being bothered then by his having a sextant, and not being quite sure why. Before I could say anything else, he tossed me the keys.

"You're the Piney. You drive."

"Still Mr. Macho, I see."

He laughed. I drove.

It's easy to get into the Pine Barrens from northern Ocean County. You just get on Route 70 and head west. About halfway between the Atlantic Ocean and Philadelphia, say, near a place known as Ongs Hat, you turn left. And wave bye-bye to the twentieth century, and civilization as you know it.

How do I describe the Pine Barrens to someone who's never been there? First of all, it's big. You have to fly over it in a small plane to appreciate just how big. The Barrens runs through seven counties, takes up one-fourth of the state, but since Jersey's not a big state, that doesn't tell the story. How does 2,000 square miles sound? Or a million acres? Almost the size of Yosemite National Park. Does that give you an idea of its vastness?

How do I describe what a wilderness this is? Maps will give you a clue. Look at a road map of New Jersey. If you don't happen to have one handy, imagine an oblong platter of spaghetti; now imagine what it looks like after someone's devoured most of the spaghetti out of the middle of the lower half, leaving only a few strands crossing the exposed plate. Same thing with a population density map—a big gaping hole in the southern half where the Pine Barrens sits. New Jersey is the most densely populated state in the U. S., averaging a thousand bodies per square mile. But the New York City suburbs in north Jersey teem with forty thousand per square mile. After you account for the crowds along the coast and in the cities and towns along the western interstate corridor, there aren't too many people left over when you get to the Pine Barrens. I've heard of an area of over a hundred thousand acres—that's in the neighborhood of 160 square miles—in the south-central Barrens with twenty-one known inhabitants. *Twenty-one.* One human being per eight square miles in an area that lies on the route through Boston, New York, Philadelphia, Baltimore, and D. C.

Even when you take a turn off one of the state or federal roads that cut through the Barrens, you feel the isolation almost immediately. The forty-foot scrub pines close in behind you and quietly but oh so effectively cut you off from the rest of the world. I'll bet there are people who've lived to ripe old ages in the Barrens who have never seen a paved road. Conversely, there are no complete topographical maps of the Barrens because there are vast areas that no human eyes have ever seen.

Are you getting the picture?

"Where do we start?" Creighton asked as we crawled past the retirement villages along Route 70. This had been an empty stretch of road when I was a kid. Now it was Wrinkle City.

"We start at the capital."

"Trenton? I don't want to go to Trenton."

"Not the state capital. The capital of the pines. Used to be called Sha-mong Station. Now it's known as Chatsworth."

He pulled out his map and squinted through the index.

"Oh, right. I see it. Right smack in the middle of the Barrens. How big is it?"

"A veritable Piney megalopolis, my friend. Three hundred souls."

Creighton smiled, and for a second or two he seemed almost . . . innocent.

"Think we can get there before rush hour?"

3. Jasper Mulliner

I stuck to the main roads, taking 70 to 72 to 563, and we were there in no time.

"You'll see something here you won't see anyplace else in the Barrens," I said as I drove down Chatsworth's main street.

"Electricity?" Creighton said.

He didn't look up from the clutter of maps on his lap. He'd been fol-lowing our progress on paper, mile by mile.

"No. Lawns. Years ago a number of families decided they wanted grass in their front yards. There's no topsoil to speak of out here; the ground's mostly sand. So they trucked in loads of topsoil and seeded themselves some lawns. Now they've got to cut them."

I drove past the general store and its three gas pumps out on the sidewalk.

"*Esso,*" Creighton said, staring at the sign over the pumps. "That says it all, doesn't it."

"That it do."

We continued on until we came to a sandy lot occupied by a single trailer. No lawn here.

"Who's this?" Creighton said, folding up his maps as I hopped out of the Wrangler.

"An old friend of the family."

This was Jasper Mulliner's place. He was some sort of an uncle—on my mother's side, I think. But distant blood relationships are nothing special in the Barrens. An awful lot of people are related in one way or another. Some said he was a descendant of the notorious bandit of the pines, Joseph Mulliner. Jasper had never confirmed that, but he'd never denied it, either.

I knocked on the door, wondering who would answer. I wasn't even sure Jasper was still alive. But when the door opened, I immediately recognized the grizzled old head that poked through the opening.

"You're not sellin' anything, are you?" he said.

"Nothing, Mr. Mulliner," I said. "I'm Kathleen McKelston. I don't know if you remember me, but—"

His eyes lit as his face broke into a toothless grin.

"Danny's girl? The one who got the college scholarship? Sure I remember you! Come on in!"

Jasper was wearing khaki shorts, a sleeveless orange T-shirt, and duck boots—no socks. His white hair was neatly combed and he was freshly shaved. He'd been a salt hay farmer in his younger days and his hands were still callused from it. He'd moved on to overseeing a cranberry bog in his later years. His skin was a weathered brown and looked tougher than saddle leather. The inside of the trailer reminded me more of a low-ceilinged freight car than a home, but it was clean. The presence of the television set told me he had electricity but I saw no phone nor any sign of running water.

I introduced him to Creighton and we settled onto a three-legged stool and a pair of ladderback chairs as I spent the better part of half an hour telling him about my life since leaving the Barrens and answering questions about my mother and how she was doing since my father died. Then he went into a soliloquy about what a great man my father was. I let him run on, pretending to be listening, but turning my mind to other things. Not because I disagreed with him, but because it had been barely a year since Dad had dropped dead and I was still hurting.

Dad had not been your typical Piney. Although he loved the Barrens as much as anyone else who grew up here, he'd known there was a bigger though not necessarily better life beyond them. That bigger world didn't interest him in the least, but just because he was content with where he was didn't mean that I'd be. He wanted to allow his only child a choice. He knew I'd need a decent education if that choice was to be meaningful. And to provide that education for me, he did what few Pineys like to do: He took a steady job.

That's not to say that Pineys are afraid of hard work. Far from it. They'll break their backs at any job they're doing. It's simply that they don't like to be tied down to the same job day after day, month after month. Most of them have grown up flowing with the cycle of the Barrens. Spring is for gathering sphagnum moss to sell to the florists and nurseries. In June and July they work the blueberry and huckleberry fields. In the fall they move into the bogs for the cranberry harvest. And in the cold of winter they cut cordwood, or cut holly and mistletoe, or go "pineballing"—collecting pine cones to sell. None of this is easy work. But it's not the same work. And that's what matters.

The Piney attitude toward jobs is the most laid back you'll ever encounter. That's because they're in such close harmony with their surroundings. They know that with all the pure water all around them and flowing beneath their feet, they'll never go thirsty. With all the wild vegetation around them, they'll never lack for fruit and vegetables. And whenever the meat supply gets low, they pick up a rifle and head into the brush for squirrel, rabbit, or venison, whatever the season.

When I neared fourteen, my father bit the bullet and moved us close to Pemberton where he took a job with a well-drilling crew. It was steady work, with benefits, and I got to go to Pemberton High. He pushed me to take my schoolwork seriously, and I did. My high grades coupled with my gender and low socioeconomic status earned me a full ride—room, board, and tuition—at Rutgers. As soon as that was settled, he was ready to move back into the Barrens. But my mother had become used to the conveniences and amenities of town living. She wanted to stay in Pemberton. So they stayed.

I still can't help but wonder whether Dad might have lived longer if he'd moved back into the woods. I've never mentioned that to my mother, of course.

When Jasper paused, I jumped in: "My friend Jon's doing a book and he's devoting a chapter to the Jersey Devil."

"Is that so?" Jasper said. "And you brought him to me, did you?"

"Well, Dad always told me there weren't many folks in the Pines you didn't know, and not much that went on that you didn't know about."

The old man beamed and did what many Pineys do: He repeated a phrase three times.

"Did he now? Did he now? Did he really now? Ain't that somethin'! I do believe that calls for a little jack."

As Jasper turned and reached into his cupboard, Creighton threw me a questioning look.

"Applejack," I told him.

He smiled. "Ah. Jersey lightning."

Jasper turned back with three glasses and a brown quart jug. With a practiced hand he poured two fingers' worth into each and handed them to us. The tumblers were smudged and maybe a little crusty, but I wasn't worried about germs. There's never been a germ that could stand up to straight jack from Jasper Mulliner's still. I remember siphoning some off from my father's jug and sneaking off into the brush at night to meet a couple of my girlfriends from high school, and we'd sit around and sing and get plastered.

I could tell by the way the vapor singed my nasal membranes that this was from a potent batch. I neglected to tell Creighton to go slow. As I took a respectful sip, he tossed his off. I watched him wince as he swallowed, saw his face grow red and his eyes begin to water.

"Whoa!" he said hoarsely. "You could etch glass with that stuff!" He caught Jasper looking at him sideways and held out his glass. "But delicious! Could I have just a drop more?"

"Help yourself," Jasper said, pouring him another couple of fingers. "Plenty more where this came from. But down it slow. This here's sippin' whiskey. You go puttin' too much of it down like that and you'll get apple palsy. Slow and leisurely does it when you're drinking Gus Sooy's best."

"This isn't yours?" I said.

"Naw! I stopped that long time ago. Too much trouble and gettin' too civilized 'round here. Besides, Gus's jack is as good as mine ever was. Maybe better."

He set the jug on the floor between us.

"About that Jersey Devil," I said, prompting him before he got off on another tangent.

"Right. The ol' Devil. He used to be known as the Leeds' Devil. I'm sure you've heard various versions of the story, but I'll tell you the real one. That ol' devil's been around a spell, better'n two and a half centuries. All started back around 1730 or so. That was when Mrs. Leeds of Estellville found herself in the family way for the thirteenth time. Now she was so fed up and angry about this that she cried out, 'I hope this time it's the Devil!' Well now, Someone must've been listenin' that night, because she got her wish. When that thirteenth baby was born, it was an ugly-faced thing, born with teeth like no one'd ever seen before, and it had a curly, sharp-pointed tail, and leathery wings like a bat. It bit its mother and flew out through the window. It grew up out in the pine wilds, stealing and eating chickens and small piglets at first, then graduating to cows, children, even growed men. All they ever found of its victims was their bones, and they was chipped and nicked by powerful sharp teeth. Some say it's dead now, some say it'll never die. Every so often someone says he shot and killed it, but most folks think it can't be killed. It gets blamed for every missing chicken and every pig or cow that wanders off, and so after a while you think it's just an ol' Piney folktale. But it's out there. It's out there. It's surely out there."

"Have you ever seen it?" Creighton asked. He was sipping his jack with respect this time around.

"Saw its shadow. It was up on Apple Pie Hill, up at the top, in the days before they put up the firetower. Before you was born, Kathleen. I'd been out doing some summer hunting, tracking a big ol' stag. You know what a climb Apple Pie is, dontcha?"

I nodded. "Sure do."

It didn't look like much of a hill. No cliffs or precipices, just a slow incline that seemed to go on forever. You didn't have to do much more than walk to get to the top, but you were bushed when you finally reached it.

"Anyways, I was about three-quarters the way up when it got too dark to do any more tracking. Well, I was tired and it was a warm summer night so's I just settled down on the pine needles and decided I'd spend the night. I had some jerky and some pone and my jug." He pointed to the floor. "Just like that one. You two be sure to help yourselves, hear me?"

"I'm fine," I said.

I saw Creighton reach for the jug. He could always handle a lot. I was already feeling my two sips. It was getting warmer in here by the minute.

"Anyways," Jasper went on, "I was sitting there chewing and sipping when I saw some pine lights."

Creighton started in midpour and spilled some applejack over his hand. He was suddenly very alert, almost tense.

"Pine lights?" he said. "You saw pine lights? Where were they?"

"So you've heard of the pine lights, have you?"

"I sure have. I've been doing my homework. Where did you see them? Were they moving?"

"They were streaming across the crest of Apple Pie Hill, just skirting the tops of the trees."

Creighton put his tumbler down and began fumbling with his map.

"Apple Pie Hill . . . I remember seeing that somewhere. Here it is." He jabbed his finger down on the map as if he were driving a spike into the hill. "Okay. So you were on Apple Pie Hill when you saw the pine lights. How many were there?"

"A whole town's worth of them, maybe a hunnert, more than I've ever seen before or since."

"How fast were they going?"

"Different speeds. Different sizes. Some gliding peacefully, some zipping along, moving past the slower ones. Looked like the turnpike on a summer weekend."

Creighton leaned forward, his eyes brighter than ever.

"Tell me about it."

Something about Creighton's intensity disturbed me. All of a sudden he'd become an avid listener. He'd been listening politely to Jasper's retelling of the Jersey Devil story, but he'd seemed more interested in the applejack than in the tale. He hadn't bothered to check the location of Apple Pie Hill when Jasper had said he'd seen the Jersey Devil there, but he'd been in a rush to find it at the first mention of the pine lights.

The pine lights. I'd heard of them but I'd never seen one. People tended to catch sight of them on summer nights, mostly toward the end of the season. Some said it was ball lightning or some form of St. Elmo's fire, some called it swamp gas, and some said it was the souls of dead Pineys coming back for periodic visits. Why was Creighton so interested?

"Well," Jasper said, "I spotted one or two moving along the crest of the hill and didn't think too much of it. I spot a couple just about every summer. Then I saw a few more. And then a few more. I got a little excited and decided to get up to the top of Apple Pie and see what was going on. I was breathing hard by the time I got there. I stopped and looked up and there they was, flowing along the treetops forty feet above me, pale yellow, some Ping-Pong size and some big as beach balls, all moving in the same direction."

"What direction?" Creighton said. If he leaned forward any farther, he was going to fall off his stool. "Which way were they going?"

"I'm getting to that, son," Jasper said. "Just hold your horses. So as I was saying, I was standing there watching them flow against the clear night sky, and I was feeling this strange tightness in my chest, like I was witnessing something I shouldn't. But I couldn't tear my eyes away. And then they thinned out and was gone. They'd all passed. So I did something crazy. I climbed a tree to see where they was going. Something in my gut told me not to, but I was filled with this wonder, almost like holy rapture. So I climbed as far as I could, until the tree started to bend with my weight and the branches got too thin to hold me. And I watched them go. They was strung out in a long trail, dipping down when the land dipped down, and moving up when the land rose, moving just above the tops of the pines, like they was being pulled along strings." He looked at Creighton. "And they was heading southwest."

"You're sure of that?"

Jasper looked insulted. "Course I'm sure of that. Bear Swamp Hill was behind my left shoulder, and everybody knows Bear Swamp is east of Apple Pie. Those lights was on their way southwest."

"And this was the summer?"

"Nigh on to Labor Day, if I 'member correct."

"And you were on the crest of Apple Pie Hill?"

"The tippy top."

"Great!" He began folding his map.

"I thought you wanted to hear about the Jersey Devil."

"I do, I do."

"Then how come you're asking me all these questions about the lights and not asking me about my meeting with the Devil?"

I hid a smile. Jasper was as sharp as ever.

Creighton looked confused for a moment. An expression darted across his face. It was only there for a second, but I caught it. Furtiveness. Then he leaned forward and spoke to Jasper in a confidential tone.

"Don't tell anybody this, but I think they're connected. The pine lights and the Jersey Devil. Connected."

Jasper leaned back. "You know, you might have something there. Cause it was while I was up that tree that I spotted the ol' Devil himself. Or at least his shadow. I was watching the lights flow out of sight when I heard this noise in the brush. It had a slithery sound to it. I looked down and there was this dark shape moving below. And you know what? It was heading in the same direction as the lights. What do you think of that?"

Creighton's voice oozed sincerity.

"I think that's damn interesting, Jasper."

I thought they both were shoveling it, but I couldn't decide who was carrying the bigger load.

"But don't you go getting too interested in those pine lights, son. Gus Sooy says they're bad medicine."

"The guy who made this jack?" I said, holding up my empty tumbler.

"The very same. Gus says there's lots of pine light activity in his neighborhood every summer. Told me I was a fool for climbing that tree. Says he wouldn't get near one of those lights for all the tea in China."

I noticed that Creighton was tense again.

"Where's this Gus Sooy's neighborhood?" he said. "Does he live in Chatsworth?"

Jasper burst out laughing.

"Gus live in Chatsworth? That's a good 'un! Gus Sooy's an old Hessian who lives way out in the wildest part of the pines. Never catch him *near* a city like this!"

City? I didn't challenge him on that.

"Where do we find him then?" Creighton said, his expression like a kid who's been told there's a cache of M&M's hidden somewhere nearby.

"Not easy," Jasper said. "Gus done a good job of getting himself well away from everybody. He's well away. Yes, he's well away. But if you go down to Apple Pie Hill and head along the road there that runs along its south flank, and you follow that about two mile and turn south onto the sand road by Applegate's cranberry bog, then follow that for about ten-twelve mile till you come to the fork where you bear left, then go right again at the cripple beyond it, then it's a good ten mile down that road till you get to the big red cedar—"

Creighton was scribbling furiously.

"I'm not sure I know what a red cedar looks like," I said.

"You'll know it," Jasper said. "Its kind don't grow naturally around here. Gus planted it there a good many year ago so people could find their way to him. The *right* people," he said, eyeing Creighton. "People who want to buy his wares, if you get my meaning."

I nodded. I got his meaning: Gus made his living off his still.

"Anyways, you turn right at the red cedar and go to the end of the road. Then you've got to get out and walk about a third of the way up the hill. That's where you'll find Gus Sooy."

I tried to drive the route across a mental map in my head. I couldn't get there. My map was blank where he was sending us. But I was amazed at how far I did get. As a Piney, even a girl, you've got to develop a good sense of where you are, got to have a store of maps in your head that you can picture by reflex, otherwise you'll spend most of your time being lost. Even with a good library of mental maps, you'll still get lost occasionally. I could still travel my old maps. The skill must be like the proverbial bicycle— once you've learned, you never forget.

I had a sense that Gus Sooy's place was somewhere far down in Burling-ton County, near Atlantic County. But county lines don't mean much in the Pinelands.

"That's *really* in the middle of nowhere!" I said.

"That it is, Kathy, that it is. That it surely is. It's on the slope of Razor-back Hill."

Creighton shuffled through his maps again.

"Razorback . . . Razorback . . . there's no Razorback Hill here."

"That's because it ain't much of a hill. But it's there all right. Just 'cause it ain't on your diddly map don't mean it ain't there. Lots of things ain't on that map."

Creighton rose to his feet.

"Maybe we can run out there now and buy some of this applejack from him. What do you say, Mac?"

"We've got time."

I had a feeling he truly did want to buy some of Sooy's jack, but I was sure some questions about the pine lights would come up during the transaction.

"Better bring your own jugs if you're goin'," Jasper said. "Gus don't carry no spares. You can buy some from the Buzbys at the general store."

"Will do," I said.

I thanked him and promised I'd say hello to my mom for him, then I joined Creighton out at the Wrangler. He had one of his maps unfolded on the hood and was drawing a line southwest from Apple Pie Hill through the emptiest part of the Barrens.

"What's that for?" I asked.

"I don't know just yet. We'll see if it comes to mean anything."

It would. Sooner than either of us realized.

4. The Hessian

I bought a gallon-sized brown jug at the Chatsworth general store; Creighton bought two.

"I want this Sooy fellow to be *real* glad to see me!"

I drove us down 563, then off to Apple Pie Hill. We got south of it and began following Jasper's directions. Creighton read while I drove.

"What the hell's a cripple?" he said.

"That's a spong with no cedars."

"Ah! That clears up everything!"

"A spong is a low wet spot; if it's got cedars growing around it, it's a cripple. What could be clearer?"

"I'm not sure, but I know I'll think of something. By the way, why's this Sooy fellow called a Hessian? Mulliner doesn't really think he's—?"

"Of course not. Sooy's an old German name around the Pine Barrens. Comes from the Hessians who deserted the British Army and fled into the woods after the battle of Trenton."

"The Revolution."

"Sure. This sand road we're riding on now was here three hundred–odd years ago as a wagon trail. It probably hasn't changed any since. Might even have been used by the smugglers who used to unload freight in the marshes and move it overland through the Pines to avoid port taxes in New York and Philly. A lot of them settled in here. So did a good number of Tories and Loyalists who were chased from their land after the Revolution. Some of them probably arrived dressed in tar and feathers and little else. The Lenape Indians settled in here, too, so did Quakers who were kicked out of their churches for taking up arms during the Revolution."

Creighton laughed. "Sounds like Australia! Didn't anyone besides outcasts settle here?"

"Sure. Bog iron was a major industry. This was the center of the colonial iron production. Most of the cannonballs fired against the British in the Revolution and the War of 1812 were forged right here in the Pine Barrens."

"Where'd everybody go?"

"A place called Pittsburgh. There was more iron there and it was cheaper to produce. The furnaces here tried to shift over to glass production but they were running out of wood to keep them going. Each furnace consumed something like a thousand acres of pine a year. With the charcoal industry, the lumber industry, even the cedar shake industry all adding to the daily toll on the tree population, the Barrens couldn't keep up with the demand. The whole economy collapsed after the Civil War. Which probably saved the area from becoming a desert."

I noticed the underbrush between the ruts getting higher, slapping against the front bumper as we passed, a sure sign that not many people came this way. Then I spotted the red cedar. Jasper had been right—it didn't look like it belonged here. We turned right and drove until we came to a cul-de-sac at the base of a hill. Three rusting cars hugged the bushes along the perimeter.

"This must be the place," I said.

"This is not a place. This is *no*where."

We grabbed our jugs and walked up the path. About a third of the way up the slope we broke into a clearing with a slant-roofed shack in the far left corner. It looked maybe twenty feet on a side, and was covered with tarpaper that was peeling away in spots, exposing the plywood beneath. Somewhere behind the shack a dog had begun to bark.

Creighton said, "Finally!" and started forward.

I laid a hand on his arm.

"Call out first," I told him. "Otherwise we may be ducking buckshot."

He thought I was joking at first, then saw that I meant it.

"You're serious?"

"We're dressed like city folk. We could be revenuers. He'll shoot first and ask questions later."

"Hello in the house!" Creighton cried. "Jasper Mulliner sent us! Can we come up?"

A wizened figure appeared on the front step, a twelve gauge cradled in his arms.

"How'd he send you?"

"By way of the red cedar, Mr. Sooy!" I replied.

"C'mon up then!"

Where Jasper had been neat, Gus Sooy was slovenly. His white hair looked like a deranged bird had tried to nest in it; for a shirt he wore the stained top from a set of long johns and had canvas pants secured around his waist with coarse rope. His lower face was obscured by a huge white beard, stained around the mouth. An Appalachian Santa Claus, going to seed in the off-season.

We followed him into the single room of his home. The floor was covered with a mismatched assortment of throw rugs and carpet remnants. A bed sat in the far left corner, a kerosene stove was immediately to our right. Set about the room were a number of Aladdin lamps with the tall flues. Dominating the scene was a heavy-legged kitchen table with an enamel top.

We introduced ourselves and Gus said he'd met my father years ago.

"So what brings you two kids out here to see Gus Sooy?"

I had to smile, not just at the way he managed to ignore the jugs we were carrying, but at being referred to as a "kid." A long time since anyone had called me that. I wouldn't let anyone call me a "girl" these days, but somehow I didn't mind "kid."

"Today we tasted some of the best applejack in the world," Creighton said with convincing sincerity, "and Jasper told us you were the source." He slammed his two jugs on the table. "Fill 'em up!"

I placed my own jug next to Creighton's.

"I gotta warn you," Gus said. "It's five dollars a quart."

"Five dollars!" Creighton said.

"Yeah," Gus added quickly, "but seein' as you're buying so much at once—"

"Don't get me wrong, Mr. Sooy. I wasn't saying the price is too high. I was just shocked that you'd be selling such high-grade sipping whiskey for such a low price."

"You were?" The old man beamed with delight. "It is awful good, isn't it?"

"That it is, sir. That it is. That it surely is."

I almost burst out laughing. I don't know how Creighton managed to keep a straight face.

Gus held up a finger. "You kids stay right here. I'll dip into my stock and be back in a jiffy."

We both broke down into helpless laughter as soon as he was gone.

"You're laying it on awful thick," I said when I caught my breath.

"I know, but he's lapping up every bit."

Gus returned in a few minutes with two gallon jugs of his own.

"Hadn't we ought to test this first before you begin filling our jugs?" Creighton said.

"Not a bad idea. No, sir, not a bad idea. Not a bad idea at all."

Creighton produced some paper cups from one of the pockets in his safari jacket and placed them on the table. Gus poured. We all sipped.

"This is even smoother than what Jasper served us. How do you do it, Mr. Sooy?"

"That's a secret," he said with a wink as he brought out a funnel and began decanting from his jugs into ours.

I brought up Jon's book and Gus launched into a slightly different version of the Jersey Devil story, saying it was born in Leeds, which is at the opposite end of the Pine Barrens from Estellville. Otherwise the tales were almost identical.

"Jasper says he saw the Devil once," Creighton said as Gus topped off the last of our jugs.

"If he says he did, then he did. That'll be sixty dollar."

Creighton gave him three twenties.

"And now I'd like to buy you a drink, Mr. Sooy."

"Call me Gus. And I don't mind if I do."

Creighton was overly generous, I thought, with the way he filled the three paper cups. I didn't want any more, but I felt I had to keep up appearances. I sipped while the men quaffed.

"Jasper told us about the time he saw the Jersey Devil. He mentioned seeing pine lights at the same time."

I sensed rather than saw Gus stiffen.

"Is that so?"

"Yeah. He said you see pine lights around here all the time. Is that true?"

"You interested in pine lights or the Jersey Devil, boy?"

"Both. I'm interested in all the folktales of the Pines."

"Well, don't get too interested in the pine lights."

"Why not?"

"Just don't."

I watched Creighton tip his jug and refill Gus's cup.

"A toast!" Creighton said, lifting his cup. "To the Pine Barrens!"

"I'll drink to that!" Gus said, and drained his cup.

Creighton followed suit, causing his eyes to fill with tears. I sipped while he poured another round.

"To the Jersey Devil!" Creighton cried, hoisting his cup again.

And again they both tossed off their drinks. And then another round.

"To the pine lights!"

Gus wouldn't drink to that one. I was glad. I don't think either of them would have remained standing if he had.

"Have you seen any pine lights lately, Gus," Creighton said.

"You don't give up, do you, boy," the old man said.

"It's an affliction."

"So it is. All right. Sure. I see 'em all the time. Saw some last night."

"Really? Where?"

"None of your business."

"Why not?"

"Because you'll probably try to do something stupid like catch one, and then I'll be responsible for what happened to you and this young lady here. Not on my conscience, no thank you."

"I wouldn't dream of trying to catch one of those things!" Creighton said.

"Well, if you did you wouldn't be the first. Peggy Clevenger was the first." Gus lifted his head and looked at me. "You heard of Peggy Clevenger, ain't you, Miss McKelston?"

I nodded. "Sure. The Witch of the Pines. In the old days people used to put salt over their doors to keep her away."

Creighton began scribbling.

"No kidding? This is great! What about her and the pine lights?"

"Peggy was a Hessian, like me. Lived over in Pasadena. Not the California Pasadena, the Pines Pasadena. A few miles east of Mount Misery. The town's gone now, like it never been. But she lived thereabouts by herself in a small cabin, and people said she had all sorts of strange powers, like she could change her shape and become a rabbit or a snake. I don't know about that stuff, but I heard from someone who should know that she was powerful interested in the pine lights. She told this fella one day that she had caught one of the pine lights, put a spell on it, and brought it down."

Creighton had stopped writing. He was staring at Gus.

"How could she . . . ?"

"Don't know," Gus said, draining his cup and shaking his head. "But that very night her cabin burned to the ground. They found her blackened and burned body among the ashes the next morning. So I tell you, kids, it ain't a good idea to get too interested in the pine lights."

"I don't want to capture one," Creighton said. "I don't even want to see one. I just want to know where other people have seen them. How can that be dangerous?"

Gus thought about that. And while he was thinking, Creighton poured him another cupful.

"Don't s'pose it would do any harm to show you where they was," he said after a long slow sip.

"Then it's settled. Let's go."

We gathered up the jugs and headed out into the late afternoon sunshine. The fresh air was like a tonic. It perked me up but didn't dissipate the effects of all the jack I'd consumed.

When we reached the Wrangler, Creighton pulled out his sextant and compass.

"Before we go, there's something I've got to do."

Gus and I watched in silence as he took his sightings and scribbled in his notebook. Then he spread his map out on the hood again.

"What's up?" I said.

"I'm putting Razorback Hill on the map," he said.

He jotted his readings on the map and drew a circle. Before he folded everything up, I glanced over his shoulder and noticed that the line he had drawn from Apple Pie Hill ran right by the circle that was Razorback Hill.

"You through dawdlin?" Gus said.

"Sure am. You want to ride in front?"

"No thanks," Gus said, heading for the rusty DeSoto. "I'll drive myself and you kids follow."

I said, "Won't it be easier if we all go together?"

"Hell no! You kids have been drinkin'!"

When we stopped laughing, we pulled ourselves into the Wrangler and followed the old Hessian back up his private sand road.

5. The Firing Place

"I used to make charcoal here when I was young," Gus said.

We were standing in a small clearing surrounded by young pines. Before us was a shallow sandy depression, choked with weeds.

"This used to be my firing place. It was deeper then. I made some fine charcoal here before the big companies started selling their bags of 'brickettes.' " He fairly spat the word. "Ain't no way any one of those smelly little things was ever part of a tree, I'll tell you that."

"Is this where you saw the lights, Gus?" Creighton said. "Were they moving?"

Gus said, "You got a one-track mind, don't you, boy?" He glanced around. "Yeah, this is where I saw them. Saw them here last night and I saw them here fifty years ago, and I seen them near about every summer in between. Lots of memories here. I remember how while I was letting my charcoal burn I'd use the time to hunt up box turtles."

"And sell them as snail hunters?" I said.

I'd heard of box turtle hunting—another Pinelands mini-industry—but I'd never met anyone who'd actually done it.

"Sure. Folks in Philadelphia buy all I could find. They liked to let them loose in their cellars to keep the snails and slugs under control."

"The lights, Gus," Creighton said. "Which way were they going?"

"They was goin' the same way they always went when I seen them here. That way."

He was pointing southeast.

"Are you sure?"

"Sure as shit, boy." Gus's tone was getting testy, but he quickly turned to me. " 'Scuse me, miss," then back to Creighton. "I was standing back there right where my car is when about a half dozen of them swooped in low right overhead—not a hunting swoop, but a floaty sort of swoop—and traveled away over that pitch pine there with the split top."

"Good!" said Creighton, eyeing the sky.

A thick sheet of cloud was pulling up from the west, encroaching on the sinking sun. Out came the sextant and compass. Creighton took his readings, wrote his numbers, then took a bearing on the tree Gus had pointed out. A slow, satisfied smile crept over his face as he drew the latest line on his map. He folded it up before I had a chance to see where that line went. I didn't have to see. His next question told me.

"Say, Gus," he said offhandedly. "What's on the far side of Razorback Hill?"

Gus turned on Creighton like an angry bear.

"Nothing! There's nothing there! So don't you even think about going over there!"

Creighton's smile was amused. "I was only asking. No harm in a little question, is there?"

"There is. There is. Yes, there surely is! Especially when those questions is the wrong ones. And you've been asking a whole lot of wrong questions, boy. Questions that's gonna get you in a whole mess of bad trouble if you don't get smart and learn that certain things is best left alone. You hear me?"

He sounded like a character from one of those old Frankenstein movies.

"I hear you," Creighton said, "and I appreciate your concern. But can you tell me the best way to get to the other side of that hill?"

Gus threw up his hands with an angry growl.

"That's it! I'm havin' no more to do with the two of you! I've already told you too much as it is." He turned to me, his eyes blazing. "And you, Miss McKelston, you get yourself away from this boy. He's headed straight to hell!"

With that he turned and headed for his car. He jumped in, slammed the door, and roared away with a spray of sand.

"I don't think he likes me," Creighton said.

"He seemed genuinely frightened," I told him.

Creighton shrugged and began packing away his sextant.

"Maybe he really believes in the Jersey Devil," he said. "Maybe he thinks it lives on the other side of Razorback Hill."

"I don't know about that. I got the impression he thinks the Jersey Devil is something to tell tall tales about while sitting around the stove and sipping jack. But those pine lights . . . he's scared of them."

"Just swamp gas, I'm sure," Creighton said.

Suddenly I was furious. Maybe it was all the jack I'd consumed, or maybe it was his attitude, but I think at that particular moment it was mostly his line of bull.

"Cut it, Jon!" I said. "If you really believe they're swamp gas, why are you tracking them on your map? You got me to guide you out here, so let's have it straight. What's going on?"

"I don't know what's going on, Mac. If I did, I wouldn't be here. Isn't that obvious? These pine lights mean something. Whether or not they're connected to the Jersey Devil, I don't know. Maybe they have a hallucinatory effect on people—after they pass overhead, people think they see things. I'm trying to establish a pattern."

"And after you've established this pattern, what do you think you'll find?"

"Maybe Truth," he said. "Reality. Who knows? Maybe the meaning—or meaninglessness—of life."

He looked at me with eyes so intense, so full of longing that my anger evaporated.

"Jon . . . ?"

His expression abruptly shifted back to neutral and he laughed.

"Don't worry, Mac. It's only me, Crazy Creighton, putting you on again. Let's have another snort of Gus Sooy's best and head for civilization. Okay?"

"I've had enough for the day. The *week*!"

"You don't mind if I partake, do you?"

"Help yourself."

I didn't know how he could hold so much.

While Creighton uncorked his jug, I strolled about the firing place to clear my fuzzy head. The sky was fully overcast now and the temperature was dropping to a more comfortable level.

He had everything packed away by the time I completed the circle.

"Want me to drive?" he said, tossing his paper cup onto the sand.

Normally I would have picked it up—there was something sacrilegious about leaving a Dixie cup among the pines—but I was afraid to bend over that far, afraid I'd keep on going head-first into the sand and become litter myself.

"I'm okay," I said. "You'll get us lost."

We had traveled no more than a hundred feet or so when I realized that I didn't know this road. But I kept driving. I hadn't been paying close attention while following Gus here, but I was pretty sure it wouldn't be long before I'd come to a fork or a cripple or a bog that I recognized, and then we'd be home free.

It didn't quite work out that way. I drove for maybe five miles or so, winding this way and that with the roads, making my best guess when we came to a fork—and we came to plenty of those—and generally trying to keep us heading in the same general direction. I thought I was doing a pretty good job until we drove through an area of young pines that looked familiar. I stopped the Wrangler.

"Jon," I said. "Isn't this—?"

"Damn right it is!" he said, pointing to the sand beside the road. "We're back at Gus's firing place! There's my Dixie cup!"

I turned the Jeep around and headed back the way I came.

"What are you doing?" Creighton said.

"Making sure I don't make the same mistake twice!" I told him.

I didn't know how I could have driven in a circle. I usually had an excellent sense of direction. I blamed it on too much Jersey lightning and on the thickly overcast sky. Without the sun as a marker, I'd been unable to keep us on course. But that would change here and now. I'd get us out of here this time around.

Wrong.

After a good forty-five minutes of driving, I was so embarrassed when I recognized the firing place again that I actually accelerated as we passed through, hoping Creighton wouldn't recognize the spot in the thickening dusk. But I wasn't quick enough.

"Hold it!" he cried. "Hold it just a damn minute! There's my cup again! We're right back where we started!"

"Jon," I said, "I don't understand it. Something's wrong."

"You're stewed, that's what's wrong!"

"I'm not!"

I truly believed I wasn't. I'd been feeling the effects of the jack before, true, but my head was clear now. I was sure I'd been heading due east, or at least pretty close to it. How I'd come full circle again was beyond me.

Creighton jumped out of his seat and came around the front of the Wrangler.

"Over you go, Mac. It's my turn."

I started to protest, then thought better of it. I'd blown it twice already. Maybe my sense of direction had fallen prey to the "apple palsy," as it was known. I lifted myself over the stick shift and dropped into the passenger seat.

"Be my guest."

Creighton drove like a maniac, seemingly choosing forks at random.

"Do you know where you're going?" I said.

"Yeah, Mac," he said. "I'm going whichever way you *didn't*! I think."

As darkness closed in and he turned on the headlights, I noticed that the trees were thinning out and the underbrush was closing in, rising to eight feet or better on either side of us. Creighton pulled off to the side at a widening of the road.

"You should stay on the road," I told him.

"I'm lost," he said. "We've got to think."

"Fine. But it's not as if somebody's going to be coming along and want to get by."

He laughed. "That's a fact!" He got out and looked up at the sky. "Damn! If it weren't for the clouds we could figure out where we are. Or least know where north is."

I looked around. We were surrounded by bushes. It was the Pine Barrens' equivalent of an English hedge maze. There wasn't a tree in sight. A tree can be almost as good as a compass—its moss faces north and its longest branches face south. Bushes are worse than useless for that, and the high ones only add to your confusion.

And we were confused.

"I thought Pineys never get lost," Creighton said.

"Everybody gets lost sooner or later out here."

"Well, what do Pineys do when they get lost?"

"They don't exhaust themselves or waste their gas by running around in circles. They hunker down and wait for morning."

"To hell with that!" Creighton said.

He threw the Wrangler into first and gunned it toward the road. But the vehicle didn't reach the road. It lurched forward and rocked back. He tried again and I heard the wheels spinning.

"Sugar!" I said.

Creighton looked at me and grinned.

"Stronger language is allowed and even encouraged in this sort of situation."

"I was referring to the sand."

"Don't worry. I've got four-wheel drive."

"Right. And all four wheels are spinning. We're in a patch of what's known as 'sugar sand.'"

He got out and pushed and rocked while I worked the gears and throttle, but I knew it was no use. We weren't going to get out of this superfine sand until we found some wood and piled it under the tires to give them some traction.

And we weren't going to be able to hunt up that kind of wood until morning.

I told Creighton that we'd only waste what gas we had left and that our best bet was to call it a night and pull out the sleeping bags. He seemed reluctant at first, worrying about deer ticks and catching Lyme disease, but he finally agreed.

He had no choice.

6. The Pine Lights

"I owe you one, Jon," I said.

"How was I to know we'd get lost?" he said defensively. "I don't like this any more than you!"

"No. You don't understand. I meant that in the good sense. I'm glad you talked me into coming with you."

I'd found us a small clearing not too far from the Jeep. It surrounded the gnarled trunk of an old lone pine that towered above the dominant brush.

We'd eaten the last of the sandwiches and now we sat on our respective bedrolls facing each other across the Coleman lamp sitting between us on the sand. Creighton was back to sipping his applejack. I would have killed, or at least maimed, for a cup of coffee.

I watched his face in the lamplight. His expression was puzzled.

"You must still be feeling the effects of that Jersey lightning you had this afternoon," he said.

"No. I'm perfectly sober. I've been sitting here realizing that I'm glad to be back. I've had a feeling for years that something's been missing from my life. Never had an inkling as to what it was until now. But this is it. I'm . . ." My throat constricted around the word. "I'm home."

It wasn't the jack talking, it was my heart. I'd learned something today. I'd learned that I loved the Pine Barrens. And I loved its people. So rich in history, so steeped in its own lore, somehow surviving untainted in the heart of twentieth-century urban madness. I'd turned my back on it. Why? Too proud? Too good for it now? Maybe I'd thought I'd pulled myself up by my bootstraps and gone on to bigger and better things. I could see that I hadn't. I'd taken the girl out of the Pinelands but I hadn't taken the Pinelands out of the girl.

I promised myself to come back here again. Often. I was going to look up my many relatives, renew old ties. I wasn't ready to move back here, and perhaps I never would, but I'd never turn my back on the Pinelands again.

Creighton raised his cup to me.

"I envy anyone who's found the missing piece. I'm still looking for mine."

"You'll find it," I said, crawling into my bedroll. "You've just got to keep your eyes open. Sometimes it's right under your nose."

"Go to sleep, Mac. You're starting to sound like Dorothy from *The Wizard of Oz*."

I smiled at that. For a moment there he was very much like the Jonathan Creighton I'd fallen in love with. As I closed my eyes, I saw him pull out a pair of binoculars and begin scanning the cloud-choked sky. I knew what he was looking for, and I was fairly confident he'd never find them.

It must have been a while later when I awoke, because the sky had cleared and the stars were out when Creighton's shouts yanked me to a sitting position.

"They're coming! Look at them, Mac! My God, they're coming!"

Creighton was standing on the far side of the lamp, pointing off to my left. I followed the line of his arm and saw nothing.

"What are you talking about?"

"Stand up, damn it! They're coming! There must be a dozen of them!"

I struggled to my feet and froze.

The starlit underbrush stretched away in a gentle rise for maybe a mile or two in the direction he was pointing, broken only occasionally by the angular shadows of the few scattered trees. And coming our way over that broad expanse, skimming along at treetop level, was an oblong cluster of faintly glowing lights. *Lights.* That's what they were. Not glowing spheres. Not UFOs or any of that nonsense. They had no discernible substance. They were just light. Globules of light.

I felt my hackles rise at the sight of them. Perhaps because I'd never seen light behave that way before—it didn't seem right or natural for light to concentrate itself in a ball. Or perhaps it was the way they moved, gliding through the night with such purpose, cutting through the dark, weaving from tree to tree, floating by the topmost branches, and then forging a path toward the next. Almost as if the trees were signposts. Or perhaps it was the silence. The awful silence. The Pine Barrens are quiet as far as civilized sounds are concerned, but there's always the noise of the living things, the hoots and cries and rustlings of the animals, the incessant insect susurration. That was all gone now. There wasn't even a breeze to rustle the bushes. Silence. More than a mere absence of noise. A holding of breath.

"Do you see them, Mac? Tell me I'm not hallucinating! Do you see them?"

"I see them, Jon."

My voice sounded funny. I realized my mouth was dry. And not just from sleep.

Creighton turned around in a quick circle, his arms spread.

"I don't have a camera! I need a picture of this!"

"You didn't bring a camera?" I said. "My God, you brought everything else!"

"I know, but I never dreamed—"

Suddenly he was running for the tree at the center of our clearing.

"Jon! You're not really—?"

"They're coming this way! If I can get close to them—!"

I was suddenly afraid for him. Something about those lights was warning me away. Why wasn't it warning Creighton? Or was he simply not listening?

I followed him at a reluctant lope.

"Don't be an idiot, Jon! You don't know what they are!"

"Exactly! It's about time somebody found out!"

He started climbing. It was a big old pitch pine with no branches to speak of for the first dozen feet or so of its trunk, but its bark was knobby and rough enough for Creighton's rubber-soled boots to find purchase. He slipped off twice, but he was determined. Finally he made it to the lowest branch, and from there on it looked easy.

I can't explain the crawling sensation in my gut as I watched Jonathan Creighton climbing toward a rendezvous with the approaching pine lights. He was three-quarters of the way to the top when the trunk began to shake and sway with his weight. Then a branch broke under his foot and he almost fell. When I saw that he'd regained safe footing, I sighed with relief. The branches above him were too frail to hold him. He couldn't go any higher. He'd be safe from the lights.

And the lights were here, a good dozen of them, from baseball to basketball size, gliding across our clearing in an irregular cylindrical cluster perhaps ten feet across and twenty feet long, heading straight for Creighton's tree.

And the closer they got, the faster my insides crawled. They may have been made up of light but it was not a clean light, not the golden healthy light of day. This was a wan, sickly, anemic glow, tainted with the vaguest hint of green. But thankfully it was a glow out of Creighton's reach as the lights brushed the tree's topmost needles.

I watched their glow limn Creighton's upturned face as his body strained upward, and I wondered at his recklessness, at this obsession with finding "reality." Was he flailing and floundering about in his search, or was he actually on the trail of something? And were the pine lights part of it?

As the first light passed directly above him, not five feet beyond his outstretched hand, I heard him cry out.

"They're humming, Mac! High-pitched! Can you hear it? It's almost musical! And the air up here tingles, almost as if it's charged! This is fantastic!"

I didn't hear any music or feel any tingling. All I could hear was my heart thudding in my chest, all I could feel was the cold sweat that had broken out all over my body.

Creighton spoke again—he was practically shouting now, but in a language that was not English and not like any other language I'd ever heard. He made clicks and wheezes, and the few noises that sounded like words did not seem to fit comfortably on the human tongue.

"Jon, what are you doing up there?" I cried.

He ignored me and kept up the alien gibberish, but the lights, in turn, ignored him and sailed by above him as if he didn't exist.

The cluster was almost past now, yet still I couldn't shake the dread, the dark feeling that something awful was going to happen.

And then it did.

The last light in the cluster was basketball-sized. It seemed as if it was going to trail away above Creighton just like the others, but as it approached the tree, it slowed and began to drop toward Creighton's perch.

I was panicked now.

"Jon, look out! It's coming right for you!"

"I see it!"

As the other lights flowed off toward the next treetop, this last one hung back and circled Creighton's tree at a height level with his waist.

"Get down from there!" I called.

"Are you kidding? This is more than I'd ever hoped for!"

The light suddenly stopped moving and hovered a foot or so in front of Creighton's chest.

"It's cold," he said in a more subdued tone. "Cold light."

He reached his hand toward it and I wanted to shout for him not to but my throat was locked. The tip of his index finger touched the outer edge of the glow.

"*Really* cold."

I saw his finger sink into the light to perhaps the depth of the fingernail, and then suddenly the light moved. It more than moved, it *leaped* onto Creighton's hand, engulfing it.

That's when Creighton began to scream. His words were barely intelligible but I picked out the words "cold" and "burning" again and again. I ran to the base of the tree, expecting him to lose his balance, hoping I could do something to break his fall. I saw the ball of light stretch out and slide up the length of his arm, engulfing it.

Then it disappeared.

For an instant I thought it might be over. But when Creighton clutched his chest and cried out in greater agony, I realized to my horror that the light wasn't gone—it was inside him!

And then I saw the back of his shirt begin to glow. I watched the light ooze out of him and re-form itself into a globe. Then it rose and glided off to follow the other lights into the night, leaving Creighton alone in the tree, sobbing and retching.

I called up to him. "Jon! Are you all right? Do you need help?"

When he didn't answer, I grabbed hold of the tree trunk. But before I could attempt to climb, he stopped me.

"Stay there, Mac." His voice was weak, shaky. "I'm coming down."

It took him twice as long to climb down as it had to go up. His movements were slow, unsteady, and three times he had to stop to rest. Finally, he reached the lowest branch, hung from it by one hand, and made the final drop. I grabbed him immediately to keep him from collapsing into a heap, and helped him back toward the lamp and the bedrolls.

"My God, Jon! Your arm!"

In the light from the lamp his flesh seemed to be smoking. The skin on his left hand and forearm was red, almost scalded-looking. Tiny blisters were already starting to form.

"It looks worse than it feels."

"We've got to get you to a doctor."

He dropped to his knees on his bedroll and hugged his injured arm against his chest with his good one.

"I'm all right. It only hurts a little now."

"It's going to get infected. Come on. I'll see if I can get us to civilization."

"Forget it," he said, and I sensed some of the strength returning to his voice. "Even if we get the Jeep free, we're still lost. We couldn't find our way out of here when it was daylight. What makes you think we'll do any better in the dark?"

He was right. But I felt I had to do something.

"Where's your first aid kit?"

"I don't have one."

I blew up then.

"Jesus Christ, Jon! You're crazy, you know that? You could have fallen out of that tree and been killed! And if you don't wind up with gangrene in that arm it'll be a miracle! What on God's earth made you do something so stupid?"

He grinned. "I knew it! You still love me!"

I was not amused.

"This is serious, Jon. You risked your life up there! For what?"

"I have to know, Mac."

" 'Know?' What do you have to 'know'? Will you stop giving me this bullshit?"

"I can't. I can't stop because it's true. I have to know what's real and what's not."

"Spare me—"

"I mean it. You're sure you know what's real and so you're content and complacent with that. You can't imagine what it's like not to know. To sense there's a veil across everything, a barrier that keeps you from seeing what's really there. You don't know what it's like to spend your life searching for the edge of that veil so you can lift it and peek—just peek—at what's behind it. I know it's out there, and I can't reach it. You don't know what that's like, Mac. It makes you crazy."

"Well, that's one thing we can agree on."

He laughed—it sounded strained—and reached for his jug of applejack with his good hand.

"Haven't you had enough of that tonight?"

I hated myself for sounding like an old biddy, but what I had just seen had shaken me to the core. I was still trembling.

"No, Mac. The problem is I haven't had enough. Not nearly enough."

Feeling helpless and angry, I sat down on my own bedroll and watched him take a long pull from the jug.

"What happened up there, Jon?"

"I don't know. But I don't ever want it to happen again."

"And what were you saying? It almost sounded as if you were calling to them."

He looked up sharply and stared at me.

"Did you hear what I said?"

"Not exactly. It didn't even sound like speech."

"That's because it wasn't," he said, and I was sure I detected relief in his voice. "I was trying to attract their attention."

"Well, you sure did that."

Across the top of the Coleman lamp, I thought I saw him smile.

"Yeah. I did, didn't I?"

In the night around us, I noticed that the insects were becoming vocal again.

7. The Shunned Place

I'd planned to stay awake the rest of the night, but somewhere along the way I must have faded into sleep. The next thing I knew there was sunlight in my eyes. I leaped up, disoriented for a moment, then remembered where I was.

But where was Creighton? His bedroll lay stretched out on the sand, his compass, sextant, and maps upon it, but he was nowhere in sight. I called his name a couple of times. He called back from somewhere off to my left. I followed the sound of his voice through the brush and emerged on the edge of a small pond rimmed with white cedars.

Creighton was kneeling at the edge, cupping some water in his right hand.

"How'd you find this?" I said.

"Simple." He pointed out toward a group of drakes and mallards floating on the still surface. "I followed the quacking."

"You're becoming a regular Mark Trail. How's the water?"

"Polluted." He pointed to a brownish blue slick on the surface of the pond, then held up a palmful of clear, brownish water. "Look at that color. Looks like tea."

"That's not polluted," I told him. "That's the start of some bog iron floating over there. And this is cedar water. It gets brown from the iron deposits and from the cedars but it's as pure as it comes."

I scooped up a double handful and took a long swallow.

"Almost sweet," I said. "Sea captains used to come into these parts to fill their water casks with cedar water before long voyages. They said it stayed fresher longer."

"Then I guess it's okay to bathe this in it," he said, twisting and showing me his left arm.

I gasped. I couldn't help it. I'd half convinced myself that last night's incident with the pine light had been a nightmare. But the reddened, crusted, blistered skin on Creighton's arm said otherwise.

"We've got to get you to a doctor," I said.

"It's all right, Mac. Doesn't really hurt. Just feels hot."

He sank it past his elbow into the cool cedar water.

"Now *that* feels good!"

I looked around. The sun shone from a cloudless sky. We'd have no trouble finding our way out of here this morning. I stared out over the pond. Water. The sandy floor of the Pine Barrens was like a giant sponge that absorbed a high percentage of the rain that fell on it. It was the largest untapped aquifer in the Northeast. No rivers flowed into the Pinelands, only out. The water here was glacial in its purity. I'd read somewhere that the Barrens held an amount of water equivalent to a lake with a surface area of a thousand square miles and an average depth of seventy-five feet.

This little piece of wetness here was less than fifty yards across. I watched the ducks. They were quacking peacefully, tooling around, dipping their heads. Then one of them made a different sound, more like a squawk. It flapped its wings once and was gone. It happened in the blink of an eye. One second a floating duck, next second some floating bubbles.

"Did you see that?" Creighton said.

"Yeah, I did."

"What happened to that duck?" I could see the excitement starting to glow in his eyes. "What's it mean?"

"It means a snapping turtle. A big one. Fifty pounds or better, I'm sure."

Creighton pulled his arm from the pond.

"I do believe I've soaked this enough for now."

He dipped a towel in the water and wrapped it around his scorched arm.

We walked back to the bedrolls, packed up our gear, and made our way through the brush to the Wrangler.

The Jeep was occupied.

There were people inside, and people sitting on the hood and standing on the bumpers as well. A good half-dozen in all.

Only they weren't like any people I'd ever seen.

They were dressed like typical Pineys, but dirty, raggedy. The four men in jeans or canvas pants, collared shirts of various fabrics and colors or plain white T-shirts; the two women wore cotton jumpers. But they were all deformed. Their heads were odd shapes and sizes, some way too small, others large and lopsided with bulbous protrusions. The eyes on a couple weren't lined up on the level. Everyone seemed to have one arm or leg longer than the other. Their teeth, at least in the ones who still had any, seemed to have come in at random angles.

When they spotted us, they began jabbering and pointing our way. They left the Wrangler and surrounded us. It was an intimidating group.

"Is that your car?" a young man with a lopsided head said to me.

"No." I pointed to Creighton. "It's his."

"Is that your car?" he said to Creighton.

I guessed he didn't believe me.

"It's a Jeep," Creighton said.

"Jeep! Jeep!" He laughed and kept repeating the word. The others around him took it up and chorused along.

I looked at Creighton and shrugged. We'd apparently come upon an enclave of the type of folks who'd helped turn "Piney" into a term of derision shortly before World War I. That was when Elizabeth Kite published a report titled "The Pineys" which was sensationalized by the press and led to the view that the Pinelands was a bed of alcoholism, illiteracy, degeneracy, incest, and resultant "feeble-mindedness."

Unfair and untrue. But not entirely false. There has always been illiteracy and alcoholism deep in the Pinelands. Schooling here tended to be rudimentary if at all. And as for drinking? The first "drive-thru" service originated before the Revolution in the Piney jug taverns, allowing customers to ride up to a window, get their jugs topped off with applejack, pay, and move on without ever dismounting. But after the economy of the Pine Barrens faltered, and most of the workers moved on to greener pastures, much of the social structure collapsed. Those who stayed on grew a little lax as to the whys, hows, and to-whoms of marriage. The results were inevitable.

All that had supposedly changed in modern times, except in the most isolated area of the Pines. We had stumbled upon one of those areas. Except that the deformities here were extraordinary. I'd seen a few of the inbreds in my youth. There'd been something subtly odd about them, but nothing that terribly startling. These folk would stop you in your tracks.

"Let's head for the Jeep while they're yucking it up," I said out of the corner of my mouth.

"No. Wait. This is fascinating. Besides, we need their help."

He spoke to the group as a whole and asked their aid in freeing the Jeep.

Somebody said, "Sugar sand," and this was repeated all around. But they willingly set their shoulders against the Wrangler and we were on hard ground again in minutes.

"Where do you live?" Creighton said to anyone who was listening.

Someone said, "Town," and as one they all pointed east, toward the sun. It was also the direction the lights had been headed last night.

"Will you show me?"

They nodded and jabbered and tugged on our sleeves, anxious to show us.

"Really, Jon," I said. "We should get you to—"

"My arm can wait. This won't take long."

We followed the group in a generally uphill direction along a circuitous footpath unnavigable by any vehicle other than a motorcycle. The trees thickened and soon we were in shade. And then those trees opened up and we were in their "town."

A haze of blue woodsmoke hung over a ramshackle collection of shanties made of scrap lumber and sheet metal. Garbage everywhere, and everyone coming out to look at the strangers. I'd never seen such squalor.

The fellow with the lopsided head who'd asked about the Jeep before pulled Creighton toward one of the shacks.

"Hey, mister, you know about machines. How come this don't work?"

He had an old TV set inside his one-room hut. He turned the knobs back and forth.

"Don't work. No pictures."

"You need electricity," Creighton told him.

"Got it. Got it. Got it."

He led us around to the back to show us the length of wire he had strung from a tree to the roof of the shack.

Creighton turned to me with stricken eyes.

"This is awful. No one should have to live like this. Can we do anything for them?"

His compassion surprised me. I'd never thought there was room for anyone else's concerns in his self-absorbed life. But then, Jonathan Creighton had always been a motherlode of surprises.

"Not much. They all look pretty content to me. Seem to have their own little community. If you bring them to the government's attention they'll be split up and most of them will probably be placed in institutions or group homes. I guess the best you can do is give them whatever you can think of to make the living easier here."

Creighton nodded, still staring around him.

"Speaking of 'here,' " he said, unshouldering his knapsack, "let's find out where we are."

The misshapen locals stared in frank awe and admiration as he took his readings. Someone asked him, "What is that thing?" a hundred times. At least. Another asked "What happened to your arm?" an equal number of times. Creighton was heroically patient with everyone. He knelt on the ground to transfer his readings to the map, then looked up at me.

"Know where we are?"

"The other side of Razorback Hill, I'd say."

"You got it."

He stood up and gathered the locals around him.

"I'm looking for a special place around here," he said.

Most of them nodded eagerly. Someone said, "We know every place there is around here, I reckon."

"Good. I'm looking for a place where nothing grows. Do you know a place like that?"

It was as if all of these people had a common plug and Creighton had just pulled it. The lights went out, the shades came down, the "Open" signs flipped to "Closed." They began to turn away.

"What'd I say?" he said, turning his anxious, bewildered eyes on me. "What'd I *say*?"

"You're starting to sound like Ray Charles," I told him. "Obviously they want nothing to do with this 'place where nothing grows' you're talking about. What's this all about, Jon?"

He ignored my question and laid his good hand on the shoulder of one of the small-headed men.

"Won't you take me there if you know where it is?"

"We know where it is," the fellow said in a squeaky voice. "But we never go there so we can't take you there. How can we take you there if we never go there?"

"You *never* go there? Why not?"

The others had stopped and were listening to the exchange. The small-headed fellow looked around at his neighbors and gave them a look that asked how stupid could anyone be? Then he turned back to Creighton.

"We don't go there 'cause nobody goes there."

"What's your name?" Creighton said.

"Fred."

"Fred, my name is Jon, and I'll give you . . ." He patted his pockets, then tore the watch off his wrist. "I'll give you this beautiful watch that you don't have to wind—see how the numbers change with every second?—if you'll take me to a place where you *do* go and point out the place where nothing grows. How's that sound?"

Fred took the watch and held it up close to his right eye, then smiled. "Come on! I'll show you!"

Creighton took off after Fred, and I took off after Creighton.

Again we were led along a circuitous path, this one even narrower than before, becoming less well defined as we went along. I noticed the trees becoming fewer in number and more stunted and gnarled, and the underbrush thinning out, the leaves fewer and curled on their edges. We followed Fred until he halted as abruptly as if he had run into an invisible wall. I saw why: the footpath we'd been following stopped here. He pointed ahead through what was left of the trees and underbrush.

"The bald spot's over yonder atop that there rise."

He turned and hurried back along the path.

Bald spot?

Creighton looked at me, then shrugged.

"Got your machete handy, Mac?"

"No, Bwana."

"Too bad. I guess we'll just have to bull our way through."

He rewrapped his burned arm and pushed ahead. It wasn't such rough going. The underbrush thinned out quickly and so we had an easier time of it than I'd anticipated. Soon we broke into a small field lined with scrappy weeds and occupied by the scattered, painfully gnarled trunks of dead trees. And in the center of the field was a patch of bare sand.

. . . a place where nothing grows . . .

Creighton hurried ahead. I held back, restrained by a sense of foreboding. The same something deep within me that had feared the pine lights feared this place as well. Something was wrong here, as if Nature had been careless, had made a mistake in this place and had never quite been able to rectify it. As if . . .

What was I thinking? It was an empty field. No eerie lights buzzing through the sky. No birds, either, for that matter. So what? The sun was up, a breeze was blowing—or at least it had been a moment ago.

Overruling my instincts, I followed Creighton. I touched the tortured trunk of one of the dead trees as I passed. It was hard and cold, like stone. A petrified tree. In the Pinelands.

I hurried ahead and caught up to Creighton at the edge of the "bald spot." He was staring at it as if in a trance. The spot was a rough oval, maybe thirty feet across. Nothing grew in that oval. Nothing.

"Look at that pristine sand," he said in a whisper. "Birds don't fly over it, insects and animals don't walk on it. Only the wind touches and shapes it. That's the way sand looked at the beginning of time."

It had always been my impression that sand wasn't yet sand at the beginning of time, but I didn't argue with him. He was on a roll. I remembered from college: You don't stop Crazy Creighton when he's on a roll.

I saw what he meant, though. The sand was rippled like water, like sand must look in areas of the Sahara far off the trade routes. I saw animal tracks leading up to it and then turning aside. Creighton was right: nothing trod this soil.

Except Creighton.

Without warning he stepped across the invisible line and walked to the center of the bald spot. He spread his arms, looked up at the sky, and whirled in dizzying circles. His eyes were aglow, his expression rapturous. He looked stoned out of his mind.

"This is it! I've found it! This is the place!"

"*What* place, Jon?"

I stood at the edge of the spot, unwilling to cross over, talking in the flat tone you might use to coax a druggie back from a bad trip, or a jumper down from a ledge.

"Where it all comes together and all comes apart! Where the Truth is revealed!"

"What the hell are you talking about, Jon?"

I was tired and uneasy and I wanted to go home. I'd had enough, and I guessed my voice showed it. The rapture faded. Abruptly, he was sober.

"Nothing, Mac. Nothing. Just let me take a few readings and we're out of here."

"That's the best news I've heard this morning."

He shot me a quick glance. I didn't know if it conveyed annoyance or disappointment. And I didn't care.

8. Spreading Infection

I got us back to a paved road without too much difficulty. We spoke little on the way home. He dropped me off at my house and promised to see a doctor before the day was out.

"What's next for you?" I said as I closed the passenger door and looked at him through the open window.

I hoped he wouldn't ask me to guide him back into the Pines again. I was sure he hadn't been straight with me about his research. I didn't know what he was after, but I knew it wasn't the Jersey Devil. A part of me said it was better not to know, that this man was a juggernaut on a date with disaster.

"I'm not sure. I may go back and see those people, the ones on the far side of Razorback Hill. Maybe bring them some clothing, some food."

Against my will, I was touched.

"That would be nice. Just don't bring them toaster cakes or microwave dinners."

He laughed. "I won't."

"Where are you staying?"

He hesitated, looking uncertain.

"A place called the Laurelton Circle Motor Inn."

"I know it."

A tiny place. Sporting the name of a traffic circle that no longer existed.

"I'm staying in room five if you need to get hold of me but . . . can you do me a favor? If anybody comes looking for me, don't tell them where I am. Don't tell them you've even seen me."

"Are you in some sort of trouble?"

"A misunderstanding, that's all."

"You wouldn't want to elaborate on that, would you?"

His expression was bleak.

"The less you know, Mac, the better."

"Like everything else these past two days, right?"

He shrugged. "Sorry."

"Me, too. Look. Stop by before you head back to Razorback. I may have a few old things I can donate to those folks."

He waved with his burned hand, and then he was off.

Creighton stopped by a few days later on his way back to Razorback Hill. His left arm was heavily bandaged in gauze.

"You were right," he said. "It got infected."

I gave him some old sweaters and shirts and a couple of pairs of jeans that no longer fit the way they should.

A few days later I bumped into him in the housewares aisle at Pathmark. He'd picked up some canned goods and was buying a couple of can openers for the Razorback folks. His left arm was bandaged as before, but I was concerned to see that there was gauze on his right hand now.

"The infection spread a little, but the doctor says it's okay. He's got me on this new antibiotic. Sure to kill it off."

Looking more closely now in the supermarket's fluorescent glare, I saw that he was pale and sweaty. He seemed to have lost weight.

"Who's your doctor?"

"Guy up in Neptune. A specialist."

"In pine light burns?"

His laugh was a bit too loud, a tad too long.

"No! Infections."

I wondered. But Jon Creighton was a big boy now. I couldn't be his mother.

I picked out some canned goods myself, checked out behind Creighton, and gave the bagful to him.

"Give them my best," I told him.

He smiled wanly and hurried off.

At the very tail end of August I was driving down Brick Boulevard when I spotted his Wrangler idling at the Burger King drive-thru window. I pulled into the lot and walked over.

"Jon!" I said through the window and saw him jump.

"Oh, Mac. Don't ever do that!"

He looked relieved, but he didn't look terribly glad to see me. His face seemed thinner, but maybe that was because of the beard he had started to grow. A fugitive's beard.

"Sorry," I said. "I was wondering if you wanted to get together for some *real* lunch."

"Oh. Well. Thanks, but I've got a lot of errands to run. Maybe some other time."

Despite the heat, he was wearing corduroy pants and a long-sleeved flannel shirt. I noticed that both his hands were still wrapped in gauze. An alarm went off inside me.

"Isn't that infection cleared up yet?"

"It's coming along slowly, but it's coming."

I glanced down at his feet and noticed that his ankles looked thick. His sneakers were unlaced, their tongues lolling out as the sides stretched to accommodate his swollen feet.

"What happened to your feet?"

"A little edema. Side effect of the medicine. Look, Mac, I've got to run." He threw the Wrangler into gear. "I'll call you soon."

It was a couple of weeks after Labor Day and I'd been thinking about Creighton a lot. I was worried about him, and was realizing that I still harbored deeper feelings for him than I cared to admit.

Then the state trooper showed up at my office. He was big and intimidating behind his dark glasses; his haircut came within a millimeter of complete baldness. He held out a grainy photo of Jon Creighton.

"Do you know this man?" he said in a deep voice.

My mouth was dry as I wondered if he was going to ask me if I was involved in whatever Creighton had done; or worse: if I'd care to come down and identify the body.

"Sure. We went to college together."

"Have you seen him in the past month."

I didn't hesitate. I did the stand-up thing.

"Nope. Not since graduation."

"We have reason to believe he's in the area. If you see him, contact the state police or your local police immediately."

"What's he done, officer?"

He turned and started toward the door without deigning to answer. That brand of arrogance never failed to set something off in me.

"I asked you a question, *officer*. I expect the courtesy of a reply."

He turned and looked at me, then shrugged. Some of the Dirty Harry facade slipped away with the shrug.

"Why not?" he said. "He's wanted for grand theft."

Oh, great.

"What did he steal?"

"A book."

"A *book*?"

"Yeah. Would you believe it? We've got rapes and murders and armed robberies, but this book is given a priority. I don't care how valuable it is or how much some university in Massachusetts wants it, it's only a book. But the Massachusetts people are really hot to get it back. Their governor got to our governor and . . . well, you know how it goes. We found his car abandoned out near Lakehurst a while back, so we know he's been through here."

"You think he's on foot?"

"Maybe. Or maybe he rented or stole another car. We're running it down now."

"If he shows up, I'll let you know."

"Do that. I get the impression that if he gives the book back in one piece, all will be forgiven."

"I'll tell him that if I get the chance."

As soon as he was gone, I got on the phone to Creighton's motel. His voice was thick when he said hello.

"Jon! The state cops were just here looking for you!"

He mumbled a few words I didn't understand. Something was wrong. I hung up and headed for my car.

There are only about twenty rooms in that particular motel. I spotted the Wrangler backed into a space at the far end of the tiny parking lot. Number five was on a corner of the first floor. A Do Not Disturb sign hung from the knob. I knocked on the door twice and got no answer. I tried the knob. It turned.

It was dark inside except for the daylight I'd let in. And that light revealed a disaster area. The room looked like the inside of a dumpster behind a block of fast-food stores. Smelled like one, too. There were pizza boxes, hamburger wrappers, submarine sleeves, Chinese food cartons, a sampling from every place in the area that delivered. And it was hot. Either the air conditioner had quit or it hadn't been turned on.

"Jon?" I flipped on the light. "Jon, are you here?"

He was in a chair in a corner on the far side of the bed, huddled under a pile of blankets. Papers and maps were piled on the night table beside him. His face, where visible above his matted beard, was pale and drawn. He looked as if he'd lost thirty pounds. I slammed the door closed and stood there, stunned.

"My God, Jon, what's wrong?"

"Nothing. I'm fine." His hoarse, thick voice said otherwise. "What are you doing here, Mac?"

"I came to tell you that the state police are cruising around with photos of you, but I can see that's the least of your problems! You're really sick!" I reached for the phone. "I'm calling an ambulance."

"*No!* Mac, please *don't!*"

The terror and soul-wrenching anguish in his voice stopped me. I stared at him but still kept a grip on the receiver.

"Why not?"

"Because I'm begging you not to!"

"But you're sick, you could be dying, you're out of your head!"

"No. That's one thing I'm not. Trust me when I say that no hospital in the world can help me—because I'm not dying. And if you ever loved me, if you ever had any regard for who I am and what I want from my life, then you'll put down that phone and walk out that door."

I stood there in the hot, humid squalor of that tiny room, receiver in hand, smelling the garbage, detecting the hint of another odor, a subtle sour foulness that underlay the others, and felt myself being torn apart by the choice that faced me.

"Please, Mac," he said. "You're the only person in the world who'll understand. Don't hand me over to strangers." He sobbed once. "I can't fight you. I can only beg you. Please. Put down the phone and leave."

It was the sob that did it. I slammed the receiver onto its cradle.

"Damn you!"

"Two days, Mac. In two days I'll be better. You wait and see."

"You're damn right I'll see—I'm staying here with you!"

"No! You can't! You have no right to intrude! This is *my* life! You've got to let me take it where I must! Now leave, Mac. Please."

He was right, of course. This was what we'd been all about when we'd been together. I had to back off. And it was killing me.

"All right," I said around the lump in my throat. "You win. See you in two days."

Without waiting for a reply. I opened the door and stepped out into the bright September sunlight.

"Thanks, Mac," he said. "I love you."

I didn't want to hear that. I took one last look back as I pulled the door closed. He was still swaddled from his neck to the floor in the blankets, but in the last instant before the door shut him from view, I thought I saw something white and pointed, about the circumference of a garden hose, snake out on the carpet from under the blankets and then quickly pull back under cover.

A rush of nausea slammed me against the outer wall of the motel as the door clicked closed. I leaned there, sick and dizzy, trying to catch my breath.

A trick of the light. That was what I told myself as the vertigo faded. I'd been squinting in the brightness and the light had played a trick.

Of course, I didn't have to settle for merely telling myself. I could simply open the door and check it out. I actually reached for the knob, but couldn't bring myself to turn it.

Two days. Creighton had said two days. I'd find out then.

But I didn't last two days. I was unable to concentrate the following morning and wound up canceling all my appointments. I spent the entire day pacing my office or my living room; and when I wasn't pacing, I was on the phone. I called the American Folklore Society and the New Jersey Historical Society. Not only had they not given Creighton the grants he'd told me about, they'd never heard of him.

By nightfall I'd taken all I could. I began calling Creighton's room. I got no answer. I tried a few more times, but when he still hadn't picked up by eleven o'clock, I headed for the motel.

I was almost relieved to see the Wrangler gone from the parking lot. Room five was still unlocked and still a garbage dump, which meant he was still renting it—or hadn't been gone too long.

What was he up to?

I began to search the room. I found the book under the bed. It was huge, heavy, wrapped in plastic with a scrawled note taped to the front:

Please return to Miskatonic U. archives

I slipped it out of the plastic. It was leather-bound and handwritten in Latin. I could barely decipher the title—something like *Liben Damnatus*. But inside the front cover were Creighton's maps and a sheaf of notes in his back-slanted scrawl. The notes were in disarray and probably would have been disjointed even if arranged in proper order. But certain words and phrases kept recurring: *nexus point* and *equinox* and *the lumens* and *the veil*.

It took me a while but eventually I got the drift of the jottings. Apparently a section of the book Creighton had stolen concerned "nexus points" around the globe where twice a year at the vernal and autumnal equinoxes "the veil" that obscures reality becomes detached for a short while, allowing an intrepid soul to peek under the hem and see the true nature of the world around us, the world we are not "allowed" to see. These "nexus points" are few and widely scattered. Of the four known, there's one near each pole, one in Tibet, and one near the east coast of North America.

I sighed. Crazy Creighton had really started living up to his name. It was sad. This was so unlike him. He'd been the ultimate cynic, and now he was risking his health and his freedom pursuing this mystical garbage.

And what was even sadder was how he had lied to me. Obviously he hadn't been searching for tales of the Jersey Devil—he'd been searching for one of these "nexus points." And he was probably convinced he'd found one behind Razorback Hill.

I pitied him. But I read on.

According to the notes, these "nexus points" can be located by following "the lumens" to a place shunned equally by man, beast, and vegetation.

Suddenly I was uneasy. "The lumens." Could that refer to the pine lights? And the "bald spot" that Fred had showed us—that was certainly a place shunned by man, beast, and vegetation.

I found a whole sheet filled with notes about the Razorback folk. The last paragraph was especially upsetting:

The folks behind Razorback Hill aren't deformed from inbreeding, although I'm sure that's contributed its share. I believe they're misshapen as a result of living near the nexus point for generations. The semi-annual lifting of the veil must have caused genetic damage over the years.

I pulled out Creighton's maps and unfolded them on the bed. I followed the lines he had drawn from Apple Pie Hill, from Gus's firing place, and from our campsite. All three lines represented paths of pine lights, and all three intersected at a spot near the circle he had drawn and labeled as Razorback Hill. And right near the intersection of the pine light paths, almost on top of it, he had drawn another circle, a tiny one, penciled in the latitude and longitude, and labeled it *Nexus!*

I was worried now. Even my own skepticism was beginning to waver. Everything was fitting too neatly. I looked at my watch. Eleven thirty-two. The date read "21." September 21. When was the equinox? I grabbed the phone and called an old clam digger who'd been a client since I'd opened my office. He knew the answer right off:

"The autumnal equinox. That's September twenty-second. 'Bout a half hour from now."

I dropped the phone and ran for my car. I knew exactly where to find Jon Creighton.

9. The Hem of the Veil

I raced down the Parkway to the Bass River exit and tried to find my way back to Gus Sooy's place. What had been a difficult trip in the day proved to be several orders of magnitude more difficult in the dark. But I managed to find Gus's red cedar. It was my plan to convince him to show me a short way to the far side of Razorback Hill, figuring the fact that Creighton was already there might make him more tractable. But when I rushed up to Gus Sooy's clearing, I discovered that he wasn't alone.

The Razorback folk were there. All of them, from the looks of the crowd.

I found Gus standing on his front step, a jug dangling from his hand. He was obviously shocked to see me, and was anything but hospitable.

"What do you want?"

Before I could answer, the Razorback folks recognized me and a small horde of them crowded around.

"Why are they all here?" I asked Gus.

"Just visiting," he said casually, but did not look me in the eye.

"It wouldn't have anything to do with what's happening at the bald spot on the other side of Razorback Hill, would it?"

"Damn you! You've been snoopin' around, haven't you? You and your friend. They told me he was coming around, askin' all sorts of questions. Where's he now? Hidin' in the bushes?"

"He's over there," I said, pointing to the top of Razorback Hill. "And if my guess is correct, he's standing right in the middle of the bald spot."

Gus dropped his jug. It shattered on the boards of his front step.

"Do you know what'll happen to him?"

"No," I said. "Do you?" I looked around at the Razorback folk. "Do they?"

"I don't think anyone knows, leastmost them. But they're scared. They come here twice a year, when that bald spot starts acting up."

"Have you ever seen what happens there?"

"Once. Never want to see it again."

"Why haven't you ever told anyone?"

"What? And bring all sorts of pointyheads here to look and gawk and build and ruin the place. We'd all rather put up with the bald spot craziness twice a year than pointyhead craziness every day all year long."

I didn't have time to get into Creighton's theory that the bald spot was genetically damaging the Razorback folks. I had to find Creighton.

"How do I get there? What's the fastest way?"

"You can't—"

"*They* got here!" I pointed to the Razorback folks.

"All right!" he said with open hostility. "Suit yourself. There's a trail behind my cabin here. Follow it over the left flank of the hill."

"And then?"

"And then you won't need any directions. You'll know where to go."

His words had an ominous ring, but I couldn't press him. I was being propelled by a sense of enormous urgency. Time was running out. Quickly. I already had my flashlight, so I hurried to the rear of his shanty and followed the trail.

Gus was right. As I crossed the flank of the hill I saw flashes through the trees ahead, like lightning, as if a very tiny and very violent electrical storm had been brought to ground and anchored there. I increased my pace, running when the terrain would allow. The wind picked up as I neared the storm area, growing from a fitful breeze to a full-scale gale by the time I broke through the brush and stumbled into the clearing that surrounded the bald spot.

Chaos. That's the only way I can describe it. A nightmare of cascading lights and roaring wind. The pine lights—or *lumens*—were there, hundreds of them, all sizes, unaffected by the rushing vortex of air as they swirled about in wild arcs, each flaring brilliantly as it looped through the space above the bald spot. And the bald spot itself—it glowed with a faint purplish light that reached thirty or forty feet into the air before fading into the night.

The stolen book, Creighton's notes—they weren't mystical madness. Something cataclysmic was happening here, something that defied all the laws of nature—if indeed those laws had any real meaning. Whether this was one of the nexus points he had described, a fleeting rent in the reality that surrounded us, only Creighton could say for sure right now.

For I could see someone in the bald spot. I couldn't make out his features from where I was, but I knew it was Jonathan Creighton.

I dashed forward until I reached the edge but slowed to a halt in the sand before actually crossing into the glow. Creighton was there, on his knees, his hands and feet buried in the sand. He was staring about him, his expression an uneasy mix of fear and wonder. I shouted his name but he didn't hear me above the roar of the wind. Twice he looked directly at me but despite my frantic shouting and waving, did not see me.

I saw no other choice. I had to step onto the bald spot . . . the nexus point. It wasn't easy. Every instinct I possessed screamed at me to run in the other direction, but I couldn't leave him there like that. He looked helpless, trapped like an insect on flypaper. I had to help him.

Taking a deep breath, I closed my eyes and stepped across—

—and began to stumble forward. Up and down seemed to have a slightly different orientation here. I opened my eyes and dropped to my knees, nearly landing on Creighton. I looked around and froze.

The Pine Barrens were gone. *Night* was gone. It seemed to be predawn or dusk here, but the wind still howled about us and the pine lights flashed around us, appearing and disappearing above as though passing through invisible walls. We were someplace . . . *else:* on a huge misty plain that seemed to stretch on forever, interrupted only by clumps of vegetation and huge fog banks, one of which was nearby on my left and seemed to go on and up forever. Off in the immeasurable distance, mountains the size of the moon reached up and disappeared into the haze of the purple sky. The horizon—or what I imagined to be the horizon—didn't curve as it should. This place seemed so much *bigger* than the world—our world—that waited just a few feet away.

"My God, Jon, where are we!"

He started and turned his head. His hands and feet remained buried in the sand. His eyes went wide with shock at the sight of me.

"No! You shouldn't be here!"

His voice was thicker and more distorted than yesterday. Oddly enough, his pale skin looked almost healthy in the mauve light.

"Neither should you!"

I heard something then. Above the shriek of the wind came another sound. A rumble like an avalanche. It came from somewhere within the fog bank to our left. There was something massive, something immense moving about in there, and the fog seemed to be drifting this way.

"We've got to get out of here, Jon!"

"No! I'm staying!"

"No way! Come on!"

He was wracked with infection and obviously deranged. I didn't care what he said, I wasn't going to let him risk his life in this place. I'd pull him out of here and let him think about it for six months. *Then* if he still wanted to try this, it would be his choice. But he wasn't competent now.

I looped my arms around his chest and tried to pull him to his feet.

"Mac, please! Don't!"

His hands remained fixed in the sand. He must have been holding onto something. I grabbed his right elbow and yanked. He screamed as his hand pulled free of the sand. Then I screamed, too, and let him go and threw myself back on the sand away from him.

Because his hand wasn't a hand anymore.

It was big and white and had these long, ropey, tapered, rootlike projections, something like an eye on a potato when it sprouts after being left under the sink too long, only these things were moving, twisting and writhing like a handful of albino snakes.

"Go, Mac!" he said in that distorted voice, and I could tell from his face and eyes that he hadn't wanted me to see him like this. "You don't belong here!"

"And you do?"

"*Now* I do!"

I couldn't bring myself to touch his hand, so I reached forward and grabbed some of his shirt. I pulled.

"We can find doctors! They can fix you! You can—"

"*NO!*"

It was a shout and it was something else. Something long and white and hard as flexed muscle, much like the things protruding from his shirt sleeve, darted out of his mouth and slammed against my chest, bruising my breasts as it thrust me away. Then it whipped back into his mouth.

I snapped then. I scrambled to my feet and blindly lurched away in the direction I'd come. Suddenly I was back in the Pine Barrens, in the cool night with the lights swirling madly above my head. I stumbled for the bushes, away from the nexus point, away from Jonathan Creighton.

At the edge of the clearing, I forced myself to stop and look back. I saw Creighton. His awful transformed hand was raised. I knew he couldn't see me, but it was almost as if he was waving good-bye. Then he lowered his hand and worked the tendrils back into the sand.

The last thing I remember of that night is vomiting.

10. Aftermath

I awoke among the Razorback folk who'd found me the next morning and watched over me until I was conscious and lucid again. They offered me food but I couldn't eat. I walked back up to the clearing, to the bald spot.

It looked exactly as it had when Creighton and I had first seen it in August. No lights, no wind, no purple glow. Just bare sand.

And no Jonathan Creighton.

I could have convinced myself that last night had never happened if not for the swollen, tender, violet bruise on my chest. Would that I had. But as much as my mind shrank from it, I could not deny the truth. I'd seen the other side of the veil and my life would never be the same.

I looked around and knew that everything I saw was a sham, an elaborate illusion. Why? Why was the veil there? To protect us from harm? Or to shield us from madness? The truth had brought me no peace. Who could find comfort in the knowledge that huge, immeasurable forces beyond our comprehension were out there, moving about us, beyond the reach of our senses?

I wanted to run . . . but where?

I ran home. I've been home for months now. Housebound. Moving beyond my door only for groceries. My accounting clients have all left me. I'm living on my savings, learning Latin, translating Jon's stolen book. Was what I saw the true reality of our existence, or another dimension, or what? I don't know. Creighton was right: Knowing that you don't know is maddening. It consumes you.

So I'm waiting for spring. Waiting for the vernal equinox. Maybe I'll leave the house before then and hunt up some pine lights—or *lumens*, as the book calls them. Maybe I'll touch one, maybe I won't. Maybe when the equinox comes, I'll return to Razorback Hill, to the bald spot. Maybe I'll look for Jon. He may be there, he may not. I may cross into the bald spot, I may not. And if I do, I may not come back. Or I may.

I don't know what I'll do. I don't know anything anymore. I've come to the point now where I'm sure of only one thing: Nothing is sure anymore.

At least on this side of the veil.

So here it was September and already I'd done three stories this year with Marty Greenberg involved. Then he called, looking for a fourth.

Martin H. Greenberg could be considered the novelist's Satan. Not that he's an evil man. Far from it. He's a good-natured soul with boundless energy, a sharp mind, and an endless font of ideas for collections of stories. And that's the problem.

Picture this: There you are, toiling away on a novel, wrapped up in the characters and the plot, riding the flow, building the momentum. Suddenly the phone rings. It's Marty. He's got a contract from Avon for an anthology about haunted woodstoves—going to be the definitive haunted woodstove anthology—paying a dime a word, with a deadline in four months. Can you come up with something? You say, Sorry, I'm up to my lower lip in overdue contracts and unfulfilled promises and no way can I squeeze out another five thousand words of fiction before the end of the year. Marty displays his characteristic equanimity and accepts this without the slightest squawk. You make small talk about the kids, the biz, and sundry other matters, then hang up and go back to your novel.

But over the course of the next few days and weeks Marty's proposal nibbles and gnaws at you. Haunted woodstoves . . . hmmmm. You remember how Grandma's used to look like it had two glowing eyes. What if . . . ?

Before you know it, you've got a story bouncing off the inner walls of your skull, and if you don't write it out now and send it to Marty you'll never sell it anywhere else because Marty's anthology will be definitive, without question, the very last word on haunted woodstoves. So you break off from your novel and write Marty's goddamn story.

Yes . . . the novelist's Satan.

But I had no one but myself to blame this time. Marty had edited *The Further Adventures of Batman* the year before, and at one time or another I'd taken him to task for not asking me to contribute. He said he'd assumed I never read comic books. Never read them? Hell, I've *written* them. So when he got a contract for *The Further Adventures of the Joker*, I was on his list of writers to call.

It wasn't a good time for me to write a short story. I was knee-deep in *Reprisal*, rewriting and restructuring everything I'd done the preceding winter. I needed to focus myself completely to get this right. But the Joker . . . one of my all-time favorite villains . . . I couldn't resist. I put *Reprisal* aside.

But I wanted to do *my* Joker. I disliked Jack Nicholson's portrayal in 1989 almost as much as Cesar Romero's back in the sixties. Sure, the bizarre murders, the bad jokes, and psychopathic clowning were all there in abundance, but no sense of anything truly evil beating beneath the surface. I decided to take the Joker out of his element, drain off some of his control, make him a prisoner/patient in the notorious Arkham Asylum. Here we would see a subtler, less flamboyant Joker, but more deeply and darkly evil . . . coldly maleficent. Batman would not appear. I'd offer no prose equivalent of comic-book splash-page action. My Joker would chill instead of thrill. My story would be a tabletop psychomachy.

Read on and decide which Joker you'd rather deal with. Mine, or Nicholson's?

DEFINITIVE THERAPY

ARKHAM ASYLUM

MEDICAL HISTORY

NAME: "The Joker"   **DATE OF BIRTH:** Unknown
MR#   20073

ATTENDING PHYSICIAN: Dr. R. Hills & staff

CHIEF COMPLAINT: Committed to life internment by court order. Returned to this facility after the most recent of his periodic escapes.

HISTORY OF CHIEF COMPLAINT: A career criminal with a long, well-publicized, well-documented history of anti-social and sociopathic behavior in the guise of a self-created public persona known as "The Joker." Convicted of multiple murders. Multiple escapes and readmissions to this facility. See old charts.

PAST HISTORY: Little available besides what is in the public record. The patient relates a history of juvenile delinquency, which meets the criteria for Severe Conduct Disorder, undifferentiated type (312.90).

ALLERGIES: None known.   **MEDICATIONS:** On no meds.

PREVIOUS HOSPITALIZATIONS: Many to this facility. See previous charts.

FAMILY HISTORY: Unknown. Patient uncooperative as historian.

SOCIAL HISTORY: No external stigmata of alcoholism or drug abuse.

SYSTEMIC REVIEW: According to what little history can be gleaned from the patient, he has been in generally good health for most of his life. He has a past history of facial trauma combined with toxic chemical exposure resulting in permanent disfigurement of the facies, the integument, and its appendages. No history of hearing loss or visual impairment. No thyroid disease or diabetes. No asthma, emphysema, or chronic lung disease. No heart disease or hypertension. No history of ulcer or colitis. No GU infections or past disease. No seizures or strokes. His psychiatric history has been exhaustively explored and documented at this facility. His facial/chemical trauma was once posited as the source of his psychopathy, but the patient relates a long history (undocumented) of criminal antisocial behavior since his early teens, long predating the trauma.

DICTATED BY: Harold Lewis, M.D.
SIGNATURE: _____

PHYSICAL EXAM

NAME: "The Joker" (legal name unknown)   **MR#** 20073

ATTENDING PHYSICIAN: Dr. R. Hills & staff

VITAL SIGNS: BP: 122/78   P: 82   R: 10   T: 98.6

PHYSICAL FINDINGS: A thin, facially disfigured Caucasian male, apparently in his midthirties, alert, well-oriented, in no distress. The head is normocephalic with slight evidence of proptosis. Neuromuscular paresis and cicatricial disfigurement of the facial tissues have resulted in a permanent rictus. Ears, nose, and throat are negative. The neck is supple, the thyroid is negative to palpation. The chest shows a moderate pectus excavatum. The heart is normal in size and rhythm with no murmurs. The lungs are clear to auscultation and percussion. The abdomen is soft, no masses, no organomegaly, no tenderness. Normal uncircumcised male genitalia. The lymph nodes are negative. The limbs are intact and freely movable. The deep tendon reflexes are + 2 bilaterally, the pupils are equally reactive to light and accommodation. The skin is markedly pale. Its appendages—the hair and nails—are green. This does not appear to be factitial since there is no sign of natural color under the cuticles or at the roots.

PROVISIONAL DIAGNOSIS:
1. Antisocial Personality Disorder (301.70)
2. Probable Delusion Disorder, grandiose type (297.10)
3. Rule out Bipolar Disorder, manic, mood congruent with psychotic features (296.44)
4. Rule out Intermittent Explosive Disorder (312.34)

DICTATED BY: Harold Lewis, M.D.
SIGNATURE: _____

Session One

He was painfully thin, and taller than I'd expected.

I remained standing as the guards led the gaunt, manacled figure into the interview cell.

The Joker's appearance is positively shocking at close range. I'd seen his face before. Who hasn't? But to find myself standing across a small table from the man, to have his eyes scan me from a distance of only three feet as if I were some kind of insect, was a jolt. The smile . . . that was what did it. We've all seen that soulless, mirthless grin countless times, shining at us in black and white from the front page of the *Gotham Gazette* or in never-quite-true color from the TV screen during the evening news, but nothing in the media prepares you for the original. The smile . . . the corners of the mouth are drawn up and back, fully halfway into the cheeks. And the teeth—so big and white. Bigger than Morton Downey Jr.'s. But they're not as white as his skin. So pale. Not so much in the bleached, albino sense; more like a white stain. I could not help feeling that with a little cold cream on a cloth I could wipe it off. But I knew that had been tried many times. The seaweed green of his hair and fingernails were the garnish on this bizarre human concoction.

During my five years of psychiatric residency in New York's Downstate Medical Center, and in various maximum security facilities about the country, I have encountered mental illness in its most violent manifestations. But I could not remember actually *feeling* madness as I did in my first seconds in the room with the Joker. Nothing in the media prepared me for the power of the man. In fact, the never-ending stream of stories about him in the press only serves to trivialize him. We've become used to the Joker; we've become almost comfortable with him. We all know that he is a career criminal and a multiple murderer, to boot, yet his face is so familiar that he has become part of the background noise of Gotham. His latest outrage does not stir us to as much anger as it would had it been perpetrated by a stranger. Better the devil you know . . .

My task was to get to know this devil.

With two armed guards watching closely, I thrust my hand across the table.

"I'm Dr. Lewis, Mr. Joker. I'll be—"

"Call me 'Joker,' " he said in a surprisingly soft voice as he stared at me, ignoring my hand. The contrast between his grave tone and his grinning face was disconcerting.

"But that's not your real name. I'd prefer to address you by that."

"That name is gone. Call me the Joker if you wish to have any meaningful communication with me."

I was reluctant to do that. The patient's Joker persona appeared to be the axis upon which his criminal career turned. I did not want to reinforce that persona. Yet I had to communicate with him. I had little choice but to acquiesce.

"Very well, Mr. Joker. I—"

"*Just* . . . 'Joker.' "

I thrust out my hand again.

"Joker, I'm Dr. Lewis. I'll be handling your therapy."

He ignored my hand and appeared suddenly agitated.

"When did you arrive? I've never seen you before. Where is Dr. Hills? Why isn't he treating me?"

"Dr. Hills sent me. I'm new to the staff since your last . . . escape."

I could read fury in his eyes, but the grin never wavered.

"I want the head man. I *always* get the head man. I deserve it! I'm not just another petty crook, you know. I'm the Joker. I'm the king of crime in this burg and I want Dr. Hills!"

Grandiosity and entitlement. I considered adding Narcissistic Personality Disorder (301.81) to my list of diagnoses.

I shrugged and tried to be disarming.

"Sorry, Joker. He sent me in his place. Looks like we're stuck with each other."

Suddenly he relaxed.

"Okay."

Emotional lability.

For the third time, I stuck out my hand. This time, to the accompaniment of small clinks from the chains on his manacles, he took it. As we shook, I heard a buzz and felt a sting in my palm. I cried out in surprise and snatched my hand away. The Joker began to laugh.

That laugh. His speaking voice had been so soft, almost soothing. But the laugh—a broken, high-pitched keen that makes the small hairs rise.

The guards leaped forward and thrust him into the chair. He laughed maniacally as they ripped something from one of his fingers. The older of the two guards handed it to me, then they searched him for anything else he might be carrying.

I stared at the object in my hand. A joy buzzer. A simple, corny, old-time practical joke.

"He's clean, Doc," the older guard said as they finished their search.

I stared at the buzzer.

"He was supposed to be 'clean' when you brought him in here."

They said nothing but took up new positions, closer now, flanking him on each side.

I held up the buzzer.

"How did you get this?"

"I had it sent in."

"You can't just have things 'sent in.' Inpatients are severely restricted as to possessions."

"You mean *other* inpatients," he said. "I'm the Joker. What I want, I get. Security here is a joke." His eyes lit. "Get it? A joke!"

The guards looked uncomfortable as he laughed. And they deserved to. He should never have arrived at this interview carrying something like that. What if the prong had been poisoned?

He seemed to read my mind.

"All in good, clean, harmless fun, Dr. Lewis. I'm as harmless as a pussycat."

I gave him a level stare.

"I believe Colin Whittier might take exception to that . . . if he could."

The Joker snorted and waved a hand in dismissal.

"Whittier! A fraud! A charlatan posing as an artist. He left his mark on the art world—like acne. I put a finishing touch to his work—a match. Get it?"

He began to laugh.

"You murdered him!"

"No loss. He deserved to die. A destroyer of true art. The world is far better off without him."

Complete lack of remorse or guilt.

I remembered his latest atrocity so well. I'd joined the staff shortly after the Joker's last escape and it wasn't too long thereafter that he raided an art gallery that was showing the work of an immensely talented young artist named Colin Whittier. The Joker pulled all of Whittier's work from the walls and burned the canvases in the center of the gallery floor. Then he replaced them with a collection of dark abstracts, each signed, *The Joker.*

The next morning, Whittier flew into a justifiable rage. He yanked all the Joker's paintings and ripped them to shreds. An eye for an eye. And that should have been that. But it wasn't. Whittier was found in the gallery two days later, dead. Murdered. But not by any means so simple as a bullet or a knife. No, his mouth and nose had been poured full of thick green paint, asphyxiating him. And then he was nailed to the gallery wall within a large, ornate gilt frame. On the wall next to the corpse was written:

Colin Whittier
RIP
An artist who really
threw himself into his work

The casual brutality of the crime still blew an icy wind through my soul whenever I thought of it. And the perpetrator was sitting not three feet away from me. Grinning.

Grinning . . .

I'd quietly admired Whittier's work for years. His paintings spoke to me. I'd even bid on one or two of his early works a few years ago when they were still within reach, but lost out to deeper pockets. Now they were permanently out of reach. Well, at least there were posters. But when I thought of all the paintings he would never do, I felt a rage seep through to my very soul—

Stop!

This was no good. I was becoming emotional. I couldn't allow that. I had to help this man, and I couldn't do it if I remained angry. I terminated the first session then and there.

Session Two

"He's clean this time, Doc," said the older guard as he sat the Joker in front of me.

"You're sure of that?" I said.

"Yeah. Pretty much."

I did not offer to shake hands with the patient.

"Good morning, Joker," I said, cheerily addressing him by the name he preferred.

The Joker stared at me, his eyes twinkling as I took my place on the far side of the table.

"I've decided to accept you as my physician for this stay, Dr. Lewis."

"Be still, my heart."

"I was getting tired of Dr. Hills, anyway. Such an egotist—an I-sore. Always letting off esteem. Get it?"

"Unfortunately, yes."

"But seriously, folks, if I am to cooperate in therapy, we must have privacy." He glanced at the two guards who flanked him. "I can't have a couple of screws eavesdropping on the intimate details of my life."

He had a point, of course. But I wasn't about to take any chances. I had the guards manacle his wrists and ankles to the arms and legs of his chair, then had them wait outside the closed door.

"Your credentials are impressive," the Joker said when we were alone.

Concern began to nibble at the back of my neck.

"You know nothing of my credentials."

"*Au contraire,* Dr. Lewis. I have a complete dossier on you."

He then proceeded to recite my curriculum vitae, ticking off one by one the schools I'd attended, the awards I'd received, my class rank in medical school, my appointment as chief resident on Downstate's psychiatric service, even my starting salary here at Arkham.

"That's an insult," he said, shaking his head in disdain at the last item. "You're worth far more than that."

I knew my jaw was hanging open and slack.

"Where did you—?"

My expression must have been hilarious, for the Joker burst out laughing.

"I told you—I'm the Joker, the Clown Prince of Crime! Nothing goes on in this city without my knowledge."

Persistent grandiose delusions. But how did he . . . ?"

I shook off my shock and forced myself to focus on the matter at hand. Namely, interviewing my patient. He was uncooperative, giving nonsense answers to my questions about his childhood, and purposely bizarre responses to the Rorschach blots I showed him.

I tried probing his past history again.

"Ever been in love, Joker?"

"Always. I'm girl crazy—girls won't go out with me, and it makes me crazy! Get it?"

I pressed on: "Ever been married?"

"Dr. Jekyll, I believe you're getting under my hide."

"Answer the question, please."

"Married? Me? No. I prefer to stay single and unaltared. Get it?"

For the second time, amid wild laughter, I terminated the session early.

Conference

Later that day I had a clinical conference with Dr. Hills, the chief of psychiatry at Arkham. We discussed my two disturbing encounters with the Joker.

"Be extremely wary, Hal," Dr. Hills told me. "He's a diabolical creature."

I'd never heard Dr. Hills talk like this. It was so unclinical, so . . . unscientific.

"I know he's an incorrigible, but—"

"He's worse than that. He's a master manipulator. He makes it extremely difficult, almost impossible, to stay in command of your therapy session. He turns everything around on you. If you're not careful, he'll reverse the therapy process. Instead of you treating him, he will be influencing you, making you question yourself, your values, everything you believe in. . . ." Dr. Hill's voice trailed off and a far away look seeped into his eyes. "Everything."

I didn't know about that. What I did know was that he would not be manipulating me—although he had managed to unsettle me. That would not happen again.

"What I would like to know," I said, "is how he manages to have such easy access to outside sources from which he should be completely cut off."

"I know, I know. We don't know how he does it. But don't let that distract you. Stay on course. This is your trial by fire for Arkham Asylum. If you can weather the Joker, you can handle anything."

"You make him sound like the devil himself."

Dr. Hills looked away. "Sometimes I wonder . . ."

Session Five

I tried to hide my agitation as the session began, tried to pretend that nothing untoward had happened. The Joker, for his part, was less cooperative than usual. Despite the fact that we were alone, he said not a word. Just sat there staring at me. Grinning.

Finally, I turned off the tape recorder, ready to terminate the session.

Then he spoke.

"Don't you like your new car?"

I bit down on the insides of my cheeks to keep from shouting out my anger. I couldn't let him see how shaken I was, how he'd gotten to me.

It had happened that morning. I'd been running late and so it was especially frustrating when I couldn't find my car in the Gotham Gardens parking lot. At first I'd thought I'd simply forgotten where I'd parked it, for there was a Mercedes in the spot I usually used. Soon it became clear that my car was gone. But who would steal that old junker?

Agitated now, I walked over to my usual spot and checked out the Mercedes. It was new. A brand-new 560 SEL. Royal blue. My favorite color. I thought about how I was going to own one of those someday and I wondered which tenant in a low-rent apartment complex like Gotham Gardens could afford such a beast.

Then I saw the keys in the door lock.

I peered through the driver's window. There was an envelope on the front seat. With my name on it. I yanked open the car door and tore open the envelope. Inside was the registration card—in my name—and a sheet of purple stationery.

> *For the exclusive use*
> *of Dr. Harold Lewis.*

A playing card was attached. A joker.

"Well?" the Joker said now from the other side of the table. "Aren't you even going to say thank you?"

No. I wasn't going to say thank you.

"How'd it drive?"

I'd been running late already and had no choice but to drive the Mercedes to work. How'd it drive? Like piloting a cloud. But I'd been too angry, too unsettled by this arrogant intrusion into my life to enjoy it.

I steadied myself. Finally, I felt able to speak calmly.

"Where is my old car?"

"Gone. Dead. Kaput. Junked. Pounded into a neat little cube of twisted steel and sent back to the melting pot from which it came."

"Listen, pal," I said, "if you think such a blatant attempt at bribery will get you special treatment from me, or turn me into some sort of clandestine ally, you're sadly mistaken. I'm not for sale."

Not ever. I thought. *Especially not to the murderer of Colin Whittier.*

"Of course you're not. Do you really think I'd be so clumsy as to try to bribe you with a car? A *car*? Good gracious me, no. It's just that I simply couldn't bear to know that my personal physician was driving around in public in that 1982 Toyota. A *Celica*, no less! I've got a reputation to uphold. How do you think it looks to my organization when they see their leader's doctor driving a Jap junker? It was an intolerable situation that required an immediate remedy."

"I won't stand for it!"

"I'm afraid you have no choice, Dr. Lewis. The deed is done. Your old car is no more. You might as well use the new one. Why not enjoy it? Your conscience is clear, you ethics are unsullied. I ask nothing in return, only that you drive it. My image, you see."

"Guards," I called. I wasn't about to listen to any more of this.

"Dina will love it, too."

Dina? What did he know about Dina?

Weak and numb, I watched the guards unlock his restraints and lead him out.

Session Eight

The session was going particularly well. The Joker was opening up about his troubled, turbulent childhood. I still had no insight as yet into the mechanisms of his behavior, but we were just getting started in therapy. The important thing was that I felt that we were beginning to make progress toward a viable physician-patient relationship. Then he started with the crummy one-liners again.

"You know, Dr. Lewis, I was the kind of student who made my teachers stay after school. Get it? I was an honor student—I was saying either 'Yes, your Honor,' or 'No, your Honor.' Get it? When I was a kid I was so tough, I got thrown out of every reform school in the country."

"Can we try to be serious? Just for a moment?"

"Don't worry, Doc. I know you're trying. In fact, you're very trying. Get it?"

That did it. I made a final note prior to ending the session. But when I looked up, I saw that his hands were free. He was holding out a deck of playing cards.

"Pick a card," he said. "Any card."

Terror jolted through me. I shouted for the guards. By the time they reached us, the Joker's hands were back in the manacles. The deck of cards remained between us on the table.

"Never mind," I told the guards. After all, he hadn't tried to harm me. Maybe this was an opportunity to gain his confidence, which might put us on the quickest road to meaningful therapy. "False alarm."

As they returned to their posts outside the door, the Joker looked at me curiously. I picked up the deck and shuffled through it. All jokers.

"*How* do you get these things smuggled in?"

"I've told you: I'm the—"

" 'Clown Prince of Crime.' I know. A regular modern-day Mabuse."

"Ah. The doctor is a movie buff. Yes, I suppose I could be compared to Dr. Mabuse on a superficial level, but I am his superior in every way. Dr. Mabuse was a piker compared to the Joker."

More grandiosity. It was wearying.

"But you're real," I said. "Mabuse was fiction. He didn't have to worry about running up against Batman."

I knew immediately that I'd struck a nerve. Something changed in the Joker's eyes and demeanor. The airy, bon-vivant pose vanished. I felt a chill worm across my shoulders as cold hatred flashed from his eyes and hung like rank smog in the air between us. And then as suddenly as it had come, it was gone. Blown away by a gust of laughter.

"Batman! Talk about crazies! They put *me* in here while they let *him* run around loose in his cape and tights."

"They could have put you in the electric chair for murdering Colin Whittier," I said softly. I'd almost said *should* instead of *could*. I'd have to be careful.

"But they can't!" he said with another laugh. "Because I've been classified as insane! I'm not responsible. Isn't that wonderful? Oh, it's so good to be mad in America. I can do unto others, but they can't do unto me!"

As he giggled on, I said, "Don't you feel any remorse for the hurt you've caused people? For the artistic riches you've robbed from society by killing Colin Whittier?"

"Society? What has society ever done for me?"

"Well, you might have a point there, but you've caused untold harm in your lifetime—the deaths, the grief, the pain. Don't you feel any impulse to make reparation?"

"Not the slightest. I put the Joker first. If I don't, who will? I. Me. *Moi.* Society, the public good, the little man, they can take my leavings. And I'd prefer you not mention Batman in my presence again."

Remembering how quickly he'd gotten in and out of his manacles a moment ago, I nodded.

"And by the way," he said, "how does the lovely Dina like the new car?"

I was suddenly boiling on the inside, but I remained cool without.

"Just as you do not wish Batman mentioned, I do not wish anyone from my personal life mentioned."

"She's very attractive."

"I hope you're not thinking of threatening her."

"Threaten?" He laughed. "That sort of thing is for pistoleros and dime-a-dozen desperadoes. *Fratellezza* swine. I like you, Dr. Lewis. I have no interest in threatening anyone dear to you. Besides, why should I? What can you do for me?"

"You might think I can help you escape."

Another laugh. "I can escape any time I wish."

"Really? Then, why are you still imprisoned here?"

"Because for the time being it amuses me," he said without missing a beat. "Just as I can smuggle in anything I wish, I can leave anytime I wish. And when I decide that it's time to take my leave, I shall escape with élan, dear doctor. Without your help. No crude, petty jailbreak for the Joker. The Joker will not sneak out, nor will he crawl or tunnel out. He'll either fly or walk—at the time of his own choosing."

"We'll see."

"Yes. We will. And when are you going to ask that woman to marry you?"

"None of your business!"

"Ah! Business! I wish we were in business! Building and loan—I wish you'd get out of the building and leave me alone. Get it?"

"Good day, Joker," I said, rising.

"Good day, Dr. Lewis."

Session Ten

I could barely contain my rage. As soon as the guards left, I exploded.

"This time you've gone too far, Joker!"

"Whatever are you talking about, Dr. Lewis?"

"The ring, damn you! The goddamn ring!"

"You mean that little bauble I sent Dina? Think nothing of it."

"It wasn't 'just a bauble,' and you know it!"

When I'd answered my doorbell the night before, I'd been shocked to find Dina standing there with tears in her eyes. She threw her arms around me and told me how beautiful it was, and what a romantic way to propose. And then she showed me the ring—a huge solitaire, flawless, at least three carats. It was perfect, she said, the engagement ring she'd always dreamed of, and to think I'd sent it to her nestled in a bouquet of roses with the note: *Dina—Make my life complete. Marry me. Hal.*

I'd been planning to ask her to marry me as soon as I got on my feet financially, but I'd had nothing to do with this. I knew immediately who was behind it, though. I should have told her right then. But when I saw the look in her eyes, the joy in her face, I couldn't. How could I take that ring off her finger and say it wasn't from me? I wrapped my arms around her and said nothing.

"I won't have you interfering in my life!"

"Who's interfering?" he said through that grin. "I like you. I don't want to see you settle for second best. In a few years you'll be able to afford all these things on your own. But for now, it gives me pleasure to help you out. What's so wrong with that?"

"You're trying to compromise my judgment! And it won't work!"

"Of course it won't. We both know you've got too much integrity for that. By the way, there's an engagement gift waiting for you in your apartment."

That did it. I stormed out of the examining room.

But deep within my gut was a strange new feeling, a growing awareness that it was my duty to render this . . . this *Joker* incapable of corrupting or harming anyone again.

Conference

"A prefrontal lobotomy?" Dr. Hills said. "You must be joking!"

The irony of his choice of words was lost in the shocked silence around me. I'd gone directly from my session with the Joker to the psychiatric conference where I'd blurted out my recommendation. The rest of the psychiatric staff—Drs. Hills, Miller, and Bolland—were there, and I believe I stunned them all.

The solution had occurred to me as I'd entered the room. A prefrontal lobotomy—surgical invasion of the frontal lobe of the brain. It had been used briefly with great success in the 1930s. Violent, agitated patients had become pussycats—gentle, placid, physically and emotionally in low gear. But the procedure had fallen out of favor because it was deemed too extreme. And because it was irreversible.

"Yes, I'm aware that it's a radical suggestion," I said, "but you've got to admit that this particular case warrants a radical solution. *Demands* it, I should think. Lobotomy is definitive therapy in the case of a patient as incorrigibly violent as the Joker."

Dr. Hills said, "We'll come under heavy fire from the patients' rights groups merely for suggesting it. The ACLU, all the—"

"What about the rights of the people he will harm in the future when he escapes again?" I replied. "And we all know he will escape again. Let's be honest, gentlemen: modern psychiatry has failed society in the case of the Joker. I know. I've gone through his past records. The man seems to escape at will. Then he goes on a rampage of murder and robbery, is caught, is returned to us, only to escape again for another rampage. No matter how we chain him, drug him, psychoanalyze him, he escapes. And he never pays a price for the harm he does! Between rampages, he's given a clean, comfortable cell, three meals a day, and free medical care. For life!"

"But a lobotomy—?" Dr. Hills said.

"We've failed to contain him, we've failed to change him with therapy or control him with drugs, and the courts won't send him to the chair. As physicians charged with treating the so-called criminally insane, I think we have a duty to consider the definitive therapy for his sort of behavior disorder."

There was a long silence. Finally, Dr. Hills said, "I'll take it up with the State Board of Medical Examiners."

I left the conference room in a state of wild exhilaration. I might have

been the new man on the staff but I was making my presence felt in no uncertain terms. And beyond that, I knew that my recommendation for lobotomy would prove to the Joker once and for all that Harold Lewis,
M.D., was not for sale.

Session Nine-A

Numb, speechless, I stared across the table at the Joker. That smile . . . if
only he'd stop smiling.

"Well?" he said. "Do you like your engagement gift?"

"Where—?" My mouth was dry. "Where did you get it?"

I'd come home last night to find an original Colin Whittier hanging on
my wall. An *original*! An abstract of swirling blues and greens that made
me think of the depths of the ocean . . . the eternal cycle of birth, life, and
death . . . cold, ghastly, unutterably beautiful.

The cost of a Whittier had gone through the roof since his death at the
Joker's hands. Each was worth millions now. I'd never be able to afford a
Whittier. Never. And the Joker had given me one.

I owned a Whittier original . . . a Whittier . . .

The monetary value meant nothing to me, for selling it was out of the
question. I'd sell my soul to the devil before I'd part with it.

"I have a bunch of the things," the Joker said. "From his show at the
Gotham Gallery."

"But the papers said you burned them!"

"Don't be silly. They're far too valuable for that, although for the life of
me I can't imagine why. The man showed not the slightest trace of talent. I
burned some old canvases of my own that I was unhappy with."

"Then . . . you still have all those Whittiers?"

"Yes. Stacked up in one of my warehouses. I forget which one, actually.
I had one of my men dig that piece out for you."

A stack of them . . . I felt weak.

"Well? Do you like it? You haven't told me."

"I—I can't accept stolen goods," I said, forcing the words past my lips.

"Too bad. I was going to give the rest of them to you as a wedding present." The Joker shrugged. "Very well. I'll have my men remove it and—"

"*No!*" I said—almost a shout. "I mean, not yet. Let me live with it
awhile."

The Joker's smile seemed to broaden. "As you wish, Dr. Lewis."

Conference

Whittiers . . . a stack of Whittiers . . . sitting in a warehouse . . . collecting dust . . . rats nibbling at the canvases . . . clawing at the paint . . .

The image roamed my mind at will as I sat at the conference table and waited for Dr. Hills to arrive. Finally, he burst in.

"They approved it!" he cried. "The State Board of Medical Examiners approved a prefrontal lobotomy on the Joker! Any other patient and they would have said no, but the Joker—yes! Within weeks Arkham Asylum is going to be in all the medical journals!"

As excited chatter swept the table, I felt my blood run cold. The paintings. The Whittiers. A lobotomized Joker would be so passive and tractable that he'd tell the police the whereabouts of all his stashes of loot. The Whittiers . . . *my* Whittiers . . . they'd be returned to the gallery . . . to be sold for millions apiece.

"When is the surgery scheduled?"

"Tomorrow morning. Dr. Robinson is flying in from Toronto tonight."

"Maybe we should give electroshock a try," I said.

"ECT has failed already. What's the matter, Hal? The lobotomy was your idea. Having a change of heart?"

I hesitated. How could I protest the implementation of my own suggestion?

But that had been before I'd known about the Whittiers.

"Maybe. I think ECT deserves another chance. It could be we're rushing this too much."

"We have to move quickly. It was the Board's opinion that delay will only allow opposition to organize and cause legal obstruction. They feel that if we present the world with a lobotomized Joker as a fait accompli, there will be far less protest. And we will have discharged our duty to the public. As you so eloquently stated, Hal, we need definitive therapy in the Joker's case. And that's just what we're providing."

What could I say? I decided to risk everything.

"I'd like to go on record right now as being opposed to the surgery. At least at this time. I think we should explore other options first. And I'd like to call for a vote."

They all stared at me in shock. I didn't care. I had to stop the surgery—at least until I got my hands on the Whittiers. They were all I could think of. Even if I could only delay the surgery, it would give me time to convince

Dina to move up our marriage so that the Joker could make good on his promised wedding gift. After that, I'd push again for the lobotomy.

But when the vote came, mine was the only hand raised in opposition.

Session Nine-B

That night I arranged another session with the Joker. I didn't even bother going through the motions of turning on the tape recorder.

"Did you really mean what you said about giving me the other Whittiers as a wedding gift?"

"Of course," the Joker said. "Have you set a date yet?"

I clasped my hands together to keep them from trembling. I'd always been a terrible liar.

"Yes. Tomorrow. We've decided we can't wait any longer. We're getting married before a justice of the peace in the morning."

"Really? Congratulations! I'm very happy for you."

"Thank you. So . . . I was wondering . . . could you tell me where you've stored those stolen Whittiers? I'll pick them up tonight, if you don't mind."

"No. Of course not. Do you know where Wrightson Street is?"

I could barely contain my excitement.

"No. But I'll find it."

"Here," the Joker said, casually freeing his hands from the restraints and picking up a pencil. "I'll draw you a map."

As he began to draw, I leaned forward. Suddenly his other hand flashed forward. I felt a sting in my neck. As I jerked back I saw the dripping syringe in his hand. I opened my mouth to shout for the guards but the words wouldn't come. A roar like a subway charging into a station filled my ears as everything faded to black.

A voice, faraway, calling me through the blackness. I move toward it and come into the light.

A bizarre, twisted face, half Joker, half normal, floating before me.

"Time to wake up, Dr. Lewis," it says in the Joker's voice. "Time to rise and shine."

I try to speak. My lips feel strange as they move, and the only sounds I can make are garbled, unintelligible.

I try to move, but my hands are cuffed to the chair. I can only sit and watch.

And as I watch, the Joker stares into a mirror and fits pieces of flesh-colored latex over his chin and left cheek. I see him only in profile, but as each piece is affixed, he looks less and less like the Joker, and more and more like someone else. Someone I know.

"You gave me some very bad moments there, Dr. Lewis," he says. "For a full twenty-four hours you had me believing I'd misjudged you, underestimated you. Self-doubt is most unpleasant, even in a minuscule dose. I don't know how other people put up with a lifetime full of it."

I try again to speak but the result is still gibberish.

"Don't bother," he says. "One of the effects of that injection is a disorganization of the speech centers of the brain. But let me get back to the story of my brief episode of inner turmoil. You see, all through these past few weeks I've been thinking that I had you, really had you. For instance, you kept the Mercedes. I mean, if you'd really wanted to show me up, you could have sold it, bought another old Toyota junker, and given the balance to charity. That would have put me in my place. Same with the engagement ring. Oh, I know I put you in a tough spot then, but if you really had the courage of your convictions, you'd have told the lovely Dina the truth. But you didn't. You were willing to let the very first step of your marriage be a false one. Oh, I was sure I had you."

He pauses as he begins brushing makeup over his latex mask, then continues:

"Then you go storming into the staff conference and drop your bombshell. I was shocked, believe me. A prefrontal lobotomy, Dr. Lewis? How audacious! It would have worked, I'm sure. I was almost proud of you when I heard. None of the other incompetents here had the brains to think of it, or the guts to suggest it. But you charged right in and told it like it was. I like that. Reminds me of me."

I try to speak again, with the same results.

"What's that?" he says. "You're not like me? Oh, but you are. A while back you took me to task for being indifferent to the consequences of my actions, their tragic effects upon the individuals directly involved and upon society at large. And I told you, quite honestly, that I didn't care. You were so self-righteous. And then what did you go and do? When you discovered that I had something you wanted, you tried to turn the staff away from your 'definitive therapy.' Up to that moment, I'd planned simply to disappear and, as usual, leave you all wondering how. But now I see that you weren't concerned with what was best for society; you weren't concerned with the responsibilities of your position here. You were concerned only with what Dr. Harold Lewis wanted. And you weren't even honest with yourself about it."

He lifts the mirror and holds it before his made-up face as he turns toward me. Hidden behind the mirror, he says, "See? Didn't I say you were just like me?"

And in the mirror I see the pale, distorted features of the Joker grinning back at me.

Horror rips through me. I try to scream but it's useless.

"That injection contained a nonlethal variation on my tried-and-true Joker venom," he says, staying behind the mirror. "So, besides scrambling your speech areas, it has also pulled your lips into a handsome smile. I've completed the picture by bleaching your skin and dying your hair and fingernails green."

Then he lowers the mirror.

I gasp as I see my own face on the Joker's body.

"How do I look?" he says.

I struggle frantically with the manacles, trying to pull free, trying to break the arms of the chair so I can get my hands around his throat.

"Guards!" he calls in my voice. The two uniformed men rush in and the Joker says, "The patient has become violent. I think it best to carry him back to his cell as is, chair and all. I'll order a sedative that will hold him until his surgery tomorrow morning."

The lobotomy! Please, God! Not the lobotomy!

As they drag me from the room, I hear his soft voice behind me.

"And I'll be sure to give Dina your best tonight."

Gary Raisor called in October about the anthology he was editing for Dark Harvest. He'd titled it *Obsessions*, and that was what it was about: obsessions. This was his third call this year. Could I contribute?

At that time my major obsession was still *Reprisal*. I'd worked out most of the kinks in the novel, and the writing was picking up momentum. I didn't want to lose that. I had no time for a story about an obsession. But Gary's such an engaging guy I told him I'd give it a shot if I found the time.

I went back to *Reprisal* but frequently found myself distracted by thoughts of food. You see, Mary and I had started a strict low-fat diet that summer in an effort to drop ten pounds each. The diet was working, but I was *hungry*. Always. There were times when all I could think about was food. Eating was gradually becoming . . . an obsession.

I started "Topsy" before the World Fantasy Convention in Seattle and finished it when I returned to Jersey. The story is written entirely in first-person vernacular. That can wear you out if it goes on too long. But "Topsy" is only three thousand words, just the right length. It was recently reprinted in *100 Hair-Raising Little Horror Stories*.

(Hint: The key to clarity here is to read the words phonetically and *listen* to what you're reading.)

TOPSY

I'm inna middle a chewing on dis giant lasagna noodle when Nurse Delores appears.

"Morning, Topsy!" she says as she marches inta da room in her white uniform.

Dey call me Topsy.

Don't ax why dey call me dat. My name's Bruno. But evybody here calls me Topsy.

"Oh, no," she says. "You've been eating your sheets again!"

I look down an see she's right. My sheets is all chewed up. I guess dat weren't no giant lasagna noodle after all.

God I'm hungry.

"Ready for breakfast?" she says all bright an cheery.

Course I'm ready for breakfast—I'm *dyin* for breakfast—but I don't say nuttin. Cause what dey call breakfast here ain't. Ain't lunch or dinner neither. Just liquid. Not even a shake. I amember when I useta eat diet shakes. Useta drink ten a dem fa breakfast. An anotha fa coffee break. Dey're junk. I neva lost weight on dem. Not once.

But no shakes roun here. Just dis clear glop. And here she comes wit a whole glass of it.

"Here, Topsy. Open your mouth and drink this," she says, all Mary Sunshine perkiness.

If my hands weren't strapped to da side of da bed I'd grab her an make her drink it herself an see how much *she* likes dat shit.

She tilts da glass toward my lips but I turn away.

"Come on, Topsy," she says. "I know you don't like it, but it's this or nothing."

"No!"

"Come on, Topsy. Do it for Delores. Don't be mad at me. The protein hydrosylate isn't my idea. It's doctors orders. And it's working. You're down to twelve hundred and thirty pounds now."

Still I don't open.

"Come on, baby. It's this or go hungry. Open up."

Sometimes she calls me baby, but dat don't make it taste better, believe me.

I open an pretend it's a milk shake. A big double chocolate praline shake laced wit wet walnuts.

Don't help. I gag an wanna barf it all ova da place but manage to choke it down. Gotta. It's all I'll get til lunch. An dat'll only be a salad.

God I'm so hungry.

Dey don't unnerstan aroun here. Don't seemta realize dat I gotta eat. Dey say dey're helpin me by stickin needles in my arms an feedin me teeny bits of veggies an barely a mouthful of whole-grain sumpin-or-otha an dis liquid protein shit, but dey ain't helpin. Ain't helpin me one bit.

Guy's gotta eat.

Useta be so good when my brotha Sal an his wife Marie was takin care a me. I was happy den. Dat's cause dey unnerstood. Dey knew I hadda eat. Boy could dey cook. No limit, man. Anyting I wanted, it was dere on da bed tray soon as I said.

Dey unnerstood me, know'm sayin?

Breakfast was da best. On regula days Marie'd whip me up a coupla dozen eggs over easy wit a coupla poundsa bacon an lotsa dose spicy Jimmy Dean sausage patties. *Love* dat Jimmy Dean sausage. Den she'd make me a gigantic stack a ten-inch pancakes swimmin in butta an Vermont maple syrup. An on special days, like Satadays an Sundays, she'd go all out an add in a whole platterful a eggs Benedict. *Love* eggs Benedict. All dat Hollandaise sauce over dose poached eggs on English muffins an Canadian bacon. Heaven, man. Absolute heaven.

Midmornings dere'd be Entenmann's sugar crumb cake or cheese babka or my favorite, All Butter French Crumb cake. Or sometimes lox an bagels wit cream cheese an herring in cream sauce.

Neva could tell what lunch was gonna be. Sometimes a coupla family-size buckets of da Colonel's Extra Crispy fried chicken, but most times Sal'd bring me in tree or four sausage an pepperoni pizzas or half a dozen subs from Vinnie's. Da subs were da best, man. Pepper an egg, veal parmesian, Italian delight, an da Kitchen Sink sub wit evyting on it.

Loved lunch, man.

Midafternoons I'd do it kinda light. Jus some coffee an a coupla packages a Oreos. Or maybe some Little Debbie Satellite bars. When it was hot, Sal'd get me a gallon a Welsh Farms peanut butter swirl ice cream. He'd mix it up wit a can of Hershey's chocolate syrup an I'd be in heaven, man.

Dinner'd start aroun five cause I couldn't wait no longer. Marie'd cut me up a nice cold antipasta while Sal'd broil up a coupla dozen garlic clams oreganata. Den da pasta—a coupla poundsa Marie's super linguine wit white clam sauce, da noodles swimmin in butter an garlic, an da diced clams piled all over da top. Next da fish, usually a coupla tree- or four-pound lobsters or half a dozen pounds a shrimp done up scampi style. After dat, a meat, maybe steak or veal or a nice Krakus ham. For dessert, maybe anotha gallon a da peanut butter swirl or a nice cherry cheesecake, or a coupla peach pies a la mode wit some cannoli onna side.

My bedtime snack was always candy. Sal'd let me have all da Snickers bars I wanted. He'd buy dem by da case an leave a whole box right by my bed so's I could grab one anytime I got hungry. An let me tell you, I got hungry a lot durin da night. But I neva woke Sal or Marie. I knew dey needed deir sleep. I was a good guy. I hung on an starved till breakfast.

Sal an Marie knew how to take care of me. Dey knew what I needed. Dat I hadda eat. Dey understood about eatin, know'm sayin?

Evyting was great till dat day when dey was both out at once. Dey hardly ever left me alone. I mean, sure dey went out togetha once inna while, but neva for long. Dis time dey was gone a long time. A coupla hours, maybe, an I was starvin. Not jus hungry, man. I mean *starvin*!

An I couldn't get outta bed.

Wasn't always dis big. I mean, like I was always big accordin to Ma. Born big an jus kept gettin bigger, she always said. But now I'm *huge*, man. Take up a whole damn king-size bed. Can't get outta bed on my own. Always needed help from Sal or Marie. Good ting Marie's real strong—good

Sicilian stock—or she'd've been no help. But all I needed was for one of dem ta give me a little boost an someone to lean on while I shuffled to da batroom. Dey took off da doorframe but still I can barely turn aroun in dere. Lucky I only go twice a day. An it don't matter if I'm doin number one or number two, man, I gotta sit. First of all, I can't stand dat long. An second, well, I mean, I ain't seen my dick in at least ten years, so da only way I can be sure I ain't peein onna floor is to sit. An even den I sometimes miss da bowl. And when I take a dump . . .

Let's not talk about dat.

Anyways, Sal an Marie was gone fa hours an I was starvin so I tried to get outta bed on my own. Took forever, but I managed to sit up by myself. Made me feel good. Hadn't done dat on my own in years. Den by holdin onta da bedpost I somehow got myself to my feet. I started shufflin cross da bedroom, takin little teeny steps so's I wouldn't lose my balance. God, I din't want to tink what would happena me if I toppled over an wound up onna floor. I mean, man, dey'd hafta bring in a crane or sumpin ta get me up again.

An just as I was tinkin about it, it started happenin. I started swayin. Little sways at first, den bigger ones. I tell ya I was scared to det. I aimed myself for da doorway, figrin I could hold onta da jamb, but started tee-terin as I stumbled an I slammed inna da doorway wit a awful crack. I saw da wallboard crack an heard da studs inside groan an creak, but da wall held an I was still on my feet. I hadn't fallen!

But I was stuck. Usually I went troo dat door sideways. Now I was jammed inta it at a angle an no matter how I tried I couldn't move out or in. I was scared. I started gettin pains in my chest an my heart started racin like crazy. I hadn't been on my feet for dat long a time in more years dan I could amemba. Couldn't breathe. I yelled fa help. Screamed my freakin lungs out, but not fa long. My chest was gettin all congested, like I was fillin up wit water or sometin. I couldn't scream no more. Evyting got fuzzy, den evyting got black.

Next ting I knew I was in dis place.

It's a hospital room. Actually it's not a room, it's what dey call a suite. Two rooms. I'm in da big room, but dere's a smaller one straight ahead a me dat's like a little kitchen wit a fridge an a microwave an stuff. An dere's a batroom off to my right but in all da time I'm here I ain't been in it yet. Dey told me what hospital I'm in but I forgot. Who cares, anyway? Da im-portant ting is dey're *starvin* me!

"Time for your bed bath," Delores says as she comes in carryin a basin of soapy water. She stops an stares at me. "Good Lord, Topsy! You're eating your pillow!"

I look. Oh, yeah. I guess I am. I tought it was a big marshmallow.

I spit feathers.

"Never mind," she says wit a sigh. "Let's get to the ablutions."

Most guys would get off bein washed down by a blonde dish like Delores, but I gotta admit I'm too hungry ta tink about anyting but food.

"Gimme a treat, Delores."

"Shush!" she says, glancin around my room. "What if one of the doctors heard you?"

"Don't care. Need a treat."

"After your bath."

"No. Now. Gotta have sometin."

"Oh, all right."

As she reaches into her uniform pocket I can feel da juices pour into my mout. She pulls out one of dose little low-sugar caramels she sneaks in for me an unwraps it.

"Stop it, Topsy," she says. "You're droolin all over yourself. Open up."

I open an she pops it into my mout, jerkin her fingers back real quick cause I accidently bit her once.

I taste da caramel. Da sweetness runs all over da inside of my mout. *OhGodohGodohGodohGodohGodohGodohGodohGod!*

I near start ta cry.

"Come on, Topsy," Delores says, pattin my arm. She's a good nurse. She feels for me. I can tell. "You'll be all right."

"Need food!"

"You need to lose weight, that's what you need. You almost died of congestive heart failure back in your house. It's lose weight or die, Topsy."

I figure I'd ratha die cause starvin like dis is worse dan det.

"Where's Sal? Where's Marie?"

"Do we have to go through that again?" Delores says as she starts rubbin a soapy washcloth on my belly. I look down at my bare skin. Looks like acres a ice cream.

"Troo what again?"

"I know you don't want to accept it, Topsy, but your brother and his wife have been indicted for attempted murder and they're out on bail awaiting trial. They are forbidden by the court to come anywhere near you. They were trying to kill you, Topsy."

"No. Dey treated me good! Dey fed me!"

"They were feeding you to death, that's what they were doing. A nifty little scheme, I've got to admit. You kept signing checks so they could buy you food, big checks that allowed them to live high while they kept pumping you full of the worst kind of food you can imagine."

"Good food," I told her. "Da best!"

"The *worst*! High fat, high calorie. Your blood sugar and cholesterol and triglycerides were through the roof! And when they got you to fifteen hundred pounds, they left you for a day. They knew you'd try to get out of bed, and they figured you'd fall and die on the floor. Well, it almost worked. Lucky for you that you got stuck in the doorway and someone heard you yell. Even then you almost didn't make it. By the time they broke through the wall of the house and hoisted you out, you were so far gone into heart failure you almost died in the back of the truck on the way to the hospital. It almost worked, Topsy. The rats almost got your money."

"Ain't got no money."

"Oh, really? Folks with no money can't afford a private hospital suite like this. What do you call that twelve million dollars you won?"

Oh, yeah. Dat. I won dat inna state lotto a few years ago. I forget tings sometimes. I amemba Sal an Marie bein real happy for me. Dat's when dey moved in an started takin care of me. Dey treated me real good. Dey unnerstood dat I gotta eat.

I always hadda eat. Evyting I amemba bout bein a kid is food. Ma cooked for me alla time, an when she ran outta food I'd go over my fren's houses and deir moms'd fix me stuff. I lost my first job as a kid makin deliveries for Angelo's Grocery because I useta eat half da stuff along da way. And whateva job I had, I always spent da money on food.

Food was evyting ta me. I amemba how I useta give people directions back in da days when I could still get aroun. It'd be "Go down to da Dunkin Donuts an turn left, den go bout tree blocks an turn right at da Dairy Queen an it's bout half a mile downa street, a block past Paisan's Pizza." All my landmarks hadda do wit food.

But afta I won da lotto an we moved out to Long Island, I got so fat dat my whole world became my bedroom, an time got measured by meals an TV shows.

Da TV's on now. I useta love to watch TV. All da game shows an talk shows inna mornin, an da soaps inna aftanoon. Loved dem all. Now I hate 'em. Not da shows—da commercials. Food! All dey seemta be sellin is freakin *food*! Like torture, man! I go crazy wit da little remote control but evytime I switch I see dis food bein shoved at me in livin color! I'm bout t'go crazy, know'm sayin? I mean, if it ain't McDonald's it's Burger King or Wendy's or Red Lobster wit dose shrimp just oozin butta onna enda da fork. Or da Pillsbury Doughboy's got some new cinnamon ting he's pushin, or dere's microwave chocolate cake or Reese's Pieces or Eat Beef It's Real Food or Domino's Pizza or Peter Pan Peanut Butter or Holly Farms Chicken or Downyflake Waffles or Dorito Nacho Chips an on an on.

Know'm sayin?

Tell ya it ain't fair, man. Guy could go *crazy*!

"Okay, Topsy," Delores is sayin. "It's time to do your back. Now I know you can't turn over, but I want you to help me. I'm going to unstrap your right hand so I can do some of your back."

Dey been keepin my hands strapped downta da bed frame. Dat's cause da diet's been makin me kinda goofy. I got bandages on da middle finger and pointer a my right hand cause I tried to eat dem.

Kid you not, man. I been goin a little squirrelly here. I mean, da otha night I really tought dose fingers was hot dogs. S'true. Jus like I tought my sheet was a big lasagna noodle an my pillow was a giant marshmallow, I coulda sworn dat night my two fingers was hot dogs. It was dark. I started chewin on dem an screamin at da same time. Da docs said I was hallucinatin. Closed me up wit ten stitches. Now dey keep my hands tied down so's I don't do it again.

Dey shouldn't worry. I won't. It hurt too much.

"Gimme a candy first," I tell her.

"No," Delores says. "After, Topsy. *After.*"

"Okay," I say. But I don't really mean it.

When she unstraps my right wrist, I roll left, like I'm lettin her wash da part of my back she can reach. But while I'm twisted dat way, I work on da left strap an get it undone. Now I'm ready.

"Okay, Topsy," she says. "Roll back now."

I roll. An keep on rollin. As I rock to da right, I grab Delores.

"Candy!" I shout. "Gimme! Now!"

Delores squeals an twists away. She's strong but I got a good grip on her. She pulls away but I stretch after her. Her feet slip an she goes down but I lean over da edge of da bed, keepin my grip, never lettin go, reachin wit my free hand for da pocket wit da caramels.

But suddenly I feel myself slippin. I mean da bed's tiltin, da whole freakin hospital bed's tippin ova wit me on it. An I'm headin right down on toppa Delores. I try to stop myself but I can't. Da bed's tilted too far. I'm outta control. I'm fallin. Delores screams as I land on her.

It ain't a long scream. More like a quick little yelp, like your pooch makes when you accidently step on its foot. Den she cuts off.

But she don't stop movin. She's strugglin an kickin an clawin unda me, tryna get out, tryna breathe. An I'm tryna get offa her, really an truly I am, but it's so hard. Finally I edge myself back an to da side. It's slow work, but finally I get offa her face.

Too late. Poor Delores has stopped strugglin by den. An when I manage to get a look at her face, it's kinda blue. Real blue, in fact. I mean, like she's sorta dead.

I like start ta cry. I can't help it. I loved Delores an now she's gone. I specially loved her caramels.

Which reminds me of her goody pocket. So while I'm cryin, I reach for her pocket. I push my hand inside but I can't find no caramels. Not a one.

No way, man! I know dere's candy in dere!

I push deeper inta da pocket but it's empty, man! Freakin *empty*!

I'm kinda upset now. I pull on da pocket. I mean, I *know* dere's candy in dere. Da pocket rips an still no caramels. I rip deepa, layer afta layer till I reach . . .

. . . skin.

Smooth white skin. It's a leg. Turkey leg. Big white meat turkey leg. Never heard of such a ting, but here it is right in fronta me. Waitin for me. An I can't resist. I take a bite—

Gaa! Ain't cooked. Raw and bloody. God, I'm freakin hungry but I can't eat raw turkey!

I look up an around. Da utility room is only a dozen or so feet away. If I can make it to da microwave . . .

Marty Greenberg again. The fifth time this year. But again, I asked for it. It was November 16 at another of SFWA's annual editor-publisher receptions. I was sitting with some of the mystery guys who'd dropped by—Bob Randisi, Michael Seidman among them—when Heather Woods of Tor mentioned a Dick Tracy anthology in the works, deadline end of December so they could time its release with the Warren Beatty film next year.

I straightened in my chair. Dick Tracy? Who's editing it? She told me Max Allan Collins and Marty Greenberg. I was rolling on *Reprisal*, I was diddling with a story for Jeff Gelb's *Shock Rock*, and only six weeks left before the Tracy deadline. None of that mattered. I had to be in it.

In all the long history of dramatic comic strips, two titles stand head and shoulders above the rest. *Little Orphan Annie* is tops. Whether or not you agree with Harold Gray's politics is irrelevant. The *LOA* strips from the thirties are a folksy chronicle of the Great Depression, challenging Dickens in their portrait of the poles of human venality and nobility. With limited wordage crammed cheek by jowl with drawings into the confined space of four little boxes, with only the stark blacks and whites of newsprint at his disposal, Harold Gray somehow managed on a daily basis to produce minimasterpieces of dramatic expressionism.

Dick Tracy is the second standout. Although Chester Gould also used light and shadow to excellent advantage, his characters lacked the depth of Gray's. But with the rogues' gallery of grotesque villains he flung against his hero through the years, who noticed? Flattop, the Brow, Flyface, Coffeehead, Shakey, the Mole, Pruneface . . . everybody has a personal favorite. Mine has always been Mumbles.

I had to do a Mumbles story.

I didn't know personally the coeditor, Max Allan Collins, though I did know his work—his mystery novels and his scripting of the current *Dick Tracy* strip. So I called Marty and said I wanted in. He said, No problem, but hurry, and he gave me Collins's phone number.

Al (that what he's called) and I discussed Mumbles. He had drowned in the strip in the midfifties, but Al had brought him back later on. He told me Mumbles would be in the film, played by Dustin Hoffman, no less. No one else was doing a Mumbles story so I was welcome to him.

But hurry.

I hurried. I put *Reprisal* aside once more (amazing the book ever got finished) and dove into Chester Gould's characters. My story takes place in October 1956. It's a bit tongue in cheek, but I slipped in a tiny lesson in sociology for those in the under-thirty crowd who take it for granted that rock has always played up and down the radio dial, who remain unaware of the racial storms that raged around the music in the early days.

I was there. I may have been only ten in '56 but I'd already experienced my rock and roll epiphany (see *Soft & Others*) and remember buying a copy of "Hound Dog"/"Don't Be Cruel"—on a ten-inch 78, no less. (Wish I still had it.) I remember rock and roll being called "race music" in polite circles and "nigger music" on the street. But all that was a sidebar to the story. Uppermost in my mind was remaining true to Gould's sense of the grandiose and the outré.

Al was delighted to get a story with a classic Chester Gould death trap.

ROCKABILLY

Detectives Helmsly and DeSalvo had formed a two-man Committee to End the Noise.

"That racket's gotta go, Tracy," DeSalvo was saying.

"Yeah," said Helmsly.

Tracy couldn't look at these two without thinking of Abbott and Costello—Helmsly as the former, pudgy DeSalvo the latter. In fact they once did the "Who's On First" routine at a PBA talent show. But they were good cops, even if they were a little rough around the edges.

"You know we like the kid as much as anybody," DeSalvo said, "but either he takes his jungle-bunny music somewhere else or one of us goes in there and accidentally sits on his pipsqueak phonograph."

Tracy put down the newspaper. The news from Hungary was pretty depressing—martial law and mass arrests since the Soviets marched in—and the presidential campaign at home was boring, with Ike and Nixon looking like shoo-ins.

He stared at DeSalvo. He didn't like the jungle-bunny reference but he let it slide. A lot of people were getting pretty worked up about this new rock and roll music the kids were playing, calling it jigaboo jive and nigger music. He'd even heard some preachers and teachers on the radio calling it the devil's music. Tracy didn't know about that. All he knew was that it wasn't his kind of music.

The trouble started when Junior brought his little, fat-spindled phonograph into the locker area off the squad room and started playing these funny-looking pancake-size records with big holes in the middle—"forty-fives," he called them. There were times when the music coming out of that tiny little speaker made Tracy want to try a forty-five of his own on that thing—something .45 caliber.

Obviously Tracy wasn't the only one bothered by it. DeSalvo was still carrying on.

"Bad enough we have to listen to it half the day workin' on the Wonder Records case, but we'd like a break when we come back to the squad room."

"Okay," Tracy said. "Send him out here. I'll talk to him."

"Thanks, Tracy," said Helmsly. "Peace and quiet again, huh?"

"Peace on earth," Tracy said.

Tracy thought about Junior as he waited for him to appear. He was a little concerned about some of the changes he was seeing in the boy. The most obvious was his hair. Junior was starting to look like some of the JDs they were picking up on car thefts and in gang rumbles on the north side. What was next—a studded black leather jacket and engineer boots? Tracy would have to draw the line there.

Not that Junior wasn't a good kid—he was the best. But Tracy couldn't help feeling uneasy when he saw him looking like a young hood.

And listening to hood music.

Ye gods, that rock and roll stuff was enough to drive any sane man up the wall! Junior played it endlessly at home. You couldn't pass his bedroom on the second floor without hearing twangy guitars, thumping drums, and wailing voices. Tess seemed to tolerate it better, even claimed to like some of it. But it set Tracy's teeth on edge. Especially that Little Richard fellow.

"Hi, Tracy," Junior said as he opened the door to Tracy's office. "You wanted to see me?"

"Yes, Junior. Sit down a minute."

Tracy was at once fascinated and repelled by Junior's hair. What formerly had been a wild red shock was now a carefully combed masterpiece of . . . what? The kid had let it grow and now it was Brylcreemed to within an inch of its life. Parted high up on each side, combed toward the center and a little forward so that some carrot-colored curls hung over the forehead; the sides were slicked back above the ears to meet at the rear of his head in what was being called a D.A.—and it didn't stand for District Attorney.

Tracy didn't like any of it.

"This music you've been playing. Do you like it?"

Junior's freckled face lit with enthusiasm. "You bet! All the kids like it."

"Surely not all of them."

Junior's smile broadened. "You know that Elvis Presley song you hate—'Hound Dog'?"

Tracy winced. "How can I forget? You play it a hundred times a day."

"Well, it's the number one song in the country right now."

"There goes the country. Can you tell me why?"

"It's cool. It's a gas."

Tracy laughed. "Ah! That explains it. And that's why you listen to it all day long?"

"And all night too. At least till I fall asleep."

A thought struck Tracy.

"Would you consider yourself an authority on rock and roll, Junior?"

The kid shrugged. "Sure. An expert even."

"Good. I want you to look at something."

Tracy called to DeSalvo to bring him the evidence in the Wonder Records case. DeSalvo came in lugging the box.

"Hey, Junior," he said as he placed the box on Tracy's desk. "This is the kind of stuff you listen to. Maybe you can have them when the case is done."

Junior's eyes lit as he peered into the box. He glanced at Tracy. "Can I look?"

"Sure," Tracy said. "Handle them as much as you want."

Junior fished out a stack of 45s and shuffled through them like cards. Tracy noticed the kid's enthusiasm fading.

"Aw, these are all copies."

If the statement startled Tracy, it shocked DeSalvo.

"How do *you* know?" the detective said.

"Just look at the labels. 'Long Tall Sally' by Mark Butler, 'Blueberry Hill' and 'Ain't That a Shame' by Kevin Coyle, 'Maybellene' by Buster Squillace, 'I Hear You Knockin'' by Eleanor Robinson, 'Eddie, My Love' by Diane Gormley, 'Sh-Boom' by the Flat-tops? These aren't the real records. I *have* the real records, the ones that were done first—and best—and they're sung by Little Richard, Fats Domino, Chuck Berry, Smiley Lewis, the Teen Queens, and the Chords."

Suddenly Tracy saw what Junior meant.

"Oh, I get it. You're saying these are copies because they're sung by different artists than the originals."

"Right. They're put out for radio stations who want to play the top hits but don't want to play the originals."

DeSalvo ran a hand through his thinning hair.

"Why on earth would they want to do that?"

"Because all the originals were sung by Negroes," Junior said, looking DeSalvo straight in the eye. "Some folks call it jungle-bunny jive and so the big stations won't play it unless it's rerecorded note for note by white guys."

Tracy could see that Junior's sense of fair play was deeply offended, and he had to admit the kid had a point.

"That's not the kind of copying we're concerned with here," Tracy said before DeSalvo could reply. "The president of Wonder Records, Mr. William B. Cover, came to us with a complaint that someone is pressing perfect copies of his records and then selling them to all the stores in the city."

"If they're perfect copies," Junior said, "how did he find out?"

"Sales reports," DeSalvo said. "He read where a store reported sales far above what he'd shipped to them. He checked further and found out it was going on all over town."

"Serves him right," Junior said under his breath.

"No talk like that, understand?" Tracy said. "Whether you approve of what Wonder Records is doing or not, it's perfectly legal. Bootlegging copies of his product is not."

Junior looked down. "Sorry. You're right."

"We know it's an inside job," DeSalvo said. "Mr. Cover is positive someone's 'borrowing' his masters and pressing the copies."

"Borrowing?" Junior said.

"Yes," Tracy said. "None of the masters is missing, but Cover says someone must be pulling them one set at a time, pressing off the copies in a secret plant, then returning them. He says that's the only way the crooks could make such perfect copies."

DeSalvo snapped his fingers. "Say! What if we put Junior inside and—"

Helmsly burst in before Tracy could tell DeSalvo to forget it. "Just got a call from the Wonder Records. They found William B. Cover dead in his office."

Tracy was on his feet. "Foul play?"

"Strangled."

"Find Sam," Tracy said. "Tell him to meet me down at the Wonder offices."

As Tracy pulled into the parking lot at Wonder Records, he marveled again at the design that had made it one of the city's landmark buildings. The upper two-thirds of its north wall had been designed to look like the top of a phonograph. The huge black disc representing a record was the most arresting feature. A giant tone arm rested beside it; once every five minutes it would swing over and land on the disc. The disc itself didn't spin, but the bright orange Wonder Records label at its center did, giving the illusion that the whole gargantuan record was turning on its spindle.

Inside, Sam Catchem was waiting for him on the top floor. Cover's office took up most of the level. There was a small lobby outside the elevator vestibule where a receptionist's desk guarded the passage to a set of oak double doors. These opened on a suite of richly appointed rooms. In the rearmost office a team from Forensics was dusting everything in sight while a pair of morgue attendants waited for the signal to load the sheeted body onto their stretcher and take it down to the meat wagon.

Tracy went down on one knee beside the body and pulled back the sheet. He'd met William B. Cover only once before, at headquarters. A bluff, hearty man of about fifty with thick brown hair and apple-red cheeks.

"Strangulation didn't do much for his complexion," Catchem said in his usual laconic tone, talking around the lighted cigarette that dangled from the corner of his mouth.

Tracy had to agree. The big red cheeks were now a dusky blue mottled with tiny purple hemorrhages in the skin.

"What have we got, Sam?"

"One dead rock and roll record mogul, done in with the cord from his telephone."

"How long?"

"Still got some warmth left in him. I'd say about two hours. How about you?"

Tracy pressed the back of his fingers against Cover's throat. Not completely cold yet. He glanced at his watch.

"I'll go with that—which puts time of death right in the middle of lunch hour. Witnesses?"

"None."

"No secretary by the door?"

"Yeah, but there's a private elevator at the back end of the suite. According to his secretary—who found the body, by the way—he often brought his new talent in and out via that route. Seems he liked to keep them secret till he went public with them."

"She never heard anything?"

"I don't know. She was still pretty hysterical when I got here. She's down on the next floor. Maybe she's pulled herself together now."

Tracy threw the white sheet back over the corpse and nodded to the morgue attendants to take it away.

"Let's see what she can tell us."

The receptionist was Carolyn Typo, a pert brunette, young, barely out of secretarial school. She was shivering like someone with total body frostbite. After a few soothing remarks and reassurances, Tracy got to the point.

"I understand, Carolyn, that you saw no one enter Mr. Cover's office."

"That's right," she said, nodding and sobbing. "They must've come up the private elevator."

"Do you remember hearing anything strange, any sounds of a struggle?"

"No struggle, but they were talking pretty loud in there. In fact they were arguing."

"Did you hear any of the words?"

"Mr. Cover said something like, 'You'll never work in this town again, or in any other for that matter!' "

"Did you hear the other voice?"

"Yes, but I didn't understand what he was saying. Neither did Mr. Cover, I guess, 'cause he kept saying, 'What he say?' I guess the other man was foreign or something. Every time the other man spoke, Mr. Cover would ask over and over again: 'What he say?' "

In the far recesses of Tracy's mind, a bell of recognition chimed faintly. He shook it off.

"Would you recognize that voice again?"

"Oh, yes."

"Good. There might come a time when we'll need you for that. But right now, I want you to go down to police headquarters and make a complete statement."

After the receptionist had been led away, Tracy turned to Catchem. "Who's the number two man around here, Sam?"

Catchem checked his list.

"Hyram Figh. His office is on—"

"Did someone say my name?" said a short, slim, dapper man standing nearby. He appeared to be in his midtwenties.

"I'm Detective Tracy, this is Detective Catchem, Mr. Figh."

"Just call me Hy. Everyone does."

"Okay, Hy. Do you have any knowledge of any associate of Mr. Cover's who doesn't speak English?"

"No. Not a one."

"How about some new act he might have been auditioning?" Catchem said.

"Well, I do know he was pretty excited about a new rockabilly quartet he was secretly rehearsing in one of our recording studios."

"What on earth is 'rockabilly'?" Sam said.

"Hmmm." Hy scratched his chin. "I guess you could best describe it as a hillbilly white kid singing rhythm and blues to a rock and roll beat."

"Oh. Thanks. That clears it up perfectly."

"Any time. Anyway, W.B.—we called him W.B.—was grooming this quartet to cut the first all-original recording in the history of Wonder Records. He'd always said the key to a hit rockabilly record was to make the lyrics unintelligible. He told me he'd found a singer no one would *ever* understand. Said the kids would go crazy wondering what he was saying. They'd play the song over and over on jukeboxes all over the country, trying to figure out the lyrics. He was *very* excited."

Again that bell rang in Tracy's brain, louder now. He glanced at Catchem, who shook his head.

"I know what you're thinking, but it ain't possible."

Tracy turned back to Mr. Figh.

"Thanks, Hy. You've been a big help. Please don't leave town for the next few days. We may have some other questions for you."

"Anything I can do to help. Anything. Just call."

As the young executive headed for his office down the hall, Tracy turned to Catchem.

"Who does that sound like to you, Sam?"

"Mumbles," Catchem said, lighting another cigarette. "Who else? But Mumbles is dead, remember? He drowned over a year ago and almost took you with him."

"I know, I know. But it fits so perfectly. A guy no one can understand: That was Mumbles. Sings with a quartet: That was Mumbles. Crooked enough to have been 'borrowing' the Wonder Records masters and making illegal copies of Wonder hits—"

"I know," Catchem said. "Mumbles. But he drowned, he was buried, and neither of us believe in ghosts."

"And violent enough to kill when cornered," Tracy said. "That would fit Mumbles too." Tracy pushed back his yellow fedora and scratched his head. "Yeah. A crazy thought."

"No argument there," Catchem said. "But until Mumbles shows up, what say we get back up to the murder scene and see if we can find anything to point us toward a *living* suspect."

Tracy couldn't sleep. The William B. Cover murder wouldn't permit it. Finally he gave up trying. He left Tess slumbering peacefully in their bed and wandered down the hall to Junior's room. He put his ear against the door and listened. A radio was playing low. He knocked and stuck his head in the darkened room.

"Got any rockabilly records?"

The light came on and Junior sat up in bed.

"Sure. Want to hear some?"

"Just a couple of samplings. And real low. We don't want to wake the sleeping, let alone the dead."

Junior hopped out of bed and pulled out his record box. He showed Tracy the labels with the titles and artists and played snatches of the songs.

They all sounded pretty much the same to Tracy. Junior ran through "Blue Suede Shoes" by Carl Perkins, "Tongue Tied Jill" by Charlie Feathers, "Ooby Dooby" by Roy Orbison, "Be-Bop-a-Lula" by Gene Vincent . . .

"Enough," Tracy said. "That's all I can take. But thanks for the lesson, Junior."

He tousled the kid's hair affectionately, the way he used to, but came away with a hand coated with grease. Wiping his palm on his pajama pants leg, he returned to his own bedroom.

And still he couldn't sleep.

Mumbles . . . was it even remotely possible that he was still alive?

Tracy thought back to July of last year when he and Mumbles had been caught in that salt marsh at high tide. Tracy had survived but Mumbles had drowned because he wouldn't—or couldn't—let go of the loot he had dug up. Tracy racked his brain now trying to remember if he or Sam or anyone for that matter had officially identified the body. They'd found it strapped to the barrel of jewels, they'd shaken their heads and said that Mumbles's greed had finally killed him, then they'd sent the body off to the coroner—tagged as Mumbles.

Tracy dragged himself back to the present. This was fruitless. All it did was distract him from zeroing on a real suspect in the Cover murder.

And yet . . . rockabilly, with all its hiccuping vocals and nonsense lyrics, was almost custom made for Mumbles, wasn't it? If he were alive, he could very well have been rehearsing in the Wonder Records recording studios—

Tracy bolted upright in bed.

Rehearsing! Wouldn't they be recording those rehearsals? At least parts of them? After all, the quartet in question was slated to be a recording sensation. Wouldn't W.B. have wanted to hear what they sounded like on vinyl?

Tracy was out of bed again, this time reaching for his clothes. Those tapes might break this case.

The all-night security guard at the main entrance let Tracy in and directed him to the recording studios on the tenth floor.

"On the way in I noticed that the big record player isn't working," Tracy said.

"We turned it off in mourning for Mr. Cover. The big Wonder record won't play again until after his funeral."

"I'm sure he'd have appreciated that."

Tracy headed directly to the recording studios. All the tapes and masters in W.B. Cover's office vault had been accounted for this afternoon, so Tracy figured that the mystery quartet's rehearsal tape, if it existed, might still be in the studio.

But which studio? There were eight of them on the floor.

He realized he should have brought Sam along to help go through the hundreds, perhaps thousands of tapes that were stored here. But better to let Sam sleep so he'd be fresh for the morning. Tracy hadn't been getting any sleep anyway.

Where to start? He decided to begin at the end. As he walked down the hall toward Studio H he heard a noise. He stopped and heard it again. A clatter . . . very faint. Coming from Studio C.

Tracy pulled his snub-nosed .357 and edged the door open.

The studio was a shambles. Empty tape cannisters were everywhere; the entire studio was festooned with tangled garlands of recording tape. As Tracy watched, a ten-inch reel, trailing a shiny brown ribbon behind it, sailed across the room and clattered against the wall.

To his left, out of sight, he heard someone shouting.

"Fina fug inape!"

A chill crawled over Tracy's skin. He knew that voice. But it couldn't be. Without thinking, he shoved the door open and stepped inside.

There were four men in the room. Three of them—one wearing a gray fedora, one with a knitted cap, and one bald and bareheaded—were tearing through the studio's tape library. But it was the fourth, standing in the center of the studio floor, who seized Tracy's attention. Short, medium-framed, close-cropped blond hair, heavy-lidded eyes, dark eyebrows, and a small, thin-lipped mouth.

"Mumbles!"

The man's eyes widened. "Syoo!"

Tracy shook off the shock of seeing Mumbles alive and covered the room with his pistol. He realized he'd made a rookie-level error: no backup. But he had the drop on them so maybe he could pull this off.

"Hands up and into the middle there—all of you!"

They hesitated, looking to Mumbles for direction.

"Doozee sz," Mumbles said.

"What he say?" whispered the one with the knitted cap.

"What'sa matter? You deaf?" the bald one replied. "He said 'Do what he says,' So let's do it."

They joined Mumbles in the center.

"Now—everybody facedown on the floor."

When he had all of them down he could use the wrist radio to call for backup. This would be a good collar, even if it wasn't by the book.

Three of them went face down on the rug. Only their leader refused to comply.

"You too, Mumbles," Tracy said.

Mumbles stepped to his left behind a microphone on a chrome stand. He stayed on his feet.

"Newt beoo, Trce."

"What he say?" said the knitted cap.

Baldhead said, "He said, 'I knew it'd be you, Tracy.' "

Tracy said, "How did you survive that tide? That's what I want to know, Mumbles. And who did we bury if it wasn't you?"

"Yoofih grout, cppr."

"What he say?"

"Shuddup," said the fedora.

"Down, Mumbles," Tracy said.

Mumbles' stare was coolly defiant.

"Nway, cppr."

Tracy approached Mumbles warily, keeping the three on the floor in full view.

"I'm warning you, Mumbles. Don't try anything foolish. You're now the prime suspect in the W.B. Cover murder. And if that isn't enough, you'll be tried for Cinn's murder and as an accomplice in the George Ozone murder. *Now get down on that floor!*"

Mumbles sidestepped, keeping the mike stand between Tracy and himself.

"Kz maz, cppr."

Tracy reached out to knock the mike stand out of the way. The instant he touched it, he knew he'd been suckered. He heard the buzz, felt the electric current shoot up his arm, saw Mumbles' sneering face dissolve in a cascade of blinding white, yellow, blue, and orange explosions.

Then everything went black.

Tracy awoke slowly, to the chilly caress of a city-flavored October breeze, to the sound of faraway voices, and to the throb of a thundering headache. He opened his eyes and immediately snapped them shut against the sudden, overpowering rush of vertigo.

He took a deep breath. For a moment there, he'd almost thought—

Tracy opened his eyes again. To his left the sun was rising. The dark, sleeping city was spread out above him . . .

No—*below* him. He was upside down—trussed up and being lowered by his ankles on a long rope from the roof of the Wonder building. He could feel the grooves of the giant record logo jouncing against his back as he was lowered along the north wall.

Voices filtered down from above. He picked out Mumbles's voice immediately.

"Hole air."

"What he say?"

"He said to hold it there. C'mon. We'll tie it to this vent stack here."

"Hey, that's pretty swell, Mumbles. You got him right over the dent where the needle hits. When the arm comes over it'll nail him good!"

"Lemring amurwep innacor!"

"What he say?"

"He said, 'Let them bring that murder weapon into court!' "

There was laughter from above.

"Swaj blow," said Mumbles and the voices faded out.

Tracy's hands were tied behind his back. He probed the depth of the pit in the surface of the giant record where the tone arm's "needle" impacted twelve times an hour. A deep pit. He glanced over at the metal spike that served as the needle. It wasn't sharp, but it had to come down with considerable force to wear a pocket like this. Force enough to punch a hole in Tracy's gut.

But the laugh was on Mumbles. The giant phonograph had been shut off.

Just then Tracy felt a hum through the back of his head. The giant record vibrated as the label at its center began to turn. To Tracy's right, the tone arm shuddered to life.

Mumbles had turned on the power!

As the arm began to lift, Tracy began to swing his body left and right. Soon he had a bit of a pendulum motion established. The arc was small, but he hoped it would be enough to give him a fighting chance to be out of harm's way when the tone arm came down.

It was swinging toward him now, looming over him. He augmented his pendulum motion with a quarter roll to the right just as the needle slammed down onto the record.

Missed me!

Now he had a couple of minutes to work at the ropes around his wrists. The left was not looped quite as tightly as the right. He made an all-out bid to pull it loose, clenching his teeth against the pain as the upper layer of the skin over his wrist tore away. He groaned and broke out in a cold sweat as something popped inside his wrist, but suddenly his left hand was free. Seconds later the right was also free.

Using mostly his right hand, Tracy pulled himself up inside the tone arm. He twisted himself around to an upright position and wedged his body into the metal struts of the supporting framework. His legs and ankles were still trussed up like a roast but he left the ropes where they were for now. He had to close his eyes and let this sick feeling pass. Good to be right side up again, but his left wrist was swollen and puffy and throbbing like an elephant's migraine. At least he still had his wrist radio. He flicked the transmitter switch.

"Headquarters, this is Tracy. I'm at the Wonder Records building. I need immediate backup. Repeat: Immediate backup requested. Do you copy?"

But when he switched to receive, he heard only static. He tried again with similar results. Maybe he'd damaged the radio getting out of the ropes. Maybe just the receiver was out of commission. He hoped that was all.

Because things were a bit dicey up here.

Voices . . . from far below. Angry shouts. Tracy peeked down at the gesticulating forms in the parking lot below. He realized with a grin that they couldn't see him from down there. Couldn't even see the rope. They probably thought he'd escaped.

Well, in a few minutes they'll be right!

He went to work on the rope around his legs, doing the best he could without putting too much stress on his left wrist.

Just then the tone arm began to rise. He heard the motor groan with the strain of lifting his extra weight. The arm was just starting back toward its rest position when something snapped in its base. The motor screeched and died as the arm jolted partially free of its supports and tilted at an angle.

Tracy hung on by his fingertips, then got his feet braced against the framework again. Renewed shouts rose from below as he realized his hiding place was now exposed in the growing dawn light.

He saw two figures, one blond, one bald-headed, dart for the rear of the building. It looked like Mumbles and one of his gang were coming back up to finish the job—probably by way of W.B. Cover's private elevator.

Tracy redoubled his efforts on the ropes but they resisted him. If only he could use both hands!

Moments later he heard a clank above him. Mumbles was there, grinning maniacally as he leaned over the edge of the roof and hammered at the tone arm's remaining supports with a tire iron.

Tracy felt the structure twist and sag further. Any second now it would go, taking him down with it. And still the knots on his legs resisted him. If he could just free his legs he could climb up the arm and at least give himself a fighting chance.

And then Tracy heard a wonderful sound: sirens.

So, apparently, did Mumbles's companion.

"The cops, Mumbles. Let's get outta here!"

"Ntlee fls!"

"Are you crazy, Mumbles?" Baldhead said. "What're you doin'?"

Tracy glanced up and saw Mumbles swing his leg over the edge of the roof and begin kicking at the tone arm's base.

"Dmthns tuck!" Mumbles said.

The sirens were getting louder but every kick sent increasingly violent shudders through the arm. Its base was edging free of the support. A few more good kicks . . .

Tracy yanked on the rope that ran from his ankles up to the roof. Still tied. Suddenly he was glad he hadn't been able to conquer those knots.

Far below, Tracy saw the two other members of Mumbles's crew running for their car. He looked back up toward the roof to see Mumbles hanging from the edge of the roof by his arms, ramming both feet against the base of the tone arm.

Suddenly it twisted loose, but in twisting it caught Mumbles's foot. Mumbles lost his grip on the parapet. Baldhead made a grab for his arm but it was too late. Tracy dove free of the arm as it began to fall. The metal screeched but Mumbles's scream was louder as man and tone arm plummeted to earth.

Tracy was hanging upside down again, the blood rushing to his head. He saw the tone arm crash through the hood of the getaway car as it pulled away, saw Mumbles bounce off the car roof and land in a broken heap atop the trunk.

"That crazy bastard!" said Baldhead from above. "All because of you."

Tracy angled his neck to see the man's angry face glaring down at him. A knife snapped open in his hand.

"No reason why you shouldn't join him, cop."

As Baldhead began to saw at the rope, Tracy stuffed his right hand into the pocket the needle had made and clutched one of the record grooves with his bum left, hoping he might be able to hold on but knowing deep in his gut that there was no way in hell he could.

Suddenly there was a shot. Tracy looked up and saw part of Baldhead's scalp explode in a spray of red. Then the body slumped over the parapet. Warm blood began to drip on Tracy.

Sam Catchem's face appeared over the edge of the roof.

"You all right, Tracy?"

"Just fine, Sam. Enjoying the view."

Catchem lit a cigarette. "Yeah. Me too. You know, I was listening to a preacher on one of the news shows last night. He was warning the kids that hanging around these rock and roll joints would bring them nothing but trouble. Looking at you makes me think he may have a point."

"Pull me up, Sam. Now."

"Yes, boss."

As he was being dragged upward across the grooved surface of the giant Wonder record, Tracy stared down at Mumbles's inert form and . . .

No—not inert. His arms and legs were moving—not much, but moving all the same. He was alive. Tracy shook his head in silent wonder. Mumbles's luck never seemed to run all the way out.

Well, at least now they had a good chance of finding out who was really buried in Mumbles's grave: They could ask Mumbles himself. Either way, though, Tracy would have to get an exhumation order. But that could wait.

At least until this afternoon.

With the Dick Tracy piece sold, I went back to *Reprisal* and the short story I'd been tinkering with in November. I'd contributed "Ménage à Trois" to Jeff Gelb's *Hot Blood* a few years before (where Jeff Fazio spotted it and bought it for an episode of Showtime's *The Hunger*.) In the summer of 1989 Jeff Gelb had written asking me if I could come up with a short story for an anthology combining horror and rock. I'd already done two rock-related stories—"The Years the Music Died" and "The Last ONE MO' ONCE GOLDEN OLDIES REVIVAL" (see *Soft & Others*)—and didn't know if I had a third in me.

But it got me thinking about my days as a drummer in a garage band during the midsixties. The Pebbles were the hottest party band along the upper Barnegat Bay section of the Jersey Shore when the lead guitarist, Mike Murphy, and I walked away, found new players, and devoted the summer of '67 to seeing how far we could take this music thing. We cut a demo of two original songs; the demo got us a manager who booked us into Greenwich Village spots like the Cafe Wha? and midtown gigs at Steve Paul's Scene West, but we went nowhere.

Remembering those times, though, it occurred to me how far we could have gone if only I'd known then what I know now.

And that was how the story started.

So "Bob Dylan, Troy Jonson, and the Speed Queen" takes you back to the West Village in 1964, when Dylan is digging The Beatles and a rough beast called folk rock is slouching toward the City of Angels to be born. The Eighth Wonder was real—Murph and I used to go there to hear a friend who was in the house band—and I've tried to reconstruct it as accurately as my fogged memory will allow. But on rereading it I find I wasn't careful enough about the songs Troy rips off from the future. Imagine how something like "Life During Wartime" with its references to headphones, computers, disco, and CBGB's would have sounded to an audience in 1964.

BOB DYLAN, TROY JONSON, AND THE SPEED QUEEN

Dylan walks in and I almost choke.

I've known all along it had to happen. I mean, it was inevitable. But still, finding yourself in the same room with a legend will tend to dry up your saliva no matter how well prepared you think you are.

My band's been doing weeknights at the Eighth Wonder for two months now, a Tuesday-Wednesday-Thursday gig, and I've made sure there's an electrified Dylan song in every set every night we play. Reactions have been mixed. At worst, hostile; at best, grudging acceptance. Electric music is a touchy thing here in Greenwich Village in 1964. All these folkies who think they're so hip and radical and grass-roots wise, they'll march in Selma, but they'll boo and walk out on a song by a black man named Chuck Berry. Yet if you play the same chord progression and damn near the same melody and say it's by Howlin' Wolf or Muddy Waters or Sonny Boy Williamson, they'll stay. So, although my band's electric, I've been showing my bona fides by limiting the sets to blues and an occasional protest song.

Slowly but surely, we've been building an audience of locals. That's what I want, figuring that the more people hear us, the sooner word will get around to Dylan that somebody's doing rocked-up versions of his songs. It has to. Greenwich Village is a tight, gossipy little community, and except maybe for the gays, the folkies are just about the tightest and most gossipy of the Village's various subcultures. I figured when he heard about us, he'd have to come and listen for himself. I've been luring him. It's all part of the plan.

And tonight he's taken the bait.

So here I am in the middle of Them's version of Joe Williams's "Baby, Please Don't Go" and my voice goes hoarse and I fumble the riff when I see him, but I manage to get through the song without making a fool out of myself.

When I finish, I look up and panic for an instant because I can't find him. I search the dimness. The Eighth Wonder is your typical West Village dive, little more than a long, rectangular room with the band platform at one end, the bar right rear, and cocktail tables spread across the open floor. Then I catch his profile silhouetted against the bar lights. He's standing there talking to some gal with long, straight, dark hair who's even skinnier than he is—which isn't much of a description, because in 1964 it seems all the women in Greenwich Village are skinny with long, straight hair.

The band's ready to begin the next number on the set list, our Yardbirds-style "I'm a Man," but I turn and tell them we're doing "All I Really Want to Do." They nod and shrug. As long as they get paid, they don't give a damn what they play. They're not in on the plan.

I strap on the Rickenbacker twelve-string and start picking out Jim McGuinn's opening. I've got this choice figured to be a pretty safe one since my wire tells me that the Byrds aren't even a group yet.

Dylan's taken a table at the rear with the skinny brunette. He's slouched down. He's got no idea this is his song. Then we start to sing and I see him straighten up in his chair. When we hit the chorus with the three-part harmony, I see him put down his drink. It's not a big move. He's trying to be cool. But I'm watching for it and I catch it.

Contact.

Research told me that he liked the Byrds' version when he first heard it, so I know he's got to like our version because ours is a carbon copy of the Byrds'. And naturally, he hasn't heard theirs yet because they haven't recorded it. I'd love to play their version of "Mr. Tambourine Man," but he hasn't written it yet.

There's some decent applause from the crowd when we finish the number and I run right into a Byrds version of "The Times They Are

A-changin'." I remind myself not to use anything later than *Another Side of Bob Dylan*. We finish the set strong in full harmony on "Chimes of Freedom," and I look straight at Dylan's dim form and give him a smile and a nod. I don't see him smile or nod back, but he does join in the applause.

Got him.

We play our break number and then I head for the back of the room. But by the time I get there, his table's empty. I look around but Dylan's gone.

"Shit!" I say to myself. Missed him. I wanted a chance to talk to him.

I step over to the bar for a beer, and the girl who was sitting with Dylan sidles over. She's wearing jeans and three shirts. Hardly anybody in the Village wears a coat unless it's the dead of winter. If it's cool out, you put on another shirt over the one you're already wearing. And if it's even cooler, you throw an oversize work shirt over those.

"He sorta kinda liked your stuff," she says.

"Who?"

"Bob. He was impressed."

"Really?" I stay cool as the proverbial cucumber on the outside, but inside I want to grab her shoulders and shout, "Yeah? Yeah? What did he say?" Instead I ask, "What makes you think so?"

"Oh, I don't know. Maybe it's because as he was listening to you guys, he turned to me and said, 'I am impressed.' "

I laugh to keep from cheering. "Yeah. I guess that'd be a pretty good indication."

I like her. And now that she's close up, I recognize her. She's Sally something. I'm not sure anybody knows her last name. People around the Village just call her the Speed Queen. And by that, they don't mean she does laundry.

Sally is thin and twitchy, and she's got the sniffles. She's got big, dark eyes, too, and they're staring at me.

"I was pretty impressed with your stuff, too," she says, smiling at me. "I mean, I don't dig rock and roll at all, man, what with all the bop-shoo-boppin' and the shoo-be-dooin'. I mean, that stuff's nowhere, man. But I kinda like the Beatles. I mean, a bunch of us sat around and watched them when they were on *Ed Sullivan* and, you know, they were kinda cool. I mean, they just stood there and sang. No corny little dance steps or anything like that. If they'd done anything like that, we would've turned them right off. But no. Oh, they bounced a little to the beat, maybe, but mostly they just played and sang. Almost like folkies. Looked like they were having fun. We all kinda dug that."

I hold back from telling her that she and her folkie friends were watching the death of the folk music craze.

"I dig 'em, too," I say, dropping into the folkster patois of the period. "And I predict they're gonna be the biggest thing ever to hit the music business. Ten times bigger than Elvis and Sinatra and the Kingston Trio put together, man."

She laughs. "Sure! And I'm going to marry Bobby Dylan!"

I could tell her he's actually going to marry Sara Lowndes next year, but that would be stupid. And she wouldn't believe me, anyway.

"I like to think of what I play as 'folk rock,'" I tell her.

She nods and considers this. "Folk rock . . . that's cool. But I don't know if it'll fly around here."

"It'll fly," I tell her. "It'll fly high. I guarantee it."

She's looking at me, smiling and nodding, almost giggling.

"You're okay," she says. "Why don't we get together after your last set?"

"Meet you right here," I say.

It's Wednesday morning, three A.M., when we wind up back at my apartment on Perry Street.

"Nice pad," Sally says. "Two bedrooms. Wow."

"The second bedroom's my music room. That's where I work out all the band's material."

"Great! Can I use your bathroom?"

I show her where it is and she takes her big shoulder bag in with her. I listen for a moment and hear the clink of glass on porcelain and have a pretty good idea of what she's up to.

"You shooting up in there?" I say.

She pulls open the door. She's sitting on the edge of the tub. There's a syringe in her hand and some rubber tubing tied around her arm.

"I'm tryin' to."

"What is it?"

"Meth."

Of course. They don't call her the Speed Queen for nothing.

"Want some?"

I shake my head. "Nah. Not my brand."

She smiles. "You're pretty cool, Troy. Some guys get grossed out by needles."

"Not me."

I don't tell her that we don't even *have* needles when I come from. Of course, I knew there'd be lots of shooting up in the business I was getting into, so before coming here I programmed all its myriad permutations into my wire.

"Well, then maybe you can help me. I seem to be running out of veins here. And this is good stuff. Superpotent. Two grams per cc."

I hide my revulsion and take it from her. Such a primitive-looking thing. Even though AIDS hasn't reared its ugly head yet, I find the needle point especially terrifying. I look at the barrel of the glass syringe.

"You've got half a cc there. A gram? You're popping a whole *gram* of speed?"

"The more I use, the more I need. Check for a vein, will you?"

I rub my fingertip over the inner surface of her arm until I feel a linear swelling below the skin. My wire tells me that's the place.

I say, "I think there's one here but I can't see it."

"Feeling's better than seeing any day," she says with a smile. "Do it."

I push the needle through the skin. She doesn't even flinch.

"Pull back on the plunger a little," she says.

I do, and see a tiny red plume swirl into the chamber.

"Oh, you're beautiful!" she says. "Hit it!"

I push the plunger home. As soon as the chamber is empty, the Speed Queen yanks off her tourniquet and sighs.

"Oh, man! Oh, baby!"

She grabs me and pulls me to the floor.

I lie in bed utterly exhausted while Sally runs around the apartment stark naked, picking up the clutter, chattering on at Mach two. She is painfully thin, Dachau thin. It almost hurts to look at her. I close my eyes.

For the first time since my arrival, I feel relaxed. I feel at peace. I don't have to worry about VD because I've had the routine immunizations against syphilis and the clap and even hepatitis B and C and AIDS. About the worst I can get is a case of crabs. I can just lie here and feel good.

It wasn't easy getting here, and it's been even harder staying. I thought

I'd prepared myself for everything, but I never figured I'd be lonely. I didn't count on the loneliness. That's been the toughest to handle.

The music got me into this. I've been a fan of the old music ever since I can remember—ever since my ears started to work, probably. And I've got a good ear. Perfect pitch. You sit me down in front of a new piece of music, and guaranteed I'll be able to play it back to you note for note in less than half an hour—usually less than ten minutes for most things. I can sing, too, imitating most voices pretty closely.

Trouble is, I don't have a creative cell in my body. I can play anything that's already been played, but I can't make up anything of my own to play. That's the tragedy of my life. I should be a major musical talent of my time, but I'm an also-ran, a nothing.

To tell you the truth, I don't care to be a major musical talent of my time. And that's not sour grapes. I loathe what passes for music in my time. Push-button music—that's what I call it. Nobody actually gets their hands on the instruments and wrings the notes from them. Nobody gets together and *cooks*. It's all so cool, so dispassionate. Leaves me cold.

So I came back here. I have a couple of relatives in the temporal sequencing lab. I gained their confidence, learned the ropes, and displaced myself to the 1960s.

Not an easy decision, I can assure you. Not only have I left behind everyone and everything I know, but I'm risking death. That's the penalty for altering the past. But I was so miserable that I figured it was worth the risk. Better to die trying to carve out a niche for myself here than to do a slow rot where I was.

Of course, there was a good chance I'd do a slow rot in the 1960s as well. I'm no fool. I had no illusions that dropping back a hundred years or so would make me any more creative than I already wasn't. I'd be an also-ran in the sixties, too.

Unless I prepared myself.

Which I did. I did my homework on the period. I studied the way they dressed, the way they spoke. I got myself wired with a wetchip encoding all the biographies and discographies of anyone who was anybody in music and the arts at this time. All I have to do is think of the name and suddenly I know all about him or her.

Too bad they can't do that with music. I had to bring the music with me. I wasn't stupid, though. I didn't bring a dot player with me. No technological anachronisms—that's a sure way to cause ripples in the time stream and tip your hand to the observation teams. Do that and a reclamation squad'll be knocking on your door. Not me. I spent a whole year hunting up these ancient vinyl discs—"LPs" they call them here. Paid antique prices for them, but it was worth it. Bought myself some antique money to spend here, too.

So here I am.

And I'm on my way. It's been hard, it's been slow, but I've got only one chance at this so I've got to do it right. I picked the other band members carefully and trained them to play what I want. They need work, so they go along with me, especially since they all think I'm a genius for writing such diverse songs as "Jumpin' Jack Flash," "Summer in the City," "Taxman," "Bad Moon Rising," "Rikki Don't Lose That Number" and so many others. People are starting to talk about me. And now Dylan has heard me. I'm hoping he'll bring John Hammond with him sometime soon. That way I've got a shot at a Columbia contract. And then Dylan will send the demo of "Mr. Tambourine Man" to *me* instead of Jim McGuinn.

After that, I won't need anyone. I'll be able to anticipate every trend in rock and I'll be at the forefront of all the ones that matter.

So far, everything's going according to plan. I've even got a naked woman running around my apartment. I'm finally beginning to feel at home.

"Where'd you get these?"

It's Sally's voice. I open my eyes and see her standing over me. I smile, then freeze.

She's holding up copies of the first two Byrds albums.

"Give me those!"

"Hey, really. Where'd—"

I leap out of bed. The expression on my face must be fierce because she jumps back. I snatch them from her.

"Don't ever touch my records!"

"Hey, sorreeeee! I just thought I'd spin something, okay? I wasn't going to steal your fucking records, man!"

I force myself to cool down. Quickly. It's my fault. I should have locked the music room. But I've been so wrapped up in getting the band going that I haven't had any company, so I've been careless about keeping my not-yet-recorded "antiques" locked away.

I laugh. "Sorry, Sally. It's just that these are rarities. I get touchy about them."

Holding the records behind me, I pull her close and give her a kiss. She kisses me back, then pulls away and tries to get another look at the records.

"I'll say they are," she says. "I never heard of these Byrds. I mean, like you'd think they were a jazz group, you know, like copping Charlie Parker or something, but the title on that blue album there is *Turn, Turn, Turn*, which I've like heard Pete Seeger sing. Are they new? I mean, they've gotta be new, but the album cover looks so old. And didn't I see 'Columbia' on the spine?"

"No," I say when I can finally get a word in. "They're imports."

"A new English group?"

"No. They're Swedish. And they're pretty bad."

"But that other album looked like it had a couple of Bobby's tunes on it."

"No chance," I say, feeling my gut coil inside me. "You need to come down."

I quickly put the albums back in the other room and lock the door.

"You're a real weird cat, Troy," she says to me.

"Why? Because I take care of my records?"

"They're only records. They're not gold." She laughs. "And besides that, you wear underwear. You must be the only guy in the Village who wears underwear."

I pull Sally back to the bed. We do it again and finally she falls asleep in my arms. But I can't sleep. I'm too shaken even to close my eyes.

I like her. I really like her. But that was too close. I've got to be real careful about who I bring back to the apartment. I can't let anything screw up the plan, especially my own carelessness. My life is at stake.

No ripples, that's the key. I've got to sink into the timeline without making any ripples. Bob Dylan will go electric on his next album, just like he did before, but it will be *my* influence that nudged him to try it. "Mr. Tambourine Man" will be a big hit next summer, just as it's destined to be, but if things go according to plan, *my* band's name will be on the label instead of the Byrds. No ripples. Everything will remain much the same except that over the next few years, Troy Jonson will insinuate himself into the music scene and become a major force there. He will make millions, he will be considered a genius, the toast of both the public and his fellow artists.

Riding that thought, I drift off to sleep.

* * *

Dylan shows up at the Eighth Wonder the very next night in the middle of my note-perfect imitation of Duane Allman on "Statesboro Blues," perfect even down to the Coricidin bottle on my slide finger. There's already a good crowd in, the biggest crowd since we started playing. Word must be getting around that we're something worth listening to. Dylan has about half a dozen scruffy types along with him. I recognize Allen Ginsberg and Gregory Corso in the entourage. Which gives me an idea.

"This one's for the poets in the audience," I say into the mike; then we jump into Paul Simon's "Richard Corey," only I use Van Morrison's phrasing, you know, with the snicker after the bullet-through-his-head line. I spend the rest of the set being political, interspersing Dylan numbers with "originals" such as "American Tune," "Won't Get Fooled Again," "Life During Wartime," and so on.

I can tell they're impressed. *More* than impressed. Their jaws are hanging open.

I figure now's the time to play cool. At the break, instead of heading for the bar, I slip backstage to the doorless, cinder-block-walled cubicle euphemistically known as the dressing room.

Eventually someone knocks on the doorjamb. It's a bearded guy I recognize as one of Dylan's entourage tonight.

"Great set, man," he says. "Where'd you get some of those songs?"

"Stole them," I say, hardly glancing at him.

He laughs. "No, seriously, man. They were great. I really like that 'Southern Man' number. I mean, like I've been makin' the marches and that says it all, man. You write them?"

I nod. "Most of them. Not the Dylan numbers."

He laughs again. From the glitter in his eyes and his extraordinarily receptive sense of humor, I gather that he's been smoking a little weed at that rear table.

"Right! And speaking of Dylan, Bobby wants to talk to you."

I decide to act a little paranoid.

"He's not pissed, is he? I mean, I know they're his songs and all, but I thought I'd try to do them a little different, you know. I don't want him takin' me to court or—"

"Hey, it's cool," he says. "Bobby digs the way you're doing his stuff. He just wants to buy you a drink and talk to you about it, that's all."

I resist the urge to pump my fist in the air.

"Okay," I say. "I can handle that."

"Sure, man. And he wants to talk to you about some rare records he hears you've got."

Suddenly I'm ice cold.

"Records?"

"Yeah, says he heard about some foreign platters you've got with some of his songs on 'em."

I force a laugh and say, "Oh, he must've been talking to Sally! You know how Sally gets. The Speed Queen was really flying when she was going through my records. That wasn't music she saw, that was a record from Ireland of Dylan *Thomas* reading his stuff. I think ol' Sally's brains are getting scrambled."

He nods. "Yeah, it was Sally, all right. She says you treat them things like gold, man. They must be some kinda valuable. But the thing that got to Dylan was, she mentioned a song with 'tambourine' in the title, and he says he's been doodling with something like that."

"No kidding?" My voice sounds like a croak.

"Yeah. So he really wants to talk to you."

I'm sure he does. But what am I going to say?

And then I remember that I left Sally back at my apartment. She was going to hang out there for a while, then come over for the late sets.

I'm ready to panic. Even though I know I locked the music room before I left, I've got this urge to run back to my place.

"Hey, I really want to talk to him, too. But I got some business to attend to here. My manager's stopping by in a minute and it's the only chance we'll have to talk before he heads for the West Coast, so tell Mr. Dylan I'll be over right after the next set. Tell him to make the next set—it'll be worth the wait."

The guy shrugs. "Okay. I'll tell him, but I don't know how happy he's gonna be."

"Sorry, man. I've got no choice."

As soon as he's gone, I dash out the back door and run for Perry Street. I've got to get Sally out of the apartment and never let her back in. Maybe I can even make it back to the Eighth Wonder in time to have that drink with Dylan. I can easily convince him that the so-called Dylan song on my foreign record is a product of amphetamine craziness—everybody in the Village knows how out of control Sally is with the stuff.

As I ram the key into my apartment door, I hear something I don't want to hear, something I *can't* be hearing. But when I open up . . .

"Mr. Tambourine Man" is playing on the hi-fi.

I charge into the second bedroom, the music room. The door is open and Sally is dancing around the floor. She's startled to see me and goes into her little girl speedster act.

"Hiya, Troy, I found the key and I couldn't resist because I like really wanted to hear these weird records of yours and I love 'em, I really do, but I've never heard of these Byrds cats although one of them's named Crosby and he looks kinda like a singer I caught at a club last year only his hair was shorter then, and I never heard this 'Tambourine' song before, but it's definitely Dylan, although he's never sung it that I know of so I'll have to ask him about it. And I noticed something even weirder, I mean *really* weird, because I spotted some of these copyright dates on the records—you know, that little circle with the littler letter *c* inside them?—and like, man, some of them are in the *future*, man, isn't that wild? I mean, like there's circle-C 1965 on this one and a circle-C 1970 on that one over there, and it's like someone had a time machine and I went into the future and brought 'em back or something. I mean, is this wild or what?"

Fury like I've never known blasts through me. It steals my voice. I want to throttle her. If she were in reach I'd do it, but lucky for her she's bouncing around the room. I stay put. I clench my fists at my sides and let my mind race over my options.

How do I get out of this? Sally had one look at a couple of my albums last night and then spent all day blabbing to the whole goddamn Village about them and how rare and unique they are. And after tonight I know exactly what she'll be talking about tomorrow: Dylan songs that haven't been written yet, groups that don't exist yet, and, worst of all, albums with copyright dates in the future!

Ripples . . . I was worried about ripples in the time stream giving me away. Sally's mouth is going to cause *waves. Tsunamis!*

The whole scenario plays out inside my head: Talk spreads, Dylan gets more curious, Columbia Records gets worried about possible bootlegs, lawyers get involved, an article appears in the *Voice*, and then the inevitable—

reclamation squad knocks on my door in the middle of the night, I'm tran-
qued, brought back to my own time, and then it's bye-bye musical career.
Bye-bye Troy Jonson.

Sally's got to go.

The cold-bloodedness of the thought shocks me. But it's Sally or me.
That's what it comes down to. Sally or me. What else can I do?

I choose me.

"Are you mad?" she says.

I shake my head. "A little annoyed, maybe, but I guess it's okay." I smile.
"It's hard to say no to you."

She jumps into my arms and gives me a hug. My hands slide up to her
throat, encircle it, then slip away. Can't do it.

"Hey, like what are you doing back, man? Aren't you playing?"

"I got . . . distracted."

"Well, Troy, honey, if you're flat, you've come to the right place. I know
how to fix that."

In that instant, I know how I'll do it. No blood, no pain, no mess.

"Maybe you're right. Maybe I could use a little boost."

Her eyes light. "Groovy! I had my gear all set up in the bathroom but I
couldn't find a vein. Let's go."

"But I want you to have some, too. It's no fun being up alone."

"Hey, I'm flyin' already. I popped a bunch of black beauties before you
came."

"Yeah, but you're coming down. I can tell."

"You think so?" Her brow wrinkles with concern, then she smiles.
"Okay. A little more'll be cool—especially if it's a direct hit."

"Never too much of a good thing, right?"

"Right. You'll shoot me up like last night?"

Just the words I want to hear.

"You bet."

While Sally's adjusting her tourniquet and humming along with "Mr.
Tambourine Man," I take her biggest syringe and fill it all the way with the
methedrine solution. I find the vein first try. She's too whacked-out to notice the size of the syringe until I've got most of it into her.

She tries to pull her arm away. "Hey, that's ten fucking cc's!"

I'm cool. I'm more than cool. I'm stone-cold dead inside.

"Yeah, but it wasn't full. I only put one cc in it." I pull her off the toilet
seat. "Come on. Let's go."

"How about you, Troy? I thought you wanted—"

"Later. I'll do it at the club. I've got to get back."

As I pack up her paraphernalia, carefully wiping my prints off the syringe and bottles, she sags against the bathroom door.

"I don't feel so good, Troy. How much did you give me?"

"Not much. Come on, let's go."

Something's going to happen—twenty thousand milligrams of methamphetamine in a single dose has to have a catastrophic effect—and whatever it is, I don't want it happening in my apartment.

I hurry her out to the street. I'm glad my place is on the first floor; I'd hate to see her try a few flights of steps right now. We go half a block and she clutches her chest.

"Shit, that hurts! Troy, I think I'm having a heart attack!"

As she starts retching and shuddering, I pull her into an alley. A cat bolts from the shadows; the alley reeks of garbage. Sally shudders and sinks to her knees.

"Get me to a hospital, Troy," she says in a weak, raspy voice. "I think I overdid it this time."

I sink down beside her and fight the urge to carry her the few blocks to St. Vincent's emergency room. Instead, I hold her in my arms. She's trembling.

"I can't breathe!"

The shudders become more violent. She convulses, almost throwing me off her; then she lies still, barely breathing. Another convulsion, more violent than the last, choking sounds tearing from her throat. She's still again, but this time she's not breathing. A final shudder, and Sally the Speed Queen comes to a final, screeching halt.

As I crouch there beside her, still holding her, I begin to sob. This isn't the way I planned it, not at all the way it was supposed to be. It was all going to be peace and love and harmony, all Woodstock and no Altamont. Music, laughs, money. This isn't in the plan.

I lurch to my feet and vomit into the garbage can. I start walking. I don't look back at her. I can't. I stumble into the street and head for the Eighth Wonder, crying all the way.

The owner, the guys in the band, they all hassle me for delaying the next set. I look out into the audience and see Dylan's gone, but I don't care. Just as well. The next three sets are a mess, the worst of my life. The rest of the night is a blur. As soon as I'm done, I'm out of there, running.

I find Perry Street full of cops and flashing red lights. I don't have to ask why. The self-loathing wells up in me until I want to be sick again. I promise myself to get those records into a safety-deposit box first thing tomorrow so that something like this can never happen again.

I don't look at anybody as I pass the alley, afraid they'll see the guilt screaming in my eyes, but I'm surprised to find my landlord, Charlie, standing on the front steps to the apartment house.

"Hey, Jonson!" he says. "Where da hell ya been? Da cops is lookin' all ova for ya!"

I freeze on the bottom step.

"I've been working—all night."

"Sheesh, whatta night. First dat broad overdoses an' dies right downa street, and now dis! Anyway, da cops is in your place. Better go talk to 'em."

As much as I want to run, I don't. I can get out of this. Somebody probably saw us together, that's all. I can get out of this.

"I don't know anything about an overdose," I say. It's a form of practice. I figure I'm going to have to say it a lot of times before the cops leave.

"Not dat!" Charlie says. "About your apartment. You was broken into a few hours ago. I t'ought I heard glass break so's I come downstairs to check. Dey got in t'rough your back window, but I scared 'em off afore dey got much." He grins and slaps me on the shoulder. "You owe me one, kid. How many landlords is security guards, too?"

I'm starting to relax. I force a smile as I walk up the steps past him.

"You're the best, Charlie."

"Don't I know it. Dey did manage to make off wit your hi-fi an' your records but, hey, you can replace dose wit'out too much trouble."

I turn toward Charlie. I feel the whole world, all the weight of time itself crashing down on me. I can't help it. It comes unbidden, without warning. Charlie's eyes nearly bulge out of his head as I scream a laugh in his face.

I closed out 1989 with the only politically correct story I've ever written. I realized "Pelts" was based on a trendy idea but I wrote it anyway. It springs from the same values that fueled the very *in*correct "Buckets" (in *Soft & Others*).

"Where do you get your ideas?" It's a question we're all asked. I can tell you the instant this story began. It was the day I opened a copy of *Rolling Stone* and saw an ad placed by one of the animal rights groups. It featured an animal (a fox, I think) caught in a leg-restraint trap. In a series of photos it showed a man approach the animal and crush its throat with his heel. The casual brutality of the act sickened and appalled me. I had to say something. And since I speak through my fiction, I began to write.

The working title was "Traps II" and I finished it at the tail end of December. I knew of a dozen anthologies that would take it, but I wanted something special for this story. Then I remembered a letter from Bill Munster (yes, that's his real name) seeking a story for his Footsteps Press chapbook series. I figured that would be a perfect showcase for "Pelts."

Bill did a beautiful job with the chapbook, aided by a wonderfully subtle cover illustration from Jill Bauman. All royalties "Pelts" earns—from the Footsteps edition, the reprint in Steve Jones and Ramsey Campbell's *Best New Horror 2*, Belgium's *Phénix*, and other anthologies, a pro rata share from this collection, and any future reprints—go to Friends of Animals. You might consider sending them a check yourself. They're not crazies—they're good people. Write to them at Friends of Animals, P. O. Box 1244, Norwalk, CT 06856.

PELTS

I

"I'm scared, Pa."

"Shush!" Pa said, tossing the word over his shoulder as he walked ahead.

Gary shivered in the frozen predawn dimness and scanned the surrounding pines and brush for the thousandth time. He was heading for his twentieth year and knew he shouldn't be getting the willies like this but he couldn't help it. He didn't like this place.

"What if we get caught?"

"Only way we'll get caught is if you keep yappin', boy," Pa said. "We're almost there. Wouldna brought you along 'cept I can't do all the carryin' myself! Now hesh up!"

Their feet crunched through the half-inch shroud of frozen snow that layered the sandy ground. Gary pressed his lips tightly together, kept an extra-tight grip on the Louisville Slugger, and followed Pa through the brush. But he didn't like this one bit. Not that he didn't favor hunting and trapping. He liked them fine. Loved them, in fact. But he and Pa were on Zeb Foster's land today. And everybody knew that was bad news.

Old Foster owned thousands of acres in the Jersey Pine Barrens and didn't allow nobody to hunt them. Had "Posted" signs all around the perimeter.

Always been that way with the Fosters. Pa said old Foster's grandpa had started the no-trespassing foolishness and that the family was likely to hold to the damn stupid tradition till Judgment Day. Pa didn't think he should be fenced out of any part of the Barrens. Gary could go along with that most anywheres except old Foster's property.

There were stories . . . tales of the Jersey Devil roaming the woods here, of people poaching Foster's land and never being seen again. Those who disappeared weren't fools from Newark or Trenton who regularly got lost in the Pines and wandered in circles till they died. These were experienced trackers and hunters, Pineys just like Pa . . . and Gary.

Never seen again.

"Pa, what if we don't come out of here?" He hated the whiny sound in his voice and tried to change it. "What if somethin' gets us?"

"Ain't nothin' gonna get us! Didn't I come in here yesterday and set the traps? And didn't I come out okay?"

"Yeah, but—"

"Yeah, but *nothin'*! The Fosters done a good job of spreadin' stories for generations to scare folk off. But they don't scare me. I know bullshit when I hear it."

"Is it much farther?"

"No. Right yonder over the next rise. A whole area crawlin' with coon tracks."

Gary noticed they were passing through a thick line of calf-high vegetation, dead now; looked as if it's been dark and ferny before winterkill had turned it brittle. It ran off straight as a hunting arrow into the scrub pines on either side of them.

"Looky this, Pa. Look how straight this stuff runs. Almost like it was planted."

Pa snorted. "That wasn't planted. That's spleenwort—ebony spleenwort. Only place it grows around here is where somebody's used lime to set footings for a foundation. Soil's too acid for it otherwise. Find it growin' over all the vanished towns."

Gary knew there were lots of vanished towns in the Barrens, but this must have been one hell of a foundation. It was close to six feet wide and ran as far as he could see in either direction.

"What you think used to stand here, Pa?"

"Who knows, who cares? People was buildin' in the Barrens afore the

Revolutionary War. And I hear tell there was crumblin' ruins already here when the Indians arrived. There's some real old stuff around these parts but we ain't about to dig it up. We're here for coon. Now hesh up till we get to the traps!"

Gary couldn't believe their luck. Every damn leghold trap had a coon in it! Big fat ones with thick, silky coats the likes of which he'd never seen. A few were already dead, but most of them were still alive, lying on their sides, their black eyes wide with fear and pain; panting, bloody, exhausted from trying to pull loose from the teeth of the traps, still tugging weakly at the chains that linked the trap to its stake.

He and Pa took care of the tuckered-out ones first by crushing their throats. Gary flipped them onto their backs and watched their striped tails come up protectively over their bellies. *I ain't after your belly, Mr. Coon.* He put his heel right over the windpipe, and kicked down hard. If he was in the right spot he heard a satisfying *crunch* as the cartilage collapsed. The coons wheezed and thrashed and flopped around awhile in the traps trying to draw some air past the crushed spot but soon enough they choked to death. Gary had had some trouble doing the throat crush when he started at it years ago, but he was used to it by now. It was just the way it was done. All the trappers did it.

But you couldn't try that on the ones that still had some pepper in them. They wouldn't hold still enough for you to place your heel. That was where the Gary and his Slugger came in. He swung at one as it snapped at him.

"The head! The *head*, dammit!" Pa yelled.

"Awright, awright!"

"Don't mess the pelts!"

Some of those coons were tough suckers. Took at least half a dozen whacks each with the Slugger to kill them dead. They'd twist and squeal and squirm around and it wasn't easy to pound a direct hit on the head every single time. But they weren't going nowhere, not with one of their legs caught in a steel trap.

By the time he and Pa reached the last trap, Gary's bat was drippy red up to the taped grip, and his bag was so heavy he could barely lift it. Pa's was just about full too.

"Damn!" Pa said, standing over the last trap. "Empty!" Then he knelt for a closer look. "No, wait! Lookit that! It's been sprung! The paw's still in it! Musta chewed it off!"

Gary heard a rustle in the brush to his right and caught a glimpse of a gray-and-black-striped tail slithering away.

"There it is!"

"Get it!"

Gary dropped the sack and went after the last coon. No sweat. It was missing one of its rear paws and left a trail of blood behind on the snow wherever it went. He came upon it within twenty feet. A fat one, waddling and gimping along as fast as its three legs would carry it. He swung but the coon partially dodged the blow and squalled as the bat glanced off its skull. The next shot got it solid but it rolled away. Gary kept after it through the brush, hitting it again and again, until his arms got tired. He counted nearly thirty strokes before he got in a good one. The big coon rolled over and looked at him with glazed eyes, blood running from its ears. He saw the nipples on its belly—a female. As he lifted the Slugger again, it raised its two front paws over its face—an almost human gesture that made him hesitate for a second. Then he clocked her with a winner. He bashed her head ten more times for good measure to make sure she wouldn't be going anywhere. The snow around her was splattered with red by the time he was done.

As he lifted her by her tail to take her back, he got a look at the mangled stump of her hind leg. Chewed off. God, you really had to want to get free to do something like that.

He carried her back to Pa, passing all the other splotches of crimson along the way. Looked like some bloody-footed giant had stomped through here.

"Whooeee!" Pa said when he saw the last one. "That's a beauty! They're *all* beauties! Gary, m'boy, we're gonna have money to burn when we sell these!"

Gary glanced at the sun as he tossed the last one into the sack. It was rising brightly into a clear sky.

"Maybe we shouldn't spend it until we get off Foster's land."

"You're right," Pa said, looking uneasy for the first time. "I'll come back tomorrow and rebait the traps." He slapped Gary on the back. "We found ourselfs a gold mine, son!"

Gary groaned under the weight of the sack, but he leaned forward and struck off toward the sun. He wanted to be gone from here. Quick like.

"I'll lead the way, Pa."

"Look at these!" Pa said, holding up two pelts by their tails. "Thick as can be and not a scar or a bald spot anywhere to be seen! Primes, every single one of them!"

He swayed as he stood by the skinning table. He'd been nipping at the applejack bottle steadily during the daylong job of cutting, stripping, and washing the pelts, and now he was pretty near blitzed. Gary had taken the knife from Pa early on, doing all the cutting himself and leaving the stripping for the old man. You didn't have to be sober for stripping. Once the cuts were made—that was the hard part—a strong man could rip the pelt off like husking an ear of corn.

"Yeah," Gary said. "They're beauts all right. Full winter coats."

The dead of winter was, naturally, the best time to trap any fur animal. That was when the coats were the thickest. And these were *thick*. Gary couldn't remember seeing anything like these pelts. The light gray fur seemed to glow a pale metallic blue when the light hit it right. Touching it gave him a funny warm feeling inside. Made him want to find a woman and ride her straight on till morning.

The amazing thing was that they were all identical. No one was going to have to dye these babies to make a coat. They all matched perfectly, like these coons had been one big family.

These were going to make one *hell* of a beautiful full-length coat.

"Jake's gonna *love* these!" Pa said. "And he's gonna pay pretty for 'em, too!"

"Did you get hold of him?" Gary asked, thinking of the shotgun he wanted to buy.

"Yep. Be round first thing in the morning."

"Great, Pa. Whyn't you hit the sack and I'll clean up round here."

"You sure?"

"Sure."

"You're all right, son," Pa said. He clapped him on the shoulder and staggered for the door.

Gary shivered in the cold blast of wind that dashed past Pa on his way out of the barn. He got up and threw another log into the pot-bellied stove squatting in the corner, then surveyed the scene.

There really wasn't all that much left to be done. The furs had all been washed and all but a few were tacked up on the drying boards. The guts had been tossed out, and the meat had been put in the cold shed to feed to the dogs during the next few weeks. So all he had to—

Gary's eyes darted to the bench. Had something moved there? He watched a second but all was still. Yet he could have sworn one of the unstretched pelts piled there had moved. He rubbed his eyes and grinned.

Long day.

He went to the bench and spread out the remaining half dozen before stretching them. Most times they'd nail their catches to the barn door, but these were too valuable for that. He ran his hands over them. God, these were special. Never had he seen coon fur this thick and soft. That warm, peaceful, horny feeling slipped over him again. On a lark, he draped it over his arm. What a coat this was gonna—

The pelt moved, rippled. In a single swift smooth motion its edges curled and wrapped snugly around his forearm. A gush of horror dribbled away before he could react, drowned in a flood of peace and tranquillity.

Nothing unusual here. Everything was all right . . . all right.

He watched placidly as the three remaining unstretched furs rippled and began to move toward him. Nothing wring with that. Nothing wrong with the way they crawled over his hands and wrists and wrapped themselves around his arms. Perfectly natural. He smiled. Looked like he had caveman arms.

It was time to go back to the house. He got up and started walking. On the way out the door, he picked up the Louisville Slugger.

Pa was snoring.

Gary poked him with the bat and called to him. His own voice seemed to come from far away.

"Pa! Wake up, Pa!"

Finally Pa stirred and opened his bloodshot eyes. "What is it, boy? What the hell you want?"

Gary lifted the bat over his head. Pa screamed and raised his hands to protect himself, much like that last coon this morning. Gary swung the bat with everything he had and got Pa on the wrist and over the right ear as he tried to roll away. Pa grunted and stiffened, but Gary didn't wait to see what happened. He swung again. And again. And again, counting. His arms weren't tired at all. The pelts snuggling around them seemed to give him strength. Long before the fortieth swing, Pa's head and brains were little more than a huge smear of currant jelly across the pillows.

Then he turned and headed for the back door.

Back in the barn, he stood by the stretching boards and looked down at the gore-smeared bat, clutched tightly now in both of his fists. A small part of him screamed a warning but the rest of him knew that everything was all right. Everything was fine. Everything was—

He suddenly rotated his wrists and forearms and smashed the bat against his face. He staggered back and would have screamed if his throat had only let him. His nose and forehead were in agony! But everything was all right—

No! Everything was *not* all right! This was—

He hit himself again with the bat and felt his right cheek cave in. And again, and again. The next few blows smeared his nose and took out his eyes. He was blind now, but the damn bat wouldn't stop!

He fell backward onto the floor but still he kept battering his own head. He heard his skull splinter. But still he couldn't stop that damn bat!

And the pain! He should have been knocked cold by the first whack but he was still conscious. He felt *everything*!

He prayed he died before the bat hit him forty times.

II

No one answered his knocking at the house—house, shmouse, it was a hovel—so Jake Feldman headed for the barn. The cold early morning air chilled the inexorably widening bald spot that commanded the top of his scalp; he wrapped his unbuttoned overcoat around his ample girth and quickened his pace as much as he dared over the icy, rutted driveway.

Old man Jameson had said he'd come by some outstanding pelts. Pelts of such quality that Jake would be willing to pay ten times the going price to have them. Out of the goodness of Jameson's heart and because of their long-standing business relationship, he was going to give Jake first crack at them.

Right.

But the old Piney gonif's genuine enthusiasm had intrigued Jake. Jameson was no bullshitter. Maybe he really had something unique. And maybe not.

This better be worth it, he thought as he pulled open the barn door. He didn't have time to traipse down to the Jersey Pine Barrens on a wild goose chase.

The familiar odor of dried blood hit him as he opened the barn door. Not unexpected. Buy fresh pelts at the source for a while and you soon got used to the smell. What was unexpected was how cold it was in the barn. The lights were on but the wood stove was cold. Pelts would freeze if they stayed in this temperature too long.

Then he saw them—all lined up, all neatly nailed out on the stretching boards. The fur shimmered, reflecting glints of opalescence from the incandescent bulbs above and the cold fire of the morning light pouring through the open door behind him. They were exquisite. *Magnificent!*

Jake Feldman knew fur. He'd spent almost forty of his fifty-five years in the business, starting as a cutter and working his way up till he found the chutzpah to start his own factory. In all those years he had never seen anything like these pelts.

My God, Jameson, where did you get them and are there any more where these came from?

Jake approached the stretching boards and touched the pelts. He had to. Something about them urged his fingers forward. So soft, so shimmery, so incredibly beautiful. Jake had seen, touched, and on occasion even cut the very finest Siberian sable pelts from Russia. But they were nothing compared to these. These were beyond quality. These were beautiful in a way that was almost scary, almost . . . supernatural.

Then he saw the boots. Big, gore-encrusted rubber boots sticking out from under one of the stretching boards. Nothing unusual about that except for their position. They lay on the dirt floor with their toes pointing toward the ceiling at different angles, like the hands of a clock reading five after ten. Boots simply didn't lie like that . . . unless there were feet in them.

Jake bent and saw denim-sheathed legs running up from the boots. He smiled. One of the Jamesons—either old Jeb or young Gary. Jake bet on the elder. A fairly safe bet seeing as how old Jeb loved his Jersey lightning.

"Hey, old man," he said as he squeezed between two of the stretching boards to get behind. "What're you doing back there? You'll catch your death of—"

The rest of the sentence clogged in Jake's throat as he looked down at the corpse. All he could see at first was the red. The entire torso was drenched in clotted blood—the chest, the arms, the shoulders the—dear Lord, the head! There was almost nothing left of the head! The face and the whole upper half of the skull had been smashed to a red, oozing pulp from which the remnant of an eye and some crazily angled teeth protruded. Only a patch of smooth, clean-shaven cheek identified the corpse as Gary, not Jeb.

But who could have done this? And why? More frightening than the sight of the corpse was Jake's sudden grasp of the ungovernable fury behind all the repeated blows it must have taken to cave in Gary's head like that. With what—that baseball bat? And after pounding him so mercilessly, had the killer wrapped Gary's dead fingers around the murder weapon? What sick—?

Jeb! Where was old Jeb? Surely he'd had nothing to do with this!

Calling the old man's name, Jake ran back up to the house. His cries went unanswered. The back door was open. He stood on the stoop, calling out again. Only silence greeted him. The shack had an *empty* feeling to it. That was the only reason Jake stepped inside.

It didn't take him long to find the bedroom. And what was left of Jeb.

A moment later Jake stood panting and retching in the stretch between the house and the barn.

Dead! Both dead!

More than dead—battered, crushed, *smeared*! . . . but those pelts. Even with the horrors of what he'd just seen raging through his mind, he couldn't stop thinking about those pelts.

Exquisite!

Jake ran to his car, backed it up to the barn door, popped the trunk. It took him a while but eventually he got all the pelts off the stretching boards and into his trunk. He found a couple of loose ones on the floor near Gary's body and he grabbed those too.

And then he roared away down the twin ruts that passed for a road in these parts. He felt bad about leaving the two corpses like that, but there was nothing he could do to help the Jamesons. He'd call the State Police from the Parkway. Anonymously.

But he had the pelts. That was the important thing.

And he knew exactly what he was going to do with them.

After getting the pelts safely back to his factory in New York's garment district, Jake immediately went about turning them into a coat. He ran into only one minor snag and that was at the beginning: The Asians among his cutters refused to work with them. A couple of them took one look at the pelts and made a wide-eyed, screaming dash from the factory.

That shook him up for a little while, but he recovered quickly enough. Once he got things organized, he personally supervised every step: the cleaning and softening, the removal of the guard hairs, the letting-out process in which he actually took a knife in hand and crosscut a few pelts himself, just as he'd done when he started in the business; he oversaw the sewing of the let-out strips and the placement of the thousands of nails used in tacking out the fur according to the pattern.

With the final stitching of the silk lining nearing completion, Jake allowed himself to relax. Even unfinished, the coat—*That Coat,* as he'd come to call it—was stunning, unutterably beautiful. In less than an hour he was going to be the owner of the world's most extraordinary raccoon coat. Extraordinary not simply because of its unique sheen and texture, but because you couldn't tell it was raccoon. Even the cutters and tackers in his factory had been fooled; they'd agreed that the length of the hair and size of the pelts were similar to raccoon, but none of them had ever seen raccoon like this, or *any* fur like this.

Jake wished to hell he knew where Jameson had trapped them. He'd be willing to pay almost anything for a regular supply of those pelts. What he could sell those coats for!

But he had only one coat now, and he wasn't going to sell it. No way. This baby was going to be an exhibition piece. It was going to put Fell Furs on the map. He'd bring it to the next international show and blow the crowd away. The whole industry would be buzzing about That Coat. And Fell Furs would be known as the company with That Coat.

And God knew the company needed a boost. Business was down all over the industry. Jake couldn't remember furs ever being discounted as deeply as they were now. The animal lovers were having a definite impact. Well, hell, he was an animal lover too. Didn't he have a black lab at home?

But animal love stopped at the bottom line, bubby.

If he played it right, That Coat would turn things around for Fell Furs. But he needed the right model to strut it.

And he knew just who to call.

He sat in his office and dialed Shanna's home number. Even though she'd just moved, he didn't have to look it up. He knew it by heart already. He should have. He'd dialed it enough times.

Shanna . . . a middle-level model he'd seen at a fur show two years ago. The shoulder-length black hair with the long bangs, the white skin and knockout cheekbones, onyx eyes that promised everything. And her body—Shanna had a figure that set her far apart from the other beanpoles in the field. Jake hadn't been able to get her out of his mind since. He wanted her but it seemed like a lost cause. He always felt like some sort of warty frog next to her, and that was just how she treated him. He'd approached her countless times and each of those times he'd been rebuffed. He didn't want to own her, he just wanted to be near her, to touch her once in a while. And who knew? Maybe he'd grow on her.

At least not he had a chance. That Coat would open the door. This time would be different. He could feel it.

Her voice, soft and inviting, came on the line after the third ring.

"Yes?"

"Shanna, it's me. Jake Feldman."

"Oh." The drop in temperature within that single syllable spoke volumes. "What do you want, Jake?"

"I have a business proposition for you, Shanna."

Her voice grew even cooler. "I've heard your propositions before. I'm not the least—"

"This is straight down the line business," he said quickly. "I've got a coat for you. I want you to wear it at the international show next week."

"I don't know." She seemed the tiniest bit hesitant now. "It's been a while since I've done a fur show."

"You'll want to do them again when you see this coat. Believe me."

Maybe some of his enthusiasm for the coat was coming over the phone. Jake sensed a barely detectable thaw in her voice.

"Well . . . call the agency."

"I will. But I want you to see this coat first. You've got to see it."

"Really, Jake—"

"You've *got* to see it. I'll bring it right down."

He hung up before she could tell him no and hurried out to the workroom. As soon as the last knot was tied in the last stitch he boxed That Coat and headed for the door.

"What kind of coat you buy, Mister?" someone said as soon as he stepped out onto the sidewalk.

Oh, shit. Animal lovers. A bunch of them holding signs, milling around outside his showroom.

Somebody shoved a placard in his face:

> *The only one who can wear a fur*
> *coat gracefully and beautifully*
> *is the animal to whom it belongs.*

"How many harmless animals were trapped and beaten to death to make it?" said a guy with a beard. "How many electrocuted up the ass?"

"Fuck off!" Jake said. "You're wearing leather shoes, aren't you?"

The guy smiled, "Actually, I'm wearing sneakers, but even if they were leather it wouldn't be for pure vanity. Cows are in the human food chain. Beavers, minks, and baby seals are not."

"So what?"

"It's one thing for animals to die to provide food—that's the law of nature. It's something entirely different to kill animals so you can steal their beauty by draping yourself with their skins. Animals shouldn't suffer and die to feed human vanity."

A chant began.

"Vanity! Vanity! Vanity . . ."

Jake flipped them all the bird and grabbed a cab downtown.

Such a beautiful girl living in a place like this, Jake thought as he entered the lobby of the converted TriBeCa warehouse where Shanna had just bought a condo. Probably paid a small fortune for it too. Just because it was considered a chic area of town.

At the "Elevator" sign he found himself facing a steel panel studded with rivets. Not sure of what to do, he tried a pull on the lever under the sign. With a clank the steel panel split horizontally, dividing into a pair of huge metal doors that opened vertically, the top one sliding upward, the bottom sinking. An old freight elevator. Inside he figured out how to get the contraption to work and rode the noisy open car up to the third level.

Stepping out on the third floor he found a door marked 3B straight ahead of him. That was Shanna's. He knocked, heard footsteps approaching.

"Who's there?" said a muffled voice from the other side. Shanna's voice.

"It's me, Jake. I brought the coat."

"I told you to call the agency."

Even through the door he could sense her annoyance. This wasn't going well. He spotted the glass lens in the door and that gave him an idea.

"Look through your peephole, Shanna."

He pulled That Coat from the box. The fur seemed to ripple against his hands as he lifted it. A few unused letting-out strips fell from the sleeve, landing in the box. They looked like furry caterpillars; a couple of them even seemed to move on their own. Strange. They shouldn't have been in the coat. He shrugged it off. It didn't matter. That Coat was all that mattered. And getting past Shanna's door.

"Just take a gander at this coat. Try one peek at this beauty and then tell me you don't want to take a closer look."

He heard the peephole cover move on the other side. Ten seconds later, the door opened. Shanna stood there staring. He caught his breath at the sight of her. Even without makeup, wearing an old terry cloth robe, she was beautiful. But her wide eyes were oblivious to him. They were fixed on That Coat. She seemed to be in a trance.

"Jake, it's . . . it's beautiful. Can I . . . ?"

As she reached for it, Jake dropped the fur back into its box and slid by her into the apartment.

"Try it on in here. The light's better."

She followed him into the huge, open, loftlike space that made up the great room of her condo. Too open for Jake's tastes. Ceilings too high, not enough walls. And still not finished yet. The paperhangers were halfway through a bizarre mural on one wall; their ladders and tools were stacked by the door.

He turned and held That Coat open for her.

"Here, Shanna. I had it made in your size."

She turned and slipped her arms into the sleeves. As Jake settled it over her shoulders he noticed a few of those leftover fur strips clinging to the coat. He plucked them off and bunched them into his palm to discard later. Then he stepped back to look at her. The fur had been breathtaking before, but Shanna enhanced its beauty. And vice versa. The two of them seemed made for each other. The effect brought tears to Jake's eyes.

She glided over to a mirrored wall and did slow turns, again and again. Rapture glowed in her face. Finally she turned to him, eyes bright.

"You don't have to call the agency," she said. "I'll call. I want to show this coat."

Jake suddenly realized that he was in a much better bargaining position than he had ever imagined. Shanna no longer had the upper hand. He did. He decided to raise the stakes.

"Of course you do," he said offhandedly. "And there's a good chance you'll be the model we finally settle on."

Her face showed concern for the first time since she'd laid eyes on the coat.

" 'A good chance'?" What's that supposed to mean?"

"Well, there are other models who're very interested. We have to give them a chance to audition."

She wrapped the fur more tightly around her.

"I don't want anyone else wearing this coat!"

"Well . . ."

Slowly Shanna pulled open the coat, untied the terry cloth robe beneath it, and pulled that open too. She wore nothing under the robe. Jake barely noticed her smile.

"Believe me," she said in that honey voice, "this is the only audition you'll need."

Jake's mouth was suddenly too dry to speak. He could not take his eyes off her breasts. He reached for the buttons on his own coat and found the fur strips in his right hand. As he went to throw them away, he felt them move, wiggling like furry worms. When he looked, they had wrapped themselves around his fingers.

Tranquillity seeped through him like fine red wine. It didn't seem odd that the strips should move. Perfectly natural. Funny even.

Look. I've got fur rings.

He pulled at his coat and shirts until he was bare from the waist up. Then he realized he needed to be alone for a minute.

"Where's your bathroom?"

"That door behind you."

He needed something sharp. Why?

"Do you have a knife? A sharp one?" The words seemed to form on their own.

Her expression was quizzical, "I think so. The paperhangers were using razor blades—"

"That'll be fine." He went to the workbench and found the utility knife, then headed for the bathroom. "I'll only be a minute. Wait for me in the bedroom."

What am I doing?

In the bathroom he stood before the mirror with the utility knife gripped in the fur-wrapped fingers of his right hand. A sudden wave of cold shuddered through him. He felt half-frozen, trapped, afraid. Then he saw old Jameson's whiskered face, huge in the mirror, saw his monstrous foot ram toward him. Jake gagged with the crushing pain in his throat, he was suffocating, God, he couldn't breathe—!

And then just as suddenly he was fine again. Everything was all right. He pushed the upper corner of the utility blade through the skin at the top of his breastbone, just deep enough the pierce its full thickness through to the fatty layer beneath. Then he drew the blade straight down the length of his sternum. When he reached the top of his abdomen he angled the cut to the right, following the line of the bottom rib across his flank. He heard the tendons and ligaments in his shoulder joint creak and pop in protest as his hand extended the cut all the way around his waist to his back, but he felt no pain, not from the shoulder, not even from the gash that had begun to bleed so freely. Something within him was screaming in horror but it was far away. Everything was all right here. Everything was fine.

When he had extended the first cut all the way back to his spine he switched the blade to his left hand and made a similar cut from the front toward the left, meeting the first cut at the rear near the base of his spine. Then he made a circular cut around each shoulder—over the top and through the armpit. Then another all the way around his neck. When that was done, he gripped the edges on each side of the incision he had made over the breastbone and yanked. Amid sprays of red, the skin began to pull free of the underlying tissue.

Everything was all right . . . all right . . .

Jake kept tugging.

III

Where the hell is he?

Wrapped in the coat, Shanna stood before her bedroom mirror and waited for Jake.

She wasn't looking forward to this. No way. The thought of that flabby white body flopping around on top of her made her a little ill, but she was going through with it. Nothing was going to keep her from wearing this fur.

She snuggled the coat closer about her but it kept falling away, almost as if it didn't want to touch her. Silly thought.

She did a slow turn before the mirror.

Looking good, Shanna!

This was it. This was one of those moments you hear about when your whole future hinges on a single decision. Shanna knew what that decision had to be. Her career was stalled short of the top. She was making good money but she wanted more—she wanted her face recognized everywhere. And this coat was going to get her that recognition. A couple of international shows and she'd be known the world over as the girl in the fabulous fur. From then on she could write her own ticket.

In spite of her queasy stomach, Shanna allowed herself a sour smile. This wouldn't be the first time she'd spread to get something she wanted. Jake Feldman had been leching after her for years; if letting him get his jollies on her a couple of times assured her of exclusive rights to model his coat, tonight might be the *last* time she ever had to spread for anyone like Jake Feldman.

What was he doing in the bathroom—papering it? She wished he'd get out of there and get this over with. Then she could—

She heard the bathroom door open, heard his footsteps in the great room. He was shuffling.

"In here, Jake!" she called.

Quickly she pulled free of the coat long enough to shed the robe, then slipped back into it and stretched out on the bed. She rolled onto her side and propped herself up on one elbow but the fur kept falling away from her. Well, that was okay too. She left it open, arranging the coat so that her best stuff was displayed to the max. She knew all the provocative poses. She'd done her share of nudie sessions to pay her bills between those early fashion assignments.

Outside the door the shuffling steps were drawing closer. What was he doing—walking around with his pants around his ankles?

"Hurry up, honey! I'm waiting for you!'

Let's get this show on the road, you fat slob!

Suddenly she was cold, her leg hurt, she saw a boyish-faced giant looming over her with a raised club, saw it come crashing down on her head. As she began to scream she suddenly found herself back in her condo, sprawled on her bed with the fur.

Jake was shuffling through the door.

Shanna's mind dimly registered that he was holding something, but her attention was immediately captured by the red. Jake was all red—*dripping red*—his pants, the skin of his arm, his bare—

Oh God it was blood! He was covered with blood! And his chest and upper abdomen—they were the bloodiest. Christ! The skin was gone! Gone! Like someone had ripped the hide off his upper torso.

"I . . ." His voice was hoarse. A croak. His eyes were wide and glazed as he shuffled toward her. "I made this vest for you."

And then Shanna looked at what he held out to her, what drooped from his bloody fingers—fingers that seemed to be covered with fur.

It was indeed a vest. A white, blood-streaked, sleeveless vest. Between the streaks of blood she could see the wiry chest hairs straggling across the front . . . whorling around the nipples.

Shanna screamed and rolled off the bed, hugging the coat around her. She wished she could have pulled it over her head to hide the sight of him.

"It's for you," he said, continuing his shuffled toward her. "You can wear it under the coat . . ."

Whimpering in fear and revulsion, Shanna ran around the bed and dashed for the door. She ran across the great room and out into the hall. The elevator! She had to get away from that man, that *thing* who'd cut his skin into a—

The shuffling. He was coming!

She pressed the down button, pounded on it. Behind the steel door she heard the winches whir to life. The elevator was on its way. She turned and gagged as she saw Jake come though her apartment door and approach her, leaving a trail of red behind him, holding the bloody skin out as if expecting her to slip her arms through the openings.

A clank behind her. She turned, pulled the lever that opened the heavy steel doors, and leaped inside. An upward push on the inner lever brought the outer doors down with a deafening clang, shutting out the sight of Jake and his hideous offering.

Clutching the coat around her bare body Shanna sank to her knees and began to sob.

God, what was happening here? Why had Jake cut his skin off like that? *How* had he done it?

"Shanna, please," said the croaking voice from the other side of the doors. "I made it for you."

And then the doors started to open! Before her eyes a horizontal slit was opening between the outer doors, and two bloody arms with fur-wrapped fingers were thrusting the loathsome vest toward her through the gap.

Shanna's scream echoed up and down the open elevator shaft as she hit the *Down* button. The car lurched and started to sink.

Thank you, God!

But the third floor doors continued to open. As she passed the second floor and continued her descent, Shanna's eyes were irresistibly drawn upward. Through the open ceiling of the car she watched the ever-widening gap, watched as the two protruding arms and the vest were joined by Jake's head and upper torso.

"Shanna! It's for you!"

The car stopped with a jolt. First floor. Shanna yanked up the safety grate and pulled the lever. Five seconds . . . five seconds and she'd be running for the street, for the cops. As the outer doors slowly parted, that voice echoed again through the elevator shaft.

"Shanna!"

She chanced one last look upward.

The third-floor doors had retracted to the floor and ceiling lines. Most of Jake's torso seemed to be hanging over the edge.

"It's for—"

He leaned too far.

Oh, shit, he's falling!

"—yooooouuuuuu!"

Shanna's high-pitched scream of "Noooo!" blended with Jake's voice in a fearful harmony that ended with his head striking the upper edge of the elevator car's rear wall. As the rest of his body whipped around in a wild, blood-splattering, pinwheeling sprawl, his shoed foot slammed against Shanna's head, knocking her back against the door lever. Half-dazed, she watched the steel doors reverse their opening motion.

"No!"

And Jake . . . Jake was still moving, crawling toward her an inch at a time on twisted arms, broken legs, his shattered head raised, trying to speak, still clutching the vest in one hand, still offering it to her.

The coat seemed to ripple around her, moving on its own. She had to get *out* of here!

The doors! Shanna lunged for the opening, reaching toward the light from the deserted front foyer. She could make it through if—

She slipped on the blood, went down on one knee, still reaching as the steel doors slammed down on her wrist. Shanna heard her bones crunch as pain beyond anything she had ever known ran up her arm. She would have screamed but the agony had stolen her voice. She tried to pull free but she was caught, tried to reach the lever but it was a good foot beyond her grasp.

Something touched her foot. Jake—it was what was left of Jake holding his vest out to her with one hand, caressing her bare foot with one of the fur strips wrapped around the fingers of his other hand. She kicked at him, slid herself away from him. She couldn't let him get near her. He'd want to put that vest on her, want to try to do other things to her. And she was bare-ass naked under this coat. She had to get free, get free of these doors, anything to get free!

She began chewing at the flesh of her trapped wrist, tearing at it, unmindful of the greater pain, of the running blood. It seemed the natural thing to do, the *only* thing to do.

Free! She had to get *free*!

IV

Juanita wasn't having much luck tonight. She'd just pushed her shopping cart with all her worldly belongings the length of a narrow alley looking for a safe place to huddle for the night, an alcove or deep doorway, someplace out of sight and out of the wind. A good alley, real potential, but it was already occupied by someone very drunk and very nasty. She'd moved on.

Cold. Really felt the cold these days. Didn't know how old she was but knew that her bones creaked and her back hurt and she couldn't stand the cold like she used to. If she could find a place to hide her cart, maybe she could sneak into the subway for the night. Always warmer down there. But when she came up top again all her things might be gone.

Didn't want to be carted off to no shelter, neither. Even a safe one. Didn't like being closed in, and once they got you into those places they never let you go till morning. Liked to come and go as she pleased. Besides, she got confused indoors and her mind wouldn't work straight. She was an outdoors person. That was where she did her clearest thinking, where she intended to stay.

As she turned a corner she spotted all the flashing red and blue lights outside a building she remembered as a warehouse but was now a bunch of apartments. Like a child, she was drawn to the bright, pretty lights to see what was going on.

Took her a while to find out. Juanita allowed herself few illusions. She knew not many people want to explain things to someone who looks like a walking rag pile, but she persisted and eventually managed to pick up half a dozen variations on what had happened inside. All agreed on one thing: a gruesome double murder in the building's elevator involving a naked woman and a half-naked man. After that the stories got crazy. Some said the man had been flayed alive and the woman was wearing his skin, others said the man had cut off the woman's hand, still others said she'd *chewed* her own hand off.

Enough. Shuddering, Juanita turned and pushed her cart away. She'd gone only a few yards when she spotted movement as she was passing a shadowed doorway. Not human movement; too low to the ground. Looked like an animal but it was too big for a rat, even a New York City rat. Light from a passing EMS wagon glinted off the thing, and Juanita was struck by the thickness of its fur, by the way the light danced and flickered over its surface.

Then she realized it was a coat—a fur coat. Even in the dark she could see that it wasn't some junky fun fur. This was the real thing, a true, blue, top-of-the-line, utterly fabulous fur coat. She grabbed it and held it up. *Mira!* Even in the dark she could see how lovely it was, how the fur glistened.

She slipped into it. The coat seemed to ripple away from her for a second, then it snuggled against her. Instantly she was warm. So warm. Almost as if the fur was generating its own heat, like an electric blanket. Seemed to draw the cold right out of her bones. Must've been ages since she last felt so toasty. But she forced herself to pull free of it and hold it up again.

Sadly, Juanita shook her head. No good. Too nice. Wear this thing around and someone'd think she was rich and roll her but good. Maybe she could pawn it. But it was probably hot and that would get her busted. Couldn't take being locked up ever again. A shame, though. Such a nice warm coat and she couldn't wear it.

And then she had an idea. She found an alley like the one she'd left before and dropped the coat onto the pavement, fur side down. Then she knelt beside it and began to rub it into the filth. From top to bottom she covered the fur with any grime she could find. Practically cleaned the end of the alley with that coat. Then she held it up again.

Better. Much better. No one would recognize it and hardly anybody would bother trying to take it from her the way it looked now. But what did she care how she looked in it? As long as it served its purpose, that was all she asked. She slipped into it again and once more the warmth enveloped her.

She smiled and felt the wind whistle through the gaps between her teeth.

This is living! she thought. Nothing like a fur to keep you warm. And after all, for those of us who do our living in the outdoors, ain't that what fur is for?

APPENDIX

I'm including the next piece because it's the offspring of the preceding story. "Pelts" and its stage adaptation should be read back-to-back.

The stage version started at the tail end of March 1990 when I received a call from someone named Al Corley who'd got my number from Joe Lansdale. He said he was putting together a Grand Guignol–type production called *Screamplay* for off-Broadway, featuring state-of-the-art special effects and midgets for ushers. Would I be interested in writing a one-act play for them?

My first thought. This is a Lansdale joke. Joe is setting me up.

But as Al Corley talked on about how they had the Astor Place Theatre reserved, and how Del Close was scheduled to direct, I realized he was serious. So I sent him a copy of *Soft & Others* plus a few manuscripts of stories that were in the pipeline. He latched onto "Pelts" immediately and suggested I adapt it.

So while my agent informed the producers of all the unacceptable clauses in their contract, I began the first draft. I started on May 3 and finished it in four days. Al Corley read it and said there was one major problem: I'd written the play just like the story, which meant it had three sets. That was two too many. One set. Do it with one set.

One set? This was more restrictive than *Monsters* (I'll explain that later).

But the challenge of distilling the action and interaction down to the bare essentials intrigued me. Took me two days. The revision was completed on July 1.

The result is almost a different story. What little subtlety there is to be found in the prose version (not much, I grant you) is gone, obliterated by sprays of red. This is a very bloody, *busy* one-act play. But the special effects consultants said the bashed heads and flayings and such were no problem.

I didn't allow myself to get psyched. I wanted very badly to see this performed, but I'd learned from my experience with *The Keep* not to get emotionally involved until the opening credits begin to roll—and even then, hold back. So I downplayed *Screamplay* whenever it was brought up.

Just as well. *Screamplay* never reached the stage. And that's a damn shame. With material by Nancy Collins and Joe Lansdale and other super talents, dramatized with state-of-the-art live special effects (and let's not forget the midget ushers), *Screamplay* would have been a very hot ticket among New York's jaded theatergoers. But Wall Street's minicrash in the fall of 1990 and the deepening recession through '91 sucked off the financing. Opening was pushed back to March of '91, then postponed indefinitely.

So here's the one-act stage version of "Pelts." This, I think you'll agree, would have been *something* to see.

PELTS

A ONE-ACT PLAY

CHARACTERS

JEB ("PA") . . . . . a whiskered and whiskied old Piney
GARY . . . . Jeb's nineteen-year-old son
JAKE . . . . a middle-aged furrier (and if he sounds a little
    like Jackie Mason, how much can it hurt?)
SHANNA . . . . . . a young fashion model—beautiful face, beauti-
    ful body, looks utterly sophisticated. But when
    she opens her mouth she's pure Coney Island

SET

Jeb's barn

Rough plank walls, a door off-center midstage, a dirty window, a long, scarred workbench, a potbellied stove, and stretching boards (sheets of plywood to which pelts are tacked so they dry flat). Steel leg-restraint traps hang by their chains from the walls beside the door and around the window. A variety of skinning knives are racked by the center door. There is a door at each of the right and left extremes of the set.

GARY: *(Laughs)* No, Pa. But I been thinking. Are you sure these things ain't gonna be causin' us trouble?

JEB: Trouble? What the hell's that supposed to mean?

GARY: Well, I mean, we did poach 'em off old man Forster's land. You know what they say about his place.

As JEB replies, one of the PELTS draped over the top of one of the stretching board MOVES a little. Neither JEB nor GARY notices.

JEB: Garbage! Superstitious garbage. I heard all them stories— hunters goin' onto his land and never comin' out, strange noises, weird lights. *Garbage!* Old man Forster spreads them tales hisself, just like his daddy afore him. Wants to keep everybody off his acreage. Fine. Let the other chickenshits believe that stuff, but it ain't gonna stop me! Hell, we trapped that land today and got away scot-free with a gold mine, didn't we, boy! Didn't we?

GARY: Yeah, we sure did, Pa. Kind of a strange gold mine, though, dontcha think? I mean, we ain't even sure what kind of animals they was.

JEB: Who cares! Long as they got great fur. Look how those pelts shimmer. And thick! Winter thick! So celebrate, boy! Celebrate!

As GARY replies, the PELT MOVES and slips over the back of the stretching board.

GARY: I dunno, Pa. These things give me a weird feeling. For some reason I been thinkin' 'bout how it'd feel to have your hand caught in a trap so's you'd have to lie in the freezin' snow all night. You think animals feel much pain?

JEB: *(Laughs)* Not if you hit 'em right. One good whack to the head with a Louisville Slugger ought to do it every time.

Although I do remember this tough old coon I trapped once. Had to give him forty whacks before his skull caved in. Plumb like to wore me out. *(Shoots another hard look at GARY)* Ain't going soft on me, are you, boy?

GARY: No, Pa. It's just that when we was bustin' their heads this morning, a couple of them . . . well, sorta held up their paws like they was asking me not to hurt them. It was almost, like . . . human.

JEB: *(Makes a disgusted noise)* Speaking of paws, look at this. *(Tosses a small black object to GARY)* Found it stuck in one of the traps.

GARY: Hey! Looks like a front paw to one of them beasties.

JEB: Yep. The thing had just finished chewin' it off when we got there but I nailed it afore it got away.

GARY: *(Tosses it back to JEB)* Gonna add it to your collection of chew-offs?

JEB: *(Holds it up)* Nope. Think I'll put this on a chain and make me a necklace out of it. Or maybe I'll give it to Jake when he comes down.

GARY: Jake the furrier? He's comin'?

JEB: Yep. Sent him a piece of that first pelt you stripped. He called awhile back. Tried to act cool but I could tell he was all excited. Gonna be here first thing in the morning. Jake's gonna *love* these. Gonna pay big for 'em too. We're gonna have us some spending money, boy. *(Takes another pull on the applejack)* Yep. Gonna have some long green for once. *(Mumbling, head sinking toward the table)* Maybe we oughta catch a coupla those beasties alive, stick 'em inna cage . . . mate 'em . . . get into the fur farmin' business . . .

JEB's head sinks down on the table (the crown of his head toward the audience) and he begins to snore.

GARY begins to move the stretching boards around. As he slides one between JEB and the audience (allowing JEB to be replaced by a dummy), he stops. He lifts his arm from behind the board and sees a PELT clinging to his forearm. He tries to shake it loose as he finishes pushing the stretching board (moving it clear of the table), but another pelt begins clinging to his other arm. Suddenly GARY's expression goes slack and he stops trying to remove the pelts. He walks over by the potbellied stove, reaches for his bloody bat, then pulls back.

GARY: No!

GARY struggles with himself as his hands slowly reach out and pick up the bloody bat. He turns and approaches JEB's slumbering form. As GARY stands over JEB, he slowly raises the wavering bat, fighting it all the way.

GARY: Oh, no! Oh please, God, *no!*

With a wail of horror, he smashes the bat down on his father's head, caving it in amid a spray of red. He raises the bat and clubs JEB again. And again. When JEB's head is a bloody ruin, GARY slumps to his knees next to his father, SOBBING. Abruptly the SOBBING STOPS as GARY gets back to his feet. He holds the bat before his face.

GARY: Please, no! Sweet Jesus, no!

He slams the bat into his face with a loud, wet SMACK and an explosion of red. And again—another SMACK. And as the lights BLACK OUT we hear the bat SMACK into GARY'S face again and again . . . over and over . . .

SCENE THREE

JEB's barn—the next morning. The barn is bloody. The pelts are still there, but no bodies are in sight.
JAKE and SHANNA ENTER. Both are dressed in fur coats.

SHANNA: Eeeuuuh! Jake, lookit all the blood!

JAKE: What did you expect, Shanna? I'm a furrier. This is one
            of the places I get my pelts. Fur doesn't grow on trees. It
            grows on little animals. And it's gotta be peeled off their
            backs before you can wear it.

SHANNA: *(Grimacing)* Please. I haven't had breakfast yet.

JAKE: Wonder where Jeb and the kid are? Weren't up at the
            house. *(Picks up Jeb's jug and sniffs) Whew!* Jersey
            lightning! Looks like Jeb's been hitting the applejack
            again. Probably dead drunk somewhere. Or waking up
            with one helluva headache.

SHANNA: I don't know why I let you talk me into coming here. If
            this is another one of your dumb schemes to try and get
            into my pants—

JAKE: Hey, Shanna. Gimme a break. We've had a good
            professional relationship the last few years, haven't we? I
            told you: This is business. Purely business. The
            modeling business.

SHANNA: Then I should've had you call my agency and talk to
            them. Where the hell are we, anyway?

JAKE: The Jersey Pine Barrens. A coupla million acres of
            wilderness. *Real* wilderness. I mean there are stretches in
            here no human eye has ever seen. And all just an hour's
            drive from Manhattan.

SHANNA: *(Buffing her nails)* Fascinatin', Jake. Just fascinatin'. But
            what's this gotta do with me? You think this is a neat
            location for a shoot or something? It ain't.

JAKE: I don't care about a shoot site—

SHANNA: Then why are we here?

JAKE: Because of this. *(Holds up a piece of fur)* If old Jeb's got a stock of pelts that are anything like this . . .

JAKE's voice fades as he notices the pelts arrayed around the barn. As he strides from one stretching board to another, SHANNA pulls a pamphlet from her coat pocket and begins to read.

JAKE: *(Excited)* Look at them! *Look* at them! Where on earth did that old fox get them? They're magnificent!

JAKE inspects the last stretching board, then straightens up.

JAKE: Exquisite! What a coat these'll make! Look at the color! I never seen such a perfect match! They won't need to be dyed! Shanna! Look at these!

SHANNA: *(Glances up from the pamphlet)* Huh?

JAKE: Aren't you listening? What's that?

SHANNA: Just one of those pamphlets those animal rights nuts left all over your car. Listen to this: "Animals should not have to sacrifice their skins to feed human vanity." *(Laughs)* Are they nuts or what? *(Talks to the pamphlet)* Ay, if God didn't want us to look great in furs, why'd he make animals with great-lookin' fur? Huh? Tell me that!

JAKE: *(Taking the pamphlet from her)* Forget that. Take a look at these, will you. They're magnificent! *(Holds up a pelt)* And they're gonna make a magnificent coat, Shanna. When it's made, I want you to wear it for me.

SHANNA: Jake, I don't do fur shows anymore. I'm shooting for bigger things.

JAKE: Something bigger this'll get you. Trust Jakey. This coat

will put you on the cover of every major fashion
magazine in the world.

SHANNA: Jake—

JAKE: Wait. Just give these a look. Touch them. Feel them.
                 Aren't they fabulous?

*JAKE holds out the pelt to SHANNA. It's beautiful. The fur shimmers and glistens.
Little streaks of iridescence run through it.*

*SHANNA glances at it, turns away, then turns back. Without coming too close,
she walks around it, viewing it from all angles, almost mesmerized by it. She
looks at JAKE questioningly. He holds it out toward her, nodding encouragement. Finally SHANNA takes the pelt and runs her hands over it.*

JAKE: It's going to look fabulous on you, Shanna. Absolutely
                 fabulous!

*SHANNA's eyes glaze as she envisions the coat these will make. She knows she
must model this coat but isn't sure how to go about it with JAKE.*

SHANNA: *(Her voice soft with wonder)* I've never seen anything like
                 this, Jake . . . or *(She rubs the pelt against her cheek)* . . .
                 or *felt* anything like it. What kind of fur is it?

JAKE: I . . . I'm not sure. I don't even know if Jeb can get any
                 more.

SHANNA: You own these yet?

JAKE: Well, not yet. And if I know that Piney gonif, he'll want
                 my firstborn son in trade. God, I'd almost be willing.
                 But he'll want cash—which ain't in such good supply
                 right now. Maybe if he's not feeling his usual
                 hardheaded self we can work a deal. I know him. He'll
                 want to haggle, bat the prices around a little—

SHANNA: You got enough here?

JAKE: Yeah. Enough for one full-length coat. But no more. The coat may turn out to be one of a kind.

SHANNA: *(Eyes lighting)* One of a kind? I want it, Jake.

JAKE says nothing as he watches SHANNA drape the pelt over her arm and admire it. His expression becomes calculating.

SHANNA: Did you hear me, Jake? I want to model this coat.

Receiving no answer, SHANNA turns and faces him.

SHANNA: Aren't you listening?

Sensing that he now has the upper hand, JAKE becomes very businesslike.

JAKE: *(Clearing his throat)* Yes. Well. That's all fine and good, my dear, but as for showing the coat, you're not the only model being considered.

SHANNA: Forget the rest. Don't you let anyone else near this coat. This is *mine*. I was *born* to wear it.

JAKE: We'll see.

SHANNA: *(Losing some of her confidence)* Jake, you've got to be kidding.

JAKE: Shanna, Shanna, Shanna. Surely you realize you're not the only model in New York. This, however, may turn out to be the only coat of its kind in the *world*. It's going to put my business on the map in a big way. For something that important, I should let just anybody wear it? The International Fur Show's coming up and I've got to be convinced that you're the right girl before I let you parade that coat before all my snarling competitors.

SHANNA: *(Sarcastically)* "Convinced," ay?

JAKE: Well . . . yes . . . so to speak.

SHANNA starts strutting around him, swinging her hips mockingly.

SHANNA: And just what would it take to convince Jakey the furrier that he's found the right model for the job?

JAKE: Oh, I don't know. You should use your imagination maybe.

SHANNA: Use my imagination? Okay. I'll use *my* imagination. But just so you don't have to use yours—

SHANNA turns toward JAKE, pulls open her coat, and lifts her skirt, revealing black panties and a garter belt. JAKE's jaw drops as he stares at her. His first attempt to speak fails. Then:

JAKE: *(Voice cracking)* Convincing . . . very convincing.

SHANNA: I can be even more convincing in the car. *(Starts toward the door)* Come on. I'll show you.

JAKE: The car's too cramped. How about right here?

SHANNA: *(Startled)* Here? Now? Are you crazy?

JAKE: It's going to be a fabulous coat.

SHANNA: *(Sighing and muttering)* Well, I've done worse for less.

JAKE: What?

SHANNA: I said, "This place is a mess."

JAKE: No argument there. Lemme see if I can find a blanket back here.

JAKE moves stage left.

SHANNA: *(With a forced smile)* All right . . . but don't be long.

JAKE EXITS stage left.

SHANNA wanders the stage, toying with the pelts. Occasionally, one RIPPLES while her back is turned.

SHANNA: *(Calling over her shoulder)* YO, JAKE! I'M WAITING! HURRY UU-UP! *(Then in a lower voice, to herself)* Yeah. Hurry up and get this over with! My God, what a coat these'll make! You're a schlub-and-a-half, Jake, but you do know your fur. And Shanna's going to wear this one. You think this coat's going to put your business on the map? Let me tell you, little man, it's going to put *Shanna* on the map! She's going to be on the cover of everything from *Vogue* to *Popular Science. (Glances over her shoulder toward the doorway)* Where *is* he?

SHANNA walks halfway to the door stage left.

SHANNA: *(Calling)* JAKE? WHAT ARE YOU *DOING* IN THERE? DID YOU FORGET ABOUT ME? *(Mutters)* No such luck! You've been trying to jump my bones for two years, Jake, and now's your big chance. No way you're going to miss it. *(Sighs)* Ah, Shanna . . . won't be the first time. All part of the game. Let him get his jollies a few times and you'll be home free. *(Calls over her shoulder)* JA-AKE! I'M WAAAI-TING!

SHANNA wanders stage right to the door on the other side. She pulls on the handle.

SHANNA: Maybe there's something in—

She pulls open the door and JEB'S CORPSE—crushed bloody skull and all—falls on her. SHANNA screams and scrabbles away from it. JAKE ENTERS, rushing in from stage left. He sees the body and freezes, then approaches the corpse gingerly, almost tiptoeing.

JAKE: *(His voice cracking with fear)* Oh shit, oh my God, it's Jeb! Who did this? Who *did* this? Oh, this is terrible. We gotta get the police, gotta get *somebody*! What are we gonna do?

SHANNA: I know what *I'm* gonna do! I'm gettin' outta here!

SHANNA rushes for the door to the outside, but just as she reaches it, GARY BURSTS IN with a crash, knocking her back. GARY'S face is a bloody ruin, his clothes are covered with blood and snow, and a large steel trap is clamped on his ankle. He's half blind and completely mad with pain as the trap chain drags and clanks behind him. He's swinging the bat wildly, smashing it against the walls, the table, narrowly missing SHANNA and JAKE as they duck and run from him. He stops briefly over JEB'S CORPSE.

GARY: *(Through his ruined mouth)* Pa! They found you! They found you! They *know*!

GARY begins slamming the bloody Slugger around again.

GARY: The pain! The *pain*! Oh, God, stop the pain!

Finally JAKE grabs a KNIFE from the rack and threatens GARY.

JAKE: Stay back, kid. I'm warning you—stay back!

GARY: The pain! Oh, God, stop it!

GARY sees the knife and lunges forward, impaling himself on it. He almost seems relieved as he slumps to the floor, dead. JAKE stares in horror at the bloody knife in his hand.

SHANNA: *(Hysterical now)* Get me outta here, Jake! I want outta here right *now*!

JAKE: *(Pulling himself together)* Okay, okay. Go out and wait in the car. *(Hands her his coat)* I'll be right out.

SHANNA: You're not coming?

JAKE: *(Calculatingly)* I've got to take care of something first. Got to make sure nobody will know we were here. Don't want to leave any evidence. Don't want anyone to get the wrong idea . . .

SHANNA EXITS center stage.

JAKE: *(Continuing)* . . . and I don't want anybody else to get these pelts.

JAKE quickly drags both corpses offstage, then picks up the knife. He reaches into his pocket for a handkerchief to wipe the blade clean, but when he withdraws it he notices that the swatch of fur Jeb had sent him is stuck to his right hand. He tries to pull it off but it won't come.

JAKE: Hey, what *is* this? What the hell's going . . . on?
        (His struggle with the swatch slows, as does his speech)
        What's . . . happening?

Finally, JAKE's hands fall to his sides and he just stands there, looking dazed. Then . . . slowly, fitfully, the hands begin to move. They open his shirt, exposing his chest and abdomen. Then JAKE's right hand raises the knife toward his throat. JAKE's expression reflects his horror. The knife wavers as he tries to fight it off, but despite his efforts, it draws steadily closer to his throat.

JAKE: *(In a whisper)* No!

A CAR HORN starts to blare from outside as the blade finally reaches his throat and pierces the flesh at the notch atop the breastbone. From there it makes a deep slice down the length of the breastbone, then angles in a gradual right-ward curve across the abdomen to the belt line. Blood runs from the incision. JAKE switches the knife to his left hand and works the fingers of his right under the flap of skin. When he has a good grip, he begins ripping it away from the underlying flesh. As BLOOD POURS, JAKE GROANS and sinks to his knees. To the accompaniment of his own moans of pain and the impatient blaring of the CAR HORN, JAKE crawls offstage left and EXITS through the door.

The CAR HORN *blares some more, then stops. A moment later,* SHANNA ENTERS *center stage.*

SHANNA: *(Looking around)* Jake? What's keeping—? Jake, where are you?

The DOOR *at stage left opens slowly, swinging out creakily. The first things through the doorway are* JAKE'S ARMS, *held straight out before him. In his hands he holds a vest made out of human skin—pale and hairy on the outside, blood-red on its inner surface. The rest of* JAKE ENTERS *now, shirtless, shuffling his feet, staggering a little, holding the vest out before him.* JAKE'S *trunk is a bloody ruin where he has cut away the skin in a single vestlike piece. Only the skin on his arms, neck, and face remains intact; he holds the rest in his hands (the fur swatch is still wrapped around the right).*

JAKE: *(Hoarsely)* Brought . . . you . . . something.

SHANNA SCREAMS *and backs away.*

SHANNA: Jake! Oh-my-God, Jake, what's happened to you?

JAKE *is obviously weak from the trauma and the blood loss, but he is moving inexorably closer, shuffling around the workbench, holding out his gift.*

JAKE: Made it . . . for you . . .

SHANNA: Get away from me, Jake! My God, get away from me with that!

SHANNA *moves around to the other side, keeping the workbench between them.* JAKE *keeps after her.*

SHANNA: *(Wailing)* No! Jake, please! What're you *doing?*

JAKE *pursues her, an irresistible force.*

JAKE: Shanna . . . gift . . . made it for you . . .

SHANNA: Oh, God!

SHANNA pushes the workbench over on JAKE, knocking him down. She heads for the center door but SLIPS in the blood on the floor and goes down. JAKE crawls toward her, holding the vest out to her.

JAKE: Shanna . . .

SHANNA scrambles to her feet and lunges toward the door center stage. She stumbles, and her forearm slams against one of the foot-restraint traps hanging on the wall by the door. The trap closes on her wrist with a meaty CLANK. SHANNA SCREAMS in pain. But JAKE is still coming. She tries to leave with the trap still clamped on her wrist but the trap's four-foot chain is snagged on the door frame. Mad with pain and desperate to get free, she grabs a knife from the rack on the wall and begins to slash at her wrist. Blood spurts. JAKE is up on his feet now, approaching.

JAKE: Shanna . . . gift for you . . .

Still hacking at her wrist, SHANNA lurches out the door and out of sight—but the chain pulls tight, causing her to SCREAM again. JAKE reaches the door and looks in the direction Shanna went. A big smile lights his face when he spots her.

JAKE: Shanna . . . knew you wouldn't leave me!

Just then there's another wrenching SCREAM from SHANNA and the trap swings back around the door frame and dangles from the wall. Caught in its teeth is a dripping, bloody, human hand, sawed off at the wrist. As it swings back and forth, JAKE EXITS the door frame, holding the vest before him.

JAKE: *(Fading)* Shanna . . . come back . . . you'll get cold . . .
            here . . . wear this . . .

END

For years, Tom Allen was a phone friend. I have a number of them. People I see only rarely—or, like Ed Gorman, never see—but with whom I have regular conversations about writing, reading, politics, families, life in general. Tom and I started our phone friendship one Friday night in 1987 when I was working late at my office. Tom was a story editor with Laurel Entertainment, George Romero's company. My previous contacts with Tom had been brief conversations about the annual editor-publisher receptions that I had been running for SFWA, when I'd invite the Laurel crew to stop by for a drink.

Tonight Tom was calling because he'd just read *The Touch* and wanted to tell me how much he liked it. Here, obviously, was a man of great taste and discrimination.

During the ensuing months we had many late Friday phone conversations about books and authors we liked and didn't like (although Tom seemed to be able to find something of value in everyone), deciding who was overrated and who was underappreciated. I was continually and increasingly amazed at the depth and breadth of his knowledge of the sf/fantasy/horror field, and his genuine affection for it. As story editor for *Tales From The Darkside*, part of his job was combing the old magazines and anthologies for stories with adaptation potential. But this man had read *everything*.

In the spring of 1988 he asked me to drop by the Laurel offices on Broadway for a meeting. There I finally met the voice on the phone and found that Tom Allen looked about as he sounded—a big, gentle fellow with an easy smile. The upshot of the meeting was that Tom and the others at Laurel wanted me to do something for *Monsters*, the new half-hour syndicated show Laurel was preparing for the coming fall season. The guidelines were simple but strict: one or two lead characters, one to three supporting characters, one monster; one or two interior locations, no exteriors; three scenes with a 5–8–8 minute breakdown.

I told Tom I'd try. The challenge of all those restrictions intrigued me. I like to believe that I can write under any circumstances, that no set of preconditions can keep me from telling a story. Trouble was, none of my old stories had a monster in it except for "Faces," and that was much too strong for TV. So I'd have to come up with something new. For years I'd been kicking around an idea for an sf/monster story but never had the impetus to put it down on paper. Now I did. I sat myself down on a Thursday night, wrote out just enough to fill one single-spaced sheet, and sent the précis of "Glim-Glim" to Laurel on Friday morning.

Tom called a week later: They loved it. He had a few suggestions for some logistical and structural changes within the story to make it hew closer to the guidelines—nothing that changed the story itself, nothing I couldn't live with. But on March 7, before we could make the deal official, the Writers Guild of America went on strike.

I have decidedly mixed feelings about the WGA. It has all the inherent weaknesses and abuses of that most repressive form of union, the closed shop—if you don't belong to WGA, you can't sell a script. But to be fair, it put an end to many of the ugly abuses inflicted by the movie moguls and their underbosses upon writers in the bad old days. I'm a member now (I had to join if I wanted to see "Glim-Glim" produced) but what infuriated me then was that during the strike Tom could not discuss anything about "Glim-Glim" with me. *Nothing.* I wasn't a member of WGA but somehow I was on strike too. For five months.

But they couldn't stop me from writing. I didn't have a contract but I knew Laurel wanted the script. To maximize the impact of the story's seasonal hook, "Glim-Glim" had to play in December, yet it was already July. I figured I'd better have it ready to go as soon as the strike was over.

I started it on a Thursday and had it finished by the following Sunday night. By early August the strike was over. Soon I had a contract and was duking it out with Laurel about a third set. I wanted the penultimate scene to play out on the front steps of the library during a gentle snowfall.

No exteriors, they told me.

I explained that all you needed was a brick wall, a pair of doors, a set of steps, and some guy shaking snowflakes from the rafters.

But that makes three sets, they said. You're allotted only two. The budget won't allow more.

I felt like I was butting my head against the brick wall I wanted them to build. So I moved the scene inside the library.

But all in all my experience with Laurel was a good one. I might even say excellent. The producers there actually read books and have great respect for writers and the written word. The director checked with me every time he wanted to change a word or two of dialogue or to shift the focus of a scene—light years away from my experience with the filming of *The Keep*.

Due to the strike, "Glim-Glim" didn't run in December as originally planned. It first aired the week of January 30, 1989.

My only regret is that Tom Allen never saw "Glim-Glim." He died suddenly on September 30, 1988. I miss his warmth and wisdom and quiet intelligence. I miss talking to him on Friday nights.

So here's the script for "Glim-Glim" as I wanted it, using the doubly forbidden third exterior set.

And "Glim-Glim" was, is, and always will be dedicated to the man who nudged me into writing it.

This one's for you, Tom.

GLIM-GLIM

CHARACTERS

AMY . . . . a precocious nine-year-old with braids and big
glasses who is also an amateur astronomer.

ELLIOT . . . . Amy's father; early thirties; a high school math
teacher; average build with horn-rimmed
glasses; dressed in a white shirt, double-knit
slacks, and a cardigan sweater; slightly nerdy
and skittish, but fiercely protective of his
daughter.

CARL . . . . . . a young outdoorsman; nineteen, tall, broad-
shouldered, dressed in a flannel shirt with a
hunting knife strapped to his belt; his
machismo is not just a facade—he is a genuinely tough cookie.

GLIM-GLIM . . a seven-foot green telepathic alien, conical in
shape with a base four feet across. A ring of
four tentacles encircles his body two-thirds of
the way up. The silent mouth is a vertical slit
that we never see open. There are no eyes—at

least no human-type eyes—but rather a ring of
opalescent studs encircling the upper end of
the cone. We never get a good look at his base
but it is fringed with countless tiny, brushlike
legs.

SET 1
THE LIBRARY BASEMENT

This is a drab room with bare cinderblock walls. Mostly a simple storage
area lit by naked bulbs hanging from the unfinished ceiling. The concrete
floor is cluttered with wooden CRATES, storage BINS, and filing CABINETS.
This is where the members of the library staff took their coffee breaks and
ate their lunches.

There is a rickety TABLE surrounded by four mismatched CHAIRS. On the
table sit PAPER PLATES, a bowl of SUGAR, and a jar of DRY CREAMER. To the
left there's a half-REFRIGERATOR on top of which is a MR. COFFEE and some
SPOONS. To the right is a battered TV. Surplus LIBRARY POSTERS ("Reading
is FUNdamental" and "You've Seen The Movie—Now Read The Book!"
and so on) have been taped to the block walls in an attempt to brighten up
the place a bit. On one wall there's a CALENDAR that says "December."

At right rear is a hinged window at ground level up near the basement ceiling, covered with a blanket. At center rear is a FIRE DOOR that opens inward; it's blocked with filing cabinets. Right front is a heating duct, open
at the lower end, that runs upward out of sight.

SET 2
THE MAIN FLOOR OF THE LIBRARY

A typical small-town single-room library, divided into two sections—the
front to the right, the rear to the left. These are divided by a wall and a pair
of SWINGING DOORS.

THE FRONT SECTION: This is where the children's books and desks are
kept. The area is dominated by the CHARGE DESK near the front
doors, which are on the right; books are everywhere. Two small,

round children's TABLES are situated near the charge desk where the librarian can keep an eye on them. A large CALENDAR tells us it is December. (We have to be fair with the viewer, don't we?) At the rear of the set, behind the charge desk, is a door opening on the stairs to the basement.

THE REAR SECTION: On the other side of the wall and doors are the MAIN STACKS and large, heavy oak READING TABLES.

SET 3
THE FRONT STEPS OF THE LIBRARY

A rudimentary set. Little more than a brick wall with concrete steps leading down from double doors. Sash windows on either side of the doors; a small hinged basement window sits below and to the right at ground level.

SCENE ONE

FADE IN:

INT: THE LIBRARY CELLAR—DUSK

As the MAIN TITLE appears over a wide-angle FULL PAN of the basement, we hear GLIM-GLIM'S VOICE (a high-pitched warble, like a turkey recorded at 33 and played backward at 78) sounding faintly in the background. The PAN STOPS at the cellar window as we see CARL, ELLIOT, and AMY slide in feetfirst and drop to the floor. Carl carries a sack. They are obviously hurrying, but they are just as obviously trying to make as little noise as possible. They appear chilled, hugging themselves and rubbing their hands together.

ELLIOT *(Blowing into his hands)*:   Warmth! The only warm place in town!

CARL unloads bread, peanut butter, and canned soda from the sack.

CARL: Except that that *thing's* upstairs! It almost saw us this time! *(Nodding toward Amy)* I thought the squirt there was going to say hello to it!

AMY is oblivious to the remark. CAMERA FOLLOWS *as she moves toward the open duct against the wall.* GLIM-GLIM'S VOICE *becomes louder as she nears the duct.*

AMY: Glim-Glim's talking again.

CARL *and* ELLIOT *move toward her.*

CARL *(To Elliot, exasperated)*:   You got one weird kid there, man. I
mean, where'd she get such a cutesy name for that monster,
anyway? That thing's the reason her mothers'—

ELLIOT *(With a warning look)*:   Carl! *(To Amy)* Why don't you go
over to the window, honey, and see if Venus has risen yet.

AMY: But it's cloudy.

ELLIOT: Maybe it's cleared. Go see.

ELLIOT *watches fondly as she runs to the near wall, climbs on a crate, and looks out the small rectangular window near the ceiling. There's a* STAR MAP *taped to the wall next to the window.*

AMY: Daddy! It's starting to snow!

ELLIOT *(With forced enthusiasm)*:   Great, honey!

CUT TO:

INT: Med. Two-Shot

ELLIOT *and* CARL *square off against each other. It is obvious they are mismatched by more than age. They are poles apart in intellect and temperament, as well. Under normal circumstances it is unlikely they would even speak to each other. Chance has thrown them together, and they are trying to make the best of it. But it isn't easy.*

ELLIOT *(Grimly, in a low voice)*:   She doesn't know about her mother
yet. And besides, I told you—

CARL (*Anger flaring*):   I know what you told me, Mr. High School
     Teacher! But her mother's dead! As dead as my father! So she'd
     better get used to it!

ELLIOT: Pretty tough, aren't you.

CARL: Yeah. I was raised that way. My father—(*He breaks off with a
     catch in his voice—almost a sob*) Aw, what's the use!

GLIM-GLIM'S WARBLE *is louder.* CARL *glares at the duct.*

CARL: Damn thing! It's gonna pay!

ELLIOT: Maybe it was an accident. It came down more like a crash
     than a controlled landing.

CARL: Accident my butt! How much proof do you need? It sealed
     off the whole town like an ant farm, then infected us all with
     some sort of plague and watched us die! Everybody I ever
     knew in my whole life died in one weekend and I couldn't do
     anything!

ELLIOT *turns to the duct as the* WARBLE GETS LOUDER.

ELLIOT: Wish I knew what it was saying.

CARL: Right! Like you've got a chance. A couple more notches up
     and only *dogs* could hear its voice.

The camera CLOSES IN *on the duct.* GLIM-GLIM'S VOICE *gets louder as we* . . .

DISSOLVE TO:

INT: MAIN FLOOR OF THE LIBRARY—FRONT SECTION—DUSK

*The lighting is dim and moody. The light source is a banker's lamp on the
charge desk (off-camera at first) casting weird shadows over everything.* GLIM-
GLIM'S WARBLE *is very loud now. As the camera* TRACKS IN C.U. *across the*

countless open books that litter the floor and children's tables in the front part of the library, a VOICE-OVER TRANSLATION of Glim-Glim's warble rises in the sound track. We pass anatomy atlases, biochemistry texts, a PDR, a Home Medical Guide, humor, Shakespeare, and so on. The camera CONTINUES TRACKING up to the charge desk to an angle overlooking GLIM-GLIM'S shoulder (although he really doesn't have one) onto the top of the charge desk, which is illuminated by the banker's lamp. This desk also is cluttered with books. We see a tentacle curled around a crystal cube that pulsates with light. The CAMERA CLOSES IN on the cube.

GLIM-GLIM *(V.O. with echo)*:   Continuing ship's log for Scout 4-2-6-cube-3. Fourth local cycle since landfall. Am learning much about these primitive aliens from their books and from my autopsies of some of their dead. Had thought all in this locale wiped out but have recently sighted one or two survivors. They are in hiding and will not be easy to reach. But must find them. Must learn why—

CUT TO:

(NOTE: A quick cut here that overlaps Glim-Glim's last word and Carl's first word—both "why.")

INT: THE LIBRARY CELLAR—DUSK

CARL: Why us? How come *we* didn't get sick?

ELLIOT *(Shrugging)*:   I don't know. Something in our systems must have been able to resist the plague. But can we be the only ones left?

CARL: You've seen the town. You know—

ELLIOT *(Covering his eyes)*:   Yes! Bodies everywhere!

CARL *(Angry, determined)*:   Next time we make a food run, I'm getting us some fire power! We got scores to settle.

ELLIOT: I don't think that's—

CARL: No more "It might be an accident" speeches. I don't buy that.

ELLIOT: Then try this: If the alien dies while that force field is up,
it's just possible we could be sealed in this town forever with
seven thousand corpses!

CARL glowers and looks away.

ELLIOT: Okay. So we've got to sit tight. Maybe help will come.
Things could be worse. The power's out in the rest of town,
but not here. We'd be frozen stiff by now if we hadn't found
this place. *(Glances upward)* Now, if only there was something
I could do to—

CUT TO:

*(NOTE: As in previous cut, Elliot's last words should overlap Glim-Glim's first
two)*

INT: Main Floor of the Library—Front Section—Dusk

*GLIM-GLIM still stands at the charge desk, silhouetted against the light from the
lamp. Over his WARBLE we hear:*

GLIM-GLIM *(V.O. with echo)*:   —do with them once I find them. It
is only a matter of time, but time is short. Their armies might
find a means to pierce the force field before I am finished.
Fortunately, the survivors cannot escape this village. I threw
the force field up in time to contain all the inhabitants of this
particular village. So I must keep searching. Must stay in this
library—

CUT TO:

(NOTE: As in the previous two cuts, the last and first words will overlap.)

INT: THE LIBRARY CELLAR—DUSK

CARL: —library of all places! Never even visited it and now I'm livin' here! And that damn monster's upstairs every day, to boot!

ELLIOT: At least we've got heat and light and we've been able to sneak out for food.

CARL: Sure! Warm and well fed! Like lab rats! Once it finds us it'll want to see why its plague failed on us! *(Grins sourly)* Or maybe it just wants to eat us.

AMY *(V.O.):*   Daddy! Daddy!

CUT TO:

INT: MED. SHOT OF AMY AT THE CELLAR WINDOW

AMY is looking over her shoulder at the camera.

AMY: Come see the snow!

She turns her face back to the window.

CUT TO:

INT: MED. TWO-SHOT

CAMERA FOLLOWS ELLIOT and CARL to the window, where they all look out.

ELLIOT: It's really beautiful, but let's get some dinner together.

DISSOLVE TO:

INT: THE CELLAR—NIGHT

We PAN across CARL and ELLIOT as they sleep on their cots, but when we come to AMY, she's wide awake. Suddenly we hear GLIM-GLIM'S WARBLE faintly, and her expression brightens. She gets out of bed and runs to a crate situated by the air duct. She climbs this and squeezes her head and shoulders into the duct.

CUT TO:

INT: Main Floor of the Library—Front Section—Dusk

A CLOSE-UP of a heating vent at FLOOR LEVEL. Through its grate, AMY'S curious face is visible as she rises into view.

CUT TO:

INT: Main Floor of the Library—Amy's P.O.V.

Through the grate we get a floor-level view of GLIM-GLIM standing at the charge desk, flipping through the pages of a book. This is our first good look at the alien.

CUT TO:

Reverse Angle—C.U.

Through the grate, we see AMY react with wide-eyed astonishment.

AMY *(In a hushed whisper):* Glim-Glim!

CUT TO:

INT: Main Floor of the Library—Front Section—Dusk

GLIM-GLIM freezes, then begins gliding toward the grate with a SHUFFLING sound.

CUT TO:

INT: Main Floor of the Library—Amy's P.O.V.

Through the grate we see GLIM-GLIM approaching. The SHUFFLING sound is very loud as the alien draws nearer.

CUT TO:

INT: HIGH ANGLE OF THE HEATING GRATE—GLIM-GLIM'S P.O.V.

AMY is looking up in wonder and awe.

CUT TO:

REVERSE ANGLE—AMY'S P.O.V.

GLIM-GLIM fills the screen. The SHUFFLING STOPS. The upper half of its body bends forward for a closer look.

CUT TO:

REVERSE ANGLE—GLIM-GLIM'S P.O.V.

The light through the grate throws shadows across AMY'S face as she gazes up at Glim-Glim. Smiling shyly, she pokes two of her fingers through openings in the grate and wiggles them in the air.

CUT TO:

INT: MED. LOW ANGLE SHOT—GLIM-GLIM

The alien bends even closer to the camera.

CUT TO:

INT: THE HEATING GRATE—C.U.

We see AMY'S two wiggling fingers. Then a TENTACLE enters the frame and gently caresses the fingers. As camera MOVES IN to E.C.U. on the human-alien contact, we . . .

FADE OUT

SCENE TWO

FADE IN:

INT: THE LIBRARY CELLAR—DAWN

A close-up of AMY'S STAR MAP *by the cellar window.* AMY's *finger traces a line across the stars.* ANGLE WIDENS *to show* AMY.

> AMY: Daddy? Do you think Glim-Glim could have come from the Pleiades? *("plee-AY-dees")*

ANGLE WIDENS *further to reveal* ELLIOT *and* CARL *standing nearby.*

> ELLIOT *(Gentle but distracted)*: We'll try to figure that out later, okay, honey? (To Carl) You sure it's gone?

> CARL: I heard it go out and I haven't heard it come back. What else can I say?

> ELLIOT *(Anxiously)*: This could be dangerous.

> CARL: We've got to find out what it's doin' up there. In and out, in and out, day—after day. It's up to something. I want to know what!

> ELLIOT *(To Amy)*: Okay, Amy. We're going out for more food, but first we're going to sneak a look upstairs in the library. You know what you're supposed to do now, don't you?

> AMY *(Nodding and rolling her eyes because it's all so simple)*: Sure. As soon as I see Glim-Glim coming back, I run over there and call up to you.

> ELLIOT *(With a fatherly smile)*: Right!

> CARL: But you've got to keep a real careful watch. We don't want to

get caught upstairs by that monster. We don't want to be its next meal!

AMY *(With a sunny smile)*:   Oh, don't worry. Glim-Glim won't hurt you.

Carl throws his hands up in disgust and turns away.

CARL: I give up!

ELLIOT *(With a conspiratorial wink)*:   Just be a good lookout, honey.

AMY: I will, Daddy!

The ANGLE WIDENS as CARL and ELLIOT climb onto a crate and slither through the window to the outside. Some SNOW blows in around them.

CUT TO:

INT: MAIN FLOOR OF THE LIBRARY—FRONT SECTION—DAWN

CARL and ELLIOT enter cautiously through the front doors onto the library's main floor. The charge desk, the children's reading tables, all available surfaces, including the floor, are cluttered with open books.

CARL: God! Looks like a cyclone hit the place! *(Wrinkles his nose)* And the stink!

ELLIOT quickly goes from table to table, scanning the titles of the open books.

ELLIOT: History! Philosophy! Physiology! Public speaking! Mythology! Anthropology! It's reading everything in the library!

CARL: Yeah. Wants to know all about us, I bet. Looking for better ways to kill us. But what's that stink?

ELLIOT *(Nervously)*:   I'm not sure I want to know. Maybe we should get going before it comes back.

CARL: Not so fast. It's learning an awful lot about us. Let's see if we can find out a thing or two about *it*. My dad always said a good hunter knows his prey.

The CAMERA FOLLOWS *as the two men warily pick their way over the scattered books toward the main stacks at the rear.*

CUT TO:

INT: Main Floor of the Library—Rear Section—Dawn

CARL *and* ELLIOT *push through the doors.* ELLIOT *pauses by the stacks as* CARL *moves out of frame.*

CUT TO:

Another Angle

A TIGHT LONG SHOT *of* ELLIOT *slowly* WIDENS *to reveal the back of someone else's* HEAD *staring in his direction. As if sensing the scrutiny,* ELLIOT *turns toward the camera and reacts with horror.*

ELLIOT: Oh, Lord! Carl! *Carl!*

CUT TO:

Another Angle

A MED. SHOT *of the horrified* ELLIOT *as* CARL *rushes into the frame.*

CARL: What—?

ELLIOT *(Pointing, his mouth working to keep from retching)*:   Look!

CUT TO:

INT: Severed Head—C.U.

A severed head stares into the camera with glazed eyes, the bloody stump of its neck resting on a bookshelf.

CUT TO:

INT: Med. Two-Shot

ELLIOT: Oh, Lord, I know him! That's Doc Spruill!

CARL grabs ELLIOT'S arm and begins to drag him toward the rear of the library.

CARL: It gets worse.

CUT TO:

INT: The Library—Rear Section—Dawn

A QUICK PAN across one of the big oak reading tables revealing a headless, bloody, dismembered corpse—just enough to give a horrific impression without dwelling on it. The table is red with blood, the chest and abdomen are open, intestines are exposed. The pan is intercut as follows:

SLAM CUT TO:

INT: Elliot's Face—E.C.U.

ELLIOT reacts with horror and revulsion and begins to turn away.

SLAM CUT TO:

INT: Continuation of the Pan

SLAM CUT TO:

INT: Carl's Face—E.C.U.

CARL'S expression is grim but tougher. He has gutted his own kills before, so this isn't the first time he's seen this sort of thing.

SLAM CUT TO:

INT: Final Segment of the Pan

SLAM CUT TO:

INT: Med. Two-Shot

ELLIOT has turned away but CARL still stares at the table.

> CARL *(Awed)*:   Looks like my garage after me and my dad dressed a
> couple of bucks.

CUT TO:

INT: Reverse Angle

GLIM-GLIM suddenly appears before them, waving his tentacles and emitting a LOUD WARBLING noise. He looks fearsome and threatening.

CUT TO:

INT: Med. Two-Shot of Elliot and Carl

Both men react with terror. They turn and begin running toward the front of the library.

CUT TO:

INT: The Library—Front Section—Dawn

CARL and ELLIOT burst through the swinging doors from the rear and run past the charge desk and out the front doors. Behind them, GLIM-GLIM *slowly* SHUF-FLES *to the charge desk. He picks up the transcribing cube.*

GLIM-GLIM *(V.O. with echo):* Continuing ship's log for Scout 4-2-6-cube-3. Fifth local cycle since crash landfall. Have identified the lethal pathogen. It is virus 6-square-9, indigenous to our intestinal tracts but obviously extremely deadly to these unfortunate aliens. *(Feeling enters voice)* Is so tragic. All my fault. Worse. Force field will fail soon due to dying batteries. Then virus will contaminate entire planet. *(Exerts control again)* Note: Made contact late last cycle with a surviving native—a young female who does not fear me. Must pursue that contact. But cannot bring my voice down to level she can understand. Must find other way.

DISSOLVE TO:

INT: THE LIBRARY CELLAR—DAY

AMY *is hugging a snow-dusted* ELLIOT. *Behind them,* CARL *lowers himself into the cellar through the open window.*

AMY: What took you so long?

ELLIOT: We had to wait outside. The alien was just leaving. We didn't want him to spot us.

Next to them, CARL *places his bags of groceries down on a table, then opens his jacket and withdraws two .45 automatics and a box of shells.*

ELLIOT: Where'd you get those?

CARL *(With evident self-satisfaction):* While you were looking for an extra can-opener, I paid a visit to Murphy's Gun Shop. That was the last time I run from that monster!

As the grinning CARL *works the slide on the pistol, the* CAMERA MOVES IN *on* AMY'S *worried face.*

INT: Main Floor of the Library—Front Section—Night

AMY and GLIM-GLIM stand together at the charge desk.

>   AMY: Hey, this is working great! You keep pointing and I'll keep
>   writing.

CUT TO:

INT: C.U. of Amy

>   AMY: So far we've got that the you're from somewhere in Orion, the
>   sickness was an accident, and you need our help to make a
>   medicine to save everybody else. Okay. What can we do?

CUT TO:

INT: The Desk Top

GLIM-GLIM'S tentacle points to letters in the penmanship book.

>   AMY *(V.O.)*:   B . . . L . . . O . . . O . . .

She stops speaking when the tentacle rests on D.

CUT TO:

INT: C.U. of Amy

>   AMY: You need blood? How much? *(Looks down at table)* L . . . I . . .
>   T . . . T . . . L . . . *(Looks up again)* A little. Okay. I . . . I guess
>   I could help some, but it'll take an awful lot of convincing to
>   get Carl and my dad to come around. *(Looks down at table
>   again)* Tell . . . them . . . friend. *(Looks up again)* No. They'll
>   never believe. You'll have to *show* them! But how?

CUT TO:

INT: Med. Shot—Glim-Glim

GLIM-GLIM warbles.

CUT TO:

INT: C.U. of Amy

AMY *(Excitedly)*:   Hey! I know! I know! How could I forget! Wait
          here and I'll get a picture to show you!

As AMY rushes off, the CAMERA LINGERS on the silent GLIM-GLIM.

FADE OUT

SCENE THREE

FADE IN:

INT: The Basement—Day

*CARL has been cleaning a pistol and ELLIOT has been tinkering with a
shortwave radio. Both look up at the ceiling, listening to Glim-Glim's
SHUFFLE.*

CARL: What d'you suppose he's been up to all day?

ELLIOT *(Shrugging)*:   I don't know, but he's certainly been busy.

CARL: Yeah. Must've gone in and out a dozen times already. Almost
          sounds like he's building something.

ELLIOT *(Shuddering)*:   I'm not going up to look, that's for sure!

CARL laughs.

DISSOLVE TO:

INT: THE BASEMENT—NIGHT

A quick pan of the basement shows CARL *and* ELLIOT *sleeping, but Amy's cot is empty.*

CUT TO:

INT: THE LIBRARY—FRONT SECTION—NIGHT

The camera is in the rear section, looking out through the open doors at the front section. AMY *and* GLIM-GLIM *are framed in the doorway, looking toward the camera.*

AMY: Awesome! They gotta know you're a friend when they see that!

We don't see what she's looking at.

CUT TO:

INT: THE LIBRARY—FRONT SECTION—ANOTHER ANGLE—NIGHT

As AMY *shuts the doors,* GLIM-GLIM *proffers a sheet of paper.* AMY *takes it and looks at it.*

AMY: Hey, your writing's getting better but . . . *(Her voice trails off)*

CUT TO:

INT: ANGLED SHOT OVER AMY'S SHOULDER

We see the note. Large crude letters form the words: "YOU PLEASE GIVE ME BLOOD NOW?"

CUT TO:

INT: C.U. AMY'S FACE

Her smile falters as she looks up at Glim-Glim.

AMY: Yeah, well, I did promise, didn't I?

                                                    CUT TO:

INT: Glim-Glim—Amy's P.O.V.

GLIM-GLIM warbles.

                                                    CUT TO:

INT: C.U. Amy's Face

   AMY: And it'll save the whole world, huh?

                                                    CUT TO:

INT: Glim-Glim—Amy's P.O.V.

GLIM-GLIM warbles again.

                                                    CUT TO:

INT. Med. Shot of Amy

   AMY *(Jittery, with a pained expression)*:   Ooooh . . . okay. But don't
       hurt me!

A tentacle gently caresses her cheek.

                                                    DISSOLVE TO:

INT: The Basement—Elliot's Cot—Night

As we hear a faint WARBLE from Glim-Glim, ELLIOT stirs in his sleep.

                                                    DISSOLVE TO:

INT: The Library—C.U. of Amy's Arm—Night

GLIM-GLIM'S tentacle places a clear, hollow 2-inch-diameter globe over AMY'S ARM, inside the elbow.

AMY: Ouch!

QUICK CUT TO:

INT: The Basement—Elliot on His Cot—Night

Amy *(V.O.—far away)*:   Ouch!

ELLIOT'S eyes snap open. He sits up and looks around in the dark.

ELLIOT: Amy?

He gets up and stumbles to Amy's cot. When he finds it empty, he becomes worried.

ELLIOT: *Amy?*

Suddenly he faintly hears GLIM-GLIM'S WARBLE and whirls toward the duct.

ELLIOT *(Louder now)*:   Oh, God! Amy!

He rips the duct away from the wall and leaps to the exposed grate.

CUT TO:

INT: Elliot at the Grate—Side View

ELLIOT stretches his neck to see through the grate. Light from the library shines on his eyes.

CUT TO:

INT: FRONT LIBRARY—THRU THE GRATE—ELLIOT'S P.O.V.—NIGHT

We see GLIM-GLIM looming over AMY whose back is to us. The globe is attached to her arm. The globe is red now.

CUT TO:

INT: AMY'S ARM—E.C.U.

We see the globe half-filled with blood.

CUT TO:

INT: ELLIOT—THRU THE GRATE—C.U.

ELLIOT reacts with mute horror.

CUT TO:

INT: GLIM-GLIM'S P.O.V.

ELLIOT'S horrified face is visible through the grate.

CUT TO:

INT: FRONT LIBRARY—TWO-SHOT

GLIM-GLIM sees ELLIOT. WARBLING as he moves, GLIM-GLIM glides past AMY toward the grate. As he lifts a piece of paper from the charge desk, the blood-filled globe pops off her arm and smashes on the floor.

CUT TO:

INT: FRONT LIBRARY—THRU THE GRATE—ELLIOT'S P.O.V.

GLIM-GLIM is approaching the grate, WARBLING and waving a piece of paper, filling the frame.

CUT TO:

INT: THE BASEMENT—NIGHT

Panicked now, Elliot turns and races across the basement toward the window.

ELLIOT *(Near hysteria)*:   It's got her! Good Lord, it's got her!

CARL awakens and stumbles from his cot.

CARL: Wha? Who's got—

ELLIOT *(Fumbling with the window catch)*:   That Thing! That monster! It's got Amy!

CARL pulls ELLIOT away from the window and grabs him by the shoulders.

CARL: Only one thing to do! Blow the ugly bastard away! You still think this was all an accident?

ELLIOT *(Still frantic)*:   No! Give me a gun! I've got to go after her!

CARL picks up an automatic and gives it to ELLIOT.

CARL: Here. Now help me move those crates and we'll—

ELLIOT: No! There's no time! It's doing something to her now! Oh, God! *(Turning)* Come on!

He starts to climb through the basement window.

CUT TO:

EXT: THE LIBRARY FRONT DOORS—NIGHT

A LOW ANGLE from the men's P.O.V. as the library doors open and GLIM-GLIM emerges at the top of the steps, WARBLING, his tentacles writhing. A piece of PA-PER is wrapped in one tentacle.

CUT TO:

EXT: REVERSE ANGLE—GLIM-GLIM'S P.O.V.

A HIGH ANGLE of ELLIOT and CARL as they skid to a halt.

> ELLIOT *(Teary and raging)*:   Where's Amy? What have you done with
> her?

CUT TO:

EXT: REVERSE ANGLE—ELLIOT & CARL'S P.O.V.

LOW ANGLE of GLIM-GLIM. One tentacle holds out the piece of PAPER while his other tentacles wave about frantically in a crude attempt to invite them in.

CUT TO:

EXT: ELLIOT—HIGH ANGLE MED. SHOT

In a rage, ELLIOT raises the pistol and points it into the camera.

> ELLIOT: Give her back!

He fires once.

CUT TO:

EXT: REVERSE ANGLE—GLIM-GLIM

GLIM-GLIM'S body jolts with the impact of the bullet.

CUT TO:

EXT: REVERSE ANGLE—ELLIOT

ELLIOT fires twice more.

CUT TO:

EXT: The Library Front Steps—Night

GLIM-GLIM jolts and totters at the top of the steps. His tentacles go limp and he seems to crumple in on himself as green fluid spurts from a dozen holes. Finally he collapses. The CAMERA FOLLOWS as he rolls to the bottom of the steps to lie still at the feet of ELLIOT and CARL. ELLIOT is horrified. He drops the gun and looks up at the library doors.

    ELLIOT: Amy!

He runs up the steps. With a last look at the dead alien, CARL follows.

CUT TO:

INT: The Inner Doors of the Library's Main Floor—Night

The doors SLAM open as ELLIOT bursts through. CAMERA FOLLOWS as he runs past the charge desk toward the rear of the library.

    ELLIOT: Amy!

CARL follows him.

CUT TO:

INT: The Library Main Floor—Rear Section—Night

The lighting is subdued, with faint reds and green reflecting off the polished surfaces of the closed doors. ELLIOT and CARL rush in and stop dead in their tracks as the soft red and green lights flash on their faces. They react with silent, openmouthed awe.

CUT TO:

INT: The Library—Rear Section—Elliot's P.O.V.

A brightly lit Christmas tree, strung with garlands and blinking lights, stands between two of the stacks. AMY is before it, clutching a doll against her chest. She turns and beams at her father.

    AMY: Look, Daddy!

                                                      CUT TO:

INT: Elliot—Med. Shot

    ELLIOT *(Shocked, stammering)*:   Amy! You're all right? What—?

                                                      CUT TO:

INT: Library Main Floor Rear Section—Elliot's P.O.V.

AMY grins as she stands before the tree.

    AMY: I just plugged it in. Glim-Glim made it to show us he's our
           friend.

                                                      CUT TO:

INT: Elliot—Med. Shot

ELLIOT swallows convulsively and looks at his watch, then back at the tree.

    ELLIOT: It's the 24th! Christmas Eve! With all that's happened, I . . .
           we . . . forgot!

                                                      CUT TO:

INT: The Main Floor of the Library—Elliot's P.O.V.

AMY grins as she stands before the tree.

AMY: Glim-Glim didn't forget! See? I told you he was our friend. *(Craning her neck as if to look around them)* Where is he, Daddy? Where's my friend Glim-Glim?

CUT TO:

INT: ELLIOT & CARL—MED. TWO-SHOT—NIGHT

ELLIOT buries his face in his hands. CARL'S mouth works but he is still too stunned to speak.

AMY *(V.O.):* Daddy?

SLOW DISSOLVE TO:

EXT: THE BASE OF THE LIBRARY STEPS

The camera MOVES IN slowly on GLIM-GLIM'S still form lying in a pool of dark green liquid at the bottom of the stairs. His green has turned to gray. New snow is dusting him with white.

AMY *(V.O.):* Where's Glim-Glim?

We linger a moment on the dead alien, then CLOSE IN on the PAPER, a sheet of child's writing tablet, and the crude letters spelling: MERRY CHRISTMAS, then we . . .

FADE OUT.